C000318491

Destiny's
TALISMAN

—A NOVEL—

By

RALPH NEEDHAM

An Explanation and dedication

Destiny's Talisman is the second book by farmer/writer Ralph Needham. His first book 'Conscience Hill' was based on fact and drew on his practical knowledge and experience of farming on the marsh, East of the Lincolnshire Wolds through generations.

The first printing of a thousand books sold out in a few months and the book reprinted.

Whilst researching some of the details for that book Ralph was drawn in to ask 'why?' 'what if?' to some of the situations he saw. This has led to a completely fictitious account of a rural community. Like most good writers Ralph becomes completely involved with his subject and would like to thank his family for their forbearance. In particular Ralph would like to dedicate this book to his children Sally, Alistair and Andrea, that they may understand how history can often explain the present and the future.

First Published in Great Britain in 2013 by Tucann Books
Text © Ralph Needham All rights reserved
Design © TUCANN*design&print*

No part of this publication may be reproduced or transmitted in any way or by any means, including electronic storage and retrieval, without prior permission of the publisher.

ISBN 978-1-907516-25-2

Produced by: TUCANN*books*,
19 High Street, Heighington Lincoln LN4 1RG
Tel & Fax: 01522 790009
www.tucann.co.uk

AUTHOR'S NOTE

In Destiny's Talisman I relate the triumphs and tragedies experienced by five generations of a farming family during the 19th and the early part of the 20th century.

Bill Slade, although content with his lot, perhaps because he has never known things to be any different, struggles rather like generations of similar cottage farmers, to eke out a barely subsistent living from his few acres of land, but unfortunately things are about to change for the worse, with the arrival of Henry Vavour at the Hall.

Henry has just acquired the estate from an old established family who have owned the land for centuries and have happily coexisted with the cottager farmers in the village. However, Henry and his descendents are determined to enact changes, which make them particularly vindictive towards anyone they perceive as infringing their property, and that sets in train a series of events with far reaching consequences.

This is a book that I hope will interest the reader who would like to know more about what it was like to live during a period of great change in the English countryside. It may have had something to do with the fact that both of my respective grandparents made their first tentative steps on the farming ladder during this time, so I was fascinated to discover more about this period in our history. Incidentally, as readers of Conscience Hill will learn they responded to the remarkable changes that were occurring in agriculture by taking totally different approaches to one another.

Of course families such as the fictional Slade's, had dominated rural communities for centuries, or at least that was the situation until the effects of the industrial revolution and repeal of The Corn Laws altered their way of life forever.

In order to give greater realism to the locations, I have loosely based it on places I am familiar with. However when it came to the Hall itself, I took a considerable degree of liberty in describing both it and its surrounds as it was demolished in 1920 at the conclusion of The Great War. Fortunately, I have in my possession, photographs showing not only exterior views of the Hall itself, but also a number of internal ones with details of the sale of contents, and that helped me enormously in recreating the scene.

I'm quite certain however, that the real owners wouldn't have born the slightest resemblance to the unsavoury characters I write about in the book. But as for the mud and stud cottages, I remember one of those very clearly as it used to stand adjacent to our farmyard.

Following the success of my first book, CONSCIENCE HILL, that Tucann published in 2011, I would once again like to express my grateful thanks to Tom

Cann for his considerable help and constructive advice in producing this book. I also extend my thanks to John and Maureen Lill along with Vic Atkinson for reading the manuscript and offering their comments. Above all miranda france for gibing me the inspiration

My grateful thanks as always is extended to my wife Pat for her forbearance whilst I have been closeted away working on various drafts.

Please note that this is entirely a work of fiction and any reference to people alive or dead is purely coincidental.

Ralph Needham
August 2013

INDEX

THE SLADES

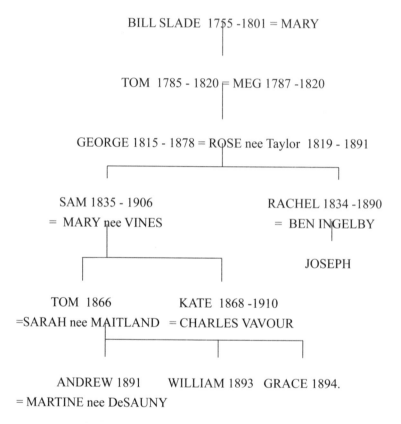

BILL SLADE 1755 -1801 = MARY

TOM 1785 - 1820 = MEG 1787 -1820

GEORGE 1815 - 1878 = ROSE nee Taylor 1819 - 1891

SAM 1835 - 1906
= MARY nee VINES

RACHEL 1834 -1890
= BEN INGELBY

JOSEPH

TOM 1866
=SARAH nee MAITLAND

KATE 1868 -1910
= CHARLES VAVOUR

ANDREW 1891
= MARTINE nee DeSAUNY

WILLIAM 1893   GRACE 1894.

THE VAVOURS

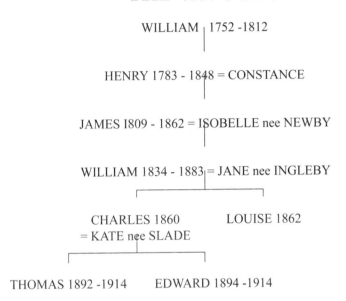

WILLIAM 1752 -1812

HENRY 1783 - 1848 = CONSTANCE

JAMES 1809 - 1862 = ISOBELLE nee NEWBY

WILLIAM 1834 - 1883 = JANE nee INGLEBY

CHARLES 1860   LOUISE 1862
= KATE nee SLADE

THOMAS 1892 -1914   EDWARD 1894 -1914

THE INGELBYS

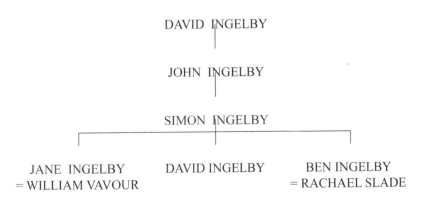

DAVID INGELBY

JOHN INGELBY

SIMON INGELBY

JANE INGELBY   DAVID INGELBY   BEN INGELBY
= WILLIAM VAVOUR   = RACHAEL SLADE

PREFACE
April 27th 1920

Neglect seemed to be everywhere; even the gravel in the driveway had succumbed to the relentless onslaught of grass and other weeds, as nature insidiously reclaimed for its own what had previously been denied. It was all further evidence, if any were really necessary, that the grounds had suffered a dramatic deterioration since the army departed. As he looked more closely at the steps leading to the west door, it was all too obvious how even they were starting to crumble away. However, it was the sight of a patch of flowering cow parsley that triggered his memory of an event in his childhood, which, little did he realise at the time, would play such a fundamental part throughout his life.

Even though more than fifty years had elapsed, the occasion had left such an impression on him that he could instantly recall the smallest detail. It had been a sunny, April morning he recalled, when he took that fateful walk by the beck. A stiff westerly wind was making the uppermost branches of the tall trees, between the Hall and the church sway so violently, that he remembered thinking that the rooks that had built their nests there must be wishing they had selected a position slightly lower down whenever a fresh gust of wind threatened to dislodge the collection of twigs that formed their nests. Following a night of heavy rain earlier in the week the beck had swollen to a raging torrent of brown water, so he knew that was the reason his mother wasn't too happy about him taking a walk by the beck alone. However in an effort to pacify her he assured her that he would be extra careful where he walked, even though he was certain that the water in the beck would be back to normal by now. He knew from past experience that it tended to drop almost as quickly as it rose. He wasn't too sure why the beck and its surrounding trees should hold such a fascination for him, but with reflection, he thought its appeal may have had something to do with the way it meandered through the wood, as it was constantly changing to reveal a new discovery around every bend. He still remembered picking his way through the clumps of lush cow parsley along the bank top and his quiet satisfaction when he noted how the water level had dropped, so that clear water now flowed over the stones in the bed of the stream. It was on these sorts of occasions, following heavy rain, that he particularly enjoyed his walks by the beck, as there was the added thrill of finding something interesting that may have been carried downstream and left suspended among the debris clinging to bushes along the banks.In the past he had never found anything of much interest other than an old shoe and on odd occasions a discarded bottle, though once he did find an almost intact clay pipe.

Little wonder therefore that his heart rate should quicken when he spotted something caught up in a particularly large clump of dead grass and twigs. From where he was standing it appeared to be partially suspended under the water by some sort of cord that was caught up among the debris. With sunlight slashing through the branches, he remembered the way it glinted whenever the current rotated it towards a shaft of sunlight. All of which added to his sense of anticipation, when even the white pebbles just below the surface of the water took on the appearance of precious stones. He still recalled his feeling of anticipation as he speculated on what the strange object might be, and bearing in mind what his mother had said about him being careful by the Beck, he wondered how he might safely retrieve it. Even though the bank on his side of the beck was quite steep, curiosity got the better of him as he scrambled down to get a better look at the object. In an endeavour to avoid getting his leather boots too wet and be reprimanded by his mother, he remembered how he had carefully picked his way across the becks stony bottom by stepping on slightly larger stones lying just below the water's surface to reach the spot. As he stretched his arm to its full extent, to grab hold of what looked rather like a piece of brown cord attached to one end of the object, he presumed that it, rather like the other objects he had discovered previously, must have been swept downstream by the recent heavy rain.

With it safely in his hand, he remembered how he had quivered with excitement when he realised that it wasn't just a piece of discarded tin, as he had at first thought, but was something a deal more interesting. At first glance it looked quite similar to the silver cross that his mother generally wore on a silver chain around her neck, except that this one was strangely different by having two bars of unequal length running across the vertical, with some kind of inscription inscribed in the metal. After giving it a vigorous rub against his sleeve he was able to decipher an elaborately scrolled "S", followed by something that may have been "auny", though the inscription was so indistinct, he would have to ask his father to read it with his magnifying glass.

Sir Charles recalled how his father, William Vavour could be quite intimidating. Ever since he had been old enough to understand he had become aware of the way the staff did their best to avoid coming into contact with him, fearing the verbal lashing he could inflict with his tongue. William Vavour, rather like his father and grandfather before him, had a reputation for treating anyone he felt to be inferior with the upmost contempt, and that certainly included all of his employees. As far as his children were concerned, well, he felt that they should be seen and not heard; little wonder therefore that Charles two younger sisters held him in such awe.

Nevertheless Charles always felt he had a special rapport with him, which may have had something to do with the fact that he was the only son. It was unsurprising therefore, that he wanted his father to be the first to see what he had discovered. So after running home as fast as his legs would carry him he rushed into the house and found him seated at his desk in the study. He remembered his feeling of pride when he asked him to close his eyes and guess what he had found before opening them again. But what he wasn't prepared for was the reaction when he pulled the cross from his coat pocket and placed it in the palm of his father's hand.

On opening his eyes a look of abject horror spread over his face, as though, judging by the speed with which he dropped it to the floor he had seen the vilest apparition. He could hardly have got rid of it quicker if it had been a red hot poker. "Don't you ever mention to anyone what you've found", he roared, barely able to control his rage. "Promise me now, that you'll never mention it to anyone in the future, not even your mother or sisters, let alone any of the servants". He remembered vividly how terribly upset he felt. He just couldn't understand why his father had reacted in that way. After promising faithfully that he would never say a word to anyone, he remembered how he had burst into tears, before fleeing from the study, up the flight of stairs to his bedroom. He could still remember how upset his mother had been when despite all her pleading he had been steadfast in refusing to say a word...

Realizing that this would probably be the last time he would be standing there, Sir Charles felt immensely sad as he took a white handkerchief from his top pocket and gently wiped away a tear.

Even though so much had happened he felt sure that people would have fully understood if he had lowered his standards, nevertheless he still kept as immaculately dressed as ever with all the sartorial elegance that befitted a gentleman who had spent the major portion of his life living in such grand surroundings. From his carefully groomed silver hair, to his black boots that shone with all the intensity of black diamonds he looked every inch to be the well respected old gentleman, villagers had come to love.

Looking back towards the Hall and what had once been carefully tended grounds, he still found it extremely difficult to come to terms with the vindictiveness that some of his forbears displayed in their treatment of folk so much less fortunate than themselves. Like him, they had enjoyed all the advantages of inherited wealth and privilege. Why then, he wondered, should they have behaved as they had.

As he picked his way across what had once been a neatly mown lawn, but was now a wilderness of long grass, to the courtyard to take a last look at the Hall's contents displayed in the specially erected marquee, he spotted the cast iron garden seat where he had often sat with Kate on summer evenings long ago. In spite of becoming partially obscured by knee high vegetation, it still like everything else that was movable, bore a lot number for the following day's sale.

Glancing towards the great west door of the Hall and the steps leading down to the gravel driveway, he closed his eyes it wouldn't take too much imagination to visualise her graceful figure bringing a cool drink for them both, when he recalled her smiling face and the laughter in her voice as she kissed him on the cheek, before taking a seat beside him. But happy as those memories were, they were overshadowed by sadder ones when he remembered the onset of her illness and his feelings of despair as he watched her health steadily decline leading eventually to her untimely death. Looking back he thought that if it wasn't a big enough blow losing the only woman that he had ever really loved, then what was to follow a few short years later had filled him with complete devastation, when both his sons were killed shortly after arriving in France in the early days of the Great War.

With no family left to follow him, he remembered how he had reluctantly come to the decision to sell the Hall, and by doing so, be rid of all the painful memories that would constantly remind him of his dear wife and sons. Turning his head, it was therefore with a heavy heart that he looked back at the great west front of the Hall, and saw how the boards crudely nailed across the windows denied it the impressive splendour it had previously portrayed. It saddened him to think that the opportunity for people to gaze from those windows and view the sweep of lawns leading down to the lake, or see cattle grazing in the park was gone forever. It reminded him of attending a concert and being sorry to see the curtain come down, when he would have really liked to see the production continue a little longer. Likewise, by blanking off the windows, he thought that nothing gave a better illustration of the buildings last act, when after tomorrow's auction of the Hall's contents, workmen would set about drawing the final curtain over the Hall, as they began the demolition of the very fabric of the building.

Momentarily closing his eyes, Sir Charles tried to conjure up a picture of the beds of roses that used to surround the lawn behind him. He remembered the delight Kate used to take in selecting the finest specimens for her magnificent flower displays, but on opening them reality set in, as dense clumps of nettles, interspersed with cow parsley and knee high couch grass had taken over the places where they once bloomed.

1795

It was market day in Hoult and throngs of common folk bustled and pushed their way along the isles of stalls in High Street. William Vavour had never been particularly happy mixing with what he disdainfully referred to as 'peasants'. On this occasion he had little choice other than to quite literally rub shoulders against their coarsely woven clothing as he searched for the entrance to Gadfly Passage. As he moved between traders and hawker's stalls that seemed to sell pretty well everything from pots to pigs, he uttered an oath when a group of ragged urchins, intent on chasing each other, cannoned into him sending him sprawling into a wall of wicker cages containing poultry. Consequently, it did little for his temper, as he searched among the market debris to find something to wipe away the worst of the sloppy chicken droppings that had fouled his smart coat. He was quite pleased therefore when he eventually spotted the narrow opening he was seeking, and made his way through its low archway.

By way of contrast to the noisy High Street, the passageway was not only a good deal quieter, but was also much narrower, making it incapable of taking anything much wider than a small handcart. Leaving the sunshine behind him, he gave an involuntary shiver as it took his eyes a few seconds to become acclimatised to the gloom caused by buildings crowding in on either side. He tried not to breathe too deeply, as his nostrils picked up the pungent smell of rotting vegetables, which judging by piles of rubbish, indicated that for quite some time the alley had become a convenient dumping ground for waste from the market stalls.

The raucous sounds of the High Street faded to a dull buzz as William moved along the passage. He scrutinized the doors until he discovered one that carried a roughly painted sign in brown lettering, indicating that the offices of Ingelby and Good, Solicitors at Law, lay beyond. Lifting the latch, he stepped inside a small entrance hall, from which despite the gloomy interior, he could see that it led onto the worn treads of a staircase which wound its way to an upper floor. At the head of the stairs he was confronted by another door which he opened to reveal a room, slightly larger than the hallway downstairs, where eight tiny window panes overlooked the brick wall of the next door building. In spite of the room being lit by its solitary north facing window it was little brighter than the downstairs hallway. However it differed by having a strange musty smell about it, which may have originated from the rows of leather bound books that William could see lining shelves across the rear wall. Although spartanly furnished, he didn't immediately notice the hunched figure of a middle aged man perched on a high backed chair to the rear of an even higher desk.

"Mr Ingelby" William said, suddenly aware of the other mans presence. He took it for granted that this must be the senior partner and therefore likely to be Ingelby. "Your name was recommended as being someone who could possibly assist me", he said, taking in the contents of the room. Ingelby peered over a pair of round pebble glasses hovering ponderously on the end of his beak like nose. Perhaps as a consequence of working in such an austere environment he frequently had to remove a handkerchief, tucked into the sleeve of his black jacket, to dab a dewdrop on his nose.

"I will do my best to assist you", David Ingelby said, inclining his head in a conspiratorial manner.

"I am William Vavour, and I have a proposition to put business your way". Ingelby gave a thin smile, as a drop of moisture fell from his nose to land on a pile of documents littering the top of his desk. "Would this have anything to do with the property that you recently acquired from Jeremy d`Enscout?"

Ignoring the question, William said "I want the peasant who lives next to the Park entrance evicted".

"That may be difficult to achieve", Ingelby pronounced, his mind buzzing with ideas on how he could protract the work in order to enhance his fee. "The d'Enscouts you know have been clients of ours for many years. Jeremy's ancestors were responsible for building the manor house and it's said they may even have been responsible for erecting the fine Norman church".

"That's all in the past, I own the property now", William declared, giving an involuntary shiver as he drew his coat a little tighter around his body in a vain effort to combat the cold draught stealing under the ill fitting door.

"I was sorry to learn of Jeremy's misfortune. I gather he made a poor judgement". Ingelby said, with a shake of his head.

"He was too greedy", William replied.

"Jeremy told me about the enterprise in South America, and how he had been assured that by purchasing shares in the company, it would be the soundest investment he ever made".

"Well, I told him that there was a slight risk, but he wouldn't listen when he saw his original investment double in value".

"But didn't you warn him it was a highly speculative venture"? Ingelby queried.

"When he saw his investment double again he beseeched me to purchase even more shares for him, but as he had used up all his money the fool borrowed from me, using the value of his estate as security".

But didn't the shares begin to drop in value"? Ingelby asked, extracting his handkerchief to dab his nose once more.

"It was like blowing up a pig's bladder", William said with a confident smirk on his face. "When it's soft and supple it will continue to stretch, but once its dry it becomes brittle and is easily burst. Suddenly everyone wanted to sell, causing the price to collapse, and very soon the shares were worthless".

"Bankrupting Jeremy in the process", Ingelby noted with a thin smile. "Weren't you one of the principle beneficiaries of those share dealings"--- his voice lowered as he rearranged a pile of papers on his desk. "You traded on your victim's, how can I put it " ---, once again he didn't finish the sentence as he held his handkerchief to his nose once more.

"Greed" William said, "Like I said, the fool was too greedy. But that's in the past. I own the estate now so I want those peasants and their hovels, cleared off the land. I'm remodelling the old manor house, so I'm not having any of them within sight of the new Hall".

"But for perhaps the last four hundred years, the d'Enscouts and cottagers have happily coexisted with the owner of the manor, why do you want the position to change?"

"They live next to the Park. I've spent good money putting up a pair of iron gates so I don't want the view spoiled by their filthy dwellings".

"Remember, their cottager's plots have been handed down from generation to generation, so it's unlikely they'll have any written title to their land. In any case, few, if any, can read or write, so they generally rely on the parson or a benevolent estate owner to guide them through any paperwork". "That's the reason I'm employing you to get them off. I think you'll know how to confuse them with legal jargon".

"I gather you wish me to produce a document to show the cottagers plot really belongs to the estate and that they are trespassing by remaining on your land," David Ingelby said, steepling his hands as he looked over his glasses in William's direction.

"You will be well rewarded provided you carry out my instructions", William said, getting up to leave.

• • • •

At first glance its unkempt thatched roof looked indistinguishable to any of the other squat mud and stud buildings that straggled along Peddars row. With half a dozen hens scratching for worms along the base of an untidy heap of rotting manure across its front, it would have been all too easy to assume that it was in fact just another dilapidated farm building. Yet a twist of smoke emerging from a chimney at one end indicated that it was also a dwelling where people lived, even though it shared its roof with livestock at one end. Whatever impression it might give from the outside, it nevertheless provided a happy home for Bill and Mary Slade and their five children. Bill was born there, and he like his father and generations of earlier Slades who had lived in the same house before him, was a cottage farmer, eking out a meagre living from his few acres of land.

One afternoon in late October as the setting sun dipped behind an ancient oak tree on the western edge of the farmyard to place the house in shadow, a sprightly horse pulling a high wheeled gig, turned into the rutted farm entrance. A thin faced man in a black, high collared coat and matching top hat lowered his reins, but before stepping to the ground fastidiously checked the ground for a comparatively clean spot to place his feet.

On hearing the sound of horse's hooves in the yard, Bill, who was about to milk their only cow, emerged from the stable to see what was happening. "Are you Slade?" The visitor enquired, disdainfully plucking an imaginary speck of dust from the sleeve of his coat.

Before Bill had an opportunity to reply, his children, dressed in an odd assortment of ragged clothing, seemed to materialize almost miraculously from nowhere. With one hand to shield the rays of the setting sun from their eyes, they huddled around their father, as they squinted up at the immaculately dressed man who had come to pay them a visit. Their pinched faces and thin bodies gave them a hungry look which seemed to be accentuated by their motley collection of tattered garments, Even Bill's rough clogs looked incongruous against the fine buckles on the visitor's shoes. The commotion, brought Mary still drying her hands on a piece of rough linen, to the doorway to see what was happening, as Tom their oldest boy, moved over to stand beside his father.

David Ingelby sniffed as he drew a fine lace edged handkerchief from his sleeve, then in order to prolong the suspense for as long as possible of why he was paying them a visit, slowly dabbed his nose. He felt in an inside pocket of his coat and extracted a metal case, from which he removed a pair of pince - nez glasses that he affixed to the bridge of his nose. Eventually, turning to Bill he opened a leather folder and extracted what looked like an official looking document bound in red tape. "I am instructed by Mr William Vavour", he read, "to tell you that you are trespassing on his land".

"Don't be bloody stupid", Bill scoffed. "Mr Viger, or whatever 'is name is, is new round ere, you can tell `im this is our place and always `as been".

"That's where I'm afraid you're mistaken", Ingelby smirked holding the document aloft. "This document proves the land belongs to the estate. Consequently he wants you and all your possessions off his land. Otherwise he will have you arrested for trespass".

"I tell yer it's our place". Bill replied. "It's not 'is to take, we've always been ere".

"Mr Vavour is merely claiming what is his, now he wants you off his land".

"But its alust belonged to us", Bill repeated, slightly less confident than he had been initially. "My father was ere and is father before im. In any case where would we go?"

"Mr Vavour's not an unreasonable man, from the goodness of his heart he says you can live in that old cottage down Peddars lane, provided you work for him and care for his swine".

"Don't be bloody daft it's a ruin! No one's lived there as long as I can remember. Any road the roof timbers are rotten and what's left o the thatch is like manure. We can't live there".

"You need to be thankful he's offered you somewhere to live. He's no obligation to offer you anything"

"You can go and tell Mr Vigerour, that we`re not leavin ere", Bill said. "Now you can git back in yer trap and git off our land".

"Then Mr Vavour will have you arrested for trespass. I must remind you that the penalty for persistently occupying another person's property is the same as that for theft, for which the punishment is imprisonment or even deportation".

Without a backward glance Ingelby turned on his heel and clambered into the gig. Wheeling his horse about he drove out of the farm entrance. When Mary looked across at Bill she saw an air of utter despair on his face. They both knew only too well how ruthless some of the estate owners could be when he remembered how unjustly his maternal grandfather had been treated for taking a rabbit from a neighbouring estate.

"We don't ave to go, - do we"? Tom pleaded tears streaming down his face, as he looked up at his father.

Although the younger children weren't quite old enough to fully understand what was happening, they were certainly old enough to see that their parents were visibly upset, so their faces crumpled into tears. Mary, unable to suppress her distress any longer, rushed over to Bill, burying her head in his smock.

"There's nowt we can do", Bill said at last. "Ees the new owner and it looks as though `e can do whativer `e wants wi the likes on us".

"Is that why you take off your cap and bow, and we have to curtsey whenever the carriage from the Hall goes by?" Jenny their oldest daughter snivelled.

"That's the way it's allust been" her mother replied. "We have to respect our superiors. It's a bit like us being on one side of a wide river. We can see them on the other side, but we haven't a boat and it's too far to swim across, so there's no way we can ever get to join them".

"It's not right", Jenny cried, "Isn't there anyone can help us? Reverend Blades is always telling us at Sunday School about fairness and how we should love our neighbours".

"I don't reckon ee`ll be a deal of help seeing ow e spends so much of is time at the 'all", her mother sighed.

The following days saw Bill pass their cow and other things they were unable to take with them to another cottager, after which, assisted by Tom, Bill loaded their few possessions on a hand cart and pushed it down the lane to the ruined cottage. However before leaving he managed to salvage what he could easily take from their old home to help repair their new one.

That night the sky glowed as their old home was torched, and the ground cleared as though their cottage had never existed.

After much effort Bill was able to fix some sort of roof over their heads by using the best of the old cottages roof timbers and covering them with reeds he scythed from a nearby ditch. Bills life became one of constant graft, because following a day's hard work caring for the estates pigs, he set about clearing the garden of weeds in order that he would be able to grow some produce the following spring.

Meanwhile, William Vavour began the reconstruction of the old Manor house, as he transformed it into an impressive Hall by adding another floor to the existing two and erecting a magnificent Georgian facade with symmetrical windows on either side of an elegant front door.

Over the course of the next couple of years, the devious lawyer was able to add extra land to William Vavour's estate by the simple expedient of producing a "Deed of title," where none previously existed, in order to establish ownership. In some instances though, where the sight of their property wouldn't directly affect him, William gave the impression of being magnanimous to the previous owners by declaring that they could continue to farm the land as one of his tenants provided they paid him a small rent.

Shortly after his sixtieth birthday, William suffered a fatal heart attack, which resulted in his son Henry and daughter in law Constance moving to the Hall in 1812. William's lasting legacy was a fine Georgian building with spacious grounds overlooking an estate of more than a thousand acres. A proportion of it, as in the days of the d'Enscouts, was farmed in hand by the estate, whilst much of the outlying land was rented to tenant farmers, some of whom had been tricked out of ownership of their land. A number of girls from the village were employed for domestic duties within the Hall, whilst fathers or brothers worked as grooms, gamekeeper or gardeners.

1815

"I don't know about you lot", the young soldier remarked to anyone still bothered to listen to another of his rants. "I'm bloody starvin".

" `Ave a word with Captain Vavour", Tom replied sarcastically. "If you ask him nicely e`l probably invite you over to join him for a meal".

Over the past few days his whining voice had become a constant irritant to members of the platoon, who in spite of everything were doing their level best to remain cheerful. It had been far from an easy time for any of them, as the majority, rather like Tom, had been coerced by their employers into becoming a part of an army that having just marched from the Channel ports was about to do battle with Napoleon.

"Wot `im what called us peasants?" He replied, a surprised look on his face.

"Ay thats im, but yer never know yer luck. `E might even tek to yer, a young fella like you,". Tom said, giving a wink at another member of the platoon.

"Yer don't sound as though yer think a deal on `im?"

"I don't, I've known the devil ever since `is father got us off our land".

"Ow did that `appen?"

Tom explained how David Ingelby had produced documents to prove that his family's small farm really belonged to the estate.

"If yer don't like `im, what are you doing `ere then?"

"Didn't `ave a deal o' choice, did I? It was a case of join the platoon, or be in the workhouse".

"Ow do you make that out".

"Well e said that if I refused to join, e would see I lost my job on the estate an' the `ouse that went with it. Then just to make sure I joined, `e said `e would make sure nobody else employed me either. So as I didn't fancy the workhouse I adnt a deal o option ad I. I asked `im ` who would care for me missus and bairns if `owt `appened to me. Better be there in the morning, was all `e said. Still Megs a sensible lass an' I know she'll do her best for the young uns, but I still worry sick about how she's coping".

It still made him fume with anger whenever he thought about the way Henry Vavour had used his position of wealth and privilege to blackmail him into joining his platoon. It seemed as though by working on the estate the Vavours had taken total control of his life making him little better than one of their slaves. He remembered how on his ninth birthday, soon after his father started to care for the estates pigs, that he began work on the estate. Whatever the weather, from first light until dusk, he had been out in the fields scaring birds from their crops. When he became a little older he helped his father with the pigs and then as the years passed by and he became stronger he was detailed to take charge of a team of horses. But now thanks to Henry Vavour, he had been transported to a foreign country miles from home, where if he listened to what some of the scaremongers were saying, very few of them were likely to survive unscathed.

In spite of being in the company of more men than he would ever have believed possible to be gathered in one place, he felt incredibly lonely and just longed to be back home in familiar surroundings with his family. Ever since he had left the ship that brought them from England he had marched alongside what seemed like thousands of other soldiers, but now on the eve of what they had been told was going to be a great battle, he constantly thought about Meg and the children back home.

Rain had fallen steadily during the afternoon, so whilst the greater proportion of Wellington's army spent an uncomfortable night drawn up in their battle positions near Waterloo, Tom, with the benefit of years spent working in the open was able to cope a good deal better than many of the men coming from the towns.

His bitterness was compounded, when he recalled Henry Vavour's short speech to the platoon the previous afternoon, when he had outlined what he wanted them to do. "We are all part of an army commanded by The Duke of Wellington", he said addressing the 120 men under his command. "We are finally going to put an end to Napoleon, because tomorrow, God willing, we're going to inflict a devastating defeat on his army". "Hold your fire until you see me drop my sword. We want the enemy to fire their muskets first, then we'll have the advantage whilst they concentrate on reloading".

It was at that point he realised that perhaps the scaremongers with their dire predictions had been right all along and he would be lucky if he ever saw his family again, as there was every possibility that he along with many other of his fellow soldiers were unlikely to survive the coming battle when the enemy started to fire their muskets. Now as they waited patiently for the enemy to attack he became aware of just how large their army was. A sea of red tunics stretched away on either side and even those areas that weren't red appeared to be populated with either horses or guns.

"What the 'ell's that", the young soldier said bringing him sharply back to reality. A rhythmical, Thump, Thump, Thump, sounded from somewhere over the brow of a hill in front of them.

"They must be coming". Tom said with a slight hesitancy in his voice, though he was determined not to show his anxiety to the younger soldier.

"They're putting the fear of God inta me, I can tell yer," the young chap replied.

Soon the tops of the French soldier's headgear began to crest the brow of the hill. When more of their bodies came into view, Tom thought the advancing army looked rather like a moving blue and yellow carpet made up of soldiers stretching as far as he could see in either direction. Still the vast army kept advancing, as it marched to that intimidating thump of their drums. On a ridge not too far to the right, Tom spotted the mounted figure of Henry Vavour silhouetted against a brilliant blue sky. The beat of the drums seemed to have increased to a crescendo, when suddenly all fell silent as the first line of French soldiers dropped to their knees.

From Tom's position the sight of the opposing army seemed to dissolve into a haze of white smoke, as thousands of muskets discharged simultaneously. Suddenly the air was filled with the sound of men screaming in agony as a hail of lead shot lacerated the forward line of soldiers. Whilst the first wave of French soldiers concentrated on reloading, Henry gave the signal for his men to fire back. Tom along with hundreds of soldiers on either side of him fired their muskets, then without waiting to reload charged with bayonets held horizontally at the opposing army.

Tom was soon in the midst of hand to hand fighting thrusting his bayonet first in one direction and then the other as he confronted the enemy for the first time. In a wild rush of adrenalin he stabbed his bayonet at any blue and yellow uniforms that came his way. For a while everything seemed to be total confusion as a melee of French and English soldiers fought hand to hand for their very lives. In the nick of time Tom parried a Frenchman's musket then with an upward movement thrust his own bayonet at the man's middle. The soft resistance of the Frenchman's body reminded him of sticking a pitch fork into a sheaf of corn.

The soldier slumped to the ground, but as Tom withdrew his bayonet he couldn't help noticing that the soldier's helmet was strangely different to those of other Frenchmen. Bugles sounded and suddenly the battlefield was full of the thrashing feet of horses, as mounted riders from both armies thrust their lances into the bodies of opposing foot soldiers. Suddenly something hit him with such force that he could hardly have collapsed a deal faster had he been pole axed.

As he slowly came round, he couldn't understand what he was doing lying on the ground, but as the mist clouding his vision began to clear, and his eyes started to focus on the bodies of dead and injured soldiers lying about him, it all began to come back. As more of his reasoning returned he was once again aware of the sound of muskets but this time their explosive crack was tempered by the screams of the injured and dying. He still wasn't exactly sure what had happened, though a burning sensation in his thigh made him realise he was injured.

As the pain settled into steady throb he reflected on his relative good fortune, after all he was still alive and that was something to be thankful for, so rolling into a foetal position he feigned death as furious fighting continued to rage all about him. After awhile, the sound of battle seemed to diminish, so in spite of feeling strangely light headed, he gingerly raised his body into a sitting position. After removing his tunic he carefully lowered his trousers to discover what was causing him so much pain. However it didn't take too long to discover that he had been stabbed through the fleshy part of his thigh. Even though his wound wasn't bleeding too severely he knew that he needed to bind it His eyes focused on the French soldier he had so recently stabbed to death and saw that his tunic was badly torn, possibly as a result of his bayonet ripping the cloth. Using his bayonet he managed to cut a length of material and bind it around his wounded thigh; however it was only then that he became aware of the cloths superior quality compared to the coarse woollen serge worn by other enemy soldiers who lay dead or injured.

Soon the pain in his thigh became so unbearable that he began to have serious doubts about his survival, yet in spite of everything else it was the thought of Meg and his family back home that sustained him. He knew that in his weakened state he would be no match for any French soldier coming his way so could expect little mercy from that quarter especially when his gaze fell on the French soldier he had so recently killed.

Nevertheless, in spite of his injury he counted himself lucky so far, after all it could so easily have been him lying there. It was only then, that he noticed what looked rather like animal entrails amidst the churned up soil. He was well accustomed to seeing pig's intestines; after all, he had watched the pig killer slaughter cottager's pigs ever since he was a small boy. It says much for his mental state, that he should assume that it was pig's intestines he was staring at, until the awful truth dawned on him, that they were human and must have come from the body of the French soldier.

His mouth filled with bile, realising that he and he alone had been responsible for disembowelling the unfortunate soldier. Burying any guilty thoughts, of what in other circumstances would be considered the vilest of murders into the back of his mind, he was buoyed by the knowledge that in this instance it was a case of either the Frenchman or him laying dead.

Feeling a little happier with this reasoning, Tom gave a closer look at the dead soldier, when he noticed an exquisite engraving of flowers along with the letters "CdS" inscribed on either side of his muskets headstock. A similar design, though on a greater scale, seemed to be engraved on the front of his helmet. Even in death, Tom thought the soldiers chiselled features marked him out as being someone important, which was surely confirmed by the quality of his dress and weapon. He looked closer at the body, noting for the first time how the ripped tunic gaped at the neck to reveal a length of cord. Intrigued, by what may be attached to it, he carefully eased the cord away from around the dead man's neck, only to discover an unusual silver cross which sparkled in the bright June sun. Slipping the cord over the French soldiers head, Tom saw that the object must have been crafted from a single piece of metal, judging by the way it was constructed. In many ways it appeared similar to the cross that stood on the altar of the church at home, except that this one strangely had two horizontal bars whilst the one at home had only one.

Tom had never held, let alone possessed, anything of such beauty, so reasoning that it could just as easily have been him that was lying dead, quickly slipped it over his head and buttoned his tunic to the collar.

Whatever else happened, he was sustained in the knowledge that he must survive for Meg and his three children waiting at home for his safe return.

1820

Following The Duke of Wellingtons famous victory, those soldiers still capable of marching, received a hero's welcome from crowds of waving people as they passed through towns and villages. A reception was laid on in Hoult, but it was a somewhat muted affair as those who had lost a husband or son remembered all too well how Henry Vavour and his friend John Ingelby had coerced them to join his platoon.

Toms wound healed amazingly well, although it left him with a severe limp which seriously affected the type of farm work that he was capable of doing on the estate. In spite of trying his best to continue working with horses, he found it virtually impossible to do the job he loved most. The trouble was, that when he was ploughing, his limp made it almost impossible to keep his balance, as it was hard enough in any case to keep a grip on the plough handles, whilst walking with one foot in the furrow and the other on the freshly upturned soil.

As a result of his handicap he was demoted to jobs where little walking was required such as the back breaking task of flailing grain. He hated the job because by necessity it entailed working between the north and south facing doors of the great barn, in order that the constant draught would blow the lighter chaff and dust from the grain. Unfortunately in doing so, it created a blizzard of airborne missiles that played havoc with his eyes. Wheat and oat glaums were bad, enough, but the serrated edges of barley awns' were a different proposition altogether, as they made him constantly rub his eyes. By the end of day they became red and inflamed making it difficult to see what he was doing.

In spite of often feeling quiet warm on a hot summers day, Tom was loathe to unbutton the top button of his shirt, consequently few fellow workers could say with any degree of certainty that they had ever caught a proper sight of the silver talisman with its strange "double cross" that he was reputed to permanently wear around his neck. For some reason that even Meg was unable to fathom, he was extremely reluctant to elaborate on how it had come into his possession. All he would ever divulge was, "I picked it up on the battlefield at Waterloo", this vagueness encouraged a sense of mystery to surround the cross's origin. In quieter moments when he had time to reflect, it troubled his sensitive nature that somewhere a mother or wife might still be grieving the loss of a son or husband and yearning for the cross as a lasting reminder of their loved one. Tom felt that by wearing it around his neck, it in some ways assuaged his conscience, by being a constant reminder of the French soldier's life he had taken and whose talisman he now wore.

"They always say like father like son", Meg remarked as both she and Tom had to hurriedly take to the grass verge to avoid being trampled by Henry Vavour followed by John Ingelby, as they raced past on a pair of sweating horses one Sunday morning, whilst they made their way to the village chapel.

"Just like their fathers, they don't give a damn for neither man nor beast", Tom observed.

"How is it they can seem to do whatever they want? People like us never stand a chance against 'em," Meg remarked.

"The servant lasses all say they like Constance, but they're frightened stiff of Henry, and as for that young James, they reckon he's a spoilt brat," Meg replied.

"'e'll be trouble, if you ask me", Tom said. "'e makes the lives of 'is governess and the servant's absolute 'ell. If they complain, 'enry believes everything 'e says and punishes 'em".

The contrast in two boys, from totally differing backgrounds, could hardly be greater. George Slade, was Tom and Megs only son and although he came from an extremely poor, though happy, family who enjoyed few in the way of home comforts, he always had a cheerful smile on his face that made him instantly likable with whoever he met. James Vavour, by way of contrast was the only son of indulgent parents who rather like small birds caring for a cuckoo, pandered to his every whim so that he lacked for nothing. He generally had a scowl on his puffy face that seemed to be accentuated by a mop of curly hair that bobbed on his shoulders as he walked. He had a mean streak within him, that when coupled with his defiant nature became the dread of all the household staff. From the youngest maid, to the most senior member of staff should they be unfortunate enough to arouse his displeasure, his father would generally believe his interpretation of the facts, even if what he said was a pack of lies.

It was therefore almost inevitable that he should have had a succession of governesses who were instantly dismissed should James make the slightest complaint about them to his father. Ann Mason was but the latest in a long line of governess's that Henry had employed to educate his son. In trying to stimulate his young sons mind, Henry had spared no expense in having James' old nursery on the upper floor of the Hall converted into a schoolroom. One morning Ann was almost at her wits end. Despite trying to interest him, he was steadfast in his refusal to pay attention to what she was saying, so in an endeavour to avoid defeat she thought a change of scene just might change his attitude by taking him into the garden. Doing her level best to keep calm, Ann somehow managed to coax him from the schoolroom down to the balcony overlooking the entrance hall. He truculently pouted his lips and became quite adamant that under no circumstances was he going to descend the sweeping flight of stairs to join her in the hallway below. After patient cajoling on Ann's part, he eventually agreed to join her, but as a further act of defiance whilst looking at Ann down below dragged his arm along the back wall of the balcony. Unfortunately in doing so he seemed oblivious to the fact that his hand in following the wall, had slipped into a recess containing a collection of green and white Bohemian glass vases that his father had acquired in settlement of one of his dubious deals. Rather like the way she had seen skittles falling at the Michaelmas fair in Hoult, Ann only became conscious of what was going to happen, when it was far too late to shout a word of warning. So she felt completely helpless as she saw the first vase topple into the next creating a chain reaction of falling vases. Some of the pieces smashed as they crashed to the ground, whilst others managed to roll across to the head of the stairs before shattering into hundreds of shards of broken glass as they fell down the marble stairway.

James, for once looked bewildered as he witnessed the mayhem which he alone had been totally responsible for causing. Unfortunately for him, in his desire to look over his shoulder and see what was happening, he overbalanced and slid untidily on his bottom down the stairway to the hallway below. Probably more surprised than hurt James began to wail when he spotted that a little nick on his hand was starting to bleed.

Everything seemed to happen so quickly that when Ann saw James falling among the broken glass at the foot of the stairs all manner of fears swept over her. Putting her hands to her face she began to scream hysterically. The sound of breaking glass followed by screaming made every servant in the house drop what they were doing and rush to the hall to see what had happened.

Quickly getting to his feet, James wasted no time in yelling for all to hear between his sobs, that Ann in attempting to strike him had caught the vases with her hand. Ann Mason's father was a prominent local business man owning warehouses by the canal basin, along with a small fleet of sloops that traded between Hoult and the Humber ports. Even though her parents had warned her of Henry Vavours fearsome reputation, and the way he patronized his son, she was a head strong girl, determined to take the position of governess, because not only was it her first appointment, but it was also quite close to home. All too late she remembered her parent's words of warning as she stood in Henrys study, and tearfully explained that she certainly hadn't assaulted his son, as James was claiming, nor had she been responsible for the destruction of the Bohemian vases, but unfortunately her denials fell on deaf ears, as Henry wouldn't hear of James being in the wrong.

"For assaulting my son", Henry exploded, his neck taking on a hue not dissimilar to a turkey's wattles, "I am immediately dismissing you, after which I will be seeking a meeting with my solicitor that hopefully should see you incarcerated. In the meantime I will be speaking to your father about recompense for the vases; they were priceless".

Ann, on hearing this became completely distraught, especially when she knew she was completely innocent, yet Henry in spite of all her protestations was determined to believe the pack of lies James had told him.

Turning his back to her, he continued in a more conciliatory tone. "There could of course be another solution that might save your father the embarrassment of seeing his daughter branded a criminal. I will be instructing John Ingleby, who I am sure your father knows, to see if another outcome might be reached".

The Ingleby's by now, had perfected their methods of persuasion to produce an outcome favourable to the Vavour's, so acquiring the Mason shipping business would be a simple operation to put in place.

The successful shipping business, now operated by Ann's father was started by her Grandfather shortly after the canal linking Hoult to the sea was opened more than fifty years earlier. Consequently it wasn't too long before trade created by the new waterway brought in a new era of prosperity to a town that had been gently decaying in a rural backwater. Prominent amongst the brick buildings surrounding the canal basin were those of Mason and Son whose name was proudly displayed in giant letters across the front of three of the great warehouses. In addition to storing commodities that had either just been delivered or were awaiting shipment, Masons warehouses also housed the offices where they administered their business. Inevitably much of their trade revolved around the export of agricultural produce and the import of bulk commodities such as coal and timber.

The threat of their only daughter Ann being hauled before the Assizes, terrified David Mason and his wife, particularly when John Ingleby hinted at a meeting held in his offices, that he had known of less serious cases of assault where the defendant had been transported.

"Now - as - for - the - Bohemian - vases", the lawyer spoke very slowly and deliberately, a chilling menace to his voice that allowed his words to hang in the air, rather like puffs of smoke from a discharged gun. "Mr Vavour tells me they were extremely valuable, having been handed down through his family for many generations". Clearing his throat for effect he added conspiratorially, "I'm sure you must be getting ready to take life a little easier, I think with the right incentive, that I just might be able to persuade Mr Vavour to forget the whole wretched business if-

– how can I put this, - - assign your shipping business over to him".

It was a confident John Ingleby, who meeting Henry Vavour at the Hall later that day, was able to report that he would shortly be preparing documents that would see the transfer of Mason and Sons old established business to Vavour estates.

• • • •

In complete contrast to the wealth and opulence displayed by Henry Vavour at the Hall, Tom Slades meagre wage was barely sufficient to provide food, let alone clothing, for his family, little wonder therefore that they sometimes went to bed cold and hungry, despite Toms best efforts growing vegetables in his garden. Such was the sense of injustice that he felt had been inflicted on his family by the underhand way William Vavour had seized their property; he never felt the slightest pangs of guilt, when on a rare occasion he ventured into one of Henry Vavour's woods to take a rabbit or pigeon.

With so little spare money, it was generally a question of Meg making do with whatever was either going to waste or was free, so it was little wonder that the families clothes were someone else's castoffs that she bought from a market stall in Hoult. As the children outgrew their clothes she patched and mended them to such an extent that by the time they were passed down to the youngest child, they were frequently little more than rags, unfit for even a scarecrow.

In much the same way that folk living by the sea shore picked up driftwood on the beach following a storm, so in order to provide their only source of fuel for the kitchen fire, Meg, after a gale, took the children with her to collect any wood that may have been blown down from roadside trees. Likewise in the autumn she could be seen picking any edible fruit and nuts from the hedgerows.

With little spare money to purchase grain for her half dozen hens, she in common with other village folk took part in the traditional country practice of gleaning any remaining ears of corn from the fields that may have been missed during the harvesting process. William Vavour, when he took possession of the Hall and its estate, reluctantly allowed villagers to continue with the ancient practice of gathering what in reality, amounted to very small quantities of grain that otherwise would have gone to waste. Henry though, seemed to so resent anyone entering estate land that when he moved into the Hall he banned the practice.

Denied access to the estates fields, Meg along with other village women resorted to collecting any stalks of grain that happened to fall from carts passing down the lanes, which resulted in the precious ears of grain becoming more valued than ever. Consequently as the available quantity of corn was strictly rationed, the hens didn't lay too well, which gave rise to arguments between the children about who was next in turn for an egg.

• • • •

It was a fine autumn day towards the end of September 1820. The current governess, like so many others before her, was doing her level best to educate James and his friend Simon Ingelby who was stopping at the Hall for a few days,. She taking them both for a walk along Peddars Lane to look for seeds and nuts and was hoping to interest them in nature. Picking up a Horse Chestnut she was carefully explaining to them how the shiny "conker" was in fact a seed, when rather than listen to what she was saying they began to toss conkers at each other.

Completely disregarding her pleas to behave, she finally threatened to tell

James' father about their disobedience if they didn't do as she requested, but of course James knew it was a hollow threat, so they continued to whoop and laugh, as they chased each other along the lane. Rounding a bend, they came across Meg and her children picking blackberries from the roadside hedge.

"Why there's a fat old cow here", James guffawed, looking over his shoulder at Simon.

"Do you think she eats grass"? Simon grinned.

To their general amusement, they both began mooing like cows, as James pulled a handful of grass from the verge and tossed it towards Meg and her two smallest daughters.

With grass landing about them the little girls began to whimper.

Meg's first instinct was to reprimand the young louts for frightening them, but mindful of their fearsome reputation swallowed her pride, knowing full well how anything connected with the pair had a nasty habit of being misrepresented, so biting her lip she managed to suppress her fury, as she bent down to comfort the little girls.

"Now, if you don't mind young sirs, I would like to get on picking some more fruit". She said respectfully.

"I'll bet she got that from a scarecrow"? Simon mocked, pointing to patches on the younger girl's simple cotton dress.

"And hers is torn", James sneered, tossing more grass in the direction of her sister, as Simon continued to moo.

Both little girls broke down in floods of tears as they gazed up at the neatly attired youths.

Laughing riotously, Simon pointed to the girl's feet.

"Why they're piglets after all", he mocked, "Look I can see their trotters", pointing to dusty toes protruding from holes in their shoes.

The governess was still some distance away, as James reached across and snatched a handful of blackberries from Meg's basket and tossed them in Simon's direction.

"I don't believe the old cow ever washes either"? James guffawed, noticing how the ripe berries had left a dark stain on Meg's fingers.

If he had bothered to look a little further up her bare arms he would have seen scratch marks where the briars had clawed her skin; ample testament, if any were needed, to the difficult task of blackberry picking. But now with both daughters crying hysterically, this was the final straw. Years of pent up frustration were suddenly released as Meg spotted James about to grab another handful of her hard won fruit. She felt so incensed by the way these privileged young men felt they could do pretty anything they wanted, that for a second she forgot all about the consequences of what might happen if she stopped him. She knew that they acted with impunity, knowing full well that it would be most unlikely they would ever be reprimanded however much distress they caused to village people such as her. Unlike the situation with her own children, she knew that they would always have a plentiful supply of food on their table and would never have known what it was like to go hungry. They seemed incapable of understanding that the blackberries, she had worked so hard to pick during the afternoon represented a rare treat in a household where food was scarce. Little wonder therefore that she should give James a push as he attempted to grab yet another handful of fruit. The unexpected nature of her actions took him completely by surprise, making him overbalance to sprawl backwards into a dense clump of briars.

"I'll tell my father you attacked me, you old cow", he screeched, not so much out of any real hurt, though the briars clung to his arms and legs, as he scrambled to his feet, but more out of sheer surprise that someone should at long last stand up to him.

Rather like most bullies, he reacted badly when he didn't get his own way, so still screaming dire consequences for Meg when he told his father what had happened, he disentangled himself from the remaining briars and with Simon in tow, raced back in the direction of the governess. Although outwardly calm for the benefit of the children, Meg was desperately worried that when Henry heard his son's version of events, he would be vindictive, which would probably mean Tom losing his job on the estate and as a consequence they would be homeless. She decided that when Tom arrived home from work she wouldn't trouble him with her concerns. After all James had been in the wrong, and in any event, the governess she reasoned, would report the true facts to Henry Vavour.

As Tom returned home from work that night he spotted a rabbit hiding within a tufted clump of grass by the roadside. Selecting a fist sized stone he took careful aim and luckily scored a direct hit on the unfortunate creature before it had time to reconsider how well it had been camouflaged. His mouth salivated at the thought of the tasty meal he knew Meg would have ready for him the following night, as he knew from past experience that cooked slowly in the side oven, her rabbit casserole prepared with onions and potatoes grown in his garden was something to look forward to. "Guess what I've got", he enthused holding the rabbit behind his back as he opened the cottage door to see his children sitting quietly on snip rugs in front of the kitchen fire. Over the years Meg had made the mats by snipping small squares of material from worn out garments, and inserting them into the coarse weave of hessian sacking. Before any of them could volunteer an answer, rather like a conjurer producing a rabbit out of a hat, he swung the dead animal from behind his back to a chorus of whoops.

The following morning after Tom had gone to work, Meg's worst fears were confirmed when John Ingelby rode up to the cottage.

"Where's your mother?" He said looking down from the saddle of his horse at Tom's grubby children playing in the dust by the roadside.

"What do yer want mam for"? George said, squinting up at him.

Hearing a disturbance Meg came to the cottage doorway, her two daughters rushing over to clutch her long grey skirt; their pinched faces looking for the entire world like frightened fawns.

John Ingleby looked down disdainfully at her, as extravagantly, he dusted a speck of nonexistent dust from his silk riding coat, then dictatorially salivating on the misery that he was imposing on the poor woman said.

"Mr Henry Vavour informs me, that yesterday; you assaulted his son James causing him injury and distress for which you will be taken to court to answer a criminal charge. I shall recommend to the court that because of the seriousness of the assault, that you be birched followed by a lengthy period of imprisonment. I'll see to it that your sentence serves as a reminder to others that you cannot go about attacking innocent people".

· · · ·

Tom had been looking forward all day to his first meat dish in ages, so was surprised at not being confronted by the delicious aroma of Megs speciality, when he opened the house door that evening.

"Where's your mother"? He asked George.

"Mam said that she had to go out and that we've got to be good children and behave until your father comes home." George said with all the authority he could muster.

Tom wasn't quite sure what to make of the children's stories about the blackberry incident the previous day, and secretly wondered why Meg hadn't mentioned it to him the previous night. He was equally mystified about the identity, of what the children described as a posh man on horseback coming to see her, after he had left for work. He knew Meg's sister was about to give birth to another child, and that Meg had promised to go over to Hanby to help for a day or two. In all probability it seemed as though she had been called urgently, and that would explain the reason that she hadn't let him know she was going.

When he was ready to leave for work the next morning, his understanding neighbour in the next door cottage told him not to worry, as she would keep an eye on the children until their mother returned. Never the less he felt a little annoyed that his brother in law hadn't sent a message regarding the birth, but on reflection he thought he was being unreasonable, after all Meg had stayed with her sister for three days at the time her previous child was born. Even so, he thought that Meg might have told their neighbour that she was going away. However he reasoned that if anything had been amiss someone would have surely contacted him by now, but in any event he resolved to return home at mid day just to check that everything was in order.

· · · ·

As he gripped his fishing rod and cast a line over the water, Bill Taylor, the senior keeper seeing mist clinging to the hedge rows and over the lake that Friday morning felt that it was a good omen for a fine autumn day. As the mist gently eddied above the lake whenever a breath of breeze caught it, he settled down to wait for that exciting moment when the float bobbed, before disappearing under the water and he knew that he had got a catch. Ever since Henry and Constance had moved into the Hall it had become one of the highlights of his week to catch a couple of perch for their Friday lunch. It was carrying out such an enjoyable task as this that made up for the cold, wet days in winter when a keeper's job was nothing like as attractive.

His father had been a keeper on the estate at the time of the d'Enscouts, so it was unsurprising that Bill should follow in his footsteps as a keeper, but now that the Vavour's owned the estate, it pained him having to enforce his employers stringent trespass rules when he knew it was to the detriment of many of his friends who he had grown up with in the village. Quietly reflecting on how lucky he was to be here on such a still autumn morning, he was idly looking through the mist, thinking that it was starting to clear a little, when out of the corner of his keen eye he spotted something unusual under the overhanging branches of a willow tree, perhaps forty five yards away. His initial thoughts were that it looked rather like a particularly large fish, he knew that Pike were in the lake, but if there was one that size he reckoned he would have to do something about it; otherwise it would clear the lake of smaller fish. Just then another filament of mist rolled across the water and he lost sight of it. Curiosity getting the better of him, he propped his fishing rod against a tree and strolled along the lakeside to get a better view of the Pike. It's not a fish after all he thought, getting closer; it's a bit of old sacking. Yet there was something odd about it that made him want to examine it more closely.

Temporally forgetting about the fish he was trying to catch, he tried to get a better view of the strange object by walking further along the water's edge. Frustratingly, whenever he thought he had a clear view his line of sight tended to be obscured by another overhanging branch from the row of willow trees that ran along this side of the lake. Determined to satisfy his curiosity, even if it was just a piece of old sacking, he found that by walking past the place where he thought it was, and looking back, that he was at last able to get a better view of the grey material. A sudden waft of breeze rippled the water over the lakes surface, and in so doing partly rotated the object. A tough keeper, he was well accustomed to seeing dead animals; after all, that was part of his job, but this was something else as he gazed into the tormented lifeless eyes of Meg Slade.

Tom was devastated when news of Meg's death was broken to him later that morning. No one had the slightest doubt that it had been anything other than a tragic accident, or at least that was everyone with the exception of Henry Vavour who knew that she had very likely committed suicide as a direct consequence of actions he had set in motion.

Henry though, was one of the first to suggest that she must have somehow become disorientated in the dense mist whilst walking around the lake causing her to slip in the water and drown. Or at least that was the widely accepted view until the following spring, when another perspective of those events began to emerge.

The governess, knowing from bitter experience how the true facts of an incident were generally distorted by Henry Vavour to favour James, was terrified of confirming Meg's version of events about the boy's loutish behaviour. She was certain that if she had done, Henry would have blamed her for being responsible for James "injury", by her incompetence in looking after them, so she decided to keep silent, by claiming that as the boys had galloped on ahead, she had lost sight of them when they disappeared around the bend in the road, consequently she was unable to see what had happened. At the time she had been secretly delighted to see, that for once James had received his comeuppance. She found it difficult to suppress a smile when she saw James wailing like a stuck pig, scramble from the briars and with Simon in tow race past her in the direction of the Hall. As a God fearing young woman, brought up with a set of high moral values it was forever on her mind that she had let Meg down by saying nothing to save her own skin, and by so doing had contributed to Meg's death by not revealing that she had seen the full sequence of events.

It was only when Henry Vavour abruptly terminated her employment as governess that she felt sufficiently confident to take her mother into her confidence, but her mother's advice was to keep quiet, pointing out that time had moved on and in any event folk would question her motives following her dismissal. John Ingleby's threats were never disclosed, although neighbours did gossip at the time about the smartly dressed man on horseback who had ridden to the Slades house the morning before Meg was found drowned.

Tom though, was faced with an impossible dilemma now that his young family were motherless. On the one hand, he needed to be at home to look after them because they were still too young to be left alone for the day whilst he was at work. On the other hand if he wasn't working and bringing in a wage, which was barely adequate at the best of times, there would be no money to feed and clothe them. In the end he was left with little choice other than to let the two girls be taken to the orphanage in Grimethorpe, whilst Fred Hoyde offered to find a job for George, now that he was nine. It tortured him to think that as soon as the girls were old enough they would be put to work picking up scraps of wool that fell under the clattering looms of the nearby weaving mills. Unless they were very lucky, the chances of surviving unscathed into their teens were quite slim, as a great many of the accidents involving children were as a result of their ragged clothing becoming entangled in the spinning shafts of the unguarded machinery.

As James got older, he became even more truculent especially when he was showing off in front of Simon Ingelby. He seemed to take a perverse delight in causing distress to his father's tenant farmers by riding through their fields of ripening grain, or panicking a field of grazing cattle. Tenants were too terrified to complain, knowing that if they were to make the slightest adverse comment about his behaviour, his father would see to it that they suffered in some way, even to the extent of evicting regular complainers from their farms. Rather than chastise him over events such as the one which led to Meg Slades death, Henry turned a blind eye to James utter contempt for anyone he regarded as being inferior to himself. Too frequently both he and Simon showed a complete lack of respect for the property or welfare of village people, as they raced their horses at breakneck speed around the village lanes.

One day they were resting their sweating horses for a few moments when James suggested they have a race around an adjoining grass field that backed on to the row of cottage gardens down Peddars Lane. However it wasn't too long before they became bored, so at James suggestion they decided to have a race over the hedges dividing the gardens to the rear of the cottages. Excitedly, thrashing their whips over the horse's flanks they tried to outdo each other regardless of the terror they were inflicting on their frightened steeds. Leaping over the hedges, their horse's hooves churned up the earth, and in the process trampled carefully nurtured vegetables, that would provide much needed food for the cottager's families.

Tom Slade returned from work just in time to see the young tyrants wheeling their horses around in the grass field ready for another mad chase over the hedges. Even the men, who had arrived home before Tom, stood alongside their families reluctant to complain, fearing the retribution Henry would meter out to them. They seemed to be rooted to the ground incapable of moving as they witnessed the destruction of crops they had so painstakingly nurtured. With rising anger, Tom saw the destruction of months of hard work, by the mindless actions of two privileged youths who had never in their lives known what it was like to go hungry. The loss of those crops would almost certainly see families running short of food during the coming winter, so he limped into the middle of his garden and stood in the path of James, as he bore down once again on his sweating stead.

"What the hell do you think you're playing at, these folk need this produce for food"? Tom said picking up a smashed cabbage plant.

For a few moments James glared defiantly at Tom standing below him, then raising his whip brought it down with all the force he could muster across Tom's body.

"Out of my way cripple; I'll ride where I want to over my father's land". He yelled.

George ran to his father, who with a streak of blood beginning to ooze from a laceration stretching across his cheek lay crumpled on the ground. Although small in stature, George wasn't short of pluck as he looked up at the tyrannical son of his father's employer.

Anger welled in his small body as he saw much of his father's hard physical labour destroyed by the loutish behaviour of the young tyrant and his friend. He remembered only too well James actions over the blackberry incident, and how he thought it was connected with his mother drowning in the lake a couple of days later.

"You'll live to regret doing that to my father", he said. "I remember what you did to my mother".

There was something about the quiet authority in George's voice that prevented James from raising his whip once again and giving the son a lesson for being so insolent.

1828

It must have had something to do with his infectious smile and willingness to help with any little task around the farm that so endeared Fred and Annie Hoyd to young George Slade. Unable to have children of their own, they were always delighted to have other village children visit them, but none of them measured up to the rapport they had with George. It was therefore unsurprising that when Annie learned of Meg's tragic death that she, should urge her husband to see if he could find a job for the young lad. She felt immensely sorry for Tom, but with the best will in the world, she realised that their limited means just wouldn't stretch to caring for the two girls as well.

Fred, in common with most cottage farmers, had inherited his small farm from his father and even though he farmed slightly more land than his neighbouring cottagers, it was still difficult to make much of a living from nine acres, four of which were rented from the Vavour estate. Over the years there had been times when birds, and particularly crows, had been especially troublesome, which had a serious effect on the yield of corn he could expect to harvest. The birds played havoc with his newly sown crops by finding the seeds of corn before the plants became fully established, only to return a little later in the year and eat the ripening grain, so Fred, in thinking of a job that young George would be able to do, remarked when he met George and his father, "I know it's not much and it'll mean spending long hours in the fields by yourself, but at least it'll find you a job until you're big enough to do something else".

George was immensely grateful for the offer as he enjoyed being with Fred and his wife, and further more could continue to live at home with his father. Although the job was often quite boring with nothing to break the tedium, he found that to help pass the time, if he stood on the highest point of Fred's top field he could follow the progress of people travelling to and from the Hall. From time to time he would spot a plume of dust, as a carriage passed along the Park drive to emerge through the wrought iron gates onto Peddars Row. It wasn't George's nature to be jealous of Henry Vavours children but at times when he was particularly cold and wet, he did envy them enjoying the warmth and security of the big house with servants to carry out almost their every wish. He knew that they would never have to be out in the middle of a cold field every day, nor did he think that they would sit down to a bowl of potato broth and dry bread at night. However, considering the fate that had befallen his two sisters, he was more than grateful that Mr and Mrs Hoyde had taken pity on him and found him employment.

From those early encounters with James, George had seen enough to realise that the Vavour's were a family to be feared, as deep down he had a feeling that there was a deal more to his mother's death than Henry Vavours claim that she must have accidentally slipped in the lake. It didn't lessen his suspicions when his father remarked from time to time about families in the district who had suffered some misfortune or other, as a consequence of crossing swords with either the Vavour's or Ingleby's.

As James was now in his teens and frequently accompanied by his friend Simon Ingleby, it was unsurprising therefore that people became wary of entangling with either of them, knowing only too well that they were likely to come away second best. Both young men were astute enough to realise that if they cried foul they generally won, and the person who had crossed their path would always finish worse off.

Constance, rather like James father, indulged his every whim, but unlike her husband she rarely learned the true facts relating to some of his wilder exploits. On the contrary, the version she heard generally portrayed him as being the innocent party in a plot designed to incriminate him in some nasty deed or other.

The acquisition of the Masons shipping business was but one of a number of shady deals that enabled Henry Vavour with the collaboration of John Ingleby to rapidly expand his commercial business ventures in Hoult. It wasn't long therefore before the name of Vavour and Co, became one of the most prominent among the names of traders emblazoned across the great brick warehouses lining the canal basin, whilst the Vavour crest on the vessels single sail became an increasing regular sight on sloops plying the canal. As the vessels were capable of carrying 40 tons, it enabled bulky commodities to be transported cheaply, which led to new businesses such as coal yards, saw mills, malt kilns and breweries being established in the town. In their endevours for more business they became totally ruthless in their drive to acquire more trade. If their strategy of undercutting prices was unsuccessful then it was left to Ingelby to devise a plan to gradually force the other party out of business.

By the age of fifteen, George Slade became indispensable to Fred Hoyde assuming an air of sensibility way beyond his years. Annie oft remarked to Fred, that if they had been blessed with children of their own they couldn't have wished for a better son than George. He was kind and considerate with an easy smile and never grumbled at any of the tasks Fred set him.

Despite the passage of weeks and then months, after his wife's tragic death and the departure of the two girls to the orphanage, Tom never fully recovered from losing them, in spite of appearing to have returned to his old self remarkably quickly. However George had good reason to know different as there were too many occasions at night when he thought he could hear his father softly weeping. Tom would frequently stop by the churchyard after leaving work, and sit by the simple headstone marking Meg's grave. As daylight faded into night and the air began to chill, he felt a peace that seemed to connect him with her.   During the quite moments that he spent there, it was only the occasional sound of carriage wheels crunching gravel at the adjacent Hall that disturbed his solitude. From where he sat in the shadows he was able to see the arrival of guests, and then the great west door opening to greet them, as light flooded down the flight of stone steps to illuminate the island of flowers set in the midst of the circular drive. He watched as the servants scurried down the steps to open a carriage door and assist laughing guests alight before they entered the great building.

Such was his feeling of injustice, that when Tom heard the radical orator William Cobbett was coming to Hoult, he took George with him to hear the great man speak at a public meeting in the market place. Agricultural labourers rubbed shoulders with men from the new factories in Hoult; all of them empathising with the sentiments Cobbett expressed.

"A minority of very wealthy and powerful people are exploiting the labour of the masses". Cobbett boomed.

In spite of all the optimistic oratory, Tom's lot didn't change; he was still poorly paid, and he still endured long hours of dusty work.

Belatedly, Henry began to realise that James drinking and womanizing with Simon Ingelby was doing little to enhance the Vavour image in Hoult, so he reasoned that he needed to find a job on the estate to occupy his mind.

The estate farms certainly didn't require any further administration, as they ran smoothly enough under the capable administration of a farm manager, who directed foremen to organise the daily work of the farm labourers, but perhaps something to do with the keepers who looked after the game might be just what he was looking for.

Ever since the time of the land enclosures, there were many cottage farmers with small acreages who had been particularly resentful when they learned that they had to surrender their small strips of land situated in the communal fields, in return for equivalent consolidated areas somewhere else. It was bad enough knowing that they would no longer be able to farm land that had been in the family for generations, but their greatest gripe was reserved for being denied access to walk over land which they regarded as being their birth right.

James wishing to show his new authority urged his keepers to rigorously enforce the estates rules on trespass, threatening that anyone caught, particularly in the woods would be prosecuted.   Never the less some village men, just for the devilment of defying the young tyrant's orders continued to exercise their age old custom. Following further exhortations to his keepers an old cottager by the name of Frank Bailey was caught one morning taking a walk by the beck side as had been his practice for over fifty years. In spite of the head keeper expressing disquiet about the old man's age, James was determined to prosecute him.

"Trespass is trespass", he declared "I don't care how old the peasant is, I'm going to make an example of him".

Frank was taken to court and had little alternative other than to plead guilty to the charge, where upon the magistrate who knew the reputation of the Vavours and their acts of retribution, fined the old man the outrageous sum of five shillings. In spite of the example made of old Frank, it only served to increase the determination of other villagers, who believed that if they ventured into the woods and took a rabbit then it represented a small victory for the little man against the wealth and power of the Vavour's. The keepers came to dread James interrogations, fearing for their jobs whenever he quizzed them about the sight of anything unusual that might indicate poaching had taken place. Although no one else was caught, the keepers had to report the sight of anything unusual, such as bloodstains or the appearance of a few feathers that might indicate poaching activity.

Although Tom occasionally saw James riding one of his sweating steeds, he rarely came into contact with either him or his father, though tales of his erratic behaviour was frequently the main topic of discussion when he and his fellow workers sat round for their breaks. George meanwhile saw even less of him, as apart from having his evening meal and sleeping at home, he spent practically all his time at the Hoyde's. After a lifetimes hard physical work, Fred's health began to deteriorate to such a degree that following the slightest exertion he became breathless. Little wonder therefore, that as George became older and gained more experience that Fred would come to increasingly rely on him to run his small farm.

"I'm afraid I'll `ave to go back to Fred's tonight", George remarked to his father, one night towards the end of October as they sat down for their evening meal. "One of the heifers was uneasy when I left, so I might even have to stop the night". Knowing only too well how much his father enjoyed his company, made George particularly loathe to leave him alone, especially now that the dark nights had arrived, but he knew that he wouldn't rest easy until the heifer had calved.

Years of hard work flailing corn were beginning to take their toll on Tom. The constant bending with a flail had given him a pronounced stoop that when coupled with his lean frame and gaunt features made him look a good deal older than his forty-six years. Harvest had been particularly late that year with few drying days during August, so that by the time the sheaves were eventually brought into the farm yard that September, many of the ears had already sprouted. Tom knew only too well that it would make the already difficult task of flailing considerably worse. He knew that the small pinched grains would not only be difficult to extract from the ears, but when combined with the green mould on the grain would make his chest ache even more.

Having completed their meal of leek and potato broth, prepared from vegetables Tom had grown in his garden, they both relaxed for a few minutes by the fire, before George said he would have to go and see how his heifer was progressing.

After washing their few pots in the sink, Tom slipped his cloak over his shoulders, in readiness for his regular evening trip to the pump that served several cottages at the other end of Peddars Row. Never knowing anything any different ever since his father was forced to move to the cottage, it had become something of a nightly ritual for him to walk the couple of hundred yards down the lane to fetch their water. Still it was at times such as these that he so dreadfully missed Meg's cheerful company, as he remembered the children's excited laughter as she prepared them for bed. His feeling of longing had been slightly relieved by the chapel minister who having recently been to the orphanage and seen both his daughters, explained to Tom that they were both well, and that his elder daughter was to be married the following year to a machine man at the mill.   It seems so very unfair, he remembered remarking to the minister, that fates dealt me such a cruel hand.

Ever since her death, it had struck him particularly hard whenever he had left the warmth of the cottage, as it seemed to draw a veil over his happy times with her and symbolised the emptiness in his life. There'll be a frost tonight; he thought, closing the door behind him and pausing for a few seconds to gaze at the stars shining like so many sparkling crystals from the inky blackness of the clear night sky.

Stepping into the cold night air made him shudder as the chill air struck his face, so pulling his cloak a little tighter over his shoulders he stood his empty bucket by the house door whilst a host of nostalgic memories flooded back. His mind was so absorbed with memories of times gone by that rather like a sleepwalker lost in a world of dreams he began to slowly stroll along the lane until with something of a shock he realized that he had somehow taken himself to the West field. It was perhaps unsurprising that he should have strolled in that direction, considering that as a child he must have gone that way countless times to see his father who had a narrow strip of land in the West Field. Following the Vavour's amalgamation of everyone's strip of land to form one large field which the estate now farmed, previous owners ran a risk of being accused of trespass if they ventured there. Beyond West Field he was just able to distinguish the dark outline of trees, through which he knew, that rather like the coils of some recumbent serpent, the beck made meandering sweeps on its way to the sea, and that brought back memories of summer evenings long ago.

It didn't take a deal of imagination to remember Meg unclasping his hand and challenging him to catch her, as she raced on ahead, her lithe figure silhouetted against the setting sun. It was perhaps a testament to his present trance like state when everything felt so real, that he should believe he could hear her voice above the sound of the water tinkling over the stones in the stream. The strange thing was though, that in spite of more than eight years passing since her death everything seemed as fresh in his mind as if it had just happened. Then in a flash the image changed to the sight of her pale face lying in a simple pine coffin on the kitchen table, but before he could dwell too long on that, the jumbled pieces rearranged themselves into a vision of members of his platoon at Waterloo, and then that also changed to the sight of the Frenchman's mutilated body.

As if for reassurance that it wasn't all a dream, he fingered the cross around his neck, and then reality set in, when he realised that in his trance like state he really had trespassed much further into the Estates land than he had ever intended. He turned, and started to retrace his steps back towards West Field as fast as his limp would allow. Was that the sound of the keepers in pursuit he could hear, or was it his imagination starting to play tricks on him? He was uncertain.

But of one thing he was certain; he didn't want a keeper to catch him here, when he remembered the episode in the gardens and how vindictive James could be, when he knew that any pleas of innocence would fall on deaf ears.

Over the previous week, gales had stripped the majority of leaves from the elm trees in the wood and blown them into drifts between the trunks. When his feet kicked into a particularly large pile of leaves it startled a rabbit, making it dart from its camouflaged hide and run furiously in the direction of the beck, rustling more leaves as it made its escape. The noise disturbed blackbirds roosting in the ivy that cloaked the beck side trees, so that with a frenzy of flapping wings and high pitched cackles they darted from their nocturnal roosts to settle in trees further away. He was only too aware that the noise they were making would surely act as an early warning alarm to the alert ears of any keepers who happened to be about, and that would be bound to set in motion an investigation to establish the cause. The trouble was that with his mind focused on so many other things, it was incredibly stupid of him to find that he was deep inside the estates wood on a perfectly still night, when he knew that James would take great delight in accusing him of poaching and sending him to court on a trumped up charge.

For some time he had come to the conclusion that the well dressed man who had confronted Meg the day before her death, must have been John Ingelby, so it seemed reasonable to assume that it was possibly something he had said to her that may have been responsible for what happened to her. If he could do that to her, then what tale was he capable of concocting to convict him? At the very least he would be evicted from his cottage and lose his job. Then where would he live? In any event who was likely to employ a lame man? The workhouse at the top of the hill in Hoult seemed the only outcome. All of these thoughts flashed through his mind as he broke into a stumbling run.

He decided that his nearest route back would bring him within yards of a bend in the beck where the wind had created a particularly large mound of leaves by funnelling them between two trees. As he stepped on the leaves, without the slightest hint of warning the leaves exploded apart, as two vice like metal jaws sprang up to clasp their interlocking teeth around his left leg. He thought he knew what pain was when he was injured at Waterloo, but this was something infinitely worse. It felt as though his leg was being severed and there was absolutely nothing he could do about it. At first he tried to pull the jaws apart but from where he lay he lacked the physical strength to prise them even a fraction of an inch sideways. In rising desperation at his predicament he tore at the soil with his fingers in a vain attempt to gain freedom, but soon realised that the effort was futile. It was only as Tom's fingers, sticky with blood, explored the interlocking teeth clamped tight to his leg, that he realised he must be caught in a mantrap similar to the one he had once seen in the loft above the great barn at the Hall farm yard. He remembered how as a youngster, not long on the farm, he had enthusiastically agreed to fetch a "wool riddle" from the loft above the barn for one of the older workers. Fetching a wool riddle was one of the regular ruses trotted out periodically for the amusement of older workers, when to their delight the young worker reported that he couldn't find it. Even in his present state, it still made him cringe to think he had been quite so daft as to fall for such a stupid request. Half a brain should have told him at the time that it was impossible to riddle wool, but there again, it, along with other hoary chestnuts seemed to act rather like an initiation test for young farm workers. It was during his unsuccessful search amongst piles of dusty rubbish for something that he wasn't exactly sure what it looked like, when he came across a metal contraption that rather resembled a giant rat trap. He remembered seeing it hung in the rafters, festooned in cobwebs, where it must have lain undisturbed for scores of years.

After a while the pain seemed to moderate a little and he became light headed. His blood felt warm to the touch as it oozed through his fingers from the gaping wound. As his strength weakened, Tom felt sure that he could hear Megs voice softly repeating his name, Tom, Tom, over and over again, - he felt confused, was it really her voice he could hear, or was it just a trick of his imagination. But then when he looked towards the dark mass of trees, he felt even more bewildered when he thought he could see Megs smiling face with an outstretched arm beckoning him towards her. As the rhythmical notes of water tinkling over the gravel bed in the beck gently lulled his senses he began to find it increasingly difficult to keep his eyes open. He felt tired and closed his eyes as the hypnotic sound in the background brought about an inner peace. After a while he slipped into unconsciousness as his life slowly ebbed away.

• • • •

The hoar frost that Tom had so accurately predicted earlier started its relentless march as the air grew colder, so that by morning the grass field by the wood was completely white. John Cane was an assistant keeper on the estate, whose first task of the day was to take a walk through the trees by the beck and check that the feeding points for the estates game birds hadn't been disturbed by predators during the night. He always enjoyed his early morning stroll through the wood because there was generally something of interest to see, especially now that autumn was well advanced. With a bit of luck now that the leaves were dropping, he thought there was a good chance that he might get a better view of a green woodpecker that he had regularly heard hammering away at the trunk of a dead tree, but had previously only caught the briefest sight of. Then if he was lucky, there was just a chance that he might catch a glimpse of a woodcock. With the onset of cooler weather, he knew that they would soon be arriving for the winter. Although as a keeper he was paid to control vermin that might destroy the estates game birds, he could never understand why James was so obsessed about village people trespassing on estate land. Did it really matter that much if someone should take the odd rabbit? He really thought James was going well over the top when he urged them all one day to report to him personally anything they saw that looked as though poaching had taken place. During all the time he had done his morning walk, the only thing he had ever seen that remotely resembled poaching, was seeing a fox carrying something in its mouth. He idly kicked a drift of leaves as he rounded one of the sharp bends on the side of the beck that morning, and in doing so, the noise disturbed a couple of carrion crows who flew into some high branches ahead. They were obviously excited as they continued to caw raucously from the safety of the tree where they had settled.

It was only when he carried on a little further that John Cane became fully aware of what they had been devouring when he disturbed them. Little wonder therefore that he stopped in his tracks and had to grip an adjacent tree trunk for support, when he was confronted by a sight that was something beyond his wildest imagination. Naturally enough over the years, there were plenty of times when he had disturbed carrion crows and magpies feasting on a dead rabbit or for that matter any other small creature that had died and had always been disgusted by the way that they always seemed to pick out the eyes and genitals first. The shepherds on the estate frequently brought a dead sheep back to the yard with bloody sockets where the eyes had once been, but what he was looking at now was something else. Before him lay the savaged remains of a man whose legs appeared to be caught in some sort of metal device. The birds hooked beaks had gouged out the eyes and by doing so had transformed the face almost beyond recognition. What he saw was so horrific that every last detail was instantly etched into his memory and would haunt him for the rest of his days. In spite of trying to avert his eyes from looking at a face that was far worse than any nightmare, he felt compelled to approach the body.

As he moved closer, Cane became aware that the mutilated corpse lying spread eagled before him was that of Tom Slade. It was quite obvious that something resembling a giant rat trap had cut deep into the flesh of one of his legs below the knee. Judging by scratch marks in the surrounding soil he could see that Tom, in a desperate effort to escape must have clawed the ground with his bare hands.

With racing heart and a dry mouth Cane bent over the out stretched figure and whilst averting his eyes from Toms face placed a hand over his chest in the forlorn hope that he might detect a heartbeat, but of course Tom's skin was stone cold. In the process of withdrawing his hand, he touched something metallic that seemed to be attached to a cord around his neck. Curiosity getting the better of him, he parted Tom's shirt to reveal the unusual silver cross that he had heard other farm workers comment on. Without considering the consequences of his actions he grabbed it, snapping the cord in the process and quickly dropped it in an inside pocket of his coat. Without a backwards glance, Cane turned on his heels and fled in a blind panic back to the Hall, arriving at the front steps, just as Henry Vavour was about to take his regular early morning walk along the Park drive.

"Whatever's the matter man"? Henry exclaimed, seeing Canes agitated state, as he rushed across flailing his arms.

"Its -- Tom Slade Sir, -- `e's dead", Cane managed to blurt out between great gulps of air.

"What! Where man...?"

"In the wood Sir, -- `ees got is legs trapped – an' its killed `im".

"Killed! His legs trapped. What the devil do you mean man? – He can't get killed in the wood.

"E is sir"

"Is it something you've done man?"

"No Sir," Cane shook his head vigorously, fearful that if he wasn't careful he was going to be held responsible for Tom's death, "`ees in a trap Sir".

"Trap! What kind of trap? Surely one of your traps couldn't possibly kill a man, - - could it"?

"I think -- it's a mantrap Sir".

"Mantrap. What the devil are you talking about?

"I'm sure it is Sir, --Years ago I remember seeing summat like it ung in the roof of the old barn Sir".

"What does this, - - this mantrap - you say, look like".

Cane started to shake even more in the face of Henry's interrogation. "It's somat like a great big rat trap, Sir. – It were old Walter, wot used to werk `ere wot tell me wot it was. Relic from the past he sez. I'm certain it wus`nt theere wen I did me rounds last night Sir".

"How do you know that man?"

"If it `ed been theer then I'd `eve seen it Sir".

"Are you quite sure that it wasn't you that set the blasted thing"? Henry said pointing an accusing finger.

"No Sir. Honest it wasn't me" Cane said, believing that Henry Vavour was about to have him convicted of the crime. Shaking even more vigorously than before, he went on– "but I reckon – an theer agen, maybe I shouldn't be sayin Sir, as ees your son".

"Come on, out with it man, what shouldn't you be saying?

"Well, James may `eve `ad a `and in setting it after I finished my rounds last night".

"What! What makes you think that"?

"Well, I spotted `im and Simon in the barn last night".

Ruin and scandal were the first thoughts to come into Henry's mind, so quickly assessing the situation said, "Pull yourself together man, and follow me to my study". With the door firmly shut, Henry instructed Cane to sit down, then reaching across to the lower drawer of his desk selected a bottle of brandy and a tumbler. After pouring a generous measure, he passed it over to the still shaking figure.

"Does anyone else know about this?" he asked in a tone more reasonable than before.

Once again, Cane gave a shake of the head, as Henry's brain went into overdrive. "Whatever's happened is obviously a tragic accident that will benefit no one if it is misconstrued" Henry said getting up and walking over to the window. I want you to swear an oath of secrecy to me now, that you will never divulge to anyone what you have seen this morning".

Cane took a much larger gulp of the brandy than he had intended, which instantly brought on a bout of coughing, as the fiery liquid ran down his throat.

Henry had many faults, but was quite astute when weighing up a difficult situation. He realised that at best his son would receive a lengthy term of imprisonment, and at worst would be hung for using an instrument that had so recently been declared illegal. John Ingelby had pointed out to him only recently, how the reforming zeal of the non conformist movement was beginning to change judge's attitudes, so that they were now less inclined to turn a blind eye to "indiscretions", as he put it, by the ruling classes.

Henry was quick to recognise that if it became known that the Vavours had had a hand in committing such a barbaric crime against a villager who had more than his share of misfortune, then it could very well seal their fate on any future business in Hoult, because local people would be united in their revulsion. By judicious use of bribes and threats, he decided to give Cane a warning.

"If you ever divulge to another person what you have seen this morning, I'll see to it that you're arrested for the offence. Without witnesses to say what you were doing in the wood, you'll have a job convincing a jury that it wasn't you who set the trap. Remember if you try to implicate others, then it's only your word against theirs. However if you keep your mouth shut I will see to it that you are promoted to the position of head keeper and I will give you forty pounds every Christmas".

Even though he couldn't clear the sight of Tom Slades face from his mind, Cane could hardly keep a smile from spreading across his face. He could hardly believe what he was hearing. It wasn't every day that he was offered forty pounds for keeping his mouth shut. An annual sum of forty pounds was as much as he earned in a year, surely a compelling argument for keeping quiet.

He quickly agreed to Henrys request and promised that he would never mention what he had seen to a living soul. He knew only too well that if he had demurred, then the Vavour's and Ingelby's between them wouldn't have taken long before they had concocted a convincing case to ensure he was found guilty of a crime, for which he would be convicted and hung for murder.

. . . .

Livid with anger, Henry strode up the stairs to James bedroom. Thrusting open the door he found his son still in bed.

"You've managed to kill a man in your trap", he said without preamble.

"What trap?" James blustered, visibly shaken by his father's sudden entrance.

"You know damn well" Henry said, in no mood to accept another of his lies.

"I don't know why you are asking me. We employ keepers to set traps".

"Don't try and make a fool of me with your stupid comments. I'm fed up with your lies. I have already asked the keepers and they deny all knowledge".

"They're lying; they're setting traps all the time. Anyway I don't even know what a mantrap looks like, let alone setting one".

Fearing that his furious father was about to strike him with his walking stick, James cowered against the far wall.

"You blithering idiot. Who mentioned a mantrap? What were you and Simon doing in the loft above the barn last night"?

James shoulders slumped as he lost his normal cocksure manner. The reality of what he had done hit him, making him much more subdued.

"I didn't think the keepers were doing their job properly, so I wanted to prove to them, that people were trespassing. Years ago when I was playing hide and seek with Simon I remembered going up into the loft above the barn and seeing a funny looking object. When I asked one of the old labourers what it was, he said it was a mantrap. I reminded Simon about it recently and he said why not take it in the woods after the keepers have completed their rounds, and see what we catch. Well that's what we did last night. We found a spot between trees by the beck where we presumed poachers would pass, so we set the trap and camouflaged it by heaping leaves over it".

"And as a result, through your stupidity, you've managed to kill a man".

"We didn't mean that to happen, it was to show the keepers that they weren't doing their jobs properly".

"That's not how a court will see it. Even with John Ingelby's best endeavours, at the very least you will be convicted of manslaughter, but far more likely it will be premeditated murder. I can tell you, that for that sort of crime you'll be lucky if you don't hang, unless we do something about it. Cane's the only person who's seen what's happened but I'm certain I've frightened him enough to ensure that he won't say a word. We can't leave the body were it is, so we have to move it somewhere else and make his death look like an accident. Go and tell the Wagoner that you want a horse harnessed to the cart that Tom Slade uses when he takes straw from the flailing barn. If he asks why you are taking it, tell him you are going to accompany Tom, because you want some straw down by the beck for the pheasants to scratch in".

A little while later father and son disappeared from sight as the farm cart with its load of straw made its ponderous way across the Park, into West Field and then into the wood.

The macabre sight of Tom's outstretched body with bloody sockets where his eyes had once been unnerved James, though his father, who had seen plenty of horrific scenes at Waterloo wasn't quite so badly affected, but even so he was shocked to see the extent of his injuries. With some difficulty they eased back the jaws of the mantrap to release the dead man's leg. It soon became apparent that his leg had been almost severed by the interlocking teeth.

After depositing some of the straw in the wood, they loaded Tom's slight frame into the cart, covering it with the remaining straw. Finally they threw the mantrap in the beck at the point where a sharp bend in the meandering stream had created a deep pool.

"I've seen these fellows taking a ride on the shafts", Henry declared, so Slade wouldn't be the first man to slip off the shafts and fall under a wheel".

Ever since his father had told him about Tom Slade's death, the thought of the hangman's noose had so swamped his mind that he could think of little else, which was in no way helped by having to assist his father extract the mutilated body from the trap and load it into the cart, but the implications of what his father was now saying suddenly lifted an enormous weight from his shoulders, when as usual he had come up with a perfect solution.

"I noticed when we came, how the cart lurched when it dropped into a rut". He remarked, sounding considerably more cheerful than a few seconds earlier.

"It would certainly be a tragic accident if a wheel dropped in a hole causing our friend to fall off and slip under one of those iron rimmed wheels". Henry smirked.

A little way down the track, well hidden from prying eyes, they removed Tom's body from the cart and positioned his legs across one of the tracks in the cart road, in such a manner that when the cart wheel passed over them it would obscure the incision made by the jaws of the mantrap.

It wasn't until much later in the day that word reached George that his father had had an accident, having presumably fallen from the shafts of the straw cart.

The Vavour's claimed that they had joined Tom that morning as he took a cart load of straw across West Field and then down to the beck side, where they had left him, preferring to walk back home together by the side of the stream. When Tom hadn't returned by mid afternoon, a fellow worker went to find out where he had got to, only to make the tragic discovery, with the horse contentedly grazing grass alongside the track.

George was devastated, as he arranged for his poor fathers broken body to be laid out on the kitchen table, in preparation for the funeral and burial next to Meg. Frank Toft the village carpenter, who also made coffins from his range of planks, stored in his workshop roof, visited the humble cottage to measure Tom whilst Beth Cummings came along to clean and dress the body. She remarked to Frank about the strange lacerations on just one of Tom's legs, but came to the conclusion that they had obviously been caused by the iron rim of the wheel. She thought little at the time of the flesh stripped from his fingers, assuming that with two broken legs he had attempted to move by clawing the ground with his hands.

It was a pity she didn't meet the man who found him under the cart until several months later, because he thought Tom must have died instantly, in view of there being no sign of a struggle.

George declined Fred and Annie Hoyde's kind invitation for him to stop with them until after the funeral, preferring to be in the cottage with his dead father for the final three nights. It wasn't until the second night that George realised there was something wrong, and then it occurred to him. Where was his father's double cross? As long as he could remember it had never left his neck. George was convinced that there was another element to his father's death, especially as the man who discovered Tom's body was adamant that the cross was not around his neck when he discovered him, because he distinctly remembered opening Tom's shirt to feel for a heartbeat. The man also remarked about the body being icy cold, but as he had had no experience of dead bodies, no one made anything of it.

Nobody from the Vavour family, as was their norm with the death of village folk, bothered to attend the simple ceremony, preferring to rely on the farm manager to represent them. Henry didn't discuss any of the events surrounding Tom Slade's death with Constance preferring for her to believe that it was just a tragic accident. He did however give a less than truthful explanation to John Ingleby, when he told him about James obsession with poachers and how he had instructed Cane to look out for them. He hinted that because of that, Tom Slade had, had his accident.

"I should keep an eye on that Cane chap" John Ingleby advised one evening after the two men had retired to the drawing room following a meal, "you don't want the fellow to cause trouble in the future".

"It's unlikely", was Henrys confident reply, adding, "He's no reason too after the way I look after him".

James for his part couldn't get the vision of Tom's tortured face out of his mind, as the sight of the dead man's bloody eye sockets seemed to haunt him all his waking hours. He knew that in spite of all his bravado, he was responsible for the poor man's death, and Simon was a willing accomplice.

Fred and Annie Hoyde made the room that George had previously occupied on a temporary basis at their home, into a permanent one, as the estate quickly reclaimed Tom's cottage and let it to another farm labourer.

Rumours began to circulate in the village about John Cane's sudden rise in fortune and why he had replaced Bill Taylor as head keeper. In particular tongues wagged at the amount he was spending at the White Hart ale house. On more than one occasion, after having too much to drink, beads of sweat would suddenly appear on his brow, then shaking his head vigorously it seemed as though he was trying to dispel an unpleasant image.

George of course heard these rumours from other villagers but they meant little to him as there was nothing in the gossip to remotely connect him to his father's death.

1836

As far back as he could remember Tom Slade had been one of Bill Taylor's best friends, which perhaps wasn't too much of a surprise, considering that they had both grown up in the same small village community and had attended the village school together. As he became older Bill fancied Meg Foster, the shy daughter of another cottage farmer, but to his regret, could never summon up sufficient courage to ask her father if he could walk her out. However when he did eventually pluck up sufficient confidence, it was all too late because Tom had already made his intentions known. It was therefore little wonder, that he would be deeply affected when he came across Meg's body that autumn morning. Naturally he heard what Henry Vavour had to say about her accidental drowning, but knowing Meg as he did, he was never convinced by his reasoning. He thought at the time that Henry had been quick, and perhaps just a little too quick to offer an explanation. He knew Meg well enough to know that it was no accident. She had lived in the village all her life, so he thought it was hardly likely that she would lose her bearings around what was really a large fish pond. In any event the water around the edge was quite shallow, so even if she had lost her bearing it was most unlikely she would have drowned in the manner that Henry was claiming.

He had been careful never to divulge his thoughts to anyone else, let alone Tom, as he knew it would only add to his distress. After all, he had no proof to back up his doubts, only a feeling that there was a deal more to it than was generally accepted. So when Henry informed him that Cane would be taking his position of head keeper after Tom's accident, he felt doubly suspicious that Henry Vavour had something to hide, but unfortunately as was the case with Meg's accident he had no proof of any malpractice, so was reluctant to share his thoughts with anyone else. In the years that followed, he had come to admire the way young George coped with the tragic deaths of both his parents. He was therefore, both proud and delighted when George asked his permission if he could walk out with his youngest daughter, Rose. Right from her earliest days, Bill and his wife had been impressed by Roses sensibility, a fact that certainly wasn't lost on Mr Wells her teacher at the village school. He was quick to recognise that in other circles Rose could have achieved great things, but given Bills limited circumstances as soon as she was ten years of age she left school to become a maid at the Hall. By her sixteenth birthday she had progressed to be the cook's principle assistant, taking full responsibility for preparing some of the Vavour's meals.

George, in spite of enjoying his work on Fred Hoyde's farm, looked forward to Sundays and his weekly visit to the service in the Wesleyan chapel, because having neither the money nor means to travel, this was the one and only occasion in the week when he had an opportunity to meet other folk. For an hour or two at least, he was able to get out of his uncomfortable working clothes and put on his one and only suit, but as the years passed by another reason developed for him to look forward to the arrival of Sunday. It was from his pew towards the rear of the chapel that he first became aware of the pretty girl seated in a family group on the second row. He couldn't help noticing that from time to time she would turn around in her seat to smile coquettishly in his direction.

At first he blushed and then nervously smiled back, until one fine day in the early spring of 1834 as they left the building, he plucked up enough courage to ask her, that if he gained her father's permission, could he walk her home. Although it was only a short stroll from the church to her home near the Hall, George was so captivated by her that it seemed like an eternity before he could meet her again the following Sunday. As the summer progressed into autumn they found that the hour or so spent together following chapel was all very well but they needed to meet more frequently. Even though Rose was expected to be on permanent call to carry out the wishes of Henry and Constance Vavour, she found that if she was careful how she went about it, she could snatch a few minutes with him, by making a prearranged liaison by the yew hedge that divided the Hall grounds from the church. Before many more months had elapsed, George asked her if she would marry him.

So it was that in June 1835 the happy couple married to the great approval of Bill and his wife. Fred and Annie Hoyde of course, were equally delighted, because over the years that he had worked for them, they had come to regard George as a surrogate son.

"If you can make it liveable, then you can have that old cottage on the other side the farm yard as a wedding present", Fred said generously.

The ruined place had lain abandoned for longer than anyone could remember, yet George fired up with the enthusiasm of youth faced the daunting challenge of repairing the old dwelling with vigour. He started by replacing the straw thatch where it had blown away and then plastered damaged areas of the mud and stud walls with the usual mixture of soil, clay and straw. Once dry, the packed earthen floors were swept clean and snip rugs, given to them by Rose's mother, were laid. The garden had long since become a wilderness of nettles, couch grass and buttercups, but rather like his father before him, when faced with a similar challenge, George set about it, realising that the more crops he could grow in his garden, then the better they would eat through the cold winter months. He was young, strong and keen, so that after a few months of hard work, he began to turn the ancient property into a comfortable home.

• • • •

"I'm afraid you're in it up to your neck now", a shocked John Ingelby remarked to Henry one evening, after a night spent drinking too much wine had loosened Henrys tongue. It was only when he saw the look of horror on his friends face, that Henry realised this was the first he knew of how both he and James had staged Tom Slade's death to look like an accident. In order that James would have no further contact with the keepers, and in particular Cane, where there was a strong possibility that in the heat of the moment something might be said that might incriminate them, John Ingelby advised Henry that James should join the Vavour shipping business.

James was more than happy to comply with the arrangement because he lived in constant dread of what might happen, if new evidence materialized linking him to the death of Tom Slade. From time to time in pursuance of his new position James travelled on one of the sloops on the two day voyage from Hoult to Hull. The trade revolved around the delivery of grain, wool and other agricultural produce, returning with coal, timber and manufactured goods. During the time the boat was being discharged and reloaded, James was invited to stay overnight at the home of Sir Joshua Newby whose family business had traded for several years with the Vavour shipping company. The Newby family wealth had originally been founded on the slave trade with the port of Hull forming a pivotal segment of the triangle, but now that slavery was about to be abolished in Britain, their business empire as a major import and exporter was being extended in other directions.

It was during one of his stays at the Newbys that he met Isabelle, Sir Joshua and Lady Jane's attractive youngest daughter. Even though she had never been short of eligible suitors from good families, it could have been something to do with the rebellious streak within her that made her want to defy her parents' wishes, especially when they were not wholly enthusiastic about the young man from south of the river. On the other hand her Latin temperament, that so excited James, might equally well have had something to do with her mother's Spanish ancestry, but in any event she derived a certain satisfaction in the knowledge that James didn't exactly fit the stereotyped young man her parents regarded as being suitable for her. James became so besotted with her, that he would seize upon the slightest excuse to make the journey to Hull, even though it meant being closeted for several days with the rough sailors manning the sloops. He was however, astute enough to realise that if he wanted to win Isabelle's hand, then he would have to suppress his demanding behaviour, and show a great deal more respect for others than he had shown in the past.

On a flaming June day in 1835, James married Isabelle in one of the grandest society weddings that the city had seen for many years. It had taken two of Hulls finest seamstresses most of a month to produce the bride's exquisite silk wedding dress which was heavily adorned with pearls and sequins on not only the dress itself, but also the fifteen foot train. Eight pure white stallions drew the Lord Mayor's fine, gilded carriage that conveyed the newly wedded couple from the church to a glittering reception in the Guildhall.

Simon Ingelby who since the death of Tom Slade had kept a much lower profile was best man, whilst both of Isabelle's sisters made radiant bridesmaids.

Although the wedding was just one week later than that of George and Rose, there could hardly have been a greater contrast between the two events. Following their simple ceremony a few guests gathered afterwards at Roses parents home, whilst over in Hull the reception was lavish with food and wine for more than six hundred guests. As if to emphasise the chasm that existed between the Vavour's and village people, no one from the village was invited to attend either the reception in Hull or another event hosted the following day by Henry and Constance in the Hall.

There was much local speculation on where the newlyweds would live, some folk, who claimed to be in the know, even suggested that Henry and Constance would leave the Hall in order that they could move in there, but it soon became clear that they would be setting up home in David Mason's grand town house in Hoult. Although David Mason had been cheated out of his business by Henry Vavour, he had continued to maintain the lifestyle of a prosperous business man. But unfortunately once his source of income dried up he found he could no longer afford the houses upkeep, so as a final humiliation he allowed his home to pass into Vavour hands.

It wasn't too long after their wedding that Isabelle began to have second thoughts about her infatuation with James. All too late she began to see a darker side to the husband who had swept her off her feet. Nowhere was her regret more keenly felt than during the hours of darkness. There were terrifying moments in the middle of the night when she was woken by a blood curdling scream as he drew the bed clothes about him in an endeavour to be rid of some imagined demons. On other occasions he would wake her by gripping her so tightly that she could hardly breathe. She found his refusal to discuss the reasons why he loathed the dark, particularly frustrating, especially when he would insist they leave friends houses for home well before dusk, and under no circumstances would he venture across the Park in darkness. Even though their relationship, which at best could be described as volatile, she nevertheless produced a son the following June who they named William after James grandfather.

• • • •

The memory of his father's accidental death had begun to fade with the passage of time, or at least that was the case, until everything changed one day when George came across Jack Barker in rather bizarre circumstances. Jack was a well known local character, who loved nothing better than stopping for a chat with anyone he could manage to waylay for a few minutes, even though his general appearance deterred those who didn't know him. However people soon warmed to him when his heavily lined face broke into a broad smile, which coupled with a mischievous twinkle to his eyes made him instantly likeable. Over the years Jack had built up something of a reputation as a poacher largely because of the way he could often be seen taking a walk along the lanes and bridleways as dusk approached. With that in mind, it was perhaps inevitable, that rather unjustly his name generally arose if a fowl mysteriously disappeared during the night, when in all probability, the more likely culprit was a fox. His hat, that was generally pulled down to his ears, may once have looked quite smart on the head for which it was originally purchased, but over the years since passing into his possession it had lost much of its appeal, as it had become stained in a kaleidoscope of colours ranging from brown through differing shades of grey to black. In spite of its generous size, it still seemed incapable of containing all his straggly grey hair which seemed to poke out in all directions from around its circumference. To add to his reputation as a poacher, Jack always wore a loose fitting grey coat, though even that may also at one time have been a different colour. However the inside pockets were of such capacity that they were capable of concealing pretty well anything he might come across on his travels. Now in his early seventies, Jack had never married living alone in an isolated cottage some distance away from other houses in the village. Given his reputation for living on whatever bird or animal he could take, it was rather apt that Georges contact with him should have a poaching connection.

One February morning, George was in one of Fred Hoyde's fields, taking extra feed to a flock of pregnant ewes, when he spotted the outstretched arm of a figure waving from the base of the large hedge boarding a ditch on the far side of the field. As George got closer it was soon apparent, that the figure was Jack, and that he seemed to be sprawled halfway down the side of the ditch, with one of his legs caught somewhere within the thick stems of the overgrown hawthorn hedge.

"I was setting another snare for a rabbit see", Jack said by way of explanation when George reached him. "I 'ad to git through this 'ere edge when soft like, I forgot all about the other snare Id set, and damn me if I didn't catch me foot in it. It made me lose me balance so that I trapped me other foot between these two branches," pointing to where one foot was held in an elongated V between two thick stems.

"I wus trapped just as fast as your poor father 'ad been, bless 'im".

"What do you mean by that"? George said sharply. "My Father wasn't trapped, he had an accident; he was run over by his straw cart. What makes you think he was caught in a trap"?

"I'm not rightly sure what I'm saying". Jack said mumbling through his few remaining teeth. "It's the damn cold, I can't be thinkin straight. I'm get mixed up with sum at else".

With some difficulty owing to Jacks weight and the awkward position in which the old fellow was laying, George managed to extract his leg from between the branches and get him into an upright position. The other leg however, was quite a different proposition, because as Jack had struggled, the wire snare had tightened around his leg cutting deep into the flesh just above the top of his boot. When George removed the boot, he was horrified to see how the old chap's foot had turned an angry shade of purple no doubt as a result of the wire constricting the flow of blood. Rather than attempt the difficult process of extricating the snare, George unfastened the other end of it, where it had been anchored to one of the thick hawthorn stems and decided to move Jack with it still attached. As it was virtually impossible for the poor old fellow to walk, George loaded him into the back of his shepherding trap and brought him back to his cottage. Rose, although heavily pregnant, quickly took charge of the situation, as she got George to carry him into their only downstairs room and lay him on a wooden bench by the fire.

"We need to fetch the doctor", Rose said her face full of concern. "I've got a little money put by for the baby's clothes".

• • • •

"Let him lay comfortable beside the fire and give him two tablespoons of this mixture every four hours", the doctor explained, handing Rose a bottle of dark green liquid, "it will help to suppress his fever. I don't care for the look of his foot though, but if you bathe it twice a day adding a little salt to the water it might give him some relief".

In spite of the doctor's best efforts Jacks foot failed to heal, in fact as the days passed by it continued to get worse, eventually turning an angry shade of green, before going black with an accompanying smell of rotting flesh that permeated the furthest reaches of the small cottage. With Annie Hoyde's assistance, Rose did her best, to make him as comfortable as possible, but his condition steadily deteriorated. Even in his more rational moments, despite sympathetic questioning, Jack refused to elaborate on his earlier statement about the death of George's father. From their bed in the loft, George and Rose were kept awake by the sound of the poor man's feverish murmurings until one night as they both lay awake; George thought he could hear the old man faintly calling his name. Even though he was desperate to hear if the old man would elaborate on his earlier statement, he was mindful of where he placed his feet as he clambered down the rough ladder to the kitchen below. It wouldn't have been the first time he had lost his footing on one of the bits of round branch that formed the rungs of the rudimentary ladder and he had landed in an untidy heap on the floor. Stepping across the kitchen to where Jack lay, he saw that the candle Rose had placed by his bed when they retired for the night had almost burned away, yet its meagre flame augmented by the first glimmer of light entering the window as dawn approached illuminated Jack's silver hair and beard in an almost luminous glow.

Bending in an endeavour to catch what the old man was mumbling, George was aware that his breathing had become much shallower than the rasping sound they had heard earlier. Very slowly the old chap turned his head and began to whisper in such a low voice that George had to hold his ear close to his sunken mouth to catch what he was saying.

"Yer father didn't die 'ow they sed".

"What"? George said suddenly wide awake. "What do you mean, are you saying it wasn't an accident after all".

Jack gave another long sigh before continuing. "No. They reckoned 'ede fallen under the wheel of is straw cart, -- but it wus a lie".

"Why was it a lie"? George asked gently, staggered at what Jack was saying.

Jack gave a low rasping cough, before carrying on in a voice that was barely audible.

"E was caught in a mantrap in the wood by the beck. I see 'im wi me own eyes, but when I found im 'e was dead and 'ad been a long time".

"Why didn't you say what you'd seen at the time"?

"I couldn't say ought, -- cos I knew that bastard James Vavour, --- would pin 'is death on me, --- 'an then 'e would 'ave 'ad me 'ung".

"Are you sure about this? Whereabouts in the wood did it happen"? George coaxed, but Bill closed his eyes as he drifted back into unconsciousness. George sat with him until day break, but long before the first rays of morning sun passed through the kitchen window Jack had long been dead. George's head buzzed with the knowledge that his father's death wasn't the accident everyone had been led to believe, but if old Jack was right, and there was little reason to doubt his word, then he had been killed in a mantrap. So who was responsible?

George had been distressed to see the way Jack suffered, but with his passing he had bequeathed a legacy of unanswered questions concerning his father's death, some of which he was sure Jack could have resolved. If the old chap really had seen what had happened to his father, and George was confident that he had, then who had set the man trap? Furthermore where did it go? Then there was the question of who moved his father's body, and placed it under the wheel of the straw cart? What part, if any, did the Vavour's play in the sordid business? Though judging by the money Cane was spending in the ale house, it was reasonable to assume that they were involved in some way. But there was something else that had troubled him ever since his father's death. What happened to his double cross?

Loads of questions, but how was he going to find the answers? After all, five years had passed since his father's death. Little wonder therefore that long after the sun had risen he was still trying to come to terms with what Jack had told him in the moments before he died. It wasn't just a case of learning that his father's death hadn't been the tragic accident that he had always believed it to be, but more that someone had deliberately caused it by setting one of the most barbaric traps known to man.

He was so deep in thought that he was oblivious of Rose climbing down the ladder, until he felt her arm around his shoulder. "Surely if it had been a keeper, father would have known about it", she reasoned, after George had related what Jack had said.

1837

Ever since hearing Jack Barkers bombshell, when he claimed that his father, rather than suffering a fatal accident as everyone was led to believe, had in fact been killed in one of the most brutal ways possible, by being trapped in a mantrap, it had rarely left George's thoughts.

"Why would `e make up a story like that, if it wasn't true"? Bill Taylor remarked in his usual straight forward manner, after George related what Jack had told him. Then, as if to reinforce the point, added. "Especially when `e knew `e was dying. I remember seein' one o' them traps once. It was fastened up in the rafters above the loft in the barn. I could niver understand what size animal it was meant to catch, until one of the old `ands said it was for catching men".

"Well, first we need to start off by finding out if it's still there", George replied.

• • • •

"I've `ad a good root around up theer", Bill reported a few days later, as he sat by the fire with his son in law to plan their next move. "There's plenty o kelter up theer, but I couldn't see ought o that trap".

"I can't see why anyone else would want to take it, so it should still be there", George reasoned. "That is of course unless it was the one that trapped my father".

"I'll bet you Cane remembered coming across it while `e was looking for somat else up theer". Bill replied. "Then when James wanted us to stop anyone going in the wood, e thought e would get in is good books by telling im about the trap".

"Well that makes good sense". George said, "It's more than likely that James would have instructed Cane to set the thing, either to catch a poacher, or at the very least scare somebody. We all know how he feels about anybody on his land".

"Just goes to show what an evil devil e is when e must ave known the terrible injury it would ave caused when them bloody jaws snapped shut", Bill said shaking his head in disbelief that anyone could be so callous.

"So Cane must have found my father in the trap next morning and reported back to James". George reasoned. "That would explain the reason they made him head keeper in place of you".

"And they give im a load of money to keep is gob shut" Bill added. "That would explain why he's spending' so much money in the White Hart drinking".

"By `ell when I git me `ands on `im, I'll gee `im` what for. The bugger won't know wither `e's comin' or goin'` when I've dun we `im'".

"Steady on Bill, I'll be first in the queue when it comes to dishing out punishment, but before we do anything we need to plan it carefully. If we wade in too soon without thinking it through properly, it'll more than likely backfire on us and then we'll find ourselves before the court. Just remember Henry Vavour and that slimy Ingelby know how to pin the blame on the likes of us".

"I see yer point", Bill said nodding his head in agreement.

The farm waggoner, when asked, confided to Bill that he thought it strange at the time that James wanted to personally collect the straw cart as requests of that nature were usually all handled by one of the coachmen. Furthermore, he said that James was supposed to have picked up Tom from the flailing barn, although no one could actually recall seeing Tom at work that morning. Bearing in mind that they were asking people to recall events that occurred several years earlier it was probably unsurprising that folk could not be more precise. Bill and George reasoned that James must have set the trap and found the body, which was the reason the Vavour's had taken the cart to pick up the body and stage the accident.

"In which case Cane isn't involved at all". George said at another of their regular meetings.

"But that wouldn't explain why 'e wus made 'ead keeper" Bill pointed out, and any road ow do you explain about the money ees spending"?

"You're quite right; he's as guilty as hell. But what about father's cross, it's never turned up"?

"If Barker didn't take it, who did, was it Cane or Vavour"? Bill said.

"I know Barker was a poacher and was often made out to be worse than he was, but I don't think he would steal from a dead man. George said. "But now that he's dead and almost certain to be the only witness, we need to find the cross because I think it'll lead us to father's killer".

"We can't go agin the word of men like 'enry Vavour, or that damned son of is, unless we 'ave some at to go on". Bill remarked philosophically.

"Any road wi men like that cunnin' devil Ingelby on their side they'll run rings round the like's o us".

"I'm sure Cane must have played a part, maybe even innocently, in my father's death". George said rubbing his chin as he pondered the implications. "I just wonder if we can set a trap to catch them." .

• • • •

A light breeze ruffled the remaining leaves in the hawthorn hedge dividing Westfield from the track where Tom had been found, as a waning moon illuminated the tense features of a shadowy figure moving furtively along its sheltered side. George was wearing a loose fitting cloak that as a testament to years of use had acquired an overall camouflaged appearance, evidenced by mud stains, interspersed with something much darker, from which one could only speculate on its origin. For the past few years the cloak had been relegated to a damp outhouse at the rear of George's cottage but tonight it was serving its purpose admirably. In spite of moving as stealthily as possible, he was unable to prevent a group of pigeons taking noisily to the wing as they flew away in panic from their nocturnal roost in a nearby tree. The disturbance spooked another group a little further down the hedge row which in turn created a chain reaction that rippled its way into the nearby wood. Through gaps in the hedge, George could see that the flickering lights of oil lamps in the upstairs windows of distant cottages were steadily being extinguished as folk retired for the night. Somewhere in the distance a dog fox gave a series of sharp, petulant yaps, as a cloud briefly passed over the face of the moon. With the light level vastly decreased it was difficult to spot the out stretched wings of a barn owl as it silently glided under the overhanging branches of trees bordering the beck, its night vision homing in on any small mammals that might form its nightly meal. George moved purposely from the hedge line into the deeper shade of a belt of gnarled chestnut trees that bordered the wood and led to the beck.

Henry and Constance after entertaining John and Laura Ingleby to an enjoyable meal of estate reared roast lamb, and drunk a fine Claret imported to Hoult on one of their own vessels, were relaxing together by the fire in the Halls south drawing room. The flickering flames of ash logs burning lazily in the ingle nook fireplace, created an almost hypnotic effect, especially when from time to time they settled into a new position, causing the fire to momentarily flare and send a shaft of light across the room to illuminate the pleats in the heavy damask curtains. When a much larger log slid sideways in a shower of sparks it created a much larger flame than usual which added another dimension to the severe features of William Vavour's portrait above the hearth. His enigmatic smile belied the ruthless passion that had made him such a feared foe in his business dealings. By using a combination of intimidation, bribes and threats he was largely responsible for creating the formidable dynasty that he bequeathed to Henry and his grandson James. Light from an ornate brass oil lamp suspended from a hook in the centre of the ceiling cast a yellow glow over the room illuminating half a dozen religious paintings displayed on other walls.

John Ingleby's round face, and small pebble glasses gave him a cosy image, which was at complete odds with those who had the misfortune to come across his devious nature. Lowering his voice he turned towards Henry and said conspiratorially in a tone that he hoped the ladies wouldn't catch. "We may have trouble".

"Surely there's nothing can possibly emerge after all this time", Henry replied sitting a little straighter in his chair as he took another sip of his brandy. Carefully wiping his moustache with a flourish of his handkerchief, he carried on in an even lower voice, "I warned Cane that if he should as much as breathe a word about what he had seen, then he could count his days before he felt the hangman's noose around his neck?

"A powerful argument for him to keep quiet, but it wasn't him that I was really thinking about"   .

"Then who else can possibly cause trouble".

"What about that fella Barker", John replied glancing across to the ladies who were still engrossed in an animated conversation.

"But he's dead", Henry replied with a broad smile on his face, "Surely you`re not suggesting that he's found a way to communicate".

"Of course not", John Ingelby replied, feeling slightly irritated by Henrys contemptuous reply, "but didn't Tom Slade's son find him injured"?

"I can't see what that's got to do with it".

"I gather he used to roam the countryside at all hours of the night, he just might have seen something".

"Don't worry old friend". Henry replied in a patronising manner, leaning across to pat John Ingelby on the knee. "Who do you thinks going to challenge my word when I've got you behind me to deal with the legal niceties".

In spite of Henrys confident attitude, John Ingelby knew of plenty instances in his professional career, where the expected rarely occurs whilst the unexpected generally does. As Laura listened in rapt attention to Lady Constance relaying another titbit of salacious gossip, both ladies were oblivious to the note of concern that was creeping into their men folk's conversation.

Drawing his cloak a little tighter around his shoulders, George shivered, as the breeze that had been quite light all day freshened from the east, heralding much colder weather. As it strengthened it brought with it a veil of cloud that soon began to reduce the light from the moon. In many ways, George thought that the conditions could hardly be better for what he had in mind, as he was reasonably confident that on such a chilly night, any keepers still on duty would more than likely be sitting by a wood fire with the groom's in their hut, rather than be out patrolling the woods. Nevertheless he still felt as tense, as he was pretty sure that tight rope walker at last spring's Candle mass Fair must have been feeling when he stepped on to that swaying wire suspended above the market place. Even though he had tried to convince himself that no one would be about, there was still a lingering doubt that he was wrong, consequently whenever his foot stepped on a twig, the noise made him jump convincing him that someone would hear. He suspected his poor father must have been experiencing similar agonies to the ones he was going through now, except that in his father's case the only thing he would be dreading would be the shout of a keeper to stand still, never in his wildest dreams would he be expecting to step into a man trap. But George, armed with the knowledge that his father had been trapped, perhaps only yards from where he now stood, was faced with the possibility, however remote, that the device, which Bill had assured him was no longer in the loft, just might be set under the next pile of leaves where he was about to step. Although George had never seen a man trap, Bill described it as being shaped rather like a giant rat trap, activated in a similar manner, by the victim stepping on a flat trigger plate in its centre, which instantly released a powerful spring, allowing two jaws armed with cruel interlocking teeth to sink into the unfortunate victim's legs. Bill told him, how in days gone by, that is before they were banned from use, that they used to be so carefully camouflaged from sight, by covering them with twigs and leaves that intruders wouldn't have the slightest idea where they were concealed, with the result that it only needed the threat of there being mantraps to serve as a sufficient deterrent without any actually being set.

"It may well 'ave been", Bill added philosophically, "that because few victims ever walked properly again, that certain landowners, on the large estates, reckoned they were so good at stopping poaching, that they continued to use 'em right up to the time of the ban coming in".

Knowing that his father had been somewhere close to where he was now, made George and Bill assume that he must have gone there on the night of his death hoping to perhaps snare a rabbit.

However taking a rabbit wasn't the reason for George Slade being on the estates land, just over seven years since his father's tragic death.

"It's not worth it, you can't beat them" Rose had pleaded earlier, but his mind was already made up.

"If only for father's sake I've got to do it".

"But think of Rachael and Sam and what will happen to us if you are caught", she begged, in a final forlorn attempt to prevent him going.

It had tugged at his heartstrings to see her tears, as she gripped Rachael's hand, whilst two year old Sam looked completely bewildered at what was happening. He paused for a second by the house door before quickly slipping out. He knew that if he didn't go through with it now he would never rest easy, as he might never get such a good opportunity again. All of this weighed heavily on Georges mind, as his eyes, now better attuned to the darker conditions under the trees could more easily identify obstacles on the ground, yet the burning desire to correct the injustice that had been done to his family was an all consuming passion. He stooped to pass under a low branch of one of the elms lining the side of the beck, before stepping clear of the trees to stare at the dark expanse of the lake ahead of him with the bulk of the Hall beyond. From the shadows George could see a couple who he presumed to be Henry and Constance standing on the steps by the front door as they bid farewell to a couple who climbing into their gig, quickly made their way down the driveway leading across the park. Beyond the house he suspected the coachmen were still attending to their horses because he could detect a weak light coming from the stables. George had never been in the Hall, but Rose had told him of the magnificent white marble entrance hall, and the red carpeted stairway that swept up in two arms to the upper levels. She told him of the Balls held there and how the sound of music echoed through the house. She talked about the ladies in their silk gowns adorned with sparkling jewellery and the way they appeared to float down the staircase as if suspended by gossamer threads.

Although he wasn't jealous of their life style, he couldn't help comparing the opulence of the Hall with his two roomed mud and stud cottage situated at the end of a muddy track where he had made a home for Rose and their young family. But that wasn't why he was embarking on such a perilous mission, nor was he doing it from any vindictive perspective; his overriding passion was to try and fight the injustice that for too long had allowed the Vavour's, with the assistance of the Ingelby's to act with impunity over the lives of anyone who caused them displeasure.

Activity in the great house had virtually ceased for the night, as kitchen staff that had been responsible for cooking and serving the meal that Henry and Constance had enjoyed with the Ingelby's retired for the night. After clearing the table and washing the dirty dishes, they trimmed the oil lamps for the night, before finally replenishing coal scuttles and log baskets with fresh fuel for the following day. Henry ruminated on John's concerns as he slowly made his way up the grand staircase. Noting the fine furnishings about him, he reflected on how much he would stand to lose if the truth ever emerged. Constance of course knew nothing of the events relating to Tom Slade's death and would have been mortified if she had.

As the servant's lights to the rear of the Hall began to be extinguished, George, whilst still keeping to the edge of the lake, moved steadily towards the Hall, his objective being the three keeper's cottages that lay beyond. They had both agreed, that the next part of his task would be the most hazardous, because if anyone should spot him within the Hall grounds at this time of night it would be difficult to argue that he wasn't intent on robbery? Further more if John Ingelby had a hand in it, there was no knowing where his catalogue of lies would lead. Plenty of people, he reasoned, had been transported to Australia for lesser crimes. This was no time to dwell on what might happen; the die was cast, so the sooner he got on with it the better. As George got closer to the Hall, apart from a faint glow showing through the curtains of a first floor window overlooking the park, the house appeared to be in darkness. Moving swiftly, he crossed the lawn and then, still undetected, skirted the driveway in front of the Hall, before gaining the shadows at the northern end. As the bank of clouds temporally cleared the moon, he suddenly felt far more exposed, realising that in order to reach his objective, it meant crossing the large open courtyard, which he presumed led to the entrance used by the servants. Plucking up courage and hoping against hope that none of the domestic staff should choose the next few seconds to either leave the building or look out the darkened windows of their quarters; he made a dash for the sanctuary of the buildings on the other side. Once there he breathed a sigh of relief because at last he had reached some sort of comparative safety.

However his objective was the row of three keeper's cottages that lay beyond the walled garden. He realised that if he kept to the northern side of the wall then he would be able to remain in shadow until he reached the cottages. On seeing Bill's cottage, which was the end one of the three, George was reminded of what his father in law had told him earlier in the evening.

"I would 'ave loved to do it mysen, but I really daren't, in case owt goes wrong. At my age I can't afford to lose me job because me 'ouse goes we it. Any road I'm a bloody rotten liar, so if I can 'onestly say I 'ad nowt to do we it I'm more likely to be believed". Bill, whilst assisting George to plan the operation, was mindful of the danger George was putting himself and his family in if anything should go wrong. After all Rose was his daughter and he certainly didn't want to see a similar outcome to that experienced by Tom when he had discovered Meg's body.

In spite of the cold, George felt a bead of sweat forming on his brow as he reached the critical part of the plan. If Peter Cane or any member of his family should leave the house now to go to the privy down the garden, or even fetch some more logs for the fire, then all would be lost. George hesitated awhile, then telling himself it was now or never, walked purposely across to one of the two downstairs windows of Cane's small cottage. Reaching inside his cloak he extracted a tin, containing a mix of clay and water, from one pocket and then from another produced an inch wide brush and commenced to paint a cross with two bars on each of the four panes of the window. Moving sharply sideways he repeated the same procedure on the other downstairs window. The job completed, George carefully retraced his steps the way that he had come mindful that detection now would ruin their carefully laid plan.

Bill Taylor was an even earlier riser than Peter Cane so he was quite familiar with his neighbour's early morning routine. He knew that Cane's first task after rising, was to draw back the coarse textured curtain cloaking his living room window, in order that he could see to light the fire. Observing the front of Cane's house from the anonymity of his privy, Bill saw the way Cane drew the curtain back as usual, but then the door to his cottage was suddenly flung open as he rushed out to stare incredulously at the symbols drawn prominently on the panes of both windows. He looked around furtively to see if anyone was watching, before disappearing into the house once more, only to quickly reappear, but this time armed with a metal bucket containing water and a cloth. His state of panic was clear to see as he thrust the cloth in the water then with rapid strokes of his arm quickly obliterated the symbol of the double cross that had so unsettled him.

The wretched thing had always been an embarrassment, he thought, wishing with all his heart that he had never succumbed to taking it.
But the sight of those crosses painted on his window panes was something else. Who could have painted them? The only person, as far as he was aware, that

knew Tom had been caught in a mantrap was Henry and James Vavour. Of course he knew that someone had removed the body to the cart track to make it look like an accident, but he didn't know, nor did he want to know who had carried out the procedure. The strange thing was, he had never mentioned anything about taking Tom Slade's cross to Henry, yet someone and presumably it was Henry himself must have known that he had taken it. Not for long they wouldn't, because he was going to do what he should have done ages ago, get rid of the damn thing. How he wished he had never risen to the temptation to remove it from Toms neck in the first place. When he had brought it home, all those years ago, he hadn't dare show it to his wife in view of Henry Vavour's dire warning of what would happen if he ever divulged to anyone what he had seen.

But then again when he thought about it, he realized that having taken it, he was caught in a terrible dilemma. On the one hand he would simply have loved to have thrown it away and be done with it. On the other hand he was frightened that if the Vavours knew of its existence, they might at some point demand its return, and if he didn't have it then he would be in even more trouble.   The result was that he hid it at the back of the wood shed in a place that he knew would be secure from prying eyes. Now this! Who could have daubed that shape on his window? Did someone see him take the cross? Could it be James Vavour, or even that treacherous Simon Ingelby, he just didn't trust any of them. God knows, none of them would have the slightest scruples about pinning a man's death on him, so without giving the matter further thought he resolved to be rid of the thing once and for all, before whoever it was that had painted on his window came to search his property. He knew from firsthand experience how meticulously they searched, as the father of a servant girl could vouch. His house had been quite literally ripped apart, after his daughter, erroneously as it turned out, was accused of stealing a silver spoon from the Hall.

A few minutes later, Bill saw Cane emerge from his house wearing a cloak tightly fastened to the neck. He disappeared in his woodshed, only to re-emerge within seconds and walk quickly by the lake to enter the wood by the beck side. Following at a discrete distance, Bill only moved in closer once Cane was safely under the cover of the trees. It was still only half light which made it difficult for Bill to see exactly how far Cane was ahead, but having spent much of his time as a gamekeeper working in the wood, he reckoned, if necessary, he would be able to navigate his way through the trees blindfolded.

Rounding another bend, Cane came to the spot where he had come across the crows pecking at Tom's mutilated body, so this had be the right place to get rid of the damn thing once and for all. The mere thought of seeing those bloodied eye sockets was sufficient to make him cringe with revulsion.

From his vantage point behind a sizable tree trunk, Bill saw Cane raise his arm and throw something in the beck, though it was impossible to see exactly what it was, though it was a fair bet to presume that it was Toms cross alright.

Completely unaware that his actions had been observed, Cane turned on his heels, and without a backward glance, swiftly retraced his steps, passing only yards from where Bill was concealed.

Bill took careful note of the position, noting that it was near a particularly sharp bend in the stream where the force of the flowing water had gouged into the bank making a much deeper channel as it underscored the opposite bank. He could hardly contain his excitement when he met up with George later that day to give a report on how Cane had reacted on discovering the outline of the double cross daubed over his windows.

"Well, it confirms what we always thought". George said, after hearing what Bill had to say. "He had the cross alright. It must have put the fear of God into him when he saw those crosses painted on his windows because he couldn't get rid of it fast enough. But why take it so far in the wood? --- Unless". His voice tailed off.

"It wus at the same place where yer Dad was trapped" Bill finished the sentence for him.

"You'll need to take a good look along the beck at that point", George said, "But be careful how you go about it, we don't want anyone to think you're taking too keen an interest, otherwise they're going to twig you're after something".

"Can't see as 'ow any body's goin' to tek any notice, when it's me job to be there". Bill said with a thoughtful expression on his face.

A couple of days later, in spite of scrutinising the beck, at the point where he was certain Cane had thrown the object, Bill was unable to see anything unusual in the water, which was really of little surprise, considering that the water in the beck at this time of year was generally turgid, when even the lightest of rainfalls gave an almost instant runoff into the stream. Over the years, Bill had seen the beck in all its moods, so he was well aware how the placid stream could be quickly transformed into a raging torrent of brown water.

"When the weather improves and the water level drops it should be easier to see if there's 'owt there", Bill observed, on meeting George sometime later to review progress.

The weeks went by and March passed into April, but in spite of Bill studiously examining the stony bed of the stream every time he passed that way, he failed to spot anything out of the ordinary, or at least that was the case until one glorious evening towards the end of April. Spring had always been Bills favourite time of year when the countryside was bursting with energy, regenerating itself after the depressing days of winter. After such a glorious day he thought he would take a walk by the beck, not necessarily to see if he could spot anything, because in all honesty he had become resigned to the fact that even if Cane had thrown the cross into the stream, it was becoming increasingly unlikely he would ever find it. He had lost count of the number of times he had walked that way since that eventful day in January and seen nothing. But walking along the bank on this particular evening, he was captivated by the way the lowering sun was casting its rays obliquely through the trees to send shafts of bright light striking across the water. It reminded him of the beams of limelight that a company of players had used when they paid a visit to Hoult a few years back. There was still a useful flow of water but where it had once been cloudy it was now crystal clear, which allowed the light to shine directly on to stones and pebbles underneath.   Suddenly out of the corner of his eye, he spotted something under the water that he was pretty certain he hadn't seen before. He was just about to dismiss it as a trick of the light highlighting perhaps a submerged log, or even a lump of clay that had been eroded from the bank when he realised that he was very close to the bend in the beck where Cane had stopped to throw what they believed to be the cross in the water. Intrigued, he scrambled down the steep bank to take a closer look at what had caught his attention.   Whatever it might be, it was obviously much too large to be the thing Cane had thrown away, but there was something about its strange shape that made his pulse race. Even though it was virtually the same colour as the pebbles lining the streams bottom, its irregular shape didn't quite fit his first analysis of it being a piece of wood. With mounting excitement, he waded into the stream, but in so doing roiled the water by disturbing the sediment on the streams bed. It wasn't until clearer water from upstream replaced the murk that he was able to see it was some kind of metal object. Seemingly oblivious of how wet he was getting, he stretched his hands under the water and took a firm grasp of the thing, then with a firm tug managed to pull it away from its watery resting place. Even if he had found a chest of hidden treasure, he could hardly have been more delighted with his unexpected discovery when he realised what he was dragging through the water to the bank.

As water dripped from its rusty jaws, it both shocked and delighted him to think that he was holding the trap which almost certainly had been responsible for killing Tom. After carefully examining the murderous device on dry land, he decided to hide it a short distance away within a dense clump of nettles.

George met a breathless, but exuberant wet father in law, a little later by his garden gate when Bill relayed the evening's remarkable turn of events.

"We've got em now", Bill explained, "It proves for certain `e `ad som`at to do we yer father's death".

"How do you make that out?" George said, looking slightly mystified".

"I know Cane didn't throw the trap in the beck the morning I followed 'im, but whatever `e threw in was in roughly the same place I found it".

· · · ·

George had to wait until mid May when the next rainy evening occurred and he could put the next part of his plan into operation.   He needed a rainy night for two reasons; first there would be no keepers or indeed anyone else about, and secondly he needed the extra cloud cover to make it even darker during the short summer nights.

Venturing out in the incessant rain, George remembered Bill's excellent directions and easily found the spot where he had hidden the trap. It was much heavier than he had expected, as he ran his hand over the interlocking teeth that had so cruelly taken his father's life. With rain dripping from his face to splash on the tread plate of the cruel device, it needed all his willpower to avoid immediately confronting Henry Vavour and seeing what he had to say about the death of his father when he saw the trap. But then sanity returned as he hoisted the instrument of death across his shoulders and strode resolutely towards the Hall, knowing that in the unlikely possibility of being challenged, the trap itself would be ample proof that he was neither poaching nor about to commit a robbery. He met no one as he mounted the steps up to the Halls impressive front door and deposited the device in the centre of the flag stoned entrance. Although soaked to the skin he felt hugely elated that morally and practically he had laid evidence of the Vavours devious actions on their very doorstep.

Following the overnight rain, the morning sun was shining brilliantly as Constance opened the front door to the Hall. There was nothing she liked better than to take an early morning stroll around the Hall gardens before breakfast, as she found the fresh air intoxicating, almost as if the action of raindrops passing through the air had cleansed it of all impurities. She particularly enjoyed her stroll on a summer's morning because she felt the smell enhanced the perfume of flowers, particular the roses that grew against the south wall, but opening the front door she was confronted by a strange shaped rusty contraption on the flag stones. "What's this metal thing doing here?" She called over her shoulder to Henry who was slowly coming down the stairs. Henry yawned as he wandered over, then the colour drained from his face and his shoulders slumped as he gazed at something that he hoped he would never see again. Prising the thing's jaws apart and extricating the dead man's stiff limbs was something he thought he had erased from his memory forever, but the sight of it once more brought it all flooding back. "Oh it's something one of the gardeners found yesterday". he said, in what he hoped was a disinterested sort of voice, though he was aware it had risen several octaves, so in an effort to offer a distraction he immediately went into a bout of coughing, hoping that by so doing his wife wouldn't spot the surprise in his voice at seeing the thing on his doorstep. "I'll get one of the gardeners to move it later." He added walking across the hallway.

Constance apparently satisfied with his innocent explanation disappeared around the end of the house intent on picking her roses. James arrived shortly after nine accompanied by Isabelle holding young Williams hand.

Beckoning him to follow, Henry led James down the corridor to his study and instructed him to sit down. "We've got a bloody disaster on our hands and it's all your doing."

"What do you mean?" James asked the colour draining from his face, as he saw how agitated his father had become.

"Someone deposited that bloody mantrap on the front doorstep last night".

"Has anyone else seen it"? The very mention of the word mantrap made the hairs on the back of his neck bristle, as a vision of Tom's mutilated face swept in his memory.

"Only your mother and she was happy, when I told her it was bit of old junk the gardeners had found."

"There's only the two of us, along with John and Simon Ingelby and Cane that know what really happened," James reasoned, quickly regaining some of his composure.

"We know it's not us or Simon so that leaves Cane," Henry said. "But why on earth would he want to put it on the doorstep, unless he's after more money."

A little later that morning they found Peter Cane re shafting a spade in an outhouse. "What's this all about, Cane"? Henry asked without preamble.

"What do you mean sir" Cane replied, totally perplexed.

"We're not daft Cane," James said taking a more aggressive line. "You know we're talking about that business with Tom Slade."

All of a sudden it came to him. He suspected at the time that it must have been them who were responsible for painting the crosses on his windows. But why had it taken them so long before they said anything? They must have somehow discovered the cross he had thrown in the beck, but just how was a mystery? Ever wary of a trap, he couldn't understand how they knew where to look, unless that is, unbeknown to him, they had somehow managed to follow him that morning. Anyway he wasn't going to be implicated with theft from a body so he reckoned the best form of defence was denial. "No I see it on the ground Sir, but chucked it in the beck before I cum for you", he hastily replied.

"What do you mean, "chucked" it in the beck". Henry said, completely mystified by Cane's answer, after all Slade was still in the trap when they got there.

Cane was sweating profusely as he suspected that the Vavours were concocting some sort of story to prove that he was responsible for Tom's death. "If yer try to pin it on me Sir, I shall tell 'em what I see we' me own eyes", Cane said his mind spinning as he tried to fathom what the Vavours were up to. He knew that with the Inglebys connivance there was no knowing what story they were capable of fabricating, if it saw him being convicted of Tom's death instead of them. At the very least, Ingleby would have him convicted of manslaughter, when he would count himself lucky not to be deported to Australia, but far more likely be hung, or failing that spend the rest of his days rotting in the hulk of a prison ship. "Why did yer paint that mark on me windows Sir." He countered.

James Vavour now also on the defensive wondered what sort of game Cane was playing."What do you mean a mark?"

Assuming they had discovered the cross and were preparing a trap, Cane said, "Why the cross of course, you lot should know, you did it."

"I don't know what the devil you're talking about man; you're telling us a pack of lies". James said, completely puzzled by what Cane was saying.

Cane, was fast becoming flustered by the rapid turn of events, "Yis I admit I took Toms cross, but you've got it now," his mumbling voice trailed off when he saw the blank expression on both Henry and James Vavour's faces.

Suddenly the horrible realisation dawned on him that until now they hadn't a clue what he was talking about.

Henry, who hadn't spoken for some time, summed up the situation. "You've lied to us Cane. I think we'll let John Ingelby have a word with you and see if he can get the real truth out of you."

They left Cane in a state of panic, as he looked over the precipice. All he could see ahead of him, was a disaster for both he and his family, when he realised that the dramatically improved life style he had enjoyed for the past few years was suddenly about to end.

Crossing the south lawn on their way back to the Hall, Henry and James, were still deep in thought, as they entered the house through the pair of French doors. A worried frown creased Henry's forehead as he stopped, and turning to his son remarked, "It's the first I've heard about this cross but someone else obviously knows something about Tom Slade's death, otherwise why would they paint on Canes window" "Unless of course, he's making the whole thing up", James remarked.

• • • •

Albert Wood was just past his twelfth birthday and had been employed since April as an apprentice gamekeeper under the tutelage of Peter Cane. Considering his age and inexperience, it was perfectly understandable that the job Peter had set him in the wood should have taken him much longer to complete than he anticipated. So after eating the pack up his mother had prepared he returned in the early afternoon to the courtyard adjacent to the stables for Cane to give him his next job. Leaving the shade of the trees it felt stifling hot out in the open, as the afternoon sun beat down mercilessly from a brilliantly blue sky. No one seemed to be about as he waited, until Peters wife, looking slightly worried came by to see if he had seen Peter during the morning. She said he hadn't been back to the house for his midday meal and wondered where he had got to. He kicked a stone around, a little surprised that Peter wasn't about, though from past experience he knew that he often had to wait quite a while for him to turn up. Occasionally a slight breeze would manage to enter the enclosed space within the courtyard and pick up dust devils that would briefly swirl around before the breath of wind dropped and they collapsed to the ground. He idly walked around the yard, then in an effort to relieve his boredom, picked up a handful of pebbles which he threw half heartedly at a flock of chattering sparrows. They seemed to enjoy the game, because they immediately took to the wing, before circling around a couple of times and landing cheekily in another part of the yard. He wished Cane would turn up and he could get out of the sweltering heat, as he knew the other two keepers were working on a different part of the estate, so he couldn't ask them what he should do next. Earlier that morning as he had left for the wood, he had seen the two coachmen collect Mrs. Vavour in the landau and take her to Hoult, so he wasn't surprised to see that the stables were also deserted. Even the under groom was exercising a young horse, so he knew that he was unlikely to be back for a while. It was so hot waiting around as the sun seemed to beat down even stronger, when he looked at the well in the middle of the courtyard and started to speculate on how appealing a refreshing drink of ice cold water might be. The more he thought about drinking the clear refreshing liquid, the more his mouth started to salivate at the prospect of taking his fill and then splashing the cool water over his sweaty face.

A large winding handle was mounted on the side of the frame covering the well, but because the stables and gardens required much greater volumes of water at a time than would normally be the case from a domestic well, everything was constructed to a much higher specification. The mechanism linking the handle to the winding bar, for example, had a reduction gear that made it easier to raise quite large volumes of water at a time, especially when the largest containers for supplying the glasshouses were fitted.

It was therefore of little surprise to Albert, to discover that in spite of the reduction gear, it still required a considerable amount of effort on his part to turn the big handle and raise the container which he assumed, judging by the difficulty he was having in turning the handle, to be one of the largest containers they had. As was frequently the case, the last person to use the well had released the ratchet, allowing the windlass to fully unwind the rope, depositing the container in the water at the bottom of the well.

Albert was a strong lad for his age, so with the thought of being able to get a drink of ice cold water and splash some of it on his hot body, put all his strength into turning the handle. As the container reached the top of the brick parapet surrounding the well head, Albert leaned over expectantly to take a long quaff of the ice cold water, only to discover that the container held the slight body of Peter Cane.

It didn't take long for news of the tragedy to reach George at Fred Hoyde's farm. He had been chopping thistles in the grass field immediately behind Fred's house when Bill ran over excitedly to tell him the news.

"I'm sorry about Pete," Bill remarked, "but 'e should 'ave told yer what he knew about your father's death all them years ago."

"Well, it confirms that the Vavours had some sort of hold over him, so that when they saw the mantrap on their doorstep it brought it all to a head." George said.

Canes death was passed off as a tragedy waiting to happen as everyone knew how he had become addicted to drink, frequently coming home drunk from the

White Hart. It was reasoned that he must have been taking a drink of water and overbalanced into the well.

Both Henry and James Vavour knew different though, realising that they were responsible for the terrified man taking his life. James for his part became even more highly strung, knowing that there was someone else out there who knew of those fateful events.

1841

In the spring of 1840, following Fred's unexpected death during the previous hard winter George assumed full control of the Hoyde's small farm. As neither Annie nor Fred had any close relatives she had been more than delighted with the arrangement, providing she was allowed to continue living in her house and for George to pay her a small rent. In any event she got on so well with Rose, that it seemed the natural thing to do.

Ironically the constant reduction of farm gate prices gave George the opportunity to expand his acreage, by renting an additional six acres, to the nine that Fred already farmed. A couple of neighbouring cottagers had reluctantly decided to give up the struggle of trying to make a living to feed their families from their few acres, so had taken a job in one of the new business enterprises that had sprung up around the canal basin in Hoult. George devoted half of his enlarged acreage to grass where he kept his horse and reared a few cattle and sheep. On the remaining acres he grew oats to feed his horse and wheat to provide grain for his pigs and a small flock of poultry.

．．．．

There was never the slightest doubt that young Sam was destined to be a farmer. Even at the tender age of six he was rarely far from his father's side, as he seemed to shadow all of George's movements around the farm. "I reckon he must be attached to you with an invisible cord"? Rose laughingly remarked one day when Sam entered the house a couple of paces behind his father. The family, although poor were largely self sufficient, living for the most part from food they produced on the farm, and selling the surplus to purchase clothes and other basic goods. Even though life was hard, they were a happy family, and generally had sufficient to eat, which thankfully, George was pleased to acknowledge, was much better than in his youth, and certainly a vast improvement on his grandfather's family following their eviction from his smallholding.

Farm work however, continued to be carried out in much the same way that it always had been. Long hours with little in the way of mechanical aids to relieve the hard physical work. Unfortunately as agricultural commodities began to arrive in the country from the new lands opening up overseas the price of those products grown on British farms fell to new levels. This meant that farms smaller than Georges where finding it increasingly difficult to generate sufficient income to cover the purchase of even the basic necessities of life.

Destiny's Talisman

Henry Vavour showed little compassion for Peter Cane's widow and her four children, because within a couple of weeks of his funeral, she was evicted, from her cottage and as a last resort had to seek refuge in the Hoult workhouse. He was able to justify her eviction of course, by claiming that the estate required the cottage for another keeper, though it cut little ice with other villagers who were aghast at his contempt for the unfortunate widow and her young children.

As the years went by and people forgot about the events surrounding Tom's death, James began to believe that those memories were firmly in the past. But suddenly with the reappearance of the trap all that changed. It was obvious that someone, other than Cane, not only knew of the mantraps existence, but was keen to demonstrate their knowledge in the most visible way possible by depositing it on the front doorstep of the Hall. Rather like a recurring nightmare set to terrify him, the sight of the wretched thing brought all those fears flooding back with a vengeance. From the moment that he once again caught sight of those clenched jaws, he found it impossible to shake the vision of Tom Slade's dead body from his mind, or at least that was the case, until Simon in his usual optimistic manner put an entirely different slant on the matter.

"Cane was no fool you know", Simon reasoned at the conclusion of yet another discussion about Canes "accidental" death. "I'll bet every time he saw either you or your father he would think that but for him keeping his mouth shut and not divulging what he had seen, you both would be imprisoned and in your case quite likely hung. He knew his evidence would be so incriminating that even my father's persuasive powers would be unable to prevent a conviction".

"But father made him head keeper and was paying him an extra forty pounds a year, which after all was more than his total year's wages", James argued.

"I know, but given the circumstances he obviously thought he deserved much more, which is generally the way with all blackmailers."

"But why should he put the mantrap on our doorstep then?"

"Simple really, he must have spotted it whilst walking by the beck on his rounds, so it gave him an excellent opportunity to visibly remind you both that his silence was crucial to you avoiding justice."

"What about the sign, he claims someone painted on his window?" James countered, "I don't think he made that up."

"I'll bet he did. It certainly suited his case to worry you after the grilling you were giving him. Remember if someone had painted anything on his windows don't you think some of the people living in the two other cottages would have noticed it? Anyway, who do you think was going to go there in the middle of the night to paint symbols on his windows. No, that was a complete fabrication; the fellow was obviously making it all up".

"I'm not so sure about that" James said far from convinced by Simon's glib answer. "Anyway, he admitted that he had taken Tom Slade's cross".

"What do you mean Tom Slade's cross"?

"Apparently it was something Slade brought back from Waterloo and always wore around his neck. They say it was a cross with two bars".

"The Cross of Lorraine." Simon replied with a self assured expression. "It's a French heraldic cross dating back to the fourteenth century. Anyway there's nothing unusual in that, lots of people wear a lucky talisman".

"But that's just the point; they say that Tom Slade always wore it around his neck. Apparently he never removed it, not even on the hottest days in summer. Funny thing is though, I'm certain it wasn't around his neck when we moved him," James said.

"That by itself doesn't prove a thing." Simon said, "He could have left it at home that day, or for that matter he may have lost it. But it just goes to show that Cane was telling a pack of lies to worry you, Don't you think that son of his would have had something to say if he thought someone had taken it".

"Perhaps you're right", James said still not entirely convinced by Simons reasoning.

"Thinking logically though" Simon continued, "I'll bet Cane was already regretting his action in placing the mantrap on the Hall steps when you two confronted him. He must have suddenly realised that it wasn't such a good idea after all, because if he wasn't careful he was going to be convicted of Slades death. No! The more I think about it, the only other person that could possibly know anything would be George Slade."

"Well that's pretty unlikely," James scoffed. "I know for a fact that on the night in question he was up at the Hoyde's farm watching his calving cows, and further more don't you think that if he had discovered his father was trapped he would either have released him or alternatively fetched help,"

Both of them were lost in thought until Simon with a flash of inspiration said, "Parker."

"What about him. Didn't he die from a leg infection a few years ago?" James said.

"I know, but didn't Slade rescue Parker, and didn't he die in their house. What if Parker had seen something, they say that at night he'd roam all over the district?" Simon pointed out.

A few days later James and Simon were racing each other down a bridle road, when they met George Slade moving his flock of ewes and lambs to one of the new fields he was renting. James deliberately wheeled his horse in front of the small flock, and in doing so made the sheep scatter.

"What the devil did you do that for?" George shouted angrily as he saw distressed ewes and lambs frantically scurrying hither and thither, bleating for either a lost lamb or mother.

"Look who we've got here then", James mocked. "I do believe it's that ignorant peasant Slade, whose stupid father managed to get himself run over".

George bridled at James comments, remembering a time all those years earlier when he had met them both whilst his mother was gathering blackberries. He was certain in his own mind that the actions of the pair had led directly to her death, and then there was that time in his father's garden when the pair of them trashed the produce his father had grown. Furthermore he knew, but at present couldn't prove it, that James and his father were in some way involved in his father's death, so he was more than prepared to release some of his pent up fury as he confronted the tyrants.

"You can get off that poor horse you've nearly flogged to death and help me round up the sheep you've managed to scatter," George thundered his normally kindly self full of loathing.

Taken aback by George's anger Simon retreated on his horse along the hedge side, yelling words of defiance to James, as he had no appetite to get involved in anything physical.

James for his part didn't wish to seem weak in front of his friend, so true to form flayed his whip at George.

His face smarting from where the leather thong had cut across his face, George made a grab for the whip before he had an opportunity to lash him once again. However it must have been a combination of adrenalin on George's part, and certainly unpreparedness on the part of James, that resulted in him becoming unseated from his saddle and falling backwards to collapse in an untidy heap on the ground. Unfortunately for him though, this was at precisely the same spot where the sheep had so recently been milling around, and in the process evacuating their bowels. Fuming with anger at the embarrassment of George bringing him to earth in front of his friend, James made a frantic scramble to regain his feet, by using one hand to support his weight, only to discover too late that he had placed it on a particularly green specimen. With slimy sheep dung oozing between his fingers, he glanced down at his white breeches and saw they were also liberally stained with similar green material. His feet sliding on the greasy surface he spotted that Simon had a broad grin on his face which only fuelled his feeling of malevolent hatred towards George.

"You're dead peasant". He screamed, trying to regain some authority, as once again he swung his whip like a man possessed.

George meanwhile, cleverly sidestepped his violent onrush, but wasn't quite quick enough to avoid more slashes striking his body. James who by now was almost out of control at the way events were unfolding, slipped on more dung, causing him to overbalance and fall head first to the ground. In an almost seamless motion George took the opportunity to snatch the whip from his hand and after throwing it over the hedge, grab one of his arms twisting it upwards behind the middle of his back. "Now you bastard tell me what you know about my father's death," George snapped, "speak or I'll break your bloody arm." Strengthening his grip, he applied even more pressure, twisting James arm ever higher. Racked with pain, James was just about to speak when the pressure was suddenly released and he was able to turn over just in time to see Simon raining punches on to George's back.

"Run," Simon yelled, as James gripping his aching arm with his other hand, scrambled to his feet and ran towards his horse.

George recovering from the crouched position where he had defended himself from Simon's frenzied punching turned on his heel, and put all of his weight into a punch that he felt connect with the soft tissue of Simon's face. With blood streaming from his nose Simon hastily retreated after James, all the while uttering dire threats of retribution on how George could expect to be charged with assault.

Sure enough the following day as Simon Ingelby had so confidently predicted, two constables from Hoult turned up at the farm to arrest him. He was charged with common assault on two law abiding citizens who were peacefully enjoying a morning ride until George made an unprovoked attack on them. Not for the first time the combined power of both the Vavour's and Ingleby's carried sufficient clout with Henry Vavours fellow magistrates to refuse George bail, as they committed him for trial at the next Quarter Sessions. From the time of his arrest, until his trial a month later, George was held in a filthy underground cell, with only the sound of wailing prisoners to accompany the monotonous drip of water from the roof as it splashed into fetid puddles on the floor. He was well accustomed to unpleasant smells on the farm, but the stench down there of putrid excrement was something beyond his wildest imagination. Initially he was relieved to discover that the stone bench against the far wall of the cell had a reasonably dry straw mattress on which to lie, but all too soon he found that it was riddled with fleas. Before long his body became covered in wheals and scratch marks, as he attempted to relieve the irritation caused by the insects biting his skin in their rabid desire to gorge on his blood. As the cells were below ground, the prisoners were kept in total darkness, bar the brief period of time when the constables brought them their meagre ration of mouldy bread and water, or changed prisoners. It was then that for a few brief moments, a pale shaft of light filtered down the stone steps to partially illuminate their cells. If it hadn't been for constantly thinking of Rose and the children and how they were coping on the farm, that George felt sure it wouldn't have been too long before he began to suffer a similar fate to the man in the next cell, who had clearly, judging by his constant wails and screams lost his sanity. With no facilities in the cells to wash and cleanse his body, it was little wonder that by the time he eventually appeared before the judge, he should look a most unsavoury character. His hair had become long and matted, whilst his unkempt beard and long finger nails made him look positively repulsive. To make matters worse he was not allowed a change of clothing so he was still wearing the same clothes in which he had been arrested. It was unsurprising therefore, that given the weeks he had spent in his squalid cell that his clothes had become coated with layers of accumulated filth, and had taken on such an odour that the judge and other court members pressed handkerchiefs to their noses to relieve the foul stench.

At his trial, John Ingelby delivered a scathing indictment about the way George had made an unprovoked attack on his son and James Vavour. Unfortunately his denials cut little ice with the immaculately attired judge, who viewed the filthy looking defendant before him with complete disdain. If appearances were any criteria of guilt, then before he had a chance to utter a word in defence of the charges levelled against him, he was already doomed. It was of little surprise therefore, that the judge decreed he should receive twenty five lashes of the cat o'nine tails and be sentenced to three years hard labour.

As they left the court building, James and Simon congratulated each other on the verdict. They thought they had pulled off a remarkable coup by so discrediting George's integrity that no one was ever going to believe the word of an ex con; if in the future he should dare to raise the issue of them being involved in his father's death.

With lack of evidence to back up his belief, George, as much as he would have liked, was careful never to mention that James and Simon were involved in some way with setting the mantrap that had killed his father. Nevertheless, Simon was shrewd enough to realise that George did know something about their involvement, because but for him coming to James aid, he knew James was about to admit the part he had played in his father's death. James for his part was only too conscious that but for Simon's timely intervention he would certainly have admitted his part in Tom Slade's death. Now though, who was going to believe the story of a convicted felon who had been imprisoned for common assault? It was with a mixture of relief and satisfaction that James reported the outcome of the trial back to his father later that evening.

"I think that we can both sleep easier now that Slade's locked up", Henry said confidently as they both drank a celebratory toast in the seclusion of his study.

Rose, as might well be expected, was completely devastated by the news of George's imprisonment. She knew, as did everyone else that these were trumped up charges illustrating once again how the Vavour's and Ingelby's between them had manipulate the facts of a situation to suit their case. Rose, and pretty well everyone else that had ever been in George's company, knew that it just wasn't in his nature to provoke an attack in the manner that James and Simon were alleging. With her father's occasional assistance once he had finished work, as well as caring for her two small children Rose managed to run the small farm single handed. From time to time neighbours rallied round and helped whenever possible, but as they all had commitments working on their own small farms, help tended to be rather limited at busy periods in the year.

James seemed to have gained an extra spring in his step as having won an easy victory; he continued to treat with disdain all he had authority over. Now that he had set up home in Hoult with Isabelle, he began to play an even greater part in the Vavour's shipping businesses, which in turn put terror into the lives of humble clerks, who fearing for their jobs, bowed and scraped as he strolled dictatorially around the offices.

It was not a good policy to cross swords with the Vavour's as the tentacles of their influence spread far and wide, causing business people in the area to view them with a great deal of trepidation.

1846

If George thought conditions in his cell at Hoult's house of correction were horrific, then his first experience of life aboard a prison ship was far in excess of anything he could have ever imagined. Of course, during the time he was awaiting trial, there were some prisoners who seemed to take a perverse delight in talking about what he could expect to find on the prison ships if he was found guilty. After a while he began to dismiss some of their wilder statements as fanciful scaremongering, only to realise when he got there, how right they had been after all. A number of the ancient vessels, were relics of the war against Napoleon, and were now serving out their days as penal institutions in various anchorages throughout the country.

Following the judges devastating sentence, he was strapped in leg irons and transported to one of the wooden hulks anchored in the river Humber. Upon arrival at the ship two swarthy warders grabbed an arm apiece and even though he offered little resistance, dragged him across the deck to spread-eagle him around the mast where his hands and feet were manacled to iron rings set in the woodwork. Out the corner of his eye George saw another warder, who rather in the manner of a leading actor taking to the stage, appeared from a hatchway to his left. After looking about him, as if to acknowledge his audience before giving a performance, slowly removed his coat, folded it and placed it on the deck, then very methodically began to roll up each sleeve in turn. Without a word being spoken he walked across to George, who just had time to feel the man's rough hands grab his shirt collar, before he was jerked violently backwards, as his shirt was ripped from his back. The warder clearly relished his role in front of his fellow colleagues, as he seemed to be salivating at Georges apprehension of what would happen next. However he wasn't kept in suspense for much longer, as from his limited vision he watched the fellow stroll leisurely across the deck. It was at that point that George's mouth went dry, as he had just spotted a whip with a collection of leather thongs attached to one end of a six foot rope which the warder was about to pick up. As was his norm at the commencement of a performance, the warder spat on his hands, and then to add further to Georges distress and the amusement of the other warders, gave a sharp flick of his wrist which caused the length of rope at the end of his whip handle snake across the deck to give a crack like a discharging musket. Suddenly, as if he had been instantly galvanised into action, he turned, clenched his teeth into a sickening smirk, gave a little run, then with all the power he could muster brought the whip down hard over George's bare back. Waiting for what he realised was going to happen had been bad enough, but even so there was nothing that could ever have prepared him for the searing pain when those strips of leather dug into the flesh of his bare back. Such was the force of the blow that it quite literally drained his lungs of air, but before he had time to take a proper intake of breath, the next blow was upon him, and striking his lacerated skin. The pain became so intense it could hardly have felt worse if a thousand knives were slashing simultaneously through his flesh. Soon the frequency of the lashes began to merge into one long tunnel of purgatory that he wished he could die and put an end to it all. Before long even the hardened warders, who had seen it all before, had to look away as George's back began to resemble something that wouldn't have looked out of place on a butchers block. The twenty five lashes sliced his back so deeply, that when the skin eventually healed, corrugated ridges were left that remained with him to the end of his days.

Barely conscious, his arms were released allowing him to collapse to the deck, then with blood flowing freely down the back of his legs, he was dragged to a hatchway and thrust down a ladder to a lower deck, where he was greeted by an overpowering stench of ammonia rising from fetid urine and faeces. One arm was secured to a short chain that in turn was attached to a bar running the full length of a small area holding the chains of a further seven prisoners. Both ankles were linked together by another chain, which over the course of the coming weeks formed blisters. The blisters developed into ulcers, and even though he tried his hardest to adjust his position, in order to slightly relieve the pressure of the coarse rings encircling his ankles the ulcers refused to heal. With so little headroom between decks it proved impossible for prisoners to straighten beyond a stooped position, all of which, George was about to learn, only served to magnify their discomfort.

He soon discovered that in common with his fellow prisoners, the chains were never released from his arms and legs, or at least that was the case, until one of their number died and was replaced by another prisoner. With such a limited amount of movement it was inevitable that they were forced to defecate where they lay. To be laid next to another prisoner passing his motions was bad enough, but when even a slight swell caused the ship to rock, it caused pools of putrid excrement to lap onto their bodies as they attempted to rest.

George soon learnt what the term chain gang meant, when he became a member of a chained group of prisoners who were daily marched off the ship to hew stone from a nearby quarry. They were expected to break the stone down to the size of a fist and then shovel it on to horse drawn carts. If anyone should slack, or was spotted talking to a fellow prisoner, there were plenty of vindictive warders who were only too happy to be provided with an excuse to snake their whips over the unfortunate man's back and pull them into line. Inevitably, some prisoners who had been incarcerated for long periods of time and hadn't either become completely brutalised by the regime, or died as a result of disease or injury, began to lose their sanity through the sheer hopelessness of their situation.

George, in spite of everything, somehow managed to keep going by never giving up hope, even though the days seemed endless as they merged into weeks, and then weeks into months, and finally months into years.

For the three long years that he endured that living hell within that prison environment, he was sustained in the knowledge that he was completely innocent of the trumped up charges brought against him. It was during those long hours of darkness whilst he lay awake listening to the clinking of prisoner's chains and the creaking of timbers, as the ancient ship gently rocked with the tide, that he resolved to rectify the injustice done to him. He lived for the day that he would be able to reveal the truth about how James had caused his father's death, when the Vavours deceit could at last be brought to light for all to see.

Over the following months he began to formulate a plan in his head that, if he were lucky enough to survive his time in this hell hole, would entrap James Vavour. His plan, if he could execute it properly, would be brilliantly simple. He would devise a scheme that would lead his quarry into thinking that it was him that had devised a brilliant plan to settle him once and for all, but would in fact backfire spectacularly. He felt confident that if he played his cards right it just might lead to the restoration of some of the wrongs done both to him and his family. What rankled more than anything else, was the way James Vavour and his father's word, abetted by the crooked Ingleby's, were believed in preference to ordinary folk such as him.

• • • •

Three long years of hard labour with poor food consisting of at best stale and at worst mouldy bread left a dramatic legacy on his appearance. His face that was once cheerful with a friendly smile was haggard and gaunt. Over the years, dirt became ingrained under his skin causing the formation of black pock marks, that when coupled with his straggly grey hair gave him the typical intimidating appearance of a convict. From the time of his arrest, to the time of his release, George neither saw nor heard from any member of his family as any communication with anyone outside the prison was strictly forbidden. Consequently Rose had no idea if he was alive or dead, neither did George have any idea how the family were coping in his absence.

On his release Rose barely recognised the shrunken shell of a man who had difficulty standing straight owing to the scars riddling his back. A lack of proper nourishment had caused his teeth to rot and become little more than black stumps. She thought it barely credible that the fit young man that had left her over three years earlier should return looking like someone who could easily pass as her grandfather.

In spite of his poor physical condition, George could hardly wait to confide with Bill the details of the plan he had spent so long hatching in his head.

Although outraged by James and Simons lies at the trial, Bill knew there was little he could do for fear of jeopardising his own job. In any event he felt that he would be of more use to George with inside knowledge, than viewing the situation from a distance. Bill was able to confirm a few days later that a cousin of his wife who for a short time had had the misfortune to be James governess, but was now a teacher at a nearby village school, would be be only too pleased to help in any way she could.

"Can you get her to insert this piece of paper in an envelope" he said passing Bill a scrap of paper with the outline of a double cross drawn prominently across it. "And then, if she would be so kind, I would like her to address it for the personal attention of James Vavour and see that it's delivered to the Vavour shipping office".

The following Monday morning the elderly clerk in the shipping office looked worried when he heard the door leading on to the street, open, then close with a slam. The way footsteps were storming up the stairs it was pretty obvious that his tyrant of an employer was in another foul moods. Whatever had upset him this time, the poor clerk knew from past experience that he would be at the receiving end of a torrent of abuse. Ever since James had assumed greater control of the canal business he dreaded these visits. He knew that try as much as he liked, James never failed to criticise some aspect of his work. He would have left years ago, but knowing the Vavour's reputation for being vindictive towards past employees, he felt certain that at his age they would make it their business to dissuade anyone who might offer him employment. Opening the office door, James was fuming, after once again coming off second best, following another heated argument with Isabelle. Trouble was, he felt unable to deal with her in the same manner that he over rid everyone else that crossed his path. As usual he had stormed out of the house feeling frustrated and angry; consequently anyone who was unfortunate enough to come into contact with him whist he was feeling this way was more than likely to feel the full force of his venom. His original infatuation with Isabelle had long since cooled to such an extent that he could barely stand the sight of her. Her small voice, that he once found so captivating, especially irritated him, not the least when she continued to carp about something not to her liking.   Even though he couldn't tell her the reason, she constantly nagged him about his reluctance to travel during the hours of darkness. If it wasn't that, then it was the children, or it was his friends, especially Simon.

"There's a letter for you Sir," the clerk said in a subservient voice, as soon as James entered the gloomy office and before he had an opportunity to open his mouth. The old clerk sifted through a pile of papers on his desk until he found a plain brown envelope with the name of James Vavour Esq prominently printed in block capitals on its cover. James impatiently snatched the envelope from the clerk's thin hands and tore it open. A look of horror, spread over his face, as he unfolded Georges scrap of paper and stared at the outline of a Cross of Lorraine.

"Are you all right sir?" the observant clerk enquired, secretly revelling at his employers discomfort at what he had just seen.

"No, no, I'm fine, just feeling a bit faint", he replied swaying sideways as he tried to regain his composure. "I must have been rushing about too much this morning," he continued, hoping that the clerk hadn't noticed the effect the contents of the letter had had on him.

The clerk had good reason to be delighted at seeing the look on James face, after the numerous occasions he had suffered the tyrant's wrath. Gripping the envelope James hurriedly left the office, and quickly made his way to see Simon, at Ingelby and Sons imposing new offices in the market square. Several years earlier the business had vacated their dismal office in Gadfly passage to occupy their present prime position.

"Well you know who this is from," Simon remarked, holding the slip of paper James had handed him. "It's obviously from Slade. He's the only person likely to let you know that the damn cross is linked to his father's death. Remember if I hadn't intervened when I did, you would have admitted the part you played in his father's death."

"What the devil can we do"? James said pacing about impatiently, as he began to realise the hold that George Slade had over him.

"Well, I bet you that like Cane, he wants money," Simon declared removing a clay pipe from his desk and beginning to methodically fill it with tobacco from a leather pouch.

"There's only one solution as I see it. You'll have to silence him for good; otherwise he's always going to be a problem."

"How on earth do you think I'm going to do that"? James said. "After our last encounter, he's hardly likely to come within a mile of me".

Simon leaned back in his chair and took several draws on his pipe, until a large cloud of white smoke drifted to the ceiling.

"Remember, he didn't send you this for the fun of it" pointing to George's scrap of paper on his desk. "To the contrary, he deliberately sent it to you because this is his way of saying he wants to talk to you. I suggest you go to his place and speak to him, then you'll see what he wants, I'm pretty certain he will demand money, and maybe even some land as well, in exchange for keeping his mouth shut".

"All right, so let's say I agree to what he wants, I still don't understand how that's going to silence him for good".

"This is where the clever bit comes in" Simon said confidently. "Once he knows there's some money in the offing, he won't be able to resist the chance to have some of your sovereigns; so it'll be a bit like baiting a mouse trap to get him to a place where you can meet him".

"I still don't understand how that's going to help"?

"Well first you must agree to all his demands. If its money he wants, then bring along a bag of sovereigns, and if its land he wants, then bring along documents for the land as well".

"I still don't understand how that's going to help me silence him permanently".

"Well in order to demonstrate that he really does know how and where his father met his death and it's not all bluff, I suggest you agree to the transfer taking place at the same spot in the wood that he died".

"And then what"?

"The money needs placing in such a position that he has to walk in front of a particular spot to collect it. Let's say you were to set a mantrap there, you would be able to catch him like a rat in a trap".

"What!" James exploded, his face suddenly drained of colour. "You're not seriously suggesting I use a mantrap after what happened last time".

A vision of Tom's ravaged face suddenly swept into his memory as the implications of what Simon was proposing hit him.

"I tell you, if you don't do something about him, you're never going to feel safe as long as he's alive." Simon said pressing his advantage.

"What happens if anything goes wrong?"

"How can it. Remember this will be different to last time. No one except us are going to know about it".

"I've got to say it would be a sort of poetic justice if he was eliminated in the same place as his father", James smirked, "but using that mantrap again, I'm not so sure".

Suddenly relishing the idea of ridding himself of George once and for all, he came to a decision. "You're right of course, and even better I know where the mantrap was put after Cane put it on father's doorstep".

Days later James made it his business to ride around the estate, taking a route that brought him past the Slade's modest cottage. He didn't recognise the stooped old man scattering grain to a group of cackling hens, so he inquired if he knew the whereabouts of George Slade. It was with something of a shock that when the man turned to face him that he saw it was George, now looking, as a direct result of his incarceration, a shadow of his former self. George was delighted in the fact that his plan was unfolding in precisely the way he had predicted, so in order to give the impression that he didn't want anything to do with him, feigned surprise when James spoke.

"I know it was you that sent me the drawing of the double cross, what do you want?"

It required the maximum amount of self control to prevent him making a lunge for James legs, but he was conscious that an instant's stupidity would undo all the countless hours of thought he had put into his plan, so he kept his hands by his side.

James, perhaps conscious of what occurred on their last meeting, retreated a little further back.

"What makes you think I should want to get involved with a bastard like you again? Have you any idea of the hell you and that slimy friend of yours put me through. George said, secretly delighted at the way things were going. "Don't you think you have done enough damage to me already," he added for good measure, as half turning his body, he lifted his shirt and exposed his scarred back.

"I expect you want some money?" James said, shocked at what he was seeing.

"There's nothing you can give me that will compensate me for the hell you've put me through, but if you're offering me money to keep my mouth shut, you can start by giving me five hundred sovereigns, and come to think of it, you can sign over the fifteen acre field that adjoins my land. I expect you can get that crooked lawyer who has helped your family to trick plenty of good people out of their land to prepare the papers." George added in a take it or leave it voice.

James had a job to suppress a smile at the way things were going. Simon as usual had been quite correct in predicting that George was after money, so in order to convey the appearance of scoffing at George's audacity for making such a ridicules request, said for effect. "That's completely ridiculous, what makes you think I should give you that amount of money, - - and the land as well?"

"You know, that I know about your involvement in my father's death, so if you want my silence to prevent you facing justice, you had better meet my demands. Just remember that prisoners and jailers care little for people like you from privileged backgrounds. I can tell you that you'd be lucky to survive a fraction of what I've been through". George was happy to give the impression that he wasn't really bothered if James accepted his terms or not, as he threw another handful of grain to his fowls.

"I'll be back this time tomorrow". James said, wheeling his horse about, visibly shaken by George's last comment.

Good as his word he rode by the following day, and seeing George once again feeding the hens, reined in his horse, then flourishing a handkerchief as if to show contempt at George's lowly status said. "All right I'll meet your demands. I will have the land signed over to you and give you your five hundred sovereigns, but there'll be two conditions".

"What are those"? George replied scornfully.

"Well to show good faith I want your fathers cross and in addition I need you to sign a document which absolves me of any blame regarding your father's death".

Believing that it was all going very well, he said, almost to make it look like an afterthought, " just to confirm that you're not bluffing and do in fact know something, we'll make the exchange in secret at the place where you claim your father was trapped".

"Alright, when?" George said. There was little point in appearing too keen, - no, - much better to appear reluctant, and then once the bait was taken, reel him in.

"It's going to take me a little while to get the necessary documents drawn up, so as it is now the fourteenth of October, I suggest that we make it six hours after sundown on the twenty sixth, the same day that your father died", James remarked.

George deliberately looked sceptical by scratching his chin and looking disinterested, "I'm not sure I trust you to have the money and the papers. I've been thinking, I won't do it for less than seven hundred and fifty sovereigns."

Believing he might lose his quarry, James grudgingly agreed to Georges request, adding, "Remember I want the cross."

"You'll see the cross alright", George replied as a parting shot.

Bill knew the Vavours had put the trap under a large laurel in the Hall shrubbery, because one of the gardeners assuming that it was some kind of fox trap left there by a keeper, had drawn Bills attention to it, but as the years past by and the bush spread its dense foliage further over the ground everyone forgot about its existence, but James remembered and so did Bill. Bill kept a surreptitious eye on the Laurels hidden secret as he went about his duties, taking note if the trap was removed. The days passed and nothing happened. He despondently reported back to George on the evening of the twenty fifth, that perhaps they had completely misread the situation and James had another plan up his sleeve. On the morning of the twenty sixth however, Bill passed the laurel as usual with a sack of grain on his back to give the appearance to anyone who may be interested in his movements that he was going about his daily task of feeding the game birds, when he spotted that the trap had disappeared overnight.

Overjoyed at his discovery he made his way to George's isolated house, meeting him just as he was completing his morning task of milking the cow. "Great news", he enthused, "the traps gone, yer were right all along, the evil devil is intending to trap yer". "I'll be ready for him", George replied with a determined smile on his face, "Only thing is we mustn't do anything that makes him think we know what he intends doing. The next part needs very careful handling if my plan is going to succeed".

While carrying out his normal daily tasks, Bill kept a wary eye on the comings and goings at the Hall. Nothing unusual happened until early afternoon when he spotted James and Simon emerge from the stables, cross the rear courtyard and enter the Hall by a side door normally used by servants for passing unobtrusively in and out the building. Bill judged it to be about an hour later, by which time the sun was sinking towards the western hills; when he saw the door open and both of them emerge to head in the direction of the stables. Consequently he was unsurprised when he next spotted the pair astride their horses, turning left out of the drive to take them away from the village.

A keeper all his life, Bill had become supremely proficient at stalking prey, so he knew how to conceal his presence, and avoid alerting his target; therefore he correctly deduced that the pair would take a circuitous route to the wood in order to allay suspicion falling on them should anything go amiss. He was well aware that in the unlikely event of him being seen, he had a perfectly legitimate reason for being there, but in any event he had no intention of anyone spotting him. He carefully made his way through the wood until he found a spot between two ivy clad trees close to the place where he had discovered the trap and almost certainly where Tom Slade had met his death. From his concealed position he knew that he would not only be out of sight, but would be able to see everything that the pair got up to.

James and Simon were feeling particularly pleased with themselves as they made their way through the woods from the opposite direction to the obvious one from the Hall. They were happy in the belief that by taking this much longer route no one would have the remotest idea that they had been in the wood, if in the unlikely event anything should go wrong with their plan. Bill however was not deceived by the naivety of their strategy, as it wasn't too long before he spotted birds taking flight heralding the pair's progress through the wood. From his hiding place he saw them both emerge on foot, carrying the mantrap that until twenty four hours earlier had lain under a laurel bush in the Hall grounds.

It was obvious that James could hardly suppress his delight at what they were about to do, as he paced around the small clearing seemingly examining each tree trunk. "This one will do", he called excitedly, as he pointed to a tree that due to a branch rotting many years earlier had left a hole in its trunk about six feet from the ground.

"The evil bastard niver ad any intention of even bringing a few coins to keep is side of the bargain", Bill murmured to himself, as he watched James pull an obviously empty white bag from his pocket and proceed to stuff one end in the hole, leaving a substantial portion of the neck draped down the trunk as a tantalisingly glimpse of what might lay within the hole. By using the side of his foot as a shovel, he proceeded to scrape loose leaves away from the base of the tree to bare the earth, before helping Simon position the trap directly below the hole where he had placed the bag. Together they pulled back the jaws of the mantrap to the horizontal position and carefully set the trigger plate, before finally camouflaging it with twigs and leaves. Satisfied with their evil work they slapped each other around the back, before retracing their steps the way they had come.

When he was certain they were well clear, Bill began to implement the plan that George had spent so long devising. With the aid of a stick he flicked away the twigs and leaves that the couple had so recently used to camouflage the trap.
Even though he braced himself for the vicious jaws shooting upwards, when he tapped the trigger plate with his stick, it still came as something of a shock to see how fast it all happened.

It was at that point that Bill set about enacting the most crucial part of George's brilliant plan. Depending on how well he carried it out, would determine whether it was going to be a success or a dismal failure leading to untold ramifications.

He started by dragging the trap to the base of another large tree some twenty-five or so feet away, then from an inside pocket, removed the small wooden cross that George had fashioned from a piece of oak beam whilst in prison, and hooked the cord that was threaded through the top of it, over the end of a piece of rough bark at roughly head height.

As he lay awake during the long nights of his incarceration, George recalled the lonely days he had spent scaring birds from Fred Hoyde's crops and how he had passed the hours by whittling at a piece of stick with a sharp piece of flint. So when he picked up a tiny sliver of flint at the quarry it seemed the most natural thing in the world to carve away at any tiny bits of wood that came his way. It was therefore quite fortunate for him, that over the years the oak beam above his head had cracked and split in several places as a direct consequence of being in a humid environment for so many years. In view of the beams condition he found it relatively easy to prise away varying sized slivers of wood to carve. It wasn't too long before he perfected his technique of carving, so when one day a slightly larger piece came away, he decided to carve a similar cross to the one his father had always worn. The result was the exquisite object that Bill now held in his hand. By constantly wearing it around his neck it had adopted a patina that made it shine with all the brilliance of polished copper.

Following George's precise instructions he extracted from another pocket a tin containing a mixture of lime and water, and set about painting a large double cross on the trunk below George's small wooden one. As he took a moment to stand back and admire his handiwork he recalled his remark, when George had revealed that part of his plan to him. "Won't they smell a rat when they see the cross I've painted," he remembered saying.

"I know it might seem that way", George replied, "but there's not going to be a deal of light with the moon in its present phase. The sight of the large cross will draw his attention to the smaller one above it, so just like a wasp is drawn to a pot of jam he will be unable to resist going over and picking it from the tree". Finally, in what Bill thought was the masterstroke in George's plan to turn the tables on the double crossing villains, he reset the trap in its new position.

Before leaving the spot and reporting back to George, he carefully camouflaged the trap once more, after which he double checked that the mound of leaves in its original position looked similar to the way they had left it. As the last of the light faded, Bill reflected on a job well done and wondered what was going to happen before the night was through. To allay any suspicion, if by chance he was spotted, he continued on his usual rounds on a route that brought him past George's far field where he made a prearranged contact with his son in law.

"Everything went exactly as yer said it would," Bill enthused. "I set the trap as yer said and I've marked the sign o' the cross on the tree where I've 'ung yer cross. Yer were dead right to the last detail, the devil even put an empty bag that was supposed to be oldin yer money above the trap, so as yer would be bound to step on the trap as yer reached up for it".

The moon was in its last quarter, consequently it shone feebly through the largely leafless elms, but in so doing, it left dark shadows behind their trunks, which rather like the backdrop to a stage would set the scene for the action that was about to take place in front of them. It was something of a relief, to find that after all the scores of hours he had spent weighing up the pros and cons of alternative strategies in his head, that the waiting was over and the moment of truth had arrived. In spite of everything he had planned, George was enough of a realist to know that if it should go wrong, then he would be in deep trouble. It didn't bear thinking about what catalogue of lies the Ingelbys would invent. No point in dwelling on that though, when he was sustained in the belief that the next few hours might be the only opportunity he would ever get to correct the injustice done to both him and his family. Little wonder therefore that it was with a great deal of trepidation he made his way by the hedge bordering West Field and into the wood. He was only too aware that he was dealing with tricky adversaries who with the law stacked in their favour would stop at nothing to achieve their ends. However looking on the positive side, he was buoyed by the fact that events were unfolding exactly as he planned. Only thing was though; he couldn't be entirely certain what James and Simon's reaction might be when they saw the large cross painted on the tree. Would they for instance, as Bill suggested smell a rat and do something he hadn't anticipated? Even more worrying was what if they suspected that the trap had been switched and they had hatched another plan? All sorts of scenarios buzzed through his head as he carefully made his way to the spot where his father had met his horrific death. "What can you expect from bastards that are as untrustworthy as rattlesnakes", he recalled saying when Bill told him about James placing an empty bag in the tree.

"Aye and ten times as slippery" Bill had replied.

Even though Bill had witnessed them setting up the mantrap to catch him, he was only too aware that they still might have another plan in mind, as some sort of insurance, if for some reason he failed to be caught in the trap.

Therefore it seemed logical to arrive there late, especially when he was hoping to turn the tables on them.

"I wouldn't do that", Bill cautioned when he told him of his intention.

"I don't reckon they'll be early. If yer set a trap yer don't hang about waitin fer somat to git in it. No I reckon they'll be late 'aving expected yer to go straight for the bag in that tree. So if you aren't in the trap when they arrive, they're goin to smell that rat I wus talkin about."
"Well then what do you propose"?

"Go a bit earlier and git the bag from the tree, then lay on the floor as if yer legs are caught in the trap and holler for all yer worth. That'll be bound to bring um running".

"But they're going to see I'm not in the trap".

"Remember they'll be expecting to see you laid down, so they're not goin' to be exactly checkin' whereabouts the traps got yer", Bill said, "in any event it's goin to be pretty dark so if yer chuck some leaves and the like over yer legs they're not goin to see ought other than what they're expecting to see.

O an yerd better take the paint jar with yer, theyll be expectin to see that somewhere near yer", he adding as an afterthought.

As George rounded another bend in the beck, he came to the place where his father had met his death. Just at that point, the moon that had been slipping in and out of clouds all evening, disappeared behind a much larger cloud, making the small clearing that was gloomy at the best of times look positively dim. George shuddered, as he paused for a moment, realising that within this space the issue of his father's death was going to be resolved one way or the other. It was immediately obvious that neither James nor Simon had arrived, so he retrieved the bag and set about doing as Bill had suggested.

His initial screams of terror subsided into a series of low moans whilst he forlornly waved a hand that still clutched James white bag.

"What's all this then," James said breathlessly, as he, with Simon in tow suddenly appeared.

"You rotten bastards" George muttered his face seemingly contorted with pain. "I ought to have realised I was dealing with sewer rats".

"You were dead right Simon", James guffawed at the word dead, "a bit of bait and it caught him, just as you said it would and since our trusting friend mentioned rats, a rat in a trap". With that he aimed a kick at the upper part of George's body.

"You bloody scum; it's doing a mis-service to sewer rats to call you one.

Just get me out of here" George screeched. "I can't stand the pain much longer".

"You won't have to stand it much longer", Simon said, this is the last anyone's going to see of you".

"What, you're going to kill me the same as you did my father"?

"You didn't really think we could let you hold us to ransom with the information you know about us", James said. The only difference this time is that we won't be putting your body under a cart wheel to make it look like an accident".

"No you'll just disappear off the face of the earth, and no one will have the remotest idea what's happened to you" Simon remarked.

"You call yourselves honourable, neither of you know the meaning of the word. You couldn't even honour the agreement you made with me", George said dropping the white bag.

"Funnily enough, against my better judgement I do have title for the land in my pocket. Simon persuaded me to bring it along just in case things didn't go to plan".

"Fancy, the stupid peasant even honoured his side of the bargain", Simon said spotting the overturned jar of paint, "Look over there the silly devils even drawn a cross on that tree to show us where his cross is".

"How thoughtful of you", James mocked, as he strolled over to the tree. But in order to reach the cross that he could see was looped over a piece of bark, he had to take a step closer to the trunk in order that he could stretch out his hand and take it.

All of a sudden the pile of leaves where he stepped erupted upwards. "What the devil" James screeched as the powerful jaws sprang up to encircle his right ankle. "You'll soon find out, you evil bastard," George replied jumping to his feet. "Who's the stupid peasant now? You pair of buggers deliberately set that trap to catch me. Furthermore you've both admitted that you intended to kill me in the same way you killed my father?"

"I don't understand what's happening?" James screeched, looking towards the tree with the hollow trunk where until seconds ago George had lain, his leg supposedly caught in the mantrap.

"I'll bet you don't", George said rubbing his ribs where his adversary had so recently kicked him.

"But you were in it over there" James, still clutching George's wooden cross; screamed in disbelief.

"What's it doing over here"? He repeated between sobs. From where he lay, he could clearly see the foot of the tree where he had reasoned George would have had to step as he stretched up his arm to reach inside the hole and retrieve his money, and in doing so activate the trap.

Looking over his shoulder George noted that Simon seemed to be mesmerised, unable to grasp exactly what was happening. Or it may just have been that he felt by moving something equally unexpected might happen to him also. "You're a bad devil, you never intended keeping your side of the bargain". George said contemptuously, walking across and dropping the empty bag beside James head. "Was it your intention to let me suffer a lingering death like my poor father? He added plucking his wooden cross from James clenched fist. "What plan had you in mind for disposing of my body? You've already said you weren't going to run a cart wheel over it like you did to father. I've a good mind to leave you here and let you experience the kind of lingering death he suffered."

As George made to walk away, James took one hand from where he was gripping his ankle and began to wave his arm furiously. "For God's sake don't leave me here; I'll give you anything you want".

"Well let's start with the title to that fifteen acre field," George said, "You said you'd got the document with you?"

"It's in my coat pocket". James said, his faced contorted with agony.

"Pull it out and throw it over here," George said. Although he had been in darkness all evening and his eyes had become accustomed to the dark he thought the already poor light had just dimmed a fraction as he bent over to pick up the document. Out of the corner of his eye George thought he detected a slight movement, but it could be that the sudden decrease in light caused by him bending over was making him even jitterier, and then suddenly he remembered Simon. His mind had been so preoccupied with the sight of his family's tormentor, now completely under his control that he had temporally forgotten all about Simon Ingelby. Suddenly, alert to the potential danger, he continued to bend down, seemingly examining the document but held his head at a slight angle in anticipation of the onslaught that he was convinced was about to come his way. Simon lunged, but George was ready for him as he threw his body sharply to one side, leaving Simon to over balance and claw fresh air. In spite of carrying little spare flesh, prison life had made his reflexes extremely sharp, as he had become ever wary of other prisoners or jailers, consequently he was able to twist round and pounce on Simon's back pulling one of his arms sharply towards him, then in a vice like pincer movement force it up his back. Rotating it further he was satisfied to hear a click higher up his shoulder as Simon screamed out with pain.

"Bit evener than last time," George said confidently, as he continued to grip Simon's arm whilst looking down at the pathetic figure of James flailing the ground with both his arms.

It was then, that James and Simon, who until seconds earlier had felt cock a hoop in the success of their planning, realised that the man Simon referred to as a stupid peasant, wasn't quite so stupid after all, because he had completely outsmarted them both, and there was absolutely nothing they could do about it.

"If you want me to release you, I need the two documents signing that I have with me. They detail how you set the trap that killed my father and how you faked his death to make it look like an accident. I am a man of honour as clearly you two are not, yet I would have been content to accept the seven hundred and fifty sovereigns as we had agreed, but in view of your treachery I want an additional five hundred. It'll go a little way to recompense me for the pain and suffering that you have put me and my family through by your lies and cheating".

"I will never agree to that," barked Simon.

"In that case, I'll leave you tied to a tree and you can watch your friend die, perhaps you'll then realize what you did to my father. The choice is yours."

"For God's sake do whatever he asks," James yelled for once in his life powerless to control events. His ankle throbbed with unimaginable pain as he felt the stickiness of his blood percolating around his toes.

George reached into his pocket and produced duplicate copies of a document that had been drawn up by Rose's cousin. He passed a quill and a small bottle of ink to Simon, who was now sitting on the ground cradling his injured arm.

"This document sets out how you laid the trap that killed my father, and how you falsified his death. It also sets the record straight on how you both conspired to have me flogged and imprisoned."

"You don't think I'm going to sign that it's a death warrant."

"The difference between you and me is that I'll keep my word," George said quietly. "I shall keep one copy and the other will be held by someone else for safe keeping. If anything should happen to me I have given instructions for it to be forwarded to someone who is not in your pocket".

Cradling his damaged shoulder with his sound hand, Ingelby looked ashen as James screeched,

"Sign the bloody thing and get me out of here before I bleed to death."

As the moon reappeared from behind a cloud to deliver a pallid light over the scene, James and Simon signed both documents.

"I don't need anything signing regarding the money," George pointed out, "these documents will ensure that you pay up."

"Stand over there Ingleby, whilst I release your friend, and then you can both leave the way you came. After you've gone I shall dispose of this murderous trap once and for all".

As Simon Ingelby stood well clear, George eased back the jaws of the trap allowing James to drag himself clear. Luckily for him, the trap had caught him just above the ankle, with the result that his leather boot gave his leg partial protection from the full impact of the inter meshing teeth. Tom had been much less fortunate, as the soft tissue of his calf had taken the full impact. As the pair hobbled away through the wood George wondered what sort of story they would concoct to explain their injuries. With the sound of their erratic progress fading into the distance, George carried the trap the short distance to the beck where he heaved it into the same deep pool where his father-in-law had discovered it.

James's and Simon circulated a story that they had both suffered an unlucky riding accident caused by James horse rearing up at a gate which brought them both down. Unfortunately the accident was responsible for breaking James's ankle and dislocating Simon's shoulder. Bill's involvement in the night's events never came to light as the second copy of the declaration was passed to Roses cousin for safe keeping.

Not long after the events of that night, the estates bailiff was puzzled when he was instructed by James, to visit George, and tell him that he could take over the fifteen acres forthwith and there would be no claim for tenant right compensation.

A little later, a messenger from Hoult arrived at the farm and handed George a heavy sealed package with no indication as to who the sender might be.

• • • •

It was on a particularly cold night shortly before Christmas when George and Rose were relaxing by the fire to the sound of driving rain beating against the window panes. The children were asleep upstairs and George's freshly acquired cattle were lying contentedly on clean straw next door.

"By God, we've suffered at the hands of the Vavour's", George said pressing another pinch of tobacco in his pipe, "but I reckon the tide's turned at last".

"Holding that document with their confession about your father's death is going to make them think twice before they abuse us again", Rose said profoundly.

1851

There was widespread excitement in Hoult in 1849 when the new station alongside the freshly constructed railway line was opened. For the first time it gave ordinary people of limited means the ability to travel cheaply to places that hitherto had been beyond their reach by horse drawn transport.

"I can't see how they can ever compete with what we can carry on the canal," James said, limping over to the warehouse window as he and Simon watched one of their sloops being loaded in the dock basin below. In spite of having to use a stick to get around, he was immensely relieved that had it not been for his stout leather boots taking most of the impact from the traps jaws, there was every likely hood he would have lost the lower part of his leg.

Several months had elapsed since that fateful night, but the shock of those jaws springing up would live with him forever. What particularly annoyed him was that once again another of Simon's brilliant plans should end in disaster with him suffering not only a physical injury, but also one to his pride. They would deal with George Slade once and for all, he claimed, yet the man he referred to as a simple peasant had skilfully out manoeuvred them both.

"It takes them all their time to pull themselves up the slightest incline, never mind carry a load," Simon guffawed, breaking his reveille. "They're only a glorified stage coach on iron tracks.   I'm a deal more concerned about the government's repeal of the Corn Laws. It's going to let cheap grain flood into the country from the prairies in North America and that'll undermine the price of our English grain".

"So that's bound to affect trade on the canal, if farmers can't compete on price," James said.

"That's what worries me, the government says it has to keep the price of food low to feed workers in the towns," Simon pointed out.

"And that's going to mean more of our farm workers leaving the country to work in the factories," James said.

"Or emigrate," Simon added, strolling into the adjoining office.

James continued to gaze out the window, his mind only partially on what they were talking about, as he couldn't get it out of his head how things had gone so disastrously wrong. Trouble with Simon was, that he had convinced him the plan would work, but the more he thought about it the less he could understand how it had failed.   And then to add insult to injury, he had been caught in the very same trap that he had intended for George; if the facts ever got out he would forever become a laughing stock. Little wonder he felt increasingly bitter and twisted, believing Simon's reasoned argument that this was a perfect plan to rid themselves of the one person who had the information necessary to convict them. He recalled how confident he felt when he heard Georges scream. Got the bugger he remembered shouting at Simon as they both rushed through the wood to discover George laid on the ground, with his leg obviously caught in the trap. Simon had been right enough when he had correctly assumed that George Slade's greed would take over as he had obviously reached up to the hole in the tree trunk to take the bag of sovereigns. But then what followed turned from being one of triumph to a terrible nightmare. It all seemed to start going wrong when Simon pointed out the outline of a cross painted prominently on a tree on the other side of the clearing. He remembered his feeling of elation as he strolled across, expecting to find George Slades cross somewhere there. In spite of the poor light, as he neared the tree he spotted it hung on a piece of bark. Although everything happened in seemingly the blink of an eye, the events that followed were so indelibly imprinted on his mind that he was still able to give instant recall to those milliseconds of terror. It was as his fingers closed around the cross that the nightmare began. He felt the sensation of his feet sinking through the drift of leaves as he stretched up to reach the cross, and then a feeling of shock, followed by the most unimaginable pain, as his lower leg was caught in a vice like grip. But the thing that staggered him most was the way that George seemed to miraculously rise from the trap he had been caught in.

• • • •

Henry Vavour died in March 1848, in the full knowledge that George Slade, if he so wished, had the power with his sons signed confession in his possession to have him arrested and tried for being an accomplice to a murder. Far too late in life he recognised his sons duplicity, though on occasions lying awake during the quiet of the night he began to realise some of the underhand practices that he had also been involved in.

James and Isabelle along with their two children moved into the Hall that autumn, whilst his mother continued to live there, though in her own apartments to the rear of the house. James passed his pathological hatred of the Slades, on to his son William, inferring, though he would never fully elaborate why, that the reason for his lameness had something to do with a strange cross that George Slade held. His hatred of the "peasants" as he collectively referred to anyone who he considered to be in a lower station than his manifested itself in him demanding ever higher rents from his already poor tenant farmers who found it increasingly difficult to make a living. It says much for his twisted logic, that he believed they were conspiring against him, and were collectively responsible for his injury. As a consequence several of the estates smaller tenant farmers were unable to pay the increased rent resulting in them having to give up their tenancies allowing the land to revert to the estate. William, unlike James when he was of a similar age, was found a clerk's job, handling shipping contracts in a warehouse by the canal.

Annie Hoyde died peacefully in her sleep six months after the death of Henry Vavour, so in thanks for the way George and Rose had looked after her and Fred she bequeathed her small cottage and land to them. George with the assistance of eleven year old Sam decided to use some of the sovereigns he had received from James to purchase a few more Red cattle from some of the area's leading breeders with a view to increasing the profitability of their limited acreage. In addition, for Roses sake primarily, it seemed only proper that he should also invest some of his money on the construction of a new brick house. By building it close to Annie's old cottage, it would be close to the well to save the chore of carrying water. It would have a proper scullery to hold outdoor clothing, a kitchen with one of the latest ranges and three bedrooms to provide one for him and Rose and the other two for Sam and Rachael. Anything would be a big improvement on the mud and stud cottage he had renovated, even though Rose had done her best to make it a comfortable home. Despite her best efforts it only consisted of two low rooms downstairs and a single bedroom under the thatch that could only be reached by means of a ladder. As the house took shape, it soon became the principle topic of gossip in the village. Folk speculated on how George Slade freshly out of prison, admittedly on a trumped up charge devised by James Vavour and that tricky Simon Ingelby, could now be building such a fine brick house, but then the wise acres among them concluded that they must have been left a pile of money in Annie Hoyde's will.

Work was completed after harvest and the family moved into their new home at the end of October on the anniversary of the event that had turned their lives around. George, who wanted to give his family a better standard of living to the one that he had experienced as a child, realised that although he had won an important battle with the Vavour's and Ingelby's he was facing determined foes who did not take defeat easily.

He had seen the evil intent in James's eye, and knew that sooner or later there would be another confrontation, probably more serious than the last one. To some degree he was always on tender hooks not knowing from which direction the enemy would attack next. He was therefore totally unprepared when the next round of the conflict involved Sam. Sam was chopping thistles in the top field when his attention was caught by a rider travelling at a furious pace across one of his neighbour's fields. Even from a distance, he could see how the rider was lashing his whip across the horse's flanks in an effort to make the terrified animal gallop even faster as it jumped hedges and ditches. Suddenly the rider changed tack and headed towards the field where he was working. Sam knew the wooden fence on their field's boundary would be too high for the horse to jump, so was unsurprised when the horse made little attempt to clear it, as it smashed its way through the rails creating a gap for the cattle to escape.

Until that moment half a dozen heifers had been quietly grazing, but when they saw a horse and rider racing across the field towards them, their ears pricked up, then with tails vertical, set off at a furious gallop around the field. Meanwhile the rider didn't slacken pace as he continued to race up the hill towards Sam. At the last moment, William Vavour swerved his sweating horse sharply to the right, causing a shower of soil and grass to spray over the young lad. Although quite small for his years, Sam was plucky and rather like his father didn't suffer fools gladly. "You've no right to be here, frightening our animals like that, when you've plenty of your own land?" Sam said defiantly, as he looked up at the mounted figure of William.

"I shall go wherever I want; I won't take advice from a little bastard like you." William replied.

Sam's blood boiled as he saw the first of their cattle, having galloped wildly around the field, arrive at the broken fence, and start to wander through the gap.

"Look what you've done; you've smashed the fence and the heifers are getting out. The least you can do is give me a hand to get em back in".

"Do it yourself squirt. If you need a hand, better get that convict father of yours to give you a hand though I don't think his cross will be much use to him this time".

"I don't know what you're talking about, but it's about what I would expect from somebody who can thrash a horse like that". Sam said, incensed at Williams arrogance. With that William turned his horse and rode directly at him, trampling the lad under the horse's hooves, before galloping away down the hill. Dishevelled, bruised and dirty, Sam returned home to be met by Rose who with typical motherly concern soon found out exactly what had happened. "What did he mean about the cross?" Sam asked.

Uncertain of how much of that fateful night's event she should divulge to her son she demurred awhile, then decided to pass the remark off lightly.

"It's nothing really, your grandfather picked up some sort of small cross when he was fighting at Waterloo and then someone stole it".

"After we've got the cattle back in their field and repaired the fence, I'm going round to the Hall to have it out with them," George said, when Rose and Sam between them had related the full story to him. "It seems that in spite of all our optimism the Vavour's aren't done with us yet" Rose said after Sam had left the room.

"I need to remind James's that I still have his confession, so if he can't control his son better than this I shall be forced to produce it" George replied.

As George lifted the cast iron door knocker on the Hall's great west door, and thumped it down into its keep he was conscious of how much had happened in the intervening years since he was last on that step. Where he would once have felt intimidated to approach James Vavour he now felt a great deal more confident. Listening to the echoes reverberating across the hallway beyond the door, George's attention was drawn to the leering expression on the face of the knocker, typical of them, George thought, for visitors to be greeted by such an unpleasant image.

"What do you want?" An immaculately attired servant remarked haughtily, on opening the door, and looking down at George's rough working clothes.

"I want to see James Vavour, is he in?"

"I will tell him that there is a person to see him", the servant said shutting the door in George's face.

The door partially opened once more, to reveal the arrogant face of James Vavour, "I've a good mind to have you arrested for trespass", he sneered, pirouetting his body around the edge of the door on his good leg to get a better view of George. "I think it's your son that needs arresting for trespass." George said evenly, "And as for riding directly over my son with a horse, that he had thrashed within an inch of its life, he needs locking up, but what can he expect from a father like you that not only killed my father, but was quite prepared to callously kill me in that murderous mantrap".

"I thought there was a smell around here, what does the con want?" William said, appearing from around the south side of the Hall.

"If God gives me strength I will see you lot brought to justice", George replied, "You have ruined too many people's lives; the day will surely come when you are both put in your place".

William sidled across to the pony and trap that had brought George to the Hall. The pony was standing patiently to attention with the reins draped loosely over the front of the trap, when suddenly William raised the whip he was carrying by his side and brought it down smartly over the poor creatures flank. The startled animal leapt forward to the raucous laughter of both Vavours, as it set off at a furious gallop down the drive.

"Clear off and don't ever set foot here again," James said his face full of malice.

George was left with little alternative other than to retreat down the drive after his pony. He was acutely aware that it would have been foolhardy to attempt any retribution as there would have been plenty of "witnesses" to claim that George was responsible for assaulting the pair.

A couple of days later Simon Ingelby decided to take advantage of a sunny morning and take a ride down to the Hall, and perhaps take a cup of coffee with James and Isabelle, but met James at the Park gates.

"Every time I drive here, I can't avoid noticing that new house Slade's built", he remarked.

"Not half as much as it annoys me every time I see it. I won't rest until I have got even with the bastard," James said.

"You're powerless to do anything whilst he holds the documents that we both signed", Simon reasoned.

"I'll find a way to get even with the devil, just you see," James declared through tightly clenched lips.

• • • •

Simon and James were meeting for one of their regular meetings, in the top floor office of the Vavour shipping company overlooking the canal basin. Sloops and barges were in the process of being loaded or unloaded by means of a series of hoists fixed to the sides of warehouses lining the basin. Simon Ingelby, in common with many other traders, still considered the railway an irrelevance. He failed to see how something little better than a stage coach on iron wheels could possibly have the capacity to transport the bulky commodities their shipping company was transporting on the canal.

"We need to think big." Simon declared expansively, thrusting his thumbs in his waistcoat pockets. "We ought to get rid our forty tonners and get some seventy's. With increased capacity we could travel much further up the Humber than Grimsby or Hull."

"I'm not so sure," James demurred, "What about the cost? Vessels of that size need a lot of trade to cover the investment," adding as an afterthought, "we've barely enough trade to keep our six vessels operating all the time, let alone increasing the capacity."

"But just think," Simon enthused, "with larger vessels we could undercut our competitors and control a deal more trade, there's enormous scope to bring even more goods up the canal, to supply even more industrial processes which we could own a share of."

James hesitated as he saw the logic of what his friend and partner was saying, and then thinking of William, and Simon's two sons said hurriedly,

"I suppose you're right, we must speculate to accumulate, that's the only way to expand the business into the future."

An order for four sloops was placed with a ship building yard in Hull, on the premise that the greater capacity would reduce their operating costs. In 1851 the first vessel was delivered but in spite of reducing their freight charges, the extra trade Simon had so confidently predicted failed to materialize. It worried James, that unless they found fresh customers, they would be left shouldering a substantial debt, having borrowed heavily to finance the purchase.

• • • •

Rachael, George and Rose's eldest daughter, had always shown a natural aptitude for needlework. Little wonder therefore that her skills were recognised by Miss Topliss, a dressmaker in Hoult, who had built up an enviable reputation for making fashionable well made garments of the highest quality and workmanship. Rather like her mother, Rachael had an easy smile and pleasant personality that instantly endeared her to even the most difficult to please of Miss Topliss discerning clientele. She was caring and conscientious, but above all thoroughly dependable, so that customers were soon requesting that the delightful young seamstress be trusted with making their new garments. Little wonder therefore that Miss Topliss began to regard Rachael as more like a family member than an employee, consequently she was more than happy to provide accommodation for her within her own home.

The wonder of the Great Exhibition in the specially built Crystal Palace was on the lips of everyone entering the dress shop in that spring of 1851. Those who had been down to London to see it were besieged with questions about how such a massive building could be constructed of glass, though more learned heads were quick to point out that it was the handiwork of an engineer by the strange name of Isambad Kingdom Brunel, and there was pretty well nothing he couldn't build. Rachael's clients talked excitedly about the many types of exotic plants and flowers they had seen. Keen gardeners amongst them were enraptured by the sight of great drifts of orchids, whilst others drooled over the orange and lemon bushes that they had seen laden with fruit. Still more couldn't get over the sight of giant palms growing under the massive domed roof.

Many ladies raved about the fine bone china, and as for the fabulous dresses manufactured from the finest fabrics imported from the far reaches of the Empire, they were a sight to behold. Everyone talked of the crowds of people whilst one lady remarked that she had even seen Prince Albert from a distance. Rachael heard so much that she desperately wanted to see this amazing spectacle that so many folk were enthusing over, especially as it was generally felt that the like of which would never again be seen in their lifetimes.

She was beside herself with excitement therefore when Miss Topliss not only encouraged her to visit London to see the exhibition, but in appreciation of her dedication to work, offered to pay not only her third class return train fare, but also her mother's fare as well. In addition she would arrange for them both to spend two nights with her younger sister who lived in the capital. Neither mother nor daughter had ever travelled much further than the villages immediately surrounding Hoult, and even though it would soon be two years since the railway line extended to the town, they were yet to travel on a train. So the prospect of taking a more than eight hour journey to London was going to be a great adventure.

Taking their seats in one of the partially covered third class carriages towards the rear of the train, the advantage of being in either a first or second class enclosed carriage soon became apparent, when smoke from the engine had a nasty habit of swirling back into their carriage. However any inconvenience posed by smoke and wind, was more than made up by the experience of the train journey itself and the anticipation of seeing London for the first time, even if the hard wooden seats began to feel very hard after a while. Although they had to stop from time to time to take on more water and coal, they revelled at the sight of towns and villages, of green fields grazing cattle and sheep, of passing over viaducts and through cuttings, that in some instances led into pitch black smoky tunnels, until at long last the full panorama of the city of London lay before them Miss Topliss sister was a wonderful host. After meeting them from the train on its arrival in London she took them by handsome cab to her home on the outskirts of the city. On their journey they passed slums the like of which they could never have imagined. Urchins wearing what looked to be little more than rags for clothes, dodged piles of decaying rubbish as they chased each other through the streets. Meanwhile cabs, such as the one they were in, picked their way between potholes full of stinking water, whilst seemingly hundreds of people oblivious of their surroundings scurried purposely about their business.

• • • •

"It's enormous," Rachael said stopping in her tracks and gazing along the vast length of the great exhibition hall, spellbound by what she was seeing. She looked up at the glistening roof way above their heads, adding excitedly, "You can certainly see why it's nicknamed The Crystal Palace". "I've never seen anything so fantastic in all my life." Hand in hand, mother and daughter joined the thousands of other ordinary people; many of whom, like them, were visiting London for the first time. The vast majority of them united by the introduction of cheap rail transport that provided the means for them to travel and view, what the newspapers were calling, the greatest show on earth.

As they made their way along avenues displaying all manner of exhibits, they were so enthralled by what they were seeing that they couldn't help but keep stopping to stare open mouthed at some fresh wonder. But it didn't stop there, because wherever they looked there was something else to feast their eyes on. They saw so many extravagant displays of exotic flowers, fruits and vegetables, exhibited on stands manned by so many colourful people from the far reaches of the empire, that their heads buzzing with excitement, found it difficult to take it all in. Such was the magnificence of the exhibition; with a fresh revelation to astound them pretty well everywhere they looked, that time passed by all too quickly. Before they knew where they were their host was saying that it was time to leave.

"I shall still be talking about what we've seen in fifty year's time". Rachael enthused as they slowly made their way to the exit.

They had been so overwhelmed with all the sights and sounds they had witnessed, that the journey home the following day seemed to pass by remarkably quickly. As they prepared to leave the train at Hoult station their euphoria at enjoying such a wonderful time together was however rudely shattered.

Walking along the platform to the station exit, they noticed that William Vavour was standing by a gig he had evidently brought to the station to collect his mother and sister, who they spotted alighting from their first class compartment. "Why if it isn't the convict's wife and daughter?" he mocked in a loud enough voice for all to hear, as Rose and Rachel hurried by. Other passengers, aghast at his remarks, looked away not wishing to become involved, when they realized it was the young Vavour making such comments. Ladies drew their skirts about them and headed for the exit whilst their men folk rapidly brought up the rear.

Unwilling to become embroiled with William's loutish insults, especially after George's confrontation with him and his father at the Hall, Rachael and her mother left the station entrance and headed for Miss Topliss house in Briar road. Rachael had arranged to take her mother there to await her father, who had agreed to collect her once he had completed his evening milking. On hearing the sound of wheels crunching stones behind them, Rachael glanced over her shoulder just in time to see William, who was driving the gig she had seen near the platform, pull out of the station yard and snap the reins over the horse's back, instantly making it accelerate from a gentle canter to a gallop. To her alarm, she saw that he was driving the gig towards them at an alarming pace. Too late she realised that the brick wall of the tannery, beside which they were walking, came to within a couple of feet of the road, which meant that there was little verge on which to stand.

Unfortunately at the pace William Vavour was driving there was insufficient time to cross the road to the marginally wider verge on the other side. "He's deliberately trying to run us over," she screamed, grabbing hold of her mother's hand and pulling her against the wall. The gigs wheel were only inches from the wall when at the last moment William swerved away but unfortunately its momentum caused both women's long dresses to billow out, resulting in the hem of Rose's dress catching the front corner of the speeding gig and pulling her towards the wheel. She was jerked violently forward and then dragged over the rough cobbles before part of her dress ripped away and released her.

As William continued on his way at full gallop, Rachael screamed hysterically. Other passengers, who had witnessed the entire incident quickly gathered around, concerned for Rose who lay crumpled on the road.

"Did you see that", a moustachioed man declared to no one in particular. "He drove at them deliberately,"

"It was that wild William Vavour," said another.

"The bugger needs locking up," yet another declared.

Meanwhile a woman, who had travelled with them in the same carriage from London, bent down and tried to comfort Rose, who was bleeding from a wound to one of her legs, whilst the other leg, judging by its angle was quite clearly broken. "Fetch doctor Finch", the smartly dressed owner of one of the town's mills said authoritatively, to a young man standing close by. As he set off at a fast sprint, another voice called after him, "Run as fast as your legs can carry you." Two more ladies comforted Rachael whose hysterical sobs were slowly beginning to moderate. Another voice from the back of the crowd that had quickly gathered around declared, "That young Vavour's a maniac he almost ran me over a while back, we need to call the constable." Fortunately doctor Finch, who only lived around the corner, was at home having his evening meal, so he was able to quickly get to the scene of the accident. After bandaging the cuts to her leg and thigh, he administered laudanum to alleviate the pain of her broken leg. Only then did he have her carried to his surgery, situated within his home, where with the assistance of his wife, they made Rose as comfortable as possible, as he set about the task of applying a splint to her broken leg. However before she was moved, one of the town's constables appeared at the scene of the accident and was soon acquainted of the facts.

The constable was a big fellow who sported a ginger moustache of such proportions that it merged with his side whiskers.

"You'll have to watch them Vavour's", a wag pointed out, "they're more slippery than eels".

"Now look here", he said turning to the fellow, "I'm afeared of no one in this town, whoever they might be, the law will prevail."

When George arrived a short while later it took the combined strength of the constable and one of his colleagues to physically restrain him, and prevent him going straight back to the Hall, were they feared that if he didn't actually kill William Vavour, whilst he was in his present frame of mind, at the very least serious injury was quite likely to be inflicted on one party or the other. Somewhat placated, it was arranged for a neighbour to tell Sam what had happened whilst George stopped by Rose's bedside.

The constable who had recruited the assistance of Sergeant Peat, accompanied him to tackle what he knew would be a difficult interview. Giving a throaty "whoa there," to the horse drawing their black gig, the constable simultaneously gave the reins a gentle pull and leaned a little further back in his seat allowing the gig to come to a halt by the steps leading to the front door of the Hall.

"Now gentlemen, what brings you both here on such a fine evening, surely you haven't managed to apprehend all the drunks and vagrants in Hoult," James said, allowing his stick to support his considerable bulk, as he stood framed in the open doorway.

"We're here to see your son, he almost killed two women this evening," Sergeant Peat declared, ignoring the jibe.

"Come into the drawing room and let us see if we can sort out this little misunderstanding," James continued with false charm.

"It's your son we're here to speak to," the sergeant continued.

James demurred before saying in a controlled voice, "I don't think that it will be possible tonight gentlemen, he suffers from severe headaches and has taken to his bed, I'm sure he'll be alright in the morning."

"In that case, tell him we'll be back first thing tomorrow morning," Sergeant Peat declared, abruptly turning back to the gig.

As the two policemen's gig disappeared up the drive, William emerged from his position behind the door where he had overheard all the conversation.

"You idiot, you've really blown it this time, not only have you terrified your mother and sisters but it seems you almost killed those two Slade women. Not that I've any time for any of the Slade's."

"I know how you hate them father, so I was only trying to scare them," William wheedled.

"I'll get hold of Simon to see if he can find a solution to the mess you're in." James continued, deep in thought.

It didn't take too long for news of the accident to travel around Hoult; little wonder therefore that it soon came to the attention of William's friend David Ingelby, who quickly told his father.

Understanding all too well how anything connected to the Vavour's had a nasty habit of rebounding on him, Simon left for the Hall immediately and in so doing, pre-empted James contacting him. He had been told in graphic detail about the incident from other passengers who had just alighted from the London train, so was unsurprised to learn of the sergeant and constable's visit.

"There are only three possible courses of action to take," Simon said closing his eyes and cradling his fingers in a prayer like attitude.

William nervously chewed the inside of his cheek, whilst James took the weight off his injured leg by sitting on the corner of his desk.

Simon hesitated for a while, then opening his eyes, appeared to be looking intently at the cornice work on the ceiling, as if it might impart some form of divine inspiration.

"The first option is to let the officers arrest you" he said looking at William.
"I will do my best of course to claim that the horse bolted or something along those lines, but I might have difficulty explaining away the disparaging remarks you made to the two ladies, especially as there are witnesses who saw the full sequence of events. However, I must warn you that if you are convicted of attempted murder, the penalty is death by hanging or at the very least a substantial sentence of hard labour".

"What's the second option?" James questioned.

"Leave the country immediately and go to the colonies".

"And the third?" prompted William after a long pause.

"I suggest you try and come to some arrangement with the injured parties to ensure that they will not press a charge," remarked Simon.

As the reality of what he had done began to sink in, William hung his head in a contrite manner. Sat on the edge of his seat, in a voice devoid of his usual bravado, he said quietly "I don't fancy the first two options, so that only leaves the third." Mindful of their financial obligations regarding the purchase of the new sloops, James was acutely aware of how damaging this sort of publicity could be in attracting new customers, even if they were to undercut their rates substantially below their competitors.

"I agree we have little option other than to go ahead with the third option", he said after a few moments reflection. "You had better meet Slade and see what he wants this time", he said looking at Simon.

Next morning the constable and sergeant appeared at the Hall door, and with the minimum of fuss arrested William, taking him back with them to face questioning in Hoult. His mother and sisters were naturally distressed at the turn of events, but as they were unaware of Simon's gloomy analysis the previous evening, they received a somewhat different version of events.

In spite of believing what the witnesses had to say, the constabulary were well aware that money and privilege would soon come into play, so they decided that in the short term they would make life as uncomfortable as possible for the arrogant young man.

Safely sandwiched between two hefty officers William was escorted down the stone steps to one of the underground cells, where rather like George before him, bile rose in his throat when he smelt the overpowering stench of ammonia laced with putrid faeces, and the sights and sounds of prisoners poking blackened arms through the rough iron bars imploring the officers for food and water.

"You'll be kept here until we have time to question you about the incident," one of the constables said, opening a cell door.

Stepping inside the cell William tripped, and instinctively thrust out his right hand to save himself from falling to the floor. Unfortunately his hand landed on something soft and squishy, which he soon realised must have come from the overflowing wooden bucket standing in the gloom at the rear of the cell.

"You'll find a straw mattress in the corner, move it if you feel water dripping on you", the other constable said with a hint of relish in his voice, he had heard plenty of tales regarding the way that the Vavour treated anyone that crossed their path, so he was in no mood to make life easier for him.

With that the outer door clanged shut as the constables disappeared upstairs plunging the dungeon into darkness once more. When other prisoners weren't wailing like demented lunatics, William could hear the constant drip of water seeping through the roof. He decided to lie down on the straw mattress, but that presented him with further discomfort because rather like George before him, he soon began to itch as a multitude of fleas set about him, gorging on a feast of fresh blood.

Rose, meanwhile, was in expert hands, after dressing her wounds and putting her leg in plaster, Dr. and Mrs. Finch made her as comfortable as possible. "You won't be able to walk for six weeks," the doctor declared, "and even then, you'll have to support your leg with a crutch. Only time will determine how it heals it was a bad break and I fear that it may leave you with a limp".

Occurring on the face of harvest, Rose's accident could hardly have come at a worse time in the farming year, but Dr Finch had taken a weight off George's shoulders by his assurance that she was in the best possible hands, and that she would be able to return home just as soon as he was satisfied that she was safely on the road to recovery. He was further reassured when the doctor said that there would be no cost to them, as a Hoult business man who had witnessed the entire episode would be settling all bills.

The following day, the constable who had helped arrest William, met George at the field gate just as he was about to start scything his first field of barley. "I bet the young devil's not sweating as much as I am", the portly constable declared mopping his brow as he alighted from his horse. "Mind you though, after a couple of days in our cells he'll be sweating with fear, wondering what's going to happen to him next."

"I know all about it," George said, "it was as a result of his father and that crooked Simon Ingelby, lying to the court, that I received these", George said pulling his shirt to one side, so that the constable could see the lines of scars where the cat a' nine tails had cut deep into his back.

"We knew you were innocent but those clever devils manipulated the evidence. You didn't stand a chance against 'em. It's for that reason I've come to see you and delayed letting Ingelby see young Vavour for as long as I can," the constable said sweating profusely under his heavy uniform.

"I'm afraid in the hands of those clever lawyers we may have a job making our case stick", he added walking over to find shade under an ash tree by the gateway.

"But surely there were plenty of witnesses who saw everything" George remarked.

"I know, but I've already heard talk of business repercussions if certain people repeat what they saw."

"So what are you saying?"

"Remember there's more than one way of skinning a cat, and at the moment they're wrong footed."

With that the constable walked back to his horse.

George was still pondering the constable's words as he set about scything the field, but before he had gone too far, he was interrupted from his work by the sight of Simon Ingelby riding towards him. Simon had good reason to remember his last encounter with George in the wood, so decided to remain seated on his horse, a safe distance away.

"Mr Vavour sends his apologies," Simon said by way of introduction.

"Hasn't that lunatic friend of yours, the common decency to apologise personally for what his sons done, instead of sending his organ grinder"? George said looking up at the lawyer, who judging by his demeanour clearly remembered only too well, his two previous painful confrontations.

"It was just an unfortunate accident", Simon replied rather lamely.

"Don't be bloody ridiculous man, you lot make me sick. If it was an accident why didn't the maniac stop immediately and offer to help, instead of driving off?

"Rather than call him a maniac you ought to be congratulating William for doing his upmost to avoid what might have been a terrible tragedy." Simon said rather unconvincingly.

"Plenty of people witnessed the way he drove directly at my wife and daughter, coming within inches of killing them both. You can't seriously think I should be offering him congratulations? The devil needs convicting of attempted murder when I hope he receives the punishment that you and his father so richly deserved. I'm sure I don't have to remind you of all people, that given the right judge, a position that even you are unable to control, that he could easily be hung or failing that receive a good many years hard labour. You seem to have forgotten that I hold a confession which both you and James signed. Anyway I'm minded to pass it on to Sergeant Peat and see what he has to say".

"Come on don't be too hasty" Simon said, fearful that the anger in Georges voice might indicate he was highly likely to carry out his threat.

"The more I think about it, it's probably the best thing to do seeing as my wife's lying seriously injured in Doctor Finch's surgery".

"Perhaps we can come to some sort of arrangement" Simon went on rather nervously. "Let's say if you and your wife were to --- how shall we say --- agree --- that it was just a very unfortunate accident. Then by way of some form of recompense for your wife's suffering I am sure that James Vavour would make you a very generous offer if you agreed to drop all charges against his son William?"

Taking note of the points the constable had made earlier, George hesitated before replying.

"Let's say we agreed to your proposal, what have you in mind"?

"Well I'm sure a farm like yours could always do with a bit more land".

"What about the twenty acre field next to my top field, and come to think of it a new set of farm buildings wouldn't come amiss".

"But that's preposterous," Simon exploded, nearly falling from his horse.

"You asked me what I wanted in recompense and now I've told you". "Anyway the choice is yours, it's his freedom or, - - it's up to you, - - oh, and just remember, I still have your signed papers that combined with this issue could easily see both you and James Vavour being hung as well, now if you don't mind I've some harvest to get on with."

Simon rode straight back to the Hall to consult James."The bastards got us over a barrel," Simon said bitterly, "and it's all thanks to that stupid son of yours, at least he won't be enjoying his experience in that hell hole of a jail."

"I don't need you to lecture me on my son's behaviour, your job is to get him out," James replied sharply.

Next morning Simon called on George once more with two documents, one of which was signed by James Vavour to confirm the transfer of the twenty acre field and a promisory note stating that he would pay for a new set of farm buildings to be erected in George's farm yard. The other was a document that he and Rose had to sign, stating that they would not be pressing charges. Rose continued to progress well, returning home in the middle of September just in time to see the last load of wheat sheaves enter the yard. If James had previously held a pathological hatred of the Slade's, then it was ten times worse now, as the mere thought of him paying for George's new farm buildings filled him with hate.

1856

The new buildings were constructed during the summer of 1853 by a builder who the Vavour's regularly employed to carry out work on the estate or their commercial premises in Hoult. On their completion George was able to winter his expanding herd of Red cattle in the most up to date conditions, whilst the stables were ready for the time he could fulfil his long held dream of breeding Shire horses. Rose made a remarkable recovery thanks to the skill of Dr Finch, although the severity of the fracture resulted in one leg becoming slightly shorter than the other making it necessary for her to walk with the aid of a stick.

Folk, who over the years had fallen foul of the Vavours, noted that Williams so called "accident" involving Rose Slade, was yet another example of how Vavour wealth, when combined with Ingelby cunning, had enabled the latest member of the Vavour family to escape justice. However what ordinary folk, lacking their wealth and privilege, found particularly galling was that if they infringed the law in the slightest way, they could expect to receive sentences that were out of all proportion to the deed. Cynical heads concluded that once again the Vavours had bought themselves out of trouble, judging by the new buildings being constructed at George Slade's farm. However the constables felt they had achieved a minor victory by succeeding in keeping William locked up in the underground cells for six days, and in so doing made him endure conditions that would remain with him for some time.

On his release he ran a gauntlet of angry town's people hurling a stream of abuse, as he ran to the safety of his father's waiting carriage. Still smarting from his ordeal, he followed his father down to his study.

"I'm sending you away until all this business calms down", James said, grimacing in pain as he sat down heavily in the chair behind his desk.

Over recent months his leg had started to ache more than usual, but he found that if he stretched it out it gave him some relief.

Receiving no reaction from William he continued. "Your grandfathers shipping connections in Hull have agreed to find a placement for you as a midshipman in the navy. Troubles brewing in the Middle East so bearing in mind you're almost eighteen, it will give you an opportunity to redeem yourself and clean the slate".

"I don't seem to have any choice in the matter" William replied looking even more subdued than when he descended the steps into the cells. "What's this about the Middle East".

"It seems that the Russians want to impose the Orthodox Church as the proper guardians of The Holy Land".

"So what's this got to do with us"?

"Well since we beat Napoleon, we are on much better terms with the French, so our governments assisting them to help the Ottoman Empire restore the influence of the Catholic Church".

Within days William quietly departed Hoult by sloop for Hull, eliminating any further requirement for him to put in an appearance at the shipping office and suffer the humiliation of sniggers and nudges behind his back that would be bound to accompany his attendance. He joined HMS Warwick and within a matter of weeks was on his way to the Black Sea where Warwick became a part of the Anglo French flotilla intended to show that the allies meant business. The allies gave Russia an ultimatum to quit the Danube principalities that had previously been under Ottoman control or face swift retribution. The Russian reaction was swift. They sank a patrol squadron of Ottoman frigates giving France and Britain ample justification to support its Ottoman ally and declare war on Russia on March 28th 1854.

Williams's ship was soon in the thick of battle during the siege of Sevastopol when the Russians scuttled their ships, using their naval cannons as field artillery. His ship came under fire as they attempted to shell the narrow corridor of land that formed the main supply route to the Crimean peninsula from the Sea of Azov. During the course of the fierce exchange of fire HMS Warwick along with two French vessels were badly damaged causing all three ships to founder close to land enabling the survivors to scramble ashore.

William pulled himself on to the beach only to be confronted by a group of wild eyed Cossacks dressed in knee length tunics, their legs covered in flared breeches that disappeared within a pair of black calf length boots.

All about him, other sailors both French and British, weighed down by their sodden clothing dragged themselves on to dry land.

Suddenly the Cossacks started firing indiscriminately at anything that moved. William was powerless to defend himself as he looked up at a particularly large individual some forty yards distant. The man in common with his fellow Cossacks may have been more adept at close combat fighting, or on the other hand it might have been the sheer exuberance of the moment that caused him to miss an easy target. William could therefore count himself lucky that the bullet intended to kill him went through his shoulder, whilst another Cossacks bullet floored the French sailor next to him. Before he had a chance to reload, the Cossack saw his fellow comrades disappearing from sight over a sand dune, so whooping with excitement he followed suit. Now as they both sat up relieved to be alive they saw the reason for the Cossacks rapid disappearance, as several smaller boats from the flotilla drew closer to the shore with soldiers discharging a hail of bullets over their heads in the direction of the fleeing Cossacks.

Stout French sailors rowed ashore picking up the dead and attending to the wounded as they bandaged William and his French colleagues wounds before transferring them both back in tenders to a larger vessel laying off shore.

As they lay side by side in a French hospital, the real killer of the Crimean war became all too apparent, as it was later revealed that the ravages of disease killed more than three times as many soldiers as died from all other causes put together. The extreme heat coupled with the high humidity of the Danube delta led to attacks of malaria, cholera, dysentery and typhoid. In their already weakened state it was not long before William and his French companion soon succumbed to first dysentery and then malaria. Although neither of them spoke the others language, they communicated in less feverish moments by signs and gesticulations. On one particularly hot and oppressive day, William turned on his side to see the Frenchman weakly beckoning him with a crooked index finger. All around him in the sultry heat orderlies with a sprinkling of nurses were offering comforting words to the wounded and dying, as they mopped brows or moistened parched lips with water. Bending closer, William saw that the Frenchman was clasping something within his hand, indicating that William should take it. As he reached over the Frenchman unclenched his fist to reveal a silver double barred cross attached to a leather cord.

William carefully took the cross from the Frenchman's hand and gazed with fascination at a design he had once heard his father remark had some sort of connection with the Slade family. Later that day the Frenchman like more than one hundred thousand of his fellow countrymen died, and his bed was swiftly filled by another sick man. William felt he could count himself lucky to be one of the fortunate few to recover from the fever so quickly. Each day he regained a little more strength enabling him before long to leave his sick bed and after several weeks of convalescence by the warm waters of the Black Sea, return back to Britain by ship in the early spring of 1856. It seemed like a lifetime had passed since he had last been in Hoult. He had seen and experienced so much, and now at long last as he stepped off the London train he was on the final leg of his journey home, a much wiser and more mature young man.

The senior Hall coachman was there to greet him, and place his bags in the back of the gig, before they both set off for the short ride home. How the familiar seemed so welcoming, as the journey took them past the barges and sloops tied up in the canal basin. Even the slab sided brick warehouses that he had previously despised now appeared welcoming, as the sunlight played over the mellow brickwork and shadows from the hoists rippled over the water. Once they were out in open country, he couldn't help marvelling at how green everything looked compared to the arid landscape in the Crimea. Rounding a bend in the road they were confronted by Dobby, who was supposed to be tenting* his cows on the roadside grass, but was snoozing on the verge in the warm spring sunshine. The scene seemed timeless, as the coachman had to shout to get Dobby to stir himself and move his cows so they could pass by. The unfortunate fellow, although mentally retarded, was gainfully employed watching his father's cows graze the roadside verges.

*Minding

Over the years, despite his affliction, he was able to control his cows with a whip using the bare minimum of effort. He had developed a remarkable skill, that by flicking his wrist he was able to send a twenty foot cord snaking across the ground to crack in front of a venturesome cow and bring her back into line.

Moving closer to home a smile flickered over his face as he recognized the hilltop field where he remembered showing young Sam Slade who was boss, all those years ago. Then they turned into Peddars Row, but this looked strangely different to how he remembered it. To the rear of the Slade's new brick house, which for some reason always made his father utter oaths whenever he saw it, stood a range of new farm buildings. His heart missed a beat as he saw picked out in different coloured bricks the symbol of the Cross of Loraine, similar to the one he now wore around his neck.

"Come inside", his mother fussed as he stepped down from the gig,

"You must be tired after your long journey. We've so much to ask you. What was it like facing those wild Russian soldiers"? Without pausing for breath she continued, "We sent you letters, did you receive them? We did get one from you saying you had been injured and that you were in hospital".

James, who was standing in the hallway to the side of the front door, couldn't help noticing that William held one arm partly over his chest as his son crossed the white marble floor and entered the south drawing room. Sparkling spring sunshine was cascading through the windows to illuminate the potted palms as William collapsed into one of the easy chairs, whilst his mother walked over to the fireplace and pulled a cord to summon a maid to bring refreshments. The room felt warm, so William unbuttoned his jacket and loosened his shirt collar exposing the cord around his neck.

Spotting the cord James, who so far had said very little got up from his chair and walked over, "See you were awarded a medal", he said plucking the cord from around William's neck, and in doing so exposed the double cross. A red haze appeared in front of his eyes making him drop it immediately as though he had burned his fingers on red hot metal. His mind went straight back to that fateful night when he had reached up the tree trunk to retrieve such another cross as this, when he had felt the explosive force of the mantrap encircling his leg. He staggered backwards making Isabelle cry out in alarm,

"Are you alright James"? She said anxiously rushing to his aid.

"Suddenly felt a trifle feint, must be the strength of the sun", he proffered by way of explanation. Only William, who was completely unaware of the man trap incident involving the cross in the wood, picked up on the fact that it was the sight of his cross that had unnerved his father. What was it about the cross that had so shaken him?

"I think that it would be better for all concerned if you continue to keep a low profile a little longer by not visiting the offices", James said later in the confines of his study.

"Why should I do that"? William said.

"You don't seem to get it", James said testily. "Simon is convinced that the reason we have lost business over the last two years is largely a consequence of your reckless actions in deliberately running over those Slade women".

"But everyone knows it was an accident".

"Do you think I'm stupid? There were plenty of people there who would testify differently. Customers listen to what people say. They don't like dealing with someone who they believe has escaped justice". James was more than happy to believe Simon, when he blamed William for being the principle reason the extra trade he had so confidently predicted for the new sloops failed to materialize. Both he and Simon failed to realise, or perhaps they just didn't want to face up to the fact, that the railways were transporting an increasing quantity of bulky products such as coal and grain that had previously been carried by canal. Every bit of extra trade the railways picked up contributed to the terminal decline of the canal trade, resulting in Vavour canal transport losing money as there would soon be insufficient trade for two of the new sloops, let alone four. The following months passed by uneventfully with William only venturing into Hoult on rare occasions to see David Ingelby, but as time went by he had another reason to visit the Ingelby home when he became attracted to David's only sister Jane. Whenever he left the Park gates he couldn't help noticing the new farm buildings to the rear of George Slade's house. He felt certain that the money for constructing them must have been the price his father had to pay to ensure the Slades didn't press any charges against him, otherwise how could they possibly have afforded them. In spite of asking his father and David Ingelby they were both steadfast in their refusal to divulge any details. But the thing that really puzzled him was why a cross, similar to the one he wore around his neck should be so prominently displayed on the gable end of the building.

• • • •

"Now we've got some decent stables, we ought to think about breeding our own Shires and maybe selling a few". George proffered one winter evening after the family had completed their evening meal.

"It's a fact that there isn't a farmer in the country that doesn't needs them", Sam added philosophically, "So if we were able to breed some really good animals, then I'm sure there would be any number of farmers keen to buy our stock".

"Unfortunately there's a fly in the ointment". Rose pointed out; glancing up from the sock she was darning.

"What's that"? Sam said.

"James and William Vavour of course, she added sagely. "Remember they live just up the road".

"I must say I'm always on edge whenever I see either them or the Ingelby's", George said, remembering only too well how William was so nearly responsible for killing both his wife and daughter.

"Ever since they finished the new building", Rose continued, "I've seen how James stops, just after he's pulled out of the Park gates and stares in our direction as though he's planning something else".

"Still, to be positive, we've out manoeuvred the devils twice, and in spite of the fact they almost killed you and me, we're here to tell the tale". George said with a smile. "It's not the best way to put the farm on a sound footing, but I reckon we've only got our just deserts". Rose added.

"I agree, but nevertheless I know what's happened in the past and how the cunning devils can turn things to their advantage if they get half a chance". George added wryly.

1859

One sunny Saturday in June 1858, William Vavour married Jane, Simon Ingelbys only daughter in a colourful ceremony at St John's, the biggest and grandest of Hoults three churches. However, as their open topped carriage passed along the street from the church to a lavish reception at the recently opened town hall, folk who would normally have waved and cheered offering their good wishes to the newly wedded couple lowered their heads and kept their hands by their sides. It still rankled with a good many law abiding townsfolk, how James Vavour and Simon Ingelby between them had conspired to prevent William facing the justice that he so obviously deserved.

"Why is your father always so insistent he leaves here before dusk"? Jane queried after her father in law made his usual rapid departure from their new home in Hoult late one afternoon.

"I really don't know", William replied, "come to think of it, as long as I can remember I've never known him want to be out after dark".

"And there's another thing that's puzzled me", Jane continued. "What is it about that range of new farm buildings we pass after leaving the Hall drive, that seems to upset him so"?

"You mean that devil Slade?

"I've noticed the way he fumes and bangs his stick against the carriage floor as soon as he catches sight of them".

"I think it's something to do with the design of this cross on the gable end that upsets him", William said withdrawing his silver cross from within his shirt".

"Didn't you tell me you got it from a French sailor in the Crimea"?

"That's right; he gave me it shortly before he died".

"But that still doesn't explain why the unusual designs has been incorporated on the gable end of their farm building. Is there some connection between the two that I'm unaware of? Furthermore, come to think of it, why are those buildings so much finer than any others in the district? Even yours at Hall farm aren't in the same league as those".

"I really don't know", William said, conveying in his voice what he hoped was just the right amount of disinterest to stop her pursuing that line of thought any further. After all he had his own thoughts, but in order to not appear disinterested in what she was saying, added, "I don't know where those jumped up peasants get their money, especially when they lie to the constabulary.

Do you know ever since that bloody George Slade was imprisoned for attacking both our fathers he has done his damnedest to get his own back".

"Didn't they accuse you of deliberately trying to run over Mrs Slade and her daughter"? Jane asked walking over to her husband.

"George Slade will try anything to get at us. I tell you if it hadn't been for your father convincing the constables that rather than treat me as a common criminal, they should be congratulating me for bringing my spooked horse under control and avoiding a much more serious accident. If it hadn't been for my skilful driving they both might have been killed".

"Some people can be so cruel", Jane said sympathetically giving him a hug.

"That wasn't the half of it though, because before it got through their thick heads that I was innocent, they had me locked in their stinking cells for nearly a week. What with all that filth down there it's the biggest wonder I didn't catch something. God knows what might have happened to me if they had believed his lies".

"You poor dear, what an ordeal it must have been for you". Jane said gently caressing his shoulder.

As memory of that time flooded back, he remembered the look of horror that spread across his father's face on seeing the cross around his neck for the first time. The trouble was, he could never understand why it had affected him in that way, except that his father had once mentioned something about George Slade's father, picking up a similar cross on the battlefield at Waterloo. Knowing how much he hated the Slade's, could that have been the reason he reacted as he did when he saw the cross around his neck? If so, then that would explain his reaction every time he saw the symbol on the Slade's farm building. But there was another thing that troubled him, how had they managed to afford such a magnificent building in the first place, unless, and that had to be the reason, - his father had paid for it.

William eventually returned to the shipping office, but this time following his father's advice, kept a low profile, sensing that certain people with long memories still resented the fact that he had appeared to escape justice. Was it because of that, that trade on the canal continued to decline, or was there a more fundamental problem James wondered. In any event it was looking increasingly obvious that there was never going to be anything like sufficient trade for even two of the new sloops they had so optimistically purchased, let alone four, so in order to reduce some of their debt, he persuaded Simon to agree the sale of two. His mounting concern over the canal wasn't the only factor that was troubling him. Whenever he drove out the Park drive, he couldn't help but catch sight of George Slades growing herd of red cattle. That alone was bad enough, but matters only became much worse when he caught sight of a Shire horse that his foreman informed him was the foundation of their Shire horse stud. Consumed with jealousy, his devious mind began to work overtime on how he could engineer the ruination of their business. God only knows if Simons plan in the woods had succeeded none of this would have arisen. But there again, it was another example of one of Simons brilliant ideas that although seeming perfectly rational at the time, was a great deal better in theory than practice. Unfortunately, as he was beginning to discover to his cost, many of Simon's solutions to problems had a horrible habit of going wrong. After all, it wasn't Simon that had been caught in the trap, neither had he to reap the consequences of his actions in the same way that he had. Then there was the cost of it all, there seemed to be no end to it. It was bad enough giving the Slade's land and funding the construction of their new house, but the deal that Simon had brokered following William's slight indiscretion was far too generous. It only made matters a great deal worse, when he couldn't fail but see the magnificent cattle buildings that he had financed every time he drove through the Hall gates. As if all of that wasn't bad enough, they had rubbed salt into his wounded pride by prominently incorporating in different coloured bricks the outline of the double cross on the gable end, as if to constantly remind him of that episode in the wood.

The mere sight of that cross haunted him, as it instantly brought back terrible memories of that fateful night. If he wasn't careful, the devils would soon be rivalling him, especially when he could see the increased numbers of their new herd of cattle and to cap it all the foundations of a Shire horse stud. "Where would it end? Something had to be done. Then like a flash it came to him. Why hadn't he thought of it before? His plan was so simple. Not only would it be easy to execute, but best of all it would be untraceable. George and Sam's cattle numbers were not only expanding, but were also starting to become recognised in the neighbourhood as a small herd producing good quality stock.

At the end of October 1858 George and Sam brought their cattle back to the farmyard for the duration of the winter, when depending on age and sex, the animals were housed in separate groups. Each day, in addition to bringing them hay to eat and straw for bedding, drinking troughs were filled with water collected from the buildings roofs and stored in three large iron tanks. One morning towards the end of November it was Sam's turn to feed the cattle when he noticed that one of the cows didn't appear her normal self. "Mary didn't get up and come to the tumbrel this morning", Sam explained to his father. "She's usually one of the first to come and will generally horn the others away". "I've noticed the way she bosses the others", George said, "perhaps she just eat too much yesterday".

"I went across and got her to her feet", Sam continued, "but her ears were down, and she staggered sideways after she got up. She sniffed the hay before lying down once more. You're probably right, she most have some pain in her guts because her mucks quite loose. Only thing is though she seems to be slavering as well, as though there's something fast in her throat".

Sam noticed that when he fed the animals again that afternoon she was clearly worse as her nose was now dry and her breathing appeared rapid as though she had a fever, so with his father's help they decided to dose her with a propriety drug that was intended to dispel fever. "She's much worse", Sam reported to his father when he went in for his breakfast the following morning. "I can't get her to stand and to make matters worse, I'm certain a couple of other cows aren't quite right either".

Later that afternoon Mary died and the other two cows in the group were visibly worse, with similar symptoms starting to show in a group of younger cattle. "We need to fetch Frank", George said as soon as he saw how bad the other animals were looking. Frank Vines, the Animal Practitioner from Holt scratched his head and looked mystified as he walked among the listless animals, until he remembered a similar case from his early days. "I reckon they poisoned"! He declared triumphantly, looking intently at two of the worst cases. "I'm sure that's what it is, they've been poisoned"

"How do you make that out" George said, his face full of concern.

"Well they're showing all the classic signs of poisoning; it could be from either the feed or the water". Frank said quite confident he'd solved the mystery.

"I don't see how it can be the feed", Sam said "they've been eating the same hay all winter".

"He's right" George added. "It was got dry, so it isn't mouldy. In fact it's probably some of the best hay we've ever made".

"Then it has to be the water, where do they drink"?

"We fill the water troughs, every morning with water from the rainwater tanks you saw as you came in", Sam explained, adding. "The tanks are cleaned out once a year when the beasts go out to grass".

"I tell yer, you won't get water purer than that", George chipped in.

"In that case I'm completely baffled", Frank said glancing about him deep in thought, before adding as an afterthought, "I don't suppose you have any Fowlers about the place by any chance".

"What the hell's that"? George said with a puzzled expression on his face.

"It's a solution of arsenic" Frank replied, "It's sometimes used in extremely low concentrations on horses".

"Never heard of the stuff, let alone used it", George said.

"Well, what I suggest you do, just in case anything has got in the water, is to completely empty all the water troughs and refill them with fresh water, and as a further precaution knock off their hay for a few days and give them some of your best oat straw".

The next morning the cattle were certainly no worse, with no fresh animals showing symptoms of illness. By the time of the afternoon feeding, Sam was overjoyed to see a significant improvement. "I reckon we're maybe over the worst". He reported to his relieved father later that afternoon.

It didn't take long for news of the mystery illness, that some of the wilder rumour mongers were declaring had already killed half of the Slades cattle, to spread like wildfire across the village and then onto farms in neighbouring parishes, with everyone paying particularly close attention to their own animal's health, fearing some kind of epidemic. So it was with understandable relief that other cattle keepers heard the good news of the animal's speedy recovery. The estate farm manager likewise, was quite elated to hear that the Slades animals were recovering, and was consequently delighted to pass on the good news to William when he met him one morning. Miserable devil he thought to himself, as William merely grunted on hearing the good news, and continued walking.

As is so often the case when the air is still in early winter, mist and fog readily forms, which not only muffles and distorts sound, but tends to swirl and eddy first in one direction and then the other. Even when a person is familiar with their own surroundings everything in the fog looks strangely different, so it's easy to lose all sense of direction and distance, little wonder therefore that if anyone's unsure of where they are they can soon become disorientated. And that's precisely what happened late one evening that November.

Sam was about to take his usual last look around the cattle before he went to bed, so closing the back door and stepping into the raw night air he was unsurprised to find that the fog had become considerably thicker since nightfall which was probably unsurprising as it had never lifted properly all day. Pulling his cloak a little tighter around his shoulders he saw the way that the pale shaft of light from inside the house, that had briefly been reflected on the fog seemed to scurry back to the warmth inside. On this occasion he was a little later than normal doing his nightly inspection as he had just enjoyed a particularly close game of Dominoes with his parents and his sister Rachael, but since the cattle had been ill he had been extra vigilant, paying particular attention to where each animal was lying. In spite of the fog deadening sound, he could hear Jess, his border collie, giving a series of low growls outside her kennel, as she pulled on her chain first in one direction and then the other. "What's up old girl", he said, patting her head, as he passed by. Continuing on his way to the cattle yards he could still hear the dog giving a succession of anxious growls as she frantically pulled on her chain. Must be the fog that's unsettling her he thought, or perhaps a fox has become slightly disorientated and Jess has picked up its scent.

Sam lifted the hooked sneck on the crew gate and stepped into the cattle yard. There was something about the smell of housed cattle that Sam found strangely intoxicating. He always found it difficult to define exactly what it was, but he thought it may have had something to do with warm bodies chewing sweet smelling hay and lying on a clean bed of fresh barley straw. Unfortunately the fog reflected the feeble light from his lantern into an opaque haze and consequently didn't travel very far, but even so it was soon apparent to him that most of the animals were standing and slightly on edge, which Sam found unusual, as normally at this time of night they would all be laid down chewing their cuds. He knew them all by name, in most cases remembering mothers and grandmothers, as he moved slowly among them gently touching a particular favourite here and having a soothing word with another. Suddenly he heard the sound of straw rustling as a group of heifers over a dividing fence surged forward. Slightly concerned, that perhaps a fox had wandered into the building and spooked them, Sam held up his lantern to see what had caused them to panic, but of course the fog prevented him seeing very far. But then he thought he could hear the sound of boots scraping the rails of the wooden fence, and that certainly wasn't a fox. Then he caught a fleeting glimpse of a hooded figure moving swiftly across the crew yard in the direction of the gate he had just come through.   He turned back, but by the time he got to the gate, he was just in time to see the fugitive head in the direction of the open yard and disappear from view in the fog. Judging by the direction in which the figure was running Sam guessed that he must be heading for a gap between two straw stacks, so pulling the gate closed behind him, he dropped his lantern and sprinted towards the other end of the stacks where he thought his quarry would emerge.

He had anticipated correctly, because the figure who was obviously unfamiliar with the layout of the farm yard was now only a dozen yards in front so Sam put on an extra spurt of speed and made a lunge for the strangers cloak as it flared out behind. "Now you bastard", Sam yelled, his heart racing, as he grabbed it by the hem to collapse over the fugitive as they both fell to the ground "What the devil do you think you're up to? The man didn't reply, but by way of an answer, rather like a wild animal that had just been captured in a net, flailed his fists at Sam's body. With his quarry squirming from side to side within his loose fitting cloak, Sam made a grab for the man's neck in order to try and obtain a better grip. All of a sudden the man kicked out striking Sam in the groin making him double up with pain. Given a slight respite he turned sideways, scrambled to his feet and disappeared into the all enveloping fog. But as he broke away Sam's hands clutched something metallic around his neck and held on to it.

"Who do you reckon it could have been", George said, when a dishevelled looking Sam recounted what had happened since he had left the house only a few minutes earlier.

"I've no idea, but this might be a clue", Sam said flourishing the double cross he had pulled from the man's neck.

"Well I'll be damned you've got fathers cross" George exclaimed. "Your grandfather Taylor thought Cane had thrown it in the beck, so either he never threw it in, or this chaps managed to retrieve it.   Come on we need to see if the beast are alright. Whoever was in there was up to no good".

With a storm lantern each to offer illumination they looked carefully at each animal, but were relieved to find that none of them were amiss. However as they walked towards the gate, light from Sam's lantern reflected on something shiny lying in the straw.

"What the devils this", he remarked bending down and picking up a blue coloured glass bottle. "The corks gone, but luckily it's landed on its side and it looks as though there's a drop of liquid still in it".

"By God I understand now", George said "whoever it was in there has been poisoning the beast, quick we need to get those water troughs emptied immediately before any more animals take a drink".

• • • •

"Unfortunately there are two slight problems", William remarked as within the seclusion of his father's study he reported the nights events to his father.

"What are those", James said impatiently, as he leaned on the corner of the desk to take the weight off his aching leg.

"As I was getting away the devil grabbed me around the neck and must have got my silver cross. At any rate it's gone".

"You blithering idiot, I knew no good would come of the damned thing when I first saw it hung around your neck. One way or another, the sight of that double cross has haunted me for close on twenty years".

"How"? William said.

"I can't tell you now", James replied, "Suffice it to say that if the Slade's have it, they're going to think it once belonged to George Slade's fathers".

"I don't understand", persisted William, "wasn't he the fellow you once said had been run over with a horse and cart, years before I was born. Are you saying he once had a cross similar to mine?"

"Apparently so, they say it was something he picked up at Waterloo. Anyway the Slades have always claimed it was stolen from his body".

"So you think that they will think mine was his. But I still don't understand what makes you think that we should have taken theirs anyway".

"Did you say there was something else happened as well". James said changing the subject, not wishing to pursue that line of conversation.

"I dropped the bottle of poison in the crew yard as I ran off".

"You stupid, stupid idiot" James said burying his head in his hands. "Can't you do anything right. You've really blown it now. Whenever I try and get even with that damned family I seem to be jinxed".

"I don't think we need worry too much about it" William said hopefully, "Anyway it's more than likely buried under the loose straw now".

Only a few weeks had passed, since James pent up frustration had resulted in him giving William his highly personalised version of the feud with the Slade's. He failed to mention, anything about either of the two incidents with the mantrap, focusing his narrative solely on the way George Slade attacked both him and Simon Ingelby, which led to George Slade being imprisoned. "George Slade demanded that I build him a new cattle yard in return for dropping charges against you", James explained referring to Williams episode with Rose and Rachael. "The devil had me over a barrel because if I didn't agree to his demands, it was more than likely that you could have spent a long time in prison; it's your fault entirely that we have got into this state of affairs".

It was then that between them they had hatched the plan that James had thought would be so simple to implement. If it worked, and there was no reason why it wouldn't, at a stroke it would ruin the Slades financially. It would see the Slades cattle becoming sick, causing all of the in calf cows to abort, and the young stock to be so emaciated, they would be unsalable. They agreed that

William would creep in to the cattle yards at night when all was quiet, and pour some Fowlers solution into the water troughs, being careful not to put in too much as they didn't want the cattle to die.

"I thought that with the dense fog tonight, it would be an ideal opportunity to pour in the second dose", William said in defence of his actions. "I thought the Slades would be less concerned now that they thought that their animals were recovering from what they assumed was a mystery illness. I decided that I would go quite a bit later than last time, but I hadn't counted on young Slade also deciding to inspect his animals much later than usual".

"If there was so much cover with the fog, then why did it go wrong?" James questioned lowering his voice.

"It could have been as a result of the fog swirling, because all of a sudden the group of animals I was in seemed to be spooked which made them rush across to the fence. I panicked because I felt sure he would see me as he moved across the crew to see what had startled them. I clambered over a fence and raced for the door, but I'm certain he couldn't see who it was because my hood was raised all the time. I thought I'd got away but he managed to grab the back of my cloak after I took a wrong turn through the stack yard. However I kicked him hard and that seemed to wind him which allowed me to escape".

After George and Sam had drained the water troughs and refilled them with clean water, they went in the house to warm up by the fire. Turning the cross over in his hands, George remarked, "Unfortunately this doesn't necessarily prove it was around William Vavour's neck, though it does seem highly likely to be the case. In any event we need to put a stopper in that bottle and show it to Frank Vines".

Back at the Hall, James and William continued to debate the likelihood of the Slade's placing the blame on them. James however, knew only too well that it seemed whenever he tangled with the Slade's that something tended to go wrong. And now it was the wretched cross that had come back to haunt him once again. What would the Slade's be thinking, now that they had it in their possession? But there again perhaps things were not quite as black as he first thought. After all, it was most unlikely they would know anything about Williams cross. The one in the tree of course was made of wood which he reasoned must have been the one belonging to George Slade's father. If William was positive that he hadn't been recognised, then the cross that young Slade had snatched from his neck could have belonged to almost anyone, and as for the bottle, well it wasn't very big, so William was probably right in thinking that there was every chance that it was now buried under the straw.

The following morning George rode across to see Frank Vines with the bottle they had found the previous night.

"This is definitely a bottle of Fowlers Solution" Frank proclaimed, as he studiously examined the contents through a pair of pince nez glasses perched on the end of his nose.

"The labels been removed, but if I show you a new bottle", he added, reaching for a bottle on a shelf behind him. After he had wiped the dust away he passed it over for George to see. "You can see it's identical to this one. We don't use much of it these days as it's such a strong poison, but in extremely low concentrations it's a marvellous remedy for a number of horse conditions." Frank went on to pour the residue of George's bottle into a clear glass flask, and then pour a little from the full bottle into another flask.

"Identical", he said bending over to smell them, "See they've both got that same characteristic smell".

George explained to Frank about the previous night's nocturnal visitor and his suspicions on who it might be.

"I don't think that you've got sufficient evidence to bring a conviction Frank said sagely, I know you think you've recovered your fathers cross but Ingelby would run rings round you, arguing that there were possibly scores, if not hundreds of those crosses around, so how can you be absolutely certain it's your fathers, and as for the bottle it would be very difficult to pin that on to Vavour as there are any number of those bottles laying about on farms. Further more you have no real evidence, apart from taking a cross from the fugitive's neck, that the person Sam brought to the ground was William Vavour's anyway".

"The evil bastards", Sam said as he and his father were having yet another protracted discussion several days later, "why do you think they wanted to poison our cattle? Was it just because of the incident with mother and Rachael".

Naturally George had confided with Sam at the time about the terms that had been agreed with Simon Ingelby for the construction of the new building, provided he and Rose declined to press charges. Sam's initial reaction had been not to do a deal, and let William go to court so that he could suffer the hardships that his father had endured at the hands of the Vavour's. After all he reasoned his mother and sister had come within inches of losing their lives, to say nothing of his mother having to endure constant pain from her injuries.

"You can't put the clock back", George reasoned, "what's done is done, it's much better we derive some benefit from it, as it will at least help the family in the long run". Adding as an afterthought, "you know the Vavour's will get their cum uppence eventually".

At nineteen, Sam had grown into a big lad with broad shoulders and a kindly face, who rather like his father, had an equally placid nature, yet he felt angry whenever he thought of William Vavour and the evil deeds he had carried out. He constantly thought back to his fight with the hooded figure and realised just how close he had been to catching him red handed.

James in turn discussed the poisoning episode with Simon Ingelby who soon put his mind at rest confirming Frank Vines prognosis that there was no real evidence against them.

"You must remember", Simon pointed out, "that although the Slade's may suspect Williams involvement, they have absolutely no concrete evidence". William for his part was less confident than his father. It worried him that perhaps Sam had recognised him and if by chance they did find the bottle; would there be any identifying marks left on it that he hadn't noticed?

The most damming evidence lay in the cross itself now that George had it. Was it possible that a member of the Hall staff had seen it around his neck? He didn't think that it was likely but there was still that lagging doubt in his mind. He would certainly be horrified to see it produced again in his company.

• • • •

Rachel continued to become a highly valued member of Miss Topliss staff rapidly gaining a reputation in her own right for the quality of the gowns she produced resulting in her travelling to clients homes, in order to take measurements and finally to fit the dresses. She was tall and slim and always dressed decorously as befitted a lady in her position. Her smiling face and easy manner gave clients confidence in valuing her opinions. Taking a dress to Elizabeth Ingelby one day in March 1859, she was shown into the drawing room by their youngest son Benjamin, who was now one of the principle clerks in the shipping office, with special responsibility for securing new business for the firm's vessels.

Their eyes met and Ben was immediately smitten by the elegant young lady. He didn't have the flamboyance of his elder brother as he had always been overshadowed by David's overpowering dominance and almost scornful attitude, of in his eyes, lesser mortals. Naturally he saw James Vavour and his son William from time to time in the shipping office, but didn't care for the duplicity of many of the deals that they and his father got involved with. As Rachael left Benjamin hurried to show her to the door and somewhat shyly asked her if she would care to accompany him to a concert in the new town hall the following week. Rachael for her part admired the fine young man who seemed so different to his father and older brother, both of whose presence disturbed her. She was acutely aware of course, that Ben's sister had married that tyrant William Vavour, who she was never likely to forget almost, killed her and her mother. But that she reasoned shouldn't be held against Ben, who in their conversations told her how much he despised his brother in law for such a reckless deed.

The young couple got on remarkably well together. Unsurprisingly by the end of the year the romance had progressed to a position of perhaps a wedding the following year.

"I'm totally against it", George said with feeling, when Rachael told her parents how much she cared for Ben, "remember it was his father that got me imprisoned and flogged, just look at these scars", he said drawing up his shirt to show her.

"I tell you I'm not going to give away a daughter of mine to an Ingelby and that's final. Over the years, young lady, both they and the Vavour's have done their upmost to devastate our family, first by causing my mother to drown herself, then killing my father and more recently nearly killing me. As if that wasn't enough they tried to kill both you and your mother. To cap it all the Vavours, more than likely abetted by the Ingelbys attempted , and nearly succeeded in poisoning our cattle with the intention of ruining us. Is there no end to their treachery. Though your mother and I love you dearly in view of all that's happened in the past we think you're making a terrible mistake becoming involved with that family".

In spite of Rachael's protestations that whatever Ben's father had done, it was unfair to judge him in the same manner, both George and Rose remained resolute in their opposition. Elizabeth, Ben's mother, however took a much more pragmatic approach to the union. She thought a great deal of the confident young lady who was always so pleasant to her despite the part her husband had played in imprisoning her father. Even though she only heard Simon and James Vavour's versions of what had happened, she was astute enough to know that things were unlikely to have been quite as they had been portrayed.

1865

Ben and Rachael were married in October 1860, the same month that Charles Vavour was born.   In complete contrast to his sister's grand affair, their wedding ceremony was a fairly low key affair, conducted in the smaller of the town's churches at the eastern end of the town.   Rachael was bitterly disappointed, that despite all her pleading, both of her parents maintained their disapproval of the marriage and refused to attend.   Sam, standing in for his father gave his sister away, but not wishing to spend a moment longer than absolutely necessary in either William Vavour or his father's company, refused to attend the reception held in the public hall near the canal basin. The young couple made their new home in one of the smaller merchants terraced houses in Briar Road, only a short distance from Ben's place of work. Rachel was a sensitive girl who despite the huge disappointment of her parent's non-attendance at her wedding realised that she had to live her own life, and just maybe in the future she would convince them that Ben was different to the rest of his family.

• • • •

Word quickly spread that the Slade's cattle hadn't been struck by a mystery illness after all, but had in fact been deliberately poisoned by an individual who either had a grievance against the Slade's, or even worse anyone who owned livestock, in which case no one was immune from his actions. Rumours and counter rumours proliferated, regarding the identity of the villain, especially when it was learned that although Sam Slade had managed to grab hold of him, the culprit had fought his way from Sam's grasp before he could be identified. It was perhaps unsurprising that whilst the names of likely suspects were bandied about, the names of James or William Vavour were never considered as possible suspects. Most folk would have thought it preposterous in any case, that a family of their standing would stoop so low as to carry out such a despicable act, to not only cause suffering to dumb animals, but also financial ruin to a good honest hard working family. Never the less the realisation that there was someone at large who was prepared to carry out such an act against farm livestock put everyone on edge, with a rapid response to any unusual sounds during the night.

"You've been extremely lucky to get away with it unscathed", James remarked to William a couple of months later following yet another of their discussions on why nothing further had developed. "It's fortunate for you that people's memories are pretty short, otherwise somebody might have started putting two and two together".

"But there's absolutely nothing for anyone to go on". William declared.

"Not if you don't count the bottle of poison you carelessly dropped and that stupid cross that young Slade managed to grab from you. Mark my words that damn things going to cause trouble in the future".

"How can it", William reasoned, "There must be hundreds if not thousands of those crosses in France. If Sam Slade had been able to prove it was mine, then he would surely have done so long before now".

"We will see", James replied far from convinced by Williams reasoning.

• • • •

Much of the Slade's land was low lying, which after heavy rain was inclined to flood, and in the process ruin any growing crops. A solution to the problem lay in opening up ditches to drain the water away, followed by the labour intensive task of digging a series of trenches across the fields. At the bottom of which a tunnel was formed by laying two bricks on their sides followed by another bridging the top. George and Sam were no exception to other farmers in the district who found it necessary to carry out the procedure on some of their fields during the winter months, so once the livestock were fed in the morning, they collected spades and other drainage tools and made their way to whichever field they were draining at the time. When a local brickyard purchased one of the new fangled pipe forming machines that made half moon shaped pipes, to replace the use of bricks, they were one of the first farms to begin laying the new pipes. However, when it came to the attention of James and William Vavour, it proved to be the catalyst for yet another confrontation. It all came to a head one raw January morning in 1864, when both George and Sam were in the midst of digging and laying their daily target of two chains of pipes.

"They don't half save some time and effort" Sam was enthusing for the umpteenth time as he lowered another pipe into the trench bottom.

"It used to be damned hard work getting them level". George replied.

"Even then it wasn't a patch on the job these are making", Sam continued hooking his pipe tool into another pipe.

"What the devil does he want", George said looking up and seeing William Vavour riding across the field towards them.

"If you lay another of those drainage pipes I'll sue you", William declared, gazing contemptuously at them from the back of his horse.

"WHAT"? George roared, angling sideways in his trench, to get a better look at the fellow who he felt certain was responsible for poisoning their cattle.

Working waist deep in a trench of wet earth that managed to stick to pretty well everything it came in contact with, was never going to put George in a good mood at the best of times, but it was something else to be told he should stop work by an individual who he justifiably despised.

"You'll make the waters get into the ditch much quicker if you put those things in the ground and then it'll probably flood our fields". William remarked.

"Don't be bloody stupid man", Sam replied walking across from where he was working a few yards along the trench. He was feeling just as uncomfortable as his father, so like him, he was in no mood to be threatened by this arrogant young fellow.

"What makes you think our water can possibly flood your fields when all your fields are upstream of here? I've never known water run uphill".

Nonplussed by a perfectly sensible observation William persisted. "You're upsetting the balance of nature by digging drains that are not supposed to be there".

Sam, who could barely contain his annoyance was fuming at not only the man's stupidity, but also his audacity at riding over their land to tell them something that was almost laughable, if William hadn't been quite so serious. "And I don't think nature intended cattle to be poisoned with Arsenic".

"What are you talking about", William responded suddenly feeling not quite as confident as a few seconds earlier. In an attempt to camouflage a slight quaver in his voice he gave his horses reins a sharp jerk.

"Oh I think you know well enough", Sam said with authority in his voice, "remember we've got the cross now, it's only ever brought your family bad luck. You can count yourself lucky that if I had managed to hold on to you, you would have been breaking rocks now, rather than coming out with this sort of drivel".

Visibly shaken, William was already beginning to regret embarking on this particular vendetta, especially when he had felt so confident that the Slade's had no real evidence that he had been involved, but now he didn't feel quite as sure. Nevertheless, the thought of his double cross in their hands did worry him.

"Now if you've finished with your nonsense", George said, "You can bugger off our land just as fast as your horse can carry you, and don't ever step on it again unless you are invited. You can tell that father of yours who seems to be so insistent that no one trespasses on his land, that we don't want you coming on to ours either".

William reported the afternoon's events back to his father, who reacted in his usual explosive way. "Whatever possessed you to embark on that sort of ridiculous confrontation, if you continue to keep poking a stick into a wasps nest don't be surprised if they come out and sting you".

On a hot Saturday afternoon in June that year Sam married Mary, Frank Vines elder daughter in the same church that he had given his sister Rachael away almost four years previously. Both Rachael and Ben attended the happy ceremony along with their two young children though George and Rose in spite of loving their daughter found it difficult to be sociable to Ben. The young couple moved into the empty cottage, adjacent to George and Roses new home that Annie Hoyde had occupied until her death.

In view of William Vavour's attempt to poison their cattle they thought it prudent that a family member always be on hand to keep an eye on their animals, especially as the herd was acquiring a reputation among local farmers for quality. Nevertheless, when ever George or Sam were working in the fields away from home, they never felt easy, knowing from bitter experience how devious the Vavours could be, and how they were capable of doing almost anything to cause them ruination.

"I've heard that there's a new sort of reaper coming into the country next year" Sam said, as the family relaxed by the fire after enjoying an excellent Christmas dinner prepared by Rose.

"What's so different about it" George said settling in his chair for a snooze, only half interested in what Sam was saying.

"Well it's called a Sail Reaper, and it's made in America by someone called the Mc Cormick Company".

"Never heard of em", George said lighting his pipe.

"Just think", Sam enthused, "It can cut four acres of corn a day compared to us scything a third of an acre if we're lucky. I reckon we ought to buy one for next year's harvest".

"We couldn't possibly justify one for the amount we grow", George replied, perking up.

"But what if we were to harvest some of our neighbour's corn as well", Sam persisted, "The money that we earn would soon pay for the machine. Just think how much time and hard work scything that we would save".

Sam went on to explain that this new machine not only cut the stalks but the sails raked the crop across the knives to eliminate the need for another man forking off the crop. Over the following weeks Sam successfully convinced his father that if they wanted to be leading farmers in the area then they must adopt the latest farm machinery. When the new machine arrived on the farm in good time before the next harvest, it instantly became the centre of local gossip. Many of the old hands, who had spent a lifetime scything, were scathing in their criticism, declaring that they couldn't see how the new fangled machine was going to work, which was at complete odds with some of the young men, who looked on it enviously wishing that they could have one on their farm. The estate farms had recently purchased a rather unreliable second hand Bell reaper, who Sam was reliably informed, had been designed by a vicar of the same name. The new Sail Reaper by way of contrast to the Bell Reaper, rather than be pushed around the field with two horses, was drawn by only one horse. That however wasn't the only difference between the two machines, because the sail reaper delivered the stalks of grain in offset rows behind the machine, to leave a cleared pathway for the horse to walk on the next pass around the field. Inevitably news of the Slades new machine soon reached the ears of William Vavour, who was quick to pass the information to his father.

"Looks like the Slade's have upstaged us once again", he remarked

"It would serve them right if it didn't work after paying all that money for it". James said. Then an idea came into his head.

"Perhaps it won't work as well as they think", he said knowingly. "If it didn't it would bring them down a peg or two".

Following several fine days in early August, Sam judged that the Six acre field of barley was about ready to harvest. So with the prospect of the fine weather continuing he decided to move the new machine up to the field in anticipation of starting the next morning once the dew had lifted.

James of course knew that the crop was barley, so had already anticipated that it would be one of the first crops for the new machine to harvest, consequently he knew it was sure to attract the attention of many of the local farmers who had agreed to let the Slade's harvest their crops with the machine. He thought that if the machine was so critically damaged, that it was rendered useless, then not only would it make the Slade's look rather foolish, but would probably put paid to any potential earnings for them. After his humiliation in the wood he could hardly wait for an opportunity to get his own back, so as William had managed to botch his two efforts, he decided to do this alone without telling William what he had in mind. He waited until Sam had left the field, then just as the sun was setting; he walked along the hedge line that separated the Slade's field from one belonging to the estate. After a while he slipped through a gap in the hedge and came face to face with their new red and yellow painted machine. Earlier, he had picked up a hammer from the estate tool shed, pretty sure, that following his time spent among the various shafts and drives in the warehouses by the canal, that the cast iron gearbox which transferred motive power from the drive wheel to the knife and sails, would be the most vulnerable part of the machine. He therefore thought that if he were to smash it, the machine would be rendered completely useless. Getting close to the machine for the first time, the four sails reminded him of six foot long combs that he could see where cranked in such a manner that at their lowest point they became horizontal. In this position they were able to draw the stalks of grain against a reciprocating knife, before conveying the crop onto a curved table that delivered it into a neat row some five feet away from the standing crop. Slightly to the off side, and above a ribbed iron wheel that provided the motive power for the sails and the knife, a seat was positioned for the driver to control the horse. As the last rays of a brilliantly red sunset disappeared behind the hills, James took the heavy hammer from his coat pocket and looked for the gearbox that he knew must be somewhere on the machine. There was nothing that looked particularly like a gearbox higher up, so he bent over to get a look underneath the machine, and there under the flat table close to the ribbed wheel he spotted what he was looking for. Unfortunately in order to reach it, he realised that he would have to lay flat on his back, and then, by using his hands to grip the underside of the machine, pull himself underneath.

He was so full of hatred that in spite of his leg aching more than usual, which made it extremely difficult for him to straighten it without getting a painful cramp, he was determined to well and truly sabotage their machine. It was therefore with considerable difficulty that he managed to pull himself under the reaper and set about striking the cast iron metal with the hammer. After several blows, he was satisfied to hear the brittle metal crack, then a few blows later was delighted to see a stream of thick viscous oil settle into a pool on the ground. As he continued to hammer, it wasn't too long before bits of casting that formed the gearbox case fell away to expose rows of intermeshing teeth, so for good measure he aimed a blow at them and was satisfied to see a tooth split off the nearest cog wheel.

Having effectively destroyed any chance that George Slade and his son would have in using their new sail reaper it was with something of a shock that he found that he was unable to move backwards. The trouble was, because of a slope in the ground he was unable to move further forward either, and as his leg kept going into spasms he began to panic. It occurred to him far too late, that in his hell bent desire to seriously damage the reaper; he hadn't considered how he was going to get out. With only his hands to provide leverage he soon discovered in any case, that he lacked sufficient power to move his considerable weight backwards. It didn't seem to matter how much he wriggled, it was a completely useless exercise, as he soon became exhausted.

It was at this point that the dreadful irony of the situation hit him because it appeared that every time he tried to do something malicious to the Slades he seemed to be fated, as it always seemed to backfire. For instance when he and Simon had set the mantrap to catch George he had been convinced the plan couldn't fail. Yet it had, and he had been caught in his own petard. The only redeeming feature was that there was someone there to save his skin, but on this occasion because he failed to tell William what he intended to do, no one had the remotest idea where he was.

James was now fifty seven and had never done a stroke of manual work in his life, let alone carry out any regular exercise, little wonder therefore, that as a consequence of consuming plenty of rich food and wine, he carried a substantial gut. Darkness fell and his night demons started to play havoc with his brain. What was that moaning sound he could hear? Was it the wind sighing through the trees or was it Tom's tormented soul mocking him? He found it impossible to clear his mind of the vision of Toms lifeless body laid in the mantrap. Even when he closed his eyes he could still see the dead man's outstretched arm and the hand imploring someone to offer help before it was too late. His heart began to pound in his chest as his leg went into yet another spasm making him break out in a cold sweat. He shook his head violently from side to side as he did his upmost to dispel the image of the bloody sockets where Tom's eyes had once been.

He was certain he could see Tom's body laid over the ruts, so was the noise he could hear, the sound of wheels crushing bones as they passed over his legs. All of a sudden his mind cleared and the pain in his leg seemed to dissolve making him feel strangely calm. He felt very tired and just wanted to go to sleep.

Sam was up bright and early the next day. He whistled cheerfully as he went about his morning task of feeding the poultry and milking the house cow. He could hardly wait to get to the Six acre field and start operating their revolutionary new reaping machine for the very first time. He gave Prince an extra feed of oats, then stood by his neck as he stroked the black shires soft ears whilst the powerful horse swept his tongue around the trough in an endeavour to lick every last oat."I need you to be on your best behaviour today Prince, because there'll be lots of people coming to see us". He explained, as though Prince would understand what he was saying.

After an early breakfast Sam fixed the harness over the Shires broad shoulders before walking the massive animal up to the Six acre field. It was as he was about to back Prince in to the shafts that he became aware of a pair of legs protruding from underneath the reaper. He smiled when he thought one of his neighbours had stuffed a scarecrow under the machine as a joke, as several of them had made fun about his new machine replacing men. He took a hold on the ankles expecting to quickly draw it out, but all too soon realised with something of a shock, that it was no scarecrow as his hands were gripping cold flesh. Sam's mind whirled. For a few seconds he was unsure what to do next, then, and only because the Hall Farmyard was nearer, decided to run there for help. Luckily he came across a couple of farm workers in the barn, who when he told them what he had found, hurried back to the field with him, then with their combined strength, managed to pull the body from under the machine.

"Bloody ell", one of them exclaimed, on seeing James Vavour. "What do you reckon e' was doin' under theer"?

"Judgin' by that 'ammer e's been beltin somat'. The other exclaimed.

"That somats the gearbox", Sam exclaimed, bending over to see bits of cast iron casing lying among a pool of oil under the reaper. "What did the silly devil have to do that for; I havn't a cat in hells chance of getting a fresh one for this harvest".

They say that bad news travels quickly, and Sam had good reason to discover that it was all too true, as people suddenly seemed to appear from all directions, with George and William arriving from different directions at roughly the same time.

"Didn't I tell you to keep away from us". George said to an ashen faced William Vavour in a voice loud enough for all to hear.

William seemed to have lost his usual bravado as he stared transfixed at his father's bloated corpse.

"You're no longer satisfied with just coming on our land, but now you want to smash our machines as well? Between you, you've killed my father, nearly killed my wife and daughter, poisoned my cattle and now this, what is it with you people"?

William had seen corpses in the Crimea, but was totally unprepared for the sight of his father lying by the hedge with a number of frothy red bubbles seeping from his puffy lips.

"What happened"? He managed to utter at last, the stinging rebuke from George Slade still ringing in his ears. "How did it happen? Has he been run over"? As he moved around the machine to get a better view, he noticed the pieces of red coloured metal lying in a pool of oil, and then his heart missed a beat when he saw the heavy hammer. William felt a dozen pair of eyes boring into his back as he realised that he had to give some sort of explanation. "My father, -- he hasn't been himself recently", he said as if in a trance, "He must have had some sort of brain storm, something must have made him lose the balance of his mind".

The constable from Hoult was called to the scene, but of course there was nothing that he could do, except hear Dr Finch's prognosis that the deceased had suffered a massive heart attack, brought about in his opinion, by the deceased overweight severely constraining him. Tongues wagged that night with all kinds of speculation, as older members of the community recalled the time of James grandfather, and how he had ruthlessly hounded the Slade's along with other folk off their land. The general feeling was that it was a despicable act, by a powerful landlord against a small farmer who was trying to get on. But it was George Slade's remarks to William Vavour that really set tongues wagging. Those who claimed to have fully overheard the conversation, were adamant that he had said the Vavour's were responsible for his father's death, but surely that was an accident, or was it? And then George had revealed that the Vavour's had been implicated in poisoning their cattle, what was that all about?

It wasn't in Rachael's nature to be bitter, though when news reached her of James death she felt little sorrow at his passing. From an early age she had been well aware of the antipathy that the Vavour's showed to any members of her family, little wonder therefore that she found the relationship with her brother in law to be particularly fraught whenever she had the misfortune to be in his company. She found it particularly difficult to erase the image of William deliberately driving his carriage full tilt towards her and her mother. But Rachael's caring nature was not one to bear a grudge, so in spite of all that had happened in the past she prayed that William might now moderate his senseless vendetta. She knew that if it was ever within her power she would do her upmost to work towards some sort of reconciliation.

Fortunately for George and Sam, the importers had taken the wise precaution of bringing in an adequate supply of spares from America, in order that there would be a trouble free launch of the revolutionary new method of harvesting, so it was possible to obtain a replacement gear box and get the machine going.

As the sail reaper far exceeded George's expectations, he was the first to acknowledge that Sam had been correct, and his earlier misgivings were totally unjustified, as it allowed them to not only reap their own crops, but also deal with several of their neighbour's fields. Sam was delighted that his enthusiasm for investing in such a labour saving machine was more than vindicated as it half paid for itself after the first season, and that was in spite of James Vavours sabotaging tactics. The Vavour's had little option other than to pick up the bill for the replaced part and pay the wages of men to scythe crops that otherwise would have been mown by the new machine until the new parts arrived.

William Vavour's problems didn't stop there, because as the railways became more reliable they were able to not only undercut the rates Vavour shipping was charging, but were able to deliver goods in a faster time to places it was impossible for the canal born traffic to reach. Simon's optimism in finding extra work for the new sloops, began to seem grossly optimistic, as the canal company was left with capacity that far exceeded the available amount of work. Inevitably the company began to lose money which wasn't helped by servicing the borrowing requirement for the purchase of the new ships. James sabotage of the Sail Reaper was never mentioned officially as a factor leading to his death, but the facts were widely known which further eroded confidence in folk wishing to trade with Vavour shipping or their merchant business.

William and Jane moved into the Hall in the autumn of James death whilst Williams mother decided to go back to Hull and start a new life away from the bad memories of the Hall and the circumstances leading up to her husband's death.

1870

George Slade's public condemnation of the catalogue of atrocities that he and his father had inflicted on the Slade family humiliated William almost as much as discovering the way his father had met his death whilst carrying out yet another outrage. This was the man and his family who he disdainfully referred to as peasants, and yet here was George Slade relating for all too hear how they had been responsible for poisoning his cattle, almost killing his mother and sister, and most damming of all, claiming that they had been responsible for killing his father. He knew that that sort of gossip would spread like wild fire, how would he ever be able to look people squarely in the face, without thinking they were sniggering behind his back? The outcome was that he severely restricted his appearances at the shipping office, relying on Ben Ingelby to largely run the business unaided.

Inevitably, George Slade's revelations reached his wife's ears. Previously Jane had been sympathetic to William, believing that her husband had being the recipient of hurtful allegations surrounding the accident with Mrs Slade and her daughter. But the stories she was hearing now were far more serious, so she urged William to do something about it. When he refused to deny George Slades allegation that he had been responsible for poisoning their cattle, she began to worry that perhaps other things were also true. After all there could be no argument regarding the act of sabotage that James had been carrying out on their new reaper. But Jane was made of sterner stuff so she was determined that whatever his shortcomings might be, and it looked with reflection as though there were plenty, she was adamant that it was not going to affect her children. She had brought Charles and his younger sister Louise up to be polite and courteous to everyone they met, irrespective of whether they lived in one of the grandest houses in Hoult or one of the humblest cottages in the village. Charles particularly was a sensitive child who had a great affinity for all living creatures, regularly bringing home small animals or birds that he had found injured. Every morning he took kitchen scraps down to the coach house to feed a couple of the semi wild farm cats that he had adopted and in so doing turned them into pets. On his seventh birthday his mother bought him a smooth haired fox terrier puppy, which from that moment on never left his side, even sleeping in a box beside his bed. He delighted in visiting his uncle Ben and Aunt Rachael in Hoult, when he could play with his cousin Joseph, who although only one year younger, was equally passionate about all living creatures. Charles desperately wanted his aunt to bring Joseph down to the Hall so that he could show his cousin some of the hidden secrets in the wood by the beck but Rachael couldn't bear the possibility of being in William's presence, even though nearly twenty years had passed since that horrific day at the station. So it was with great anxiety that his mother heard him sobbing in his bedroom one brilliant March afternoon just after his tenth birthday.

"Whatever's the matter Charles", she said in a voice full of understanding.

"I can't tell you he spluttered tearfully, "Father says I haven't to say a word to anyone".

"Well you can certainly tell your mother; surely you are not going to keep a secret from me". "No I can't possibly tell you, father made me promise that I must never tell anybody what I'd found".

"Come on Charles, what did you find that's so distressed you"? She said gently caressing his brow. But he merely buried his head in his pillow refusing to say any more, unable to comprehend what it was about his find that had so disturbed his father. Jane of course knew nothing about the existence of either of the two crosses as William had lost his at the Slades farm before she knew him, and she had never been told about the other one, so it was in complete innocence that she hurried to find William.

"What's Charles found that's so secret you've made him promise not to tell anyone"? She declared, her cheeks flushed with annoyance.

"It's none of your business woman", he replied still seething.

"Oh yes it is William Vavour, it's very much my business when I see my child reduced to tears by something you've said. What is it he's found that makes it so secret you even forbid him to tell his own mother"?

William was at a loss for what to do for the best, if he told Jane about the cross, then he would not only have to tell her how it came into his possession in the Crimea, but then how he lost it when Sam Slade pulled it from around his neck after he had poisoned their cattle. And then there was the other cross from his father's day that somehow was tied in with George Slades, father's death. Was it all part of a tantalising ploy on the Slades part to draw him out in the open? After all, he was unlikely to forget in a hurry George Slades damming testimonial about the atrocities his family had committed against them, especially when he had said it loud enough for all to hear. Could he reasonably expect a ten year old child to never reveal what he had found?

"I think it's better if only he and I know about the object that was found", William ventured, realising that as he said it, he was creating a rift between him and his wife.

"You're making a big mistake", she remarked, with grim determination on her face, as she hurried back to comfort Charles.

After Jane left the room he took the cross he had taken from Charles out of his coat pocket and set about polishing it with his handkerchief. Goodness he thought, his mind going back to his time spent laying in his hammock on the long journey back from the Crimea   I must have handled it thousands of times but

I've never seen this inscription. Fingering the cross he pondered how he could possibly have missed seeing JdS inscribed over the top lateral.

Charles steadfastly refused to divulge anything else to his mother, being in sheer terror of what his father might do to him if he said anything else. From then on Jane's relationship with her husband, which had never been easy, took a distinct turn for the worse as an invisible veil seemed to be drawn over their marriage.

Meanwhile Sam and Mary named their first child Tom in memory of Sams grandfather, followed a couple of years later by daughter Kate .

• • • •

Despite living in Hoult, it was an easy walk for Rachael along farm tracks to visit her parents in the village. Although she had always enjoyed an excellent relationship with them, none more so than when she and her mother went on that memorable trip to London, it hurt her terribly that they both continued to be stubbornly resolute in having nothing to do with Ben. As Joseph got older, it delighted her to point out interesting flowers and wild animals along the way, with particular reference to the seasonal changes of seed time and harvest. However 1870 proved to be the first of a succession of very difficult harvests when frequent bouts of rain seemed to fall most days, which in turn proved to be an opportunity for George and Sam to capitalise on their new Sail Reaper. It was under those difficult conditions that the Sail Reaper proved its worth, as it greatly speeded up the harvest process by releasing more farm workers, who otherwise would have been employed scything the corn, to bringing sheaves of grain back into the yards during the brief dryer interludes. Such was the success of their first sail reaper that they decided to purchase a second machine the following year that would be used solely for cutting other farmers corn. The machine was so efficient that they were able to set a charge per acre that was considerably less than the cost of scything, to say nothing of being so much faster. Reaping the crop was of course only part of the operation, because it still had to be gathered and tied into sheaves, before being arranged in pairs to form stooks, to speed the drying process.

Rather than be cowed by the nature of his father's death and Charles discovery of the cross Sam Slade had snatched from his neck, Williams hatred of the Slade's, or anybody connected with them seemed to increase in intensity. Rather like his father before him, the sight of the Slade's farm buildings, where he had so nearly been caught, only served to increase his bitterness further. He was determined, that having failed once; he would find another method of, if not ruining them, then at the very least making life difficult for them. His father had made a clumsy attempt at sabotaging their new reaper, an episode he was unlikely to repeat, despite them now running two machines. So much did he resent the way that they were prospering that it became an obsession with him to get at them in some way, because whatever the Slades did they seemed to forge ahead as they pioneered the latest farming techniques. Their livestock breeding was rapidly gaining local respect for high quality animals and their Shire horses started to win awards at local shows. William's hatred for all things Slade even extended to his brother in laws wife Rachael, and their children, even though they had never harmed him.

One sunny day in May, a couple of months after Charles had found the cross, Rachael decided to take Joseph with her for a walk to see their grandparents. The verges along the road leading to the village were carpeted with patches of vivid yellow vetches, whilst a little further back cowslips and pink Campion were in full bloom. She had just been telling him about the rare Orchids that she assured him grew amongst the taller grasses, when in the far distance, at the village end of the lane; she spotted the small figure of a child walking in a desultory manner towards them. As she drew closer the child recognised her, then with outstretched arms ignored Joseph and ran towards her. "What's the matter Charles"? She asked bending down and putting a comforting arm around the little boy's shoulders.

"I'm leaving home" he declared between tears, "I'm not allowed to play with children in the village, so I was coming to Hoult to find Joseph".

"Does anybody else know where you are"? She asked with concern.

"No, I came out the back through the church yard".

Rachael was faced with a terrible dilemma, she had never been anywhere near the Hall in her life so she most certainly didn't want to start now and meet up with William in the process. Yet she could hardly take Charles with her without saying something to his parents, nor could she leave him to go home by himself given the emotional state that he was in. She decided that the best thing to do would be for him to accompany them as she continued her walk to her mother's, but just before she turned into the farm entrance she met Sam leading a horse pulling a cart full of farmyard manure. "I've got a problem" she said when both boys were out of earshot, "I've just met Charles on the road and he says that he was coming to Hoult to play with his cousin, I don't know what to do". The dilemma was soon resolved as William appeared on horseback from around a bend in the road.

"What the devil do you think you're playing at boy", he bellowed on spotting Charles, "we've scoured the house looking for you. We were just about to start on the lake when young Wood remembered spotting you slipping through the hedge into the church yard". Before Charles had an opportunity to offer an explanation, William carried on angrier than ever. "What have you come here for anyway"? I've told you often enough about speaking to these people"?

"But father", Charles said, wiping away tears with his arm.

Unable to contain his flow of rhetoric William continued his voice full of contempt. "I forbid you ever to see this low life again".

"I don't like being insulted, especially with my family around me", Sam said evenly, "get down from your horse and apologise for what you've just said. Your words ill befit a man in your position, but talking of low life nothing comes much lower than some of your deeds. I don't know what you're so concerned about him telling us, but I can tell you that we have no secrets at this house. If Charles wants someone to offer a sympathetic ear to his troubles then he need go no further than me or his aunt".

Hearing raised voices George and Rose came to the door of their house to see what the commotion was all about. They were alarmed to see William Vavour agitatedly pulling his horse's reins in first one direction and then the other, as the poor animal had to take the brunt of his anger.

"Remember I pulled your cross from around your neck," Sam said, "so you know where it is now"?

William was mystified; of course he knew where it was, he had locked it away securely in the drawer of his desk. What was Slade playing at, putting the one piece of evidence that would link him to the poisoning, in the beck where Charles had found it? Crucially though, had Charles mentioned finding the cross to them? If he hadn't then all was not lost as the Slade's would be unaware that it had been found. He felt convinced that the Slade's must have put the cross in such a place that it was going to be found, - but why? With those thoughts pondering his mind he said, "Perhaps in the relief of finding Charles I have been a little hasty in saying things that should not have been said". Turning his horses head he instructed Charles to follow him.

Back at the Hall, William was quick to interrogate Charles on what he had said, and learn the reason for him leaving home. Satisfied with the boy's honesty that he had not revealed what he had found to anyone, he resolved that if Jane was agreeable then Charles should go to the Grammar School where he would have lots of friends of his own age to play with. He reasoned that Charles could either board there or stop with his grandparents Ingleby.

Even though the profitability of farming continued to decline in the face of ever lower prices George and Sam's farm prospered as they introduced the latest machines to ease some of the hard labour. Their two Sail Reapers were a great success financially, as they generated sufficient income for them to purchase another twenty four acres of land from two neighbouring cottage farmers.

In 1870 they felt sufficiently confident enough to purchase a top quality mare from one of the county's leading breeders on the coast and breed her to an especially high quality stallion, hoping that this would be the foundation of the elite Shire horse stud that George craved.

1874

Even though time had moved on since that fateful day in March 1870, by refusing to discuss with her what Charles had found, William had effectively created a barrier, cutting himself from Jane. That by itself was bad enough, but what outraged her the most, was the way he had terrified Charles into making him promise that he would not tell her either. Of course she knew now, with the benefit of hindsight, that there was something wrong when she saw the reaction of people lining the street as their carriage passed from the church to the reception. There was none of the waving from well wishers she would have expected, rather the reverse as she spotted more than one man spit in the gutter as they passed by. Still she was made of stern stuff and even if she had made a terrible mistake, she had made her bed and she would have to lay on it. But this really was the final straw; she had put up with his irrational behaviour for quiet long enough. "I shall have my own rooms at the back of the house so that I can continue to care for the children", she said soon after the incident. "You can stay at the front if you wish but I want no more to do with you".

From that time, life at the Hall took on an entirely different complexion as Jane and William although living under the same roof led entirely separate lives. William became increasingly morose, having little to do with his wife and two children. Charles for his part, wherever possible, tried to avoid meeting his father, much preferring to be in the company of his mother and sisters. Household staff feared him, terrified of what he might say to them. In spite of the relative prosperity of the estate, income from the shipping business continued to decline putting further pressure on Ben Ingelby's shoulders as he had inherited a half share in the partnership from his father and now held the position of partner. William Vavour, as equal partner in the business was more than happy to make Ben the scapegoat for not securing trade, declaring in his usual forthright manner that Ben was totally responsible for the decline in income.

Rachael was concerned that Ben began to think himself a failure whenever he talked to his older brother, who now that he had succeeded Simon as principle, constantly reminded him on how busy his law firm was in implementing the new laws that the Liberal governments led first by Palmerston, and then by Russell were introducing. Ben was quite literally stuck between a rock and a hard place, as all his own money was tied up in a declining business, of which he was only part owner. His autocratic partner had an alternative income, yet constantly berated Ben when yet another customer transferred their business to the railways.

One dank day towards the end of October 1872, William Vavour stepped from his gig outside the shipping office. A freshening easterly breeze toyed with the last of the leaves on the plane trees along the north bank, until eventually they spun off and fluttered to the ground. He was in a foul mood, as he kicked at a pile of leaves that had blown into a drift against the outer door, before entering a small hallway and taking the stairway to the first floor office. Facing north and originally painted a dark shade of brown, the office looked depressing at the best of times, which to be fair was hardly surprising, considering it was years since it had last received a coat of paint, but on a day such as this it looked even more sombre than usual.

"If you don't get more trade we'll soon be bankrupt", He said, by way of introduction to Ben who was seated behind a desk on the opposite side of the office. Walking over to the window he saw the way paintwork had peeled around the frames to reveal blackened timber underneath. "You spend far too much time on your backside", he continued irritably, "it's about time you saw the way other people can run a canal profitably. I'm going to Stafford next week to see Lord Crewe, so you'd better come along with me and learn how they manage to make good money on their canals".

"But they're not the same" Ben pointed out at last getting an opportunity to get a word in. "For a start, their waterways are on important trading routes. The Trent and Mersey canal dissects the country whilst The Staffordshire and Worcester canal links all the heavy industry around Birmingham. And of course The Shropshire Union canal also links Chester and the River Dee to the industry around Birmingham. None of them are comparable with our small canal linking the sea to a rural town like Hoult".

"Oh yes I know it's a bit different, but that's no real excuse why you can't make good money over here", William persisted, "I'm certain that if you go about it in the right manner you can generate a great deal more trade".

Ben took this as a personal affront, with the clear implication that he wasn't running the business correctly. Not wishing to be churlish he agreed to accompany William the following week.

"You would get a lot more trade if we introduced barges". William enthused looking at the stream of barges moving in either direction down the broad waterway from Chester.

That's stupid Ben thought, but said, "What happens when our barges reach the Sea"?

William merely walked on without addressing Ben's sensible observation. The following day William left Ben to examine some of the practical points on canal transportation whilst he met Lord Crewe near Mucklestone a few miles to the north.

"As you go through the village get your driver to stop so that you can see the new memorial to the plague". Lord Crewe said as William got ready to depart. "What do you mean –the plague"? William said with a puzzled expression, "I didn't think there had been a plague in England for centuries". "Just you look at the memorial as you go past", was his Lordships parting comment.

The memorial took the form of a strange shaped stone structure on which the following was inscribed; -

In this ground are buried forty head of cattle which died of Murrain in the months of Dec 1865 and Jan 1866, the property of Richard Bourne of Mucklestone- -tenant to the Right Hon Hungerford Lord Crewe.

"Lord Crewe talked about plague, so what's Murrain"? William remarked to his elderly driver. "It's a terrible disease that beast git, we calls it the cattle plague. They git covered wi sores and puss that stops em yeating and drinking. We ed it ere about eight year ago, and that's why is lordship put up this stone. Some reckon its bods or wild animals wot spread it from farm to farm, but I reckon the wind spreads it".

"How do they cure it"? William asked intrigued, recalling his earlier episode with his bottle of poison.

"They don't, there aint no cure. All they can do is kill all the beast for miles around a case and hope they've stopped it. Nearly every beast in Cheshire was killed afore they got on top on it. Aye it ruined undreds o farmers", the old chap said with a shake of his head. "I got a job as a red coat, we ad to kill all a farmers beast, then drag em to a pit an cover em in lime to kill the infection. I could tell yer some tales about the poor sods oo lost iverything when their beast wus killed. One fellow even said yuv killed me beast, yud betta kill me now cos Ive nought to live for".

"What caused it in the first place", William asked even more intrigued.

"Most folks reckon it wus becos o the railways".

"The railways! How could the railways possibly cause it"? William replied with a puzzled expression.

"Easy really, when the railway cum it meant they could git milk quickly to the folks oo ad moved into the towns".

"I still don't see how that caused it".

"Simple see, instead on it going sour afore it got to the towns with hoss and cart, it could git to Manchester on the railway in a couple o hours".

"I still don't see how it caused this, -- this cattle plague"?

"Well iverybody started milking cows, cos there wus a good trade for the milk. There were cows iveryweare, so once the infection cum it spread like them human plagues".

"But where did it come from in the first place"?

"Nobody knows for sure, but some o the chaps wot set us on reckon it wud ave come on a ship at Liverpool".

Williams mind raced, could Murrain be the fool proof method that he had been looking for? If he went about the task correctly it would be very difficult to pin any blame on to him. It would certainly knock the Slade's off their perch if it destroyed their pedigree herd of red cattle? Judging by what his driver was telling him about the outbreak here; it was quite likely that it would ruin them. Having harboured such an all consuming passion for so long, this seemed the perfect solution to his vendetta.

Ben found William to be almost like a different man when they both met up again in Stafford. To his utter astonishment William at last seemed to understand Ben's concerns about the limited scope for expansion on their Hoult canal. Ben was staggered by the transformation in William's demeanour as they relaxed in their railway compartment on their journey home. Where William had previously been critical and garrulous, he was now amenable and content to go along with Bens suggestions.

"I think that in view of the railways success we really ought to be renting some sidings in Hoult from the railway company, and expanding our business to accommodate customers who require a quicker delivery of goods. You're in charge, so I will be perfectly happy to go along with whatever you suggest". William said his mind concentrating on other matters.

At the first opportunity William made discreet enquiries and soon established that Murrain, more commonly known as cattle plague, had been a serious economic disease in Britain for centuries but due to increased vigilance farmers now recognised how infectious the disease was. This resulted in the government exercising a swift slaughter policy to control the spread of the disease. In spite of a much greater awareness, isolated cases of cattle plague continued to occur from time to time, principally in the west of the country where there were much greater concentrations of livestock.

It was by pure chance a few weeks later that William had an amazing stroke of luck. After eating his evening meal, he was relaxing by the fire in the north drawing room with a glass of his favourite brandy, when idly turning the pages of a recent copy of The Times, he spotted an almost insignificant few lines at the foot of a page. He sat bolt upright slapping his chair arm with such gusto that the glass of brandy he had placed on the arm, jumped in the air spilling its contents on the carpet below.

OUTBREAK OF MURRAIN!

On good authority Our West of England correspondent reports, an outbreak of Murrain near Plymouth. The outbreak, we understand, occurred on an isolated farm in South Oxley. The twenty five cattle involved have all been slaughtered.

Until he had been to Cheshire the word Murrain would have meant absolutely nothing to him and he would have hardly given it a second glance, but now it was as though he had discovered the Holy Grail. His mind buzzed on how he could possibly capitalise on what he had just read? Obviously he needed to visit the farm where the outbreak occurred as soon as possible. The only problem was; he would have to invent a pretty good reason for wanting to leave the Hall at such short notice. Under no circumstances must it give rise to the slightest suspicion that he had something else in mind, especially as he knew that it would involve travelling to London to change trains for the West Country. So he began to think of reasons for going to the capital. He racked his brains for the rest of the evening trying to think of a credible alibi that wouldn't arouse suspicion. Perhaps he could be looking at a new heating systems for the Hall, or maybe meeting a financial specialist. He even thought about saying he was meeting a lady friend, but immediately dismissed the idea. So many ideas went through his head, all of which had a flaw, until his eyes rested on the obituary column in the paper and he knew he had found the perfect solution.

"I read some sad news in the Times last night" he announced to the cook after she had served him his breakfast. "A fellow I served with in the Crimea has just died, so I need to make an urgent trip to London this morning".

"I am so sorry to hear that sir" she said shaking her head, "I'm always telling my Bert we never know what lies around the corner. When do you expect to be back?".

"Well the funerals tomorrow so I'll probably stop down for a couple of days. Might meet up with some of my old shipmates, you know that sort of thing".

"Still as I always tell my Bert sir, the Lord giveth and he taketh away. Still even though it's a sad occasion the break will do you good sir", the cook said leaving the breakfast room with a hand full of dirty pots.

Glancing out the carriage window, as he waited for his train to pull out of Hoult station, he was reminded of his near scrape with Mrs Slade and his sister in law. Realising now how close he came to killing either or both of them; it made him sweat just to think of what may have happened to him. Anyway that was all in the past. What he had in mind would achieve his purpose so much better, and the best thing about it was that his part was untraceable. No sooner had he arrived in the capital than he began to implement the plan he had thought through the night before, so he immediately took a horse drawn cab across the city to Paddington station and purchased a ticket for Plymouth. He had plenty of time on his train journey to the West Country to consider that by exercising a degree of subterfuge he should be able to bluff his way on to the infected farm. By claiming that he was from the government, he didn't think it should prove to be much of a problem to tell the farmer that he wished to take further samples for analysis, or something along those lines.

It was early January; consequently the Slade's cattle, in common with every other farmer's cattle in the district, were safely housed in crew yards for the duration of the winter. William was sharp enough to realise that with the animals being housed together, it presented him with a golden opportunity for the disease to be easily transmitted through the herd. Looking back, he thought he had been lucky to escape capture when Sam Slade grabbed his cloak, but there again maybe it wasn't luck after all. No, the more he thought about it, the more it thrilled him to think that he must lead a charmed life, because against all the odds he had got away with it. He still remembered that rush of adrenalin when he realised that either Sam Slade or his father had entered the cattle yard, and the fear that if he wasn't careful he was likely to be caught red handed. But then when he thought how easily he had evaded detection in the cattle yard, he had to admit that it did give him a shock to discover that Sam Slade had out foxed him by intercepting him on the other side of the straw stacks. Nevertheless despite Slade snatching the cross from his neck he thought that whenever he met up with the Slade's luck was always with him. The possibility of what might have happened if Sam had managed to hold on to him never occurred to him. The important thing was, he had escaped detection and got away with it, just as he had when he had tried to run over the two Slade women. Even though he had little doubt about his ability to carry out his latest plan he was determined not to take any unnecessary risks. After all, if it was discovered that he had been responsible for deliberately spreading the disease, then he really would be in serious trouble. But as Murrain was so infectious he knew he would only have to ensure that one animal became infected, before the disease was passed to the rest of the herd.

Once again under the cover of darkness he crept into the Slade's farm yard and found the barn where the animals concentrated feed was stored. He removed the cover from the can containing the faecal material he had collected in Devon, and emptied it among a mixture of ground oats and chaff that he felt certain would form a part of their cattle's next day rations. In spite of Jess's keen ears picking up the sound of Williams entry on the farm, her furious barking was to no avail as William quickly made his escape not wishing to be caught a second time.

Four days later Sam noticed that one of the cows was shivering and didn't come to feed at the same time as the others in her group. On closer examination he noted that her breathing was rapid with a watery discharge flowing from her eyes and nostrils. She at first appeared constipated but by the end of the second day her dung had a foul smell. Mary, naturally, had gained considerable knowledge of animal diseases from her father, little wonder therefore that when Sam told her of the animal's symptoms she insisted her father be contacted immediately.

"I'm reasonably certain your animals have Murrain", Frank Vine said, confirming Mary's worst fears.

"I need to get a second opinion but I'm ninety nine point nine per cent sure what it is. I have only seen Murrain once before, but I clearly remember how the animals dung had this distinctive foul smell".

"But I've smelt things a deal worse than that before", George said hopefully.

"Not when it's coupled with ulceration of the mouth and nasal passages", Frank said in a matter of fact voice. "I'm afraid that's the giveaway, I'm sorry to say that your animals are showing the classic symptoms of a disease commonly known as cattle plague".

"Isn't there anything we can give them"? Sam said forlornly stroking one of his favourite cows who had ambled over for a bit of attention.

"If I'm right, and as I said before I'm certain they've got it, then there is no cure as more than three quarters of the animals will die, in any event I must report the disease to the government veterinary department, and they will insist that all of your animals are slaughtered". Later that evening Frank appeared again, this time accompanied by the local government inspector, who quickly confirmed Frank's initial diagnosis,

"We need to slaughter the animals immediately" he said. You will instantly recognise the men who will be carrying out the work by their red coats. After they have left a team of Navies will come down", he continued in an emotionless voice. "They will move the carcases to a dewpond if you have one, or failing that any natural hollows about the place. After covering them with quick lime they will be buried".

"I can't take it all in" George said, tears streaming down his face. "Where's it come from"?

"All I know is that since the last major outbreak in Cheshire in 1865 and 1866, very isolated cases occasionally occur in different parts of the country", the government man continued, anxious to be away. How he hated this part of his job, when he had to break devastating news to hard working people such as this farming family. He knew from personal experience that livestock farming was difficult enough, but for this to come out of the blue was a shock of devastating proportions. It was if he was delivering them a death sentence, because all their years of scraping and thrift were going to be snuffed out in an instant. Little wonder that many of them committed suicide when they saw no future ahead of them. He straitened his hat and made ready to leave but before moving across to the door added as an afterthought, "I do believe there was an isolated case in the Plymouth area about three weeks ago but that's a long way from here".

"But neither of us have been anywhere for ages, we've been far too busy on the farm, what with feeding stock and threshing", Sam said, who rather like his father couldn't believe what was happening to them.

"It'll ruin us", George said as the government inspector stood by the door. "We've spent years getting to this stage, and now this, why us"?

"But how's it spread", Sam persisted, as the implications of what was going to happen were now all too clear.

"Oh that's easy", the official said, "It can be carried by direct contact animal to animal, or by cattle coming into contact with infected faeces, or indeed any other tissue from infected animals, and it's possible that it may even be passed on by human beings clothing that have also been in contact with infected animals".

"To think all those years of careful breeding snuffed out in an instant", Mary added putting her arms around Sam's shoulders.

The following morning the men with red coats appeared and systematically set about slaughtering all their animals. They used the strongest horses on the farm to drag the carcases across the farm yard and dump them unceremoniously into the dew pond opposite the farm entrance. It broke Sams heart when he recognised the dead carcase of Julie, one of his favourite cows, as she was dragged by her back feet across the muddy yard, her horns scratching a furrow as she joined the rest of the herd on a rising heap of slaughtered animals. And then he spotted the ten day old calf he had stopped up all night to see safely delivered. He remembered how he had helped the calf to get its first drink of milk, and how delighted he had been to see it skipping around the yard, playing chase with some of the older calves, but now it was also dead along with its young mother. The sights and sounds of their poor animals being slaughtered, traumatised George and Rose to such a degree, that rather like a death in the family, they retreated within their house and drew their curtains.

Sam and Mary, although equally devastated at the turn of events were left with little alternative other than to carry on with their other regular farm duties, after all horses and poultry still needed feeding.

"What are we going to do now"? Mary said, as the red coats, once their task was completed prepared to leave the farm.

"Well, if it's any comfort, it's not only us that's affected, they've slaughtered all the cattle in the district, direct contact or not" Sam said philosophically. "Take old Joe for instance, he's only got three cows and that was his only source of income".

"Poor man, and to think he lost his wife at Christmas and now this", Mary added.

"I'm afraid he'll end up in the workhouse, but there's a lot more like him that's got all their money tied up in the value of their animals"

"Father says that to make sure they've removed any chance of it spreading, the red coats will slaughter all the cattle for three miles around us". Mary said.

"Well it'll ruin a good many people". Sam added, "I still can't believe that all those years of breeding has gone just as quick as snuffing out a candle, and all that's left to show is a heap of carcases in the pond.   Do you think it's just possible that this outbreak wasn't accidental but could have been introduced deliberately"? He said after a lengthy pause.

"Of course not" Mary reasoned. "Who do you think would do such a terrible thing anyway"?

"What about William Vavour to start with, he doesn't have a very good track record"? Sam said.

"I know, but even he wouldn't stoop as low as that" Mary said, "remember all their cattle at the Hall have been slaughtered as well. As bad as he is he's hardly likely to do something to us that will affect him also".

"I'm not so sure about that" Sam said, gazing out the window at the navvies who were covering the last of the carcases with soil.

"Look on the bright side we've still got our Shires" Mary said with a weak smile. "You're right, we've got to be positive", Sam said looking up, "the family's had some terrible knocks in the past and survived them, so I expect we're going to survive this one".

Whilst the redcoats went about their grisly task, a team of four Government inspectors led by Abraham Wilson, were drafted in to try and establish the source of the deadly virus. "The only thing we know for certain is that cattle on the Slade's farm contracted Murrain", Abe, as he was known to his colleagues remarked, "but the question is where did it come from"? Over the years, Abraham Wilson had become something of a specialist in tracking down the spread of Murrain, to such a degree that thanks to his work the disease had virtually been eradicated from the country. "We had that isolated outbreak near Plymouth a month or so ago" he said, but that's a long, long way from here. The chances of it spreading by birds, animals or wind are virtually nil", he summarised".

"So that just leaves human contact", another member of the team pointed out. At the end of their first day's investigations they were sitting around a large table in a back room of The White Hart to review progress. The general consensus appeared to be that despite interviewing most of the farmers within the three mile radius of the Slade farm nothing unusual was immediately apparent. The vast majority of people were quickly eliminated from the list because they had neither been near, or on any other local farms, whilst many had travelled no further than Hoult for weeks past.

"Did you find anything Abe"? Someone asked.

"I'm not sure". He said, carefully refilling his pipe. "I interviewed William Vavour this afternoon, he's the fellow who lives in the big Hall and owns most of the land around here. I thought he seemed a bit on edge and indignant that I was asking him questions, but when I pointed out that everyone was being interviewed he seemed to quieten down, but there was something about his attitude that I felt wasn't quite right". Abe took another deep puff from his pipe, expelling a white plume of smoke that drifted lazily up to the low ceiling. "When I asked him if he had travelled away from the area recently, he rather indignantly said that he hadn't, but when I pressed him further he remembered that in late October or early November he visited Lord Crewe over in Cheshire". Abe extracted a pair of wire rimmed glasses from a metal case. After hooking them over his ears, he opened a pocket book and studied some notes he had made. "Apparently he was accompanied by his business partner, a man by the name of Ben Ingelby".

"But that was more than two months ago", one of his colleagues pointed out.

Pausing for effect Abe carried on, "At first he claimed he had been no further than Hoult since that time, but then he remembered that he had been to London a couple of weeks ago to attend the funeral of a friend who had served with him in the Crimea." As even more smoke spiralled upwards from his pipe, Abe continued,

"He was unwilling to elaborate many details, other than to say whose funeral it was and when it was held. When I asked him in which part of London the ceremony took place, he became quite annoyed claiming it was none of my bloody business. Of course what he was saying might be completely genuine, but on the other hand he just might have had something to hide. It could of course be that he was visiting a mistress or even a prostitute, and that is of no concern to us, but if on the other hand he was providing an alibi to cover other activities, that might explain why he was so reticent".

"What would his motive be for bringing the disease back here, after all his cattle have all been slaughtered", one of the other members of the team volunteered.

"Now that's the interesting point", Abe continued, "I understand from village gossip that there's bad blood between him and the Slades. Its claimed, though there's no proof, that William Vavour attempted to poison their cattle with arsenic a few years ago, and that on an earlier occasion he attempted to run Mrs Slade and her daughter down with a carriage".

"Reasonable ground for suspicion", another suggested.

"How do we take our enquiries forward", the first man proffered.

"I think I'll interview Mr Vavour again tomorrow morning. I'll take you with me Ted, whilst the rest of you can see what else you can find. I've a gut feeling that we've found our man, but whether we can convict him is another matter, I think that we may have to use a modicum of bluff". Next morning to his alarm William saw the inspector he had seen the previous day accompanied by one of his colleagues striding purposely up to the front door of the Hall.

"Come in gentlemen he proffered how can I help you"? The two inspectors were escorted to William's office where they were shown two hard chairs whilst William clearly ill at ease, sat on the edge of a leather upholstered chair behind his desk.

Abe decided that attack was the best policy in this situation, so gambled on his bluff being successful. "We have reason to believe that you caught a train to Plymouth, on the same day that you left Hoult station for London". His blunt statement was followed by a deathly silence as he watched William Vavours reaction. Abe was satisfied to see him take a sharp intake of breath which he attempted to camouflage by turning his head to cough. Positive he was on the right lines Abe pressed the point, "What was the purpose for your journey --- Sir"? Allowing the word "Sir", to hover in the air.

"I've already told you he said angrily I went to London to attend a funeral".

"In that case Sir, if you could just provide us with the names and addresses of someone you met there, then the matter can be quickly resolved, and you can be eliminated from our enquiries".

"I refuse to answer any more of your damn fool questions without my lawyer being present, now if you don't mind I've work to do so good day gentlemen".

William contacted David Ingelby but only told him part of the story claiming that the inspectors were trying to pin the reason for the outbreak on to him.

"You need an alibi to confirm that you were in London" David reasoned, tell them the names and addresses of the places that you visited and the people you saw, and that will be the end of the matter".

"I am afraid that it's not as simple as that", William countered.

"I had a feeling you might say that in view of the fact that you have called on me", David said, "May I ask just where were you"?

"I was stupid, incredibly stupid; Jane and I live separate lives these days, as you well know. I went to London and spent the night with a prostitute, I can't believe how stupid I've been". Although David didn't believe a word of it, he was paid to defend his client.

The following day Abe arranged to interview William Vavour once more, but this time he was accompanied by David Ingelby. Little progress was made as it soon became apparent that the devious lawyer, in confirming Williams's story, threatened to sue for defamation of character if Abe didn't withdraw his unsubstantiated allegations. So convinced was he that William Vavour was involved in some way with the introduction of the disease that Abe, in spite of the lawyer's threat, decided to follow his hunch and take a huge gamble by making the long journey down to Plymouth to see if he could find a connection.

"You're taking a bit of a risk Abe". His fellow inspector who had accompanied him at the interview warned. "That lawyer fella, he's a tricky customer, you need to be well sure of your facts, or he will cause big trouble".

Abe therefore had plenty of reason to be sceptical as he commenced his long journey, but as they had been unable to find any other clues, he felt justified in pursuing his gut feeling. Fortunately the farm where the disease had been identified was in an isolated position; consequently the only cattle that had been slaughtered in addition to those on the infected farm were those on three adjacent farms, so he decided to visit them first to see if anyone could remember seeing someone of Vavour's description. In spite of the traumas the farmers had experienced in seeing their cattle slaughtered and resultant destruction of their livelihoods, Abe was unable to find anyone who could recall seeing anyone matching William's description. He was already beginning to have serious doubts on whether his gut feeling was quite as reliable as he had at first thought, when he arrived at the farm where the disease had been identified. He was met in the farmyard by an old chap of indeterminate age who required the use of two sticks to get about. After explaining why he was there, the old fellow pointed to the dilapidated house across the farmyard where Abe learned he now lived by himself since the death of his wife. "Yis I do remember a smartly dressed young fella coming ere", The ancient confirmed, "E ask if we ad Murrain, well I tell im e should know, cos it were is fellows what ad our beast killed. E wanted to know where we kept em cos e sez e ad to take some more samples of their muck. I sez tek what yer want cos we're finished now that the beast are all dead".

"Do you think that you could describe what this chap looked like"? Abe enquired.

The old chap tilted his hat to one side and scratched his head, before declaring, "I can't rightly say, what we all our beast just been killed, that I paid that much attention, e were quite tall, and I remember e were well dressed with a real smart green hat, a right toff I would call im".

"Anything else", Abe pressed, "That you could identify him by".

"Well there was just one thing" the elderly farmer said as an afterthought, "What was that".

"Well e eld is arm a bit funny as though e ad injured it sometime". Got him Abe thought with a satisfied smile. I've pinned him down to the farm, so anything else I can find will be a bonus. On the off chance that someone may have remembered seeing him at the station, Abe called at the ticket office as he waited for his London train. Unfortunately no one could recall a man of Vavours description in the past month, but then with a flash of inspiration he thought, of course, the Station Master.

"Well, funnily enough come to think of it, I do remember the man that you are referring to", he said thoughtfully, "I remember thinking it strange that such a well dressed man of his bearing didn't have a porter carrying his luggage. I also remember, and this is what sticks in my mind about him, he was carrying one of those small white cans with a lid that workman use for carrying their tea about. He looked so pleased with himself as he swung it from side to side. I remember thinking to myself, if he swings it a deal more the lid will come off and he will spill his tea".

"Was there anything else about the man that would enable you to recognise him again", Fred enquired.

"Well he was tall and very smartly dressed, I notice all these things in my job you know, but the thing I most remember, was that he favoured one arm; he tended to hold it across his chest. I thought to myself that mans had an injury".

When he arrived back Abe made yet another appointment to interview William Vavour, who once again wished to have his lawyer in attendance. Armed with the evidence he had gathered in the West Country, Abe had no intention of being intimidated by the presence of the lecherous lawyer who looked superciliously down his beaked nose when they met again. He couldn't help giving a wry smile to himself, as he followed them both across the hallway into the south drawing room.

"Why did you lie to us Sir", Abe announced without preamble.

"My client didn't lie" David Ingelby interjected before William could reply. "Furthermore if I hear any more of these allegations I shall instigate an action for defamation of Mr Vavours character".

"I shall ignore what you have just said Sir", Abe said giving Ingelby a withering look; "because I neither care for liars nor do I think any better of those that support them. I can prove you went to Plymouth" he said addressing William, "even though, on the last occasion we spoke, you claim to have only been to London". Abe noted with satisfaction that David Ingelby had suddenly gone mute. Judging by his clasped hands he was either in deep contemplation or praying for divine intervention. The owner of the farm infected with Murrain confirms that you spoke to him before taking samples of infected dung from the building where the cattle had been housed. The Station Master at Plymouth station clearly remembers seeing you on the platform later that day carrying a workman's tea can. It didn't contain tea, did it sir? It held a lethal dose of cattle plague which you removed from the farm; do I really need to give you any more details"?

William looked forlornly in David Ingelby's direction, who after hearing Abes damming evidence could do little other than cast his eyes down to examine his shoes. "I am arresting you William Vavour on a charge that with malicious intent you did deliberately introduce Murrain, commonly known as cattle plague, a notifiable contagious disease, to cattle in this part of the country".

At the subsequent trial the evidence was so overwhelming that William was left with little alternative other than to plead guilty and was subsequently sentenced to seven years hard labour. News of William Vavour's arrest, trial and subsequent imprisonment became not only the talk of the district but even merited several columns in the national press, the irony of which might well have been lost on William as he surveyed the four walls of his prison cell, considering that it was a footnote in the same national press that led directly to his present incarceration.

Farming folk were astonished that a man with the wealth and prestige of William Vavour should stoop so low as to deliberately introduce such a devastating disease into their community. His actions had not only destroyed years of careful breeding but had caused ruin to so many people's livelihoods in the process. Other local people, who over the years had suffered at the hands of the Vavour's were delighted that for once, one of their number was being punished for their crimes, rather than as had occurred in the past, being able to buy their way out of trouble. It was perhaps the suddenness of the disease appearing on the farm that had the greatest impact on George. Everything that followed, including the fact it had been deliberately introduced, blurred into a shifting pattern of images that abruptly ended when he surveyed the results of all those years of careful breeding rotting under a covering of earth by the farm entrance.

"In farming we learn to live with the weather", he remarked to Rose one evening after yet another despondent walk around the empty cattle yards. "Sometimes its kind and makes our job easier, whilst on other occasions it's a real battle, but at least we're prepared for it, we know it's always there to test us, but since Grandfathers time we've had the extra burden of not knowing what the Vavours are going to do to us next. It seems to be an obsession with each generation of that family that they try their upmost to destroy us. It's almost as though they've got such a hatred of us they'll go to any length to ruin us".

"I know", Rose said putting an arm around his shoulders, "the two of us have more than enough reason to be bitter considering how we've suffered because of them, yet in spite of all they've done we've continued to get on with our lives and improve ourselves. Although we've had an enormous knock, we'll get over it, just you see".

Authors note

Cattle Plague (Murrain)was finally eliminated from Great Britain in 1877, by not only enforcing a rigorous slaughter policy when a case occurred, but also severely restricting ports of entry for cattle from overseas countries.

1882

When news of the Slade's loss reached one of the breeders who had supplied some of their original animals, he was so disgusted by William Vavour's actions that he immediately offered George and Sam half a dozen of his best in calf heifers to provide the foundation of a new herd, adding that he only wanted payment when circumstances permitted. With cattle back on the farm once more, it seemed ironic, that after all the knocks George had taken throughout his lifetime; his death would come as an indirect result of doing what he loved most. No one really knew for sure exactly what happened, but when Sam found him he was lying unconscious on the frozen ground having obviously sustained a serious injury. It was evident that George had been in the process of collecting a fork of straw from the top cutting of a straw stack, so it was a matter of speculation on whether he missed his step on the ladder, or had overbalanced when his leather boots slipped sideways on the frosty rungs. With the help of a neighbour Sam was able to gently ease his father on to a door and carry him into the house. The doctor was called, and after strapping George's legs to two large wooden splints, advised that he should be kept immobile as much as possible, in order that the limbs would have an opportunity to heal.

Over the years Roses married life to George had endured many setbacks, but this was one, that sadly, despite Doctor Finch's best efforts and her unstinting nursing they were destined not to overcome. Unfortunately due to his weakened state and lack of mobility, a chest infection developed that swiftly turned to pneumonia leading to his death only a few days later.

On a bitterly cold day in February 1878, a large congregation gathered in the village church to pay their last respects to George and see him buried in a plot adjacent to his poor parents Tom and Meg who had both suffered unnatural deaths. That night, after friends and relatives had returned home, Sam and the rest of the family were in sombre mood as they ate their evening meal and contemplated a life without a much loved father and grandfather. "Considering all the knocks he's taken throughout his life, it's ironic that he should meet his death by doing one of the jobs he loved most", Sam said leaning back in his chair.

"I suppose that's something to be thankful for" Mary added thoughtfully, at least we can't blame the Vavour's this time, though God only knows they tried hard enough to finish him off".

"Considering everything else that had happened to him, a lot of folks would have packed up, reckoning it was the final straw when that government bloke said Murrain hadn't occurred here by accident", Sam added, picking his clay pipe from the mantelpiece.

"I know what you mean", "Tom said. "He could always remain positive, because whatever disaster happened he always managed to look on the bright side. I remember him saying after that hailstorm stripped the heads off the barley the other year that there'd be another crop next year. He said when you think everything's going well, there always seems to be something unexpected comes out of the blue".

"He was so right", Sam said, filling his pipe with tobacco. "Those sort of things go with the job and we learn to accept it, but to learn that someone deliberately introduced such a vile disease as Murrain on to the farm, really made me wonder about carrying on, especially having to live in fear of what they might do next, but it says everything about father", he just shrugged his shoulders and told me to look forward and not backwards".

"The church was packed", Tom said changing the subject. "That showed how well Grandfather was liked".

"Young Charles Vavour was there", Sam said.

"He's not that young", Tom remarked indignantly.

"Well perhaps not. Yer right, I was forgetting that you're nearly as old as him. Any way you wouldn't think he was William's son, he's so different to both his father and grandfather; I know for sure that neither of them would have bothered to attend the service".

"Furthermore I'll guarantee they would never have expressed any sympathy at our loss". Rose added.

"Charles came to me afterwards and said if there was anything he could do we were only to ask" Sam continued, exhaling a plume of smoke that spiralled upwards to drift among the bacon hanging from the ceiling hooks. "In the meantime he said, if Kate would like to learn to play the piano at the Hall then he would arrange for the tutor who is teaching his sister to teach her also".

"I really do hope for all our sakes that now Williams imprisoned Charles continues to change things," Rosé said.

"It's not only at the Hall where changes are happening", Sam remarked, standing up and walking over to the fire, "There's so many new machines appearing now, that our work can only get easier. I remember after we bought our first sail reaper, the old hands couldn't see how it would ever work".

"What you mean that rusty old thing at the back of the yard"? Tom said pulling a face.

"You may well mock, but I can tell you it was the latest thing in its day. I'm well aware that compared to our present reaper it looks pretty primitive".

"Wasn't that the machine that killed William Vavours father"? Tom asked.

"It was", Rose said. "That's what I mean about change. Charles would never ever do anything like that".

"We owe it to your grandfather to keep looking ahead", Sam said looking in Toms direction. "Especially when you consider the changes he must have seen in his lifetime. Machines have made such a difference since he was a boy. I remember him telling me how he once helped his father flail corn in the big barn on the Hall farm".

"I didn't realise that flails were still being used when he was young" Tom said, "I thought they used one of those old threshers"?

"Well they did, but that was only after your great Grandfather was killed".

"I remember granny telling me all about that", Tom said glancing at Rose. adding "didn't a parson invent it"?

"I believe so" Sam said, taking a quill to the fire to relight his pipe. "A man called Meikle they say. I remember as a boy seeing one of the things. It wasn't a deal bigger than the harmonium in the chapel, but there again all it did was rub grain from the ear".

"I'll bet the men who'd had the rotten job of flailing couldn't believe their luck when a farm got one". Tom said.

"Certainly some did, but a good many of 'em hated the sight of these new threshing machines".

"Why was that"?

"Even though it must have been back breaking work beating stalks of corn with sticks to get grain from the ears, they reckoned it would lead to 'em losing their jobs if these new machines replaced the work they were doing. They felt so passionately about it that it led to what were called the Swing Riots in 1830. Some of the labourers from the big estates down south started smashing up the machines and threatening the owners with violence if they brought any other machines on the farm".

"Silly devils"! Tom said.

"It all came to a head when they hung nine on 'em and transported 450 of the worst offenders to Australia".

"How did the machine actually work"? Tom said intrigued by what his father was telling him.

"Well it was powered by two horses going round and round a central shaft, that rubbed grain from the stalks of corn and then delivered a mixture of grain straw and chaff on to a heap that had to be separated into the various parts. The straw part was quite easy as it could be forked away to leave a mixture of grain and chaff. They separated the grain from the lighter chaff by throwing it into the air between a North and South facing barn door. The breeze passing through was sufficient to blow away the chaff leaving the heavier grain on the ground where it could be collected up".

"I wonder what they'd have said to our new machine with its fan to blow the chaff off the riddles and then grade the corn for size. But how did it all change"?

"Well for a start, farm labourers became a deal more enlightened than there forbears had been".

"Why was that"?

"Years of seeing cottage farmers pack up, and fellow labourers leaving the land to find better paid jobs in the factory changed attitudes, and that's to say nothing of family members emigrating to the new farmlands overseas. The result was that the men generally welcomed any new invention that removed some of the hard physical work. When you think about it everything we produce has to be lifted or carried by hand".

"It's probably a lasting legacy to father that he was prepared to pioneer new ideas and machines that would make life a bit easier".

"And now we take our new thresher to farms around the area", Tom said.

"It's quite remarkable how things have changed now that Williams imprisoned, and young Charles is assuming control, even if it's only on a temporary basis", Sam said relighting his pipe. "Charles even asked me if it were possible for us to thresh their grain on the estate farms next winter".

• • • •

In June 1881 William Vavour was released from prison, having endured conditions that were way beyond anything he could ever have imagined in his worst nightmares. For a man now in his late forties, his brief spell in the cells at Hoult almost thirty years earlier had been bad enough, but the depravity that he experienced during his present seven years' incarceration was something else. He quickly discovered that the dungeon like cells of Victorian jails were not designed for comfort; to the contrary, they were specifically designed to create conditions as unpleasant as possible, in order that society could exert a full measure of retribution which they hoped might serve as a deterrent against further offending. It was doubly worse for William because other prisoners soon learned of his privileged background, and the way his family had abused their position to become rich at the expense of poorer people such as the Slade's. Many of the prison warders also resented the way the Vavour's had escaped justice in the past. However both prisoners and warders were united in their condemnation of his crime in not only inflicting suffering and death on innocent animals, but also by his actions causing distress and financial ruin to people who some of them could relate to.

William had been used to a life of dominance over others less fortunate than himself, which made it all the harder for him when he had to take commands from prison warders who took the greatest delight in making him grovel and plead for better conditions. Fellow prisoners used whatever means came their way to humiliate a man who they associated with wealth and power. Seven years hard labour meant just that. Each morning he was chained to a line of prisoners and marched to a nearby quarry where he had to hew limestone from a cliff face, before smashing it with hammers until each lump was pebble size. If a warder should spot him taking a brief rest, or even speaking to another prisoner, then the least he could expect was to feel the explosive force of a leather thong on the end of a whip snaking across his back. Food rations metered out to the prisoners were basic in the extreme, as they usually comprised a mixture of oat gruel, stale bread and water. Unfortunately for William, he found to his cost that there were occasions when his food was contaminated with human excrement by vindictive prisoners who took a perverse delight in adulterating his food. It wasn't just the shock of encountering extremely hard labour for the first time in his life, nor was it the revulsion he felt when he spat out faeces, but the thing that really wore him down was the constant verbal abuse from both prisoners and warders. If the opportunity had ever presented itself he would gladly have taken his own life to rid himself of the living hell he was experiencing.

Jane felt utterly betrayed by his despicable action in spreading such a vile disease to animals, and by so doing ruining the livelihoods of honest hardworking people. She had never forgiven him for causing so much distress to Charles over whatever he had found way back in 1870, so that she now found it impossible to have any feelings for the man that she thought she once knew. Fortunately for Ben Ingelby, after his visit with William to Cheshire, he had assumed sole responsibility for the management of the canal company; consequently he had been able to move more of the business over to the railway, as canal traffic continued its inexorable slide towards extinction. With William away, Joseph was at long last able to fulfil a long held wish to stay at the Hall and accompany Charles on rambles through the woods. During their time together at the Grammar School they became the closest of friends. Inevitably, some folk who might once have been pleased to be associated with the Vavour's were so disgusted by Williams's actions that they completely ostracised the family, though others took a much more phlegmatic view, realising that the sins of the father should not be visited on the children.

When William Vavour was eventually released from prison he was faced with two alternatives, neither of which was ideal. On the one hand, if he returned to live at the Hall he would forever, as long as he lived, be subject to the wrath of people whose livelihoods he had ruined through his actions. On the other hand he could be shot of it all and move to another country where it was unlikely that anyone would know him and he would be able to start a new life. He thought after his experience in prison, he would be able to cope with people's mutterings and sniggering, but it frightened him to think that someone, sometime, somewhere, would be waiting their opportunity to attack him. But if he wanted to avoid that threat by leaving the country he reasoned that he would require substantial funding to enjoy the standard of living he had always been accustomed to prior to his seven years in prison. The drawback to that was that almost everything he owned was tied up in his various business interests which might prove difficult to liquidate, bearing in mind that Jane would ensure she and the family weren't turned out of their home at the Hall. In any event, in the final analysis it boiled down to the fact that it was probably better to live with the devil he knew, than the unknown elsewhere.

David Ingelby was there to meet him at Hoult station and drive him back to the Hall, but the circumstances of his homecoming were totally different to those of twenty three years earlier when he had returned from the Crimea. As the gig passed along the road to the village everything seemed familiar despite his years away, nothing seemed to have changed. Even old Dobby, was lying by the roadside as his cows grazed the roadside verges. It wasn't until he passed the field adjacent to Sam Slades house, and saw half a dozen Shire horses with their foals galloping around the field, that he began to feel annoyed. However it was when he caught sight of the Slades farm buildings and The Cross of Loraine picked out in darker bricks across the gable end that his deep seated hatred returned once more. In his twisted logic he regarded them as being responsible for his years in prison, even though it was him that had been responsible for spreading the cattle plague to the Slade's and other herds of cattle in the district.   Rather than reform him, his long prison sentence had brutalised an already unpleasant character, and turned him into a very dangerous adversary.

Impatiently flicking long strands of greasy hair from his face, he stepped from the gig to pause for a few seconds as he gazed up at the great west front of the Hall, then walking up the flight of steps he pushed open the massive front door. "Where are you Jane, where have you got to women"? He bellowed, walking across to the north drawing room.

David Ingleby had dreaded this moment, as quite naturally he had been down to the Hall on many occasions since William's imprisonment and knew full well of his sister's hostility to her husband, and how the happy household would change for the worse once he assumed control again.

Jane appeared from the direction of the kitchen and showed not the slightest hint of emotion on seeing her husband once again after his long absence.

"Aren't you pleased to see your husband again"? William sneered, "Don't say you didn't miss having me around, or have you found someone else to lavish your affection on".

"I can't tell you how much shame and humiliation you have brought down on all of the family by your despicable act" she spat out, "for all I care I wouldn't mind if I never saw you again. You have no idea of the hurt that I and the children have had to endure. Whenever I go to Hoult, I see people sniggering and pointing. I can hear them remarking, that's the wife of the man who deliberately spread cattle plague".

"Well woman", he sneered, "you're either going to have to get used to seeing me about, or else move away if you can't stand the sight of me, because I'm here to stay". With that he stepped across the room and roughly grabbed her by the shoulder. "You're hurting me she gasped" as he tried to kiss her.

David, torn between two loyalties, first to his sister and then to his client, found it was no contest really, as his sister easily won.

"Lay your hands off her or you'll have me to account for", he said in a tone William had never heard before.

"Just who do you think you are Ingelby, giving me orders in my own home, if you'd done your job properly I would never have had to endure what I've been through", William replied.

"I can deal with anything that's half honest", David said sharply, but what you did was criminality of the highest order. You were extremely lucky to only get seven years. If I'd been the judge I would have given you at least double".

Williams temper flared as he grabbed a porcelain figurine from a side table and threw it with all his might at David. It had perhaps more to due with good luck, rather than taking careful aim that the object missed him, as it sailed over his shoulder to splinter into scores of pieces against the door frame before scooting in fragments along the marble floor of the hallway.

"You'll regret doing that", David remarked in carefully measured tones, wiping a sliver of blood from his cheek, where a shard of broken porcelain had ricocheted back to nick the skin, "You're going to find to your cost that I can be a force to be reckoned with".

"Get out this house, and don't ever come in here again", William roared.

"Just one thing before I leave", David remarked, "If I discover you have hurt my sister in any way, I can assure you I will see to it that your last seven years in prison will seem like a holiday compared to the punishment I will see inflicted on you".

On hearing the sound of breaking china and raised voices, the domestic staff rushed to doorways leading on to the hallway to discover what was causing all the commotion. Listening to William's tirade against David Ingelby, was graphic enough an illustration, if one were really necessary, that everyone's life was likely to suffer now that he was back. As they melted away to carry on with their work, Charles arrived at the front door, just in time to see David Ingelby impatiently snap the reins over his horse as he turned his gig on to the Park drive.

"What's happened"? Charles said, spotting his mother gently sobbing by the south drawing room doorway. "I heard shouting as I came up the drive and then David almost ran me over with his gig". Walking over to comfort his mother he caught sight of a filthy looking individual dressed in ripped clothing sitting in the room beyond. When the figure turned his way he was shocked to realise that it was his father. Seven years in prison had altered his features almost beyond recognition. What had originally been a clear skinned face with well filled cheeks had devolved into sallow features etched with deep lines and black pitted spots. He remembered how his father used to have a thick crop of carefully groomed hair, but what he saw now were greasy strands of almost white hair draped to his shoulders.

"Charles", he sneered, "I trust you'll be a bit more respectful than the rest of them here".

When he spoke, Charles saw how his remaining teeth seemed to be nothing more than blackened stumps set within cracked lips. "I didn't know you were being released just yet? He faltered. It was only then he became aware of broken shards of figurine strewn over the marble floor that his heart sank. His father hadn't altered; he was still the tyrant he remembered. The happy times that everyone had enjoyed over the last seven years looked as though they were about to abruptly end. The disturbance that had brought staff rushing to the hallway also attracted his sister Louise, along with Kate Slade from their music lesson.

"Who's she"? William snarled, as Kate trembled by the doorway.

"Its Kate Slade, she has music lessons with Louise". Charles said.

"Not any more she doesn't. Get her out. If she ever sets foot in this house again I will personally throw her out".

"She's my guest". Charles said, walking across the hallway to comfort her as she suddenly burst into tears.   Taking her arm he added. "She'll continue to come here as long as she wishes, I'm not going to have friends I've invited humiliated in this manner".

"Make no mistake as long as I'm alive and I'm in charge here, I'm not having any of those lying devils from that family in this house", William declared his voice dropping several octaves.

"I tell you this", Charles said evenly, "from the time you went away I have done my best to improve our name in the community, now it looks as though you are about to undo all the good I've done and put the clock back seven years". Charles realised he had to decide between kowtowing to his father's irrational behaviour which he knew would entail destroying all the good will he had so carefully cultivated, or take a principled stand and leave. Speaking with wisdom way beyond his years Charles declared, "If that's going to be your attitude then I'll have no alternative but leave here and live elsewhere".

"The Hall will soon be overrun with bloody Slades if it was left to you" William roared invoking years of pent up bitterness.

"Left to you, it wouldn't be long before they took over the estate".

"It would probably be no bad thing either" Charles remarked, "especially if this is an example of how you conduct yourself. By the way I have kept my word and obeyed your instructions that I should never divulge to anyone – not even my own mother – about what I found in the beck. However your present attitude means that from now on I won't feel obliged to keep that confidence. I could never understand why it provokes such anger in you"?

William dribbling saliva from the corner of his mouth twisted his face into a grotesque shape. "If I discover you have told anyone about what you found then I will see to it that you never inherit this property".

Charles decided that as a matter of principle was at stake, he was relieved when his aunt Rachael declared that she would be delighted for him to stop with them in Hoult. His uncle Ben said that due to his expanding trade as an agricultural merchant there would be a job for him there, should work at the Hall become untenable.

1885

Over the course of the next three years William became increasingly eccentric, spending much of his time either in a study he had converted from a bedroom in the North West corner of the Hall or brooding in his adjoining bedroom. Apart from speaking to Albert Wood, who had risen to the position of head keeper, he rarely ventured from his rooms during daylight hours, which was probably just as well, considering his appearance. If the sight of his long beard and matted hair weren't bad enough, then to see a man wearing clothing little better than rags was enough to intimidate any but the bravest of souls, as William had forsaken any attempt to look half respectable. Very occasionally gardeners would catch sight of him staring from one of his upstairs windows in the direction of the Slades property. It was as though he was transfixed by the sight of their farm buildings and animals grazing in the fields beyond. Even though Charles had begun to assume a degree of responsibility over running the estate during the latter years that William was imprisoned, now that he was gone the administration reverted back to the same competent farm manager who had originally handled the day to day running of the estate.

Jane for her part, although living in the same building, to all intents and purposes led a completely separate existence in a suite of rooms in the southern part of the Hall, only very rarely coming into contact with her husband. After several alarming incidents had occurred to him during the days following his arrival in prison, William became extremely frightened of what they may do next, particularly when he was asleep. Consequently by necessity he became a very light sleeper, instantly awake at the slightest unusual sound, little wonder therefore that as he continued to sleep poorly on his release, he should get into the habit of rising in the dead of night to wander among the trees beside the beck. It may have had something to do with the threats that some of the prisoners made against him, that he quite deliberately decided not to disclose to Albert and the other keepers that he was about at night. Like his father before him, William was obsessed about anyone trespassing on the Halls property and particularly the woods surrounding the Hall, so he implored Albert to impress on his keepers how important it was that they should do their upmost to deter anyone infringing his property.

In view of William's instructions, Albert Wood made it his business to patrol the woods on a random basis during the hours of darkness with the intention of catching any of the real or imagined two or four legged thieves that William had become so paranoid about. On odd occasions, over the course of the previous few months Albert thought he may have spotted the outline of a figure moving furtively among the dark trees, but whenever he reached the spot, the figure seemed to have melted from sight in the overriding gloom of the trees, so he put it down to his imagination getting the better of him. Nevertheless it bugged him that there just might be someone there after all, so determined to settle the issue one way or the other, he decided to wait in the same spot for a few nights until he was completely satisfied.

The spectacularly colourful sunsets that September and October were so impressive that it became a hot topic of conversation whenever people met. There were those of a religious belief who claimed it to be a portent of imminent global catastrophe sent as divine judgement on mankind's failure to live according to the teaching of Christ, whilst there were others who were equally keen to promote even more improbable stories. To be fair though, some of the more outlandish ones could have owed their origins more to the effects of Hewitts' best bitter following a night spent at the White Hart, rather than any more sensible observation. However it was reliably reported from Hoult by someone who was supposed to know about these things, that the vivid colours were a direct result of an enormous volcano called Krakatoa that had exploded in south East Asia and was giving spectacular sunsets all over the world. Albert paid little heed to the theories that were widely pedalled, though he did begin to have his doubts one night in early October, when he saw that the full moon had turned bright blue.

He had had always thought that tales of ghosts and the like were superstitious nonsense, or at least that had been his position until now, because he had just caught a brief glimpse of what he thought was a hooded ethereal like figure moving swiftly through the trees and that was beginning to seriously test his conviction. The moon must be affecting my judgement, he thought, shaking his head, nobody can possibly move as fast as that. He blinked and tried to refocus his eyes, then he caught another glimpse of the figure through a gap in the trees, but this time it seemed to be much further away. Am I imagining it, or is it a ghost I'm seeing, his earlier scepticism quickly eroding. He blinked again, beginning to feel just slightly alarmed. My God what the devil is it? It can't be a ghost, he thought, trying to rationalise in his mind what he was seeing, but what with the funny coloured moon and being alone in the dead of night his brain was capable of imagining all manner of things. It was then that he remembered what some of the old hands used to say about Sam Slades grandfather being killed in these woods. Something about him being caught in a mantrap they said. But that's nonsense, he's dead, he tried to convince himself.

Damn it, if it is someone then I'll catch em in a snare. He thought, pulling himself together. I've never heard of anyone snaring a ghost. Realising it was pointless using anything as small as a rabbit snare; he decided to construct a much larger one on the same principle, but using much stronger wire. He decided that he would set it where he had seen the figure pass by the previous night and then at the appropriate moment he would make his presence known. He decided that for good measure he would set up two others, so that if the first one was unsuccessful then perhaps one of the others might trap his quarry.

The following day he carefully set his three snares and settled down for a long wait in the lee of a large elm. That evening as the sun set it created one of the most spectacular displays of colour he had yet seen, as he gazed at vivid streaks of the purest violet, contrasting sharply with vermilions and ruby reds laced with bright yellow and green. He was so well camouflaged that he was able to observe small creatures continuing to move about at will, seemingly oblivious of either his presence or what was happening in the sky above them. The hours dragged by, but whereas many folk might well have lost patience and abandoned the lonely vigil, his perseverance as a keeper enabled him to remain motionless for hours on end. As the strange moon, looking more like a disc of blue veined cheese than its familiar pale colour moved towards the west, it dipped behind a group of taller trees, placing Albert in even deeper shadow than before. It was at that point he felt his hunch was more than vindicated, because he had just spotted a shadowy figure moving purposely towards him between the trees some fifty yards away. He had selected his hiding place with great care, as he allowed the figure to pass by, before standing up and shouting, "Stop where you are, don't move", at the top of his voice.

It was clearly no ghost, he realised with considerable relief, as the figure set off in a headlong gallop through the trees towards the position where he had set the snares. Running as fast as his legs would carry him Albert realised the fugitive was out pacing him, until he saw his quarry round a tree and head for the same gap between two more trees that had been taken on the previous occasion he had seen the figure. Got him, he thought confirming his assessment of the route that he thought the fugitive would take as his quarry caught a foot into the running noose of the first snare causing him to crash to the ground with a sickening thud. The figure had been travelling at such a pace that once his foot was held in a vice like grip, the sheer momentum of his movement caused him to strike the ground with such force that his head struck the trunk of one of the adjacent trees knocking him senseless. Albert wasn't quite sure what to expect when he reached the unconscious figure and turned it over to see a face, but there was one person he was totally unprepared to see and that was the bearded features of William Vavour looking up at him.

So many emotions swept over him that for a few long seconds his mind was in a complete turmoil at what he should do next. Should he just run away and deny all knowledge of the snares when William would surely want to know who had set them? On the other hand if he was injured, it was certain he would bring charges. And then what would happen to him? ..Imprisonment for sure! ..He would be bound to lose his house. ..So what would happen to his family?....
All these thoughts flashed through his head as he stared at William's prostrate figure.

It was at that point, that in spite of the poor light, he noticed the unmistakable sight of blood escaping from the corner of William's mouth and trickling down his chin into his beard. Desperately worried by this new development his heart raced even faster. What if he had killed him? That would be murder surely. It would be no excuse claiming that William had instructed him to set snares to catch a man. He realised with awful finality that if he'd killed a man in what amounted to a mantrap, then it was a good chance that it would be the hangman's noose for him. The euphoria of what had seemed such a brilliant plan only minutes earlier instantly evaporated as he began to realise the awful plight where he now found himself. How was he possibly going to explain catching his boss in a snare? It was only when he placed a hand inside William's shirt and was unable to detect anything resembling a heartbeat that his worst fears were confirmed.

Being in the early hours of the morning who could he turn to, it was no good involving his two assistant keepers, but in any case they would panic, and more than likely only make a terrible state of affairs even worse. With rising panic he became increasingly anxious as he pondered for a few minutes what he should do. His old boss, Bill Taylor, who had regained his original position of head keeper following Canes death, would have known exactly how to handle the situation had he still been alive, but unfortunately he had been dead for more than five years. His mind in a complete whirl he desperately tried to think of someone, who might help him when he thought of Sam Slade. He didn't know Sam all that well, but knew of his reputation for being a fair minded man, surely he could be relied on to do his upmost to help him, after all his mother Rose was Bills daughter.

Barking furiously, a couple of sheep dogs leapt from their kennels by the garden gate leading to Sams house, as Albert giving them a wide berth made his way to the back door. Thankful that the dogs were securely chained and couldn't reach him, he gave a hesitant knock on the door. To make matters worse, in spite of all that had happened, he felt apprehensive about Sams reaction at being disturbed in the middle of the night? His mind spinning, Albert gave the door another knock, though judging by the racket the dogs were making he felt sure they would soon wake not only all the household, but pretty well everyone else further down the lane. Very soon he heard the sound of bolts being withdrawn before the door was opened a few inches.

"Why it's Albert", Sam exclaimed with an anxious look on his face, as he held up his flickering candle to see who it was.

"Whatever brings you here at this time of night"?

"Can I have a word with you please? I reckon I've killed William Vavour"? Albert replied, his voice quavering with emotion.

"You've what?" Sam replied, suddenly wide awake, instantly recalling his own experiences with the tyrant. "How"? Better come in out the cold and tell me what's happened".

"Well for months now", Albert began, as Sam showed him to a chair by the fire, "whenever I've seen William, and to be fair it's not been all that often since e got out o prison".

"I've heard that he spends much of his time in his rooms upstairs"? Sam interjected. "Anyway sorry for interrupting, carry on"

"That's right; e's turned into a real queer devil if you ask me. When I last saw im about a couple of weeks ago e insisted that I pay special attention to the woods cos he reckoned that there might be poachers out there trying to get is birds. Well iver since e come out of prison e's kept saying that, so just to umour im as yer might say, I always agree to keep me eye up. Judging by the way e looks though and ides away upstairs I reckon e's gone clean off his rocker cos e's alust on about it. Well as usual I didn't think a lot on it, but knowing ow e is I told im I'd keep me eye up when I was on me rounds. I was pretty certain there was no one about, or at least that was until one night earlier in the week, when I thought I may have seen somebody in the wood by the beck. I couldn't be a hundred per cent certain, so I decided I would find out one way or tother. Anyroad I decided to set some big snares and thought I would lay in wait and see if anyone appeared. Sure enough, a bit after midnight tonight, somebody showed up but galloped off when I shouted for im to stand still."

"I still don't understand how William Vavour fits into this", Sam interjected looking mystified.

"Well the feller ran away like a frit rabbit", Albert continued, "But as I thought would happen, e ran straight towards the place where Id set one of the snares. Next thing I knew ed caught is foot in it, flooring im as if e ad been pole axed. When I reached im I found that e must ave struck is ead on a tree trunk as e fell, cos e seemed to be knocked out. At any rate e wasn't moving. I turned im over, and that's when I found it was William himself with blood trickling out is mouth. I felt is chest but couldn't feel ought, so I'm fairly certain e's dead, what do you reckon I can do"?

Without saying a word, Sam stretched an arm up to the top shelf of the fireside cupboard and retrieved a bottle of brandy. Deep in thought he took two cups from a shelf lower down and carefully poured two generous measures, handing one to Albert. He slowly filled his pipe with tobacco then selecting a narrow stick from the hearth poked it into the glowing embers in the fire to light it. A column of smoke rose to the kitchen ceiling, to hang among the salted hams suspended from the beams. ...Eventually Sam spoke in carefully measured words,

"I reckon you have three choices".

"What are they", Albert enquired giving a series of coughs as the brandy caught the back of his throat.

"You can report what you've just told me to the constables in Hoult. But even if you are perfectly honest in telling them exactly what happened I still reckon that they'll charge you with manslaughter, as you deliberately set snares to catch a man. The penalty for that would probably mean several years' imprisonment. A second option would be for you to bury the body in a place where it would never be discovered. Of course that would entail keeping rigidly to the story that you knew nothing about his disappearance. It's a well known fact that he's acted strangely ever since his release from prison, so people might think it feasible that he's left the country".

"That sounds a good solution", Albert said, but what's the downside to it"?

"Well for starters, he's bound to be missed at some point and that's going to involve some sort of investigation. However if the body was ever found, and a connection was made to you, it would result in your arrest and certain conviction for murder, for which you would be hung".

"I don't reckon I could face doing that". Albert said shaking his head. "In any event I'm a bloody rotten liar, so if is body was ever discovered I'd never be able to keep up the act of not knowing ought about it. So what's your third option", Albert queried.

"If his death was made to look like an accident, and that you or one of your fellow keepers just happened to find him on your morning rounds, then that would offer a tidy solution for all concerned", Sam explained.

"That sounds a good idea, but I don't see ow it can be made to look realistic", Albert said sceptically.

"Well the first thing is, you've to get rid of the snare and any others that you have laid", Sam said.

"I can soon do that", Albert said, "but I still don't know ow you're going to explain the cut on his leg where the snare caught im".

"It needs to look as though he tripped by catching his foot in something, and in doing so unfortunately struck his head against a tree", Sam said.

"It's got to be something a good deal bigger than a bit of branch", Albert observed, "otherwise no one's going to believe that a piece of wood could leave that sort of mark on is leg".

"That's a fair point," Sam reasoned. "Ideally it needs to be a piece of old metal that looks as though it's been there for years".

"I reckon I know of just such a piece", Albert said looking a great deal more relieved now than he had been a few minutes earlier. "There's somat in the bed of the beck not far from where William is now. I've often wondered ow it got there. Anyroad of the three options, I reckon the last uns the best".

"You can rest assured that you've done nothing maliciously wrong", Sam said, giving a reassuring pat on Albert's shoulder. "The trouble is though, that if the facts as you have outlined them to me were manipulated by a clever lawyer who earns his living by putting a completely different slant on to known facts, you could be convicted of manslaughter at the very least. William Vavour has done some evil things to our family, and I for one won't mourn his loss. I will be happy to assist you in staging the accident, but you must realise that if it all goes wrong I can't help you as suspicion would be bound to fall on me, given the history of trouble s that William has inflicted on us".

Although Mary was only half awake, Sam quickly explained to her that Albert Wood had a spot of trouble that he wanted a hand with, and he would explain fully when he got back in. Fortunately the water level in the beck was quite low, so it was relatively easy for Albert to locate the bend in the beck where he had seen the rusty piece of metal. The full moon was dipping low in the western sky as the light from their lanterns picked out the strange shaped object that lay submerged in a deep pool by a sharp bend.

"It looks a bit like an oversize rattrap".   Sam remarked gazing at the object they had just recovered, as it lay on the bank top.

"I reckon it's a bloody mantrap", Albert corrected him, adding, "It was rumoured by some o the old keepers when I first started that William's father once got caught in one of these".

By partially burying the trap among leaves and other woodland debris a few yards from where William lay, they didn't find it too difficult to create the impression that the metal had lain there undisturbed for years. Finally Albert removed the snare from around William's leg, and collected the other two he had set.

The next morning looking, suitably distressed, Albert rushed back to the Hall to report the discovery of William's body in the wood alongside the beck. The doctor was called and after inspecting the body, judged by the advanced state of rigor mortis that the deceased had probably died in the early hours of the morning when it would have been all too easy to trip in the current peculiar moonlight. He concluded that evidence of scraps of hair and skin still adhering to the bark of an adjacent tree trunk was adequate proof, if any more were needed, that the deceased must have tripped on the piece of metal, causing him to strike his head against the tree, resulting in his death. A constable from Hoult came down and could find little fault with the doctors analysis of the facts presented to him. It looked to be a tragic accident. Curiously though, little was made of the rusty iron object that the doctor and constable concluded had been responsible for him tripping.

Rather like a public execution from days gone by, William's funeral drew a large crowd of the curious and mawkish. There were plenty of people there who had good reason to see the back of him, so it presented them with the perfect opportunity to witness the final chapter of a man who had caused so much distress to so many in the district.

· · · ·

Farming, in spite of the introduction of several new labour saving machines, still relied almost exclusively on men and horses to carry out most of the work, unlike many town factories that benefitted by the use of steam or water power to drive quite sophisticated machinery. British farms sadly didn't have the benefit of scale and reliable weather found in North America where vast acreages encouraged greater mechanisation and less physical hand labour. Sadly for farmers struggling to make a living, things only got worse as the century progressed, with prices continuing their inexorable decline. The depressed state of British agriculture only exacerbated the estates problems, as poor returns from the estates own farms, coupled with the difficulty in raising their tenant's rents any higher, only served to increase the burden of debt.

• • • •

For the three long years following Williams return to the Hall from prison, Charles lived out his voluntary exile with his Aunt Rachael and Uncle Ben in Hoult. Ben realised that the small canal was in terminal decline, so had wisely expanded the corn marketing side of the business and now required someone to visit farmers in the district. Charles likable manner made him eminently suitable for the job. He didn't have the arrogance and pomposity of his predecessors, who quite frankly even if the opportunity had arisen would never have been capable of doing that kind of business. In his free time Charles enjoyed the company of his cousin Joseph and two younger sisters who were always full of good humour and treated him more as a brother than a cousin.

On William's death, he returned to the Hall and once more set about the difficult task of building a better relationship with village people. Much of the good work he had previously done whilst his father was imprisoned had been destroyed by William on his return, so it now demanded an even greater effort to repair trust and remove hostility. That October he invited all the estates tenants and estate workers along with their families to a grand harvest supper at the Hall. Trestle tables and chairs were erected within the spacious hallway, whilst the grand staircase and various alcoves were decorated with ears of corn and autumn flowers, interspersed with fruit and vegetables from the Hall gardens. Donning a white apron, Charles carved slices of succulent beef from the ribs of an estate reared three year old steer, whilst a couple of maids served the seated guests. Few village people had previously been within the Hall grounds, let alone set foot inside the Hall; such was the aura of exclusivity that earlier generations of Vavours had created. The meal was completed with apple pie from the estates garden, and cream from the estates Jersey milk cows. Two wooden casks of locally produced ale and cider placed by the front door ensured that no one went thirsty.

At a stroke Charles's generosity and consideration for others not as fortunate as himself, endeared him to villagers who had previously resented his forebear's dictatorial attitude. The harvest supper was so successful that during Charles time at the Hall it became an annual event on the third Friday of October, quickly earning a well justified reputation as being the social highlight of the farming year.

On Christmas morning Charles welcomed everyone back to the Hall once more, when the entrance hall and principle downstairs rooms were decorated with festive Holly and Ivy. Whilst the adults enjoyed mince pies and glasses of hot punch ladled by one of the maids from a steaming saucepan set on the kitchen range, the children excitedly ran around the house clutching gifts that Charles distributed from under a tall tree set up in the entrance hall. After all these acts of generosity it was unsurprising, that at the conclusion of his second Christmas party that everyone stood to a rousing chorus of, "He's a jolly good fellow".

Charles restored the Halls grounds to something approaching their original splendour. He got his gardeners to grow exotic fruits and vegetables within a heated greenhouse situated on the south facing wall of the walled garden. Laughter and gaiety once again echoed throughout the great house as Charles was generous in his invitations. Not only did friends and relations come but village folk were invited also. Such was Charles popularity as an eligible bachelor that inevitably people began to romantically link his name with eligible young ladies in the district. The young lady who eventually won his heart was eight years his junior. He had first met her after asking her father if she would care to come to the Hall and learn to play the piano with his sister Louise. Their music tutor quickly recognised that Kate Slade had great natural talent in not only music but all the performing arts. As she became older, Charles enjoyed the company of the tall young woman with her friendly smile. He found her easy to talk to and liked the graceful way she moved. He loved the way she sang and put such expression into her words, but when she played she seemed to give the notes a special quality. He noted the way, that like him, she cared for small creatures and always had time for a friendly word with the humblest of visitors. Sadly his father's despicable outburst of invective severely shook her sensitive nature, for which Charles never forgave him. It was only when he moved back to the Hall that she was able to resume her music lessons.

Such was her natural talent that in spite of only occasionally playing for the previous three years she soon regained her earlier proficiency. Charles so enjoyed listening to her, that he began to hold regular concerts at the Hall where both Kate and Louise gave regular recitals.

Sam Slade was now ably assisted on the farm by his nineteen year old son Tom whose enterprise and dedication to detail continued to further their reputation as leading Shire horse breeders and pioneers of the latest harvesting and threshing machinery. The constant erosion of farm gate prices, hastened an already contracting farm labour force to seek employment in the fast growing towns and cities.

By using the Slade's latest machines to harvest their corn, followed by their threshing machine during the winter month's local farmers were able to reduce their labour costs. Even so, low prices for farm commodities made an already tough life even more challenging; to such an extent it became increasingly difficult for the very small farms to operate profitably. The demise of those small farms provided opportunities for some of their neighbouring farms to expand their acreage. In this way Sam and Tom were able to increase their farm area to almost eighty acres by renting another twelve acres from another cottage farmer who found it impossible to eke out a living from his small acreage of land.

. . . .

It had been one of those dank dreary days, so common in November when pretty well everything seemed wet to the touch. With little breeze to change the static air, a veil of mist continued to hang along the hedge rows, throughout the day leaving an air of mystery to not only where they ended, but what lay beyond. Even the remaining leaves on the elms lining the Hall drive gave up the struggle and gently fluttered down to join a carpet of rotting vegetation on the ground, whilst as if to defy gravity, spider's jetted their gossamer like threads from hedgerow twigs to tall grass stalks, where they became garlanded in a necklace of tiny water droplets. Though not yet two thirty in the afternoon, the light that had never been particularly good all day was already beginning to fade, as Charles feeling quite chilled in the raw air, decided to come inside and idle away the remainder of the afternoon by taking another look at his father's old upstairs study. Following his father's death he had briefly looked through the papers on his desk, but noting the amount of rubbish littered about the place, came to the conclusion there was little there of any merit. As many other areas of the house were in much greater need of attention, he decided that he would defer examining it more closely until some future date, consequently the room had remained locked ever since. In any case since returning to the Hall to live, he had used the original downstairs study, after all it was a great deal handier than having to go all the way upstairs and then along the corridor to the bedroom his father had adapted. Quite apart from any other consideration, he much preferred his modern flat topped partner's desk to the one his father used upstairs with its sloping top.

The first thing Charles noticed as he pushed open the door and stepped into the room was a decidedly unpleasant musty odour, that coupled with a mass of cobwebs festooning the walls, window and ceiling was adequate proof if any were really necessary that several years had passed since his father had sat at the desk, or for that matter since anyone else had been inside the room. Little wonder we haven't touched the place he thought surveying the heaps of rubbish his father had accumulated and left where he had last used it.   Piles of old papers were littered across the floor and half hidden below a pile of browning newspapers Charles spotted a pair of old boots caked in dried mud. There must have been scores of times he came in this room with his boots lathered with mud, he thought, judging by the brown footmarks and caked lumps of dried mud that had presumably dropped from his feet.

Realising that his father was probably the last person to be at the desk, Charles lifted the lid to reveal an untidy mass of loose papers at the front, behind which were a row of small compartments stuffed with more bundles of papers. He selected a bundle and idly leafed through the papers discovering that they largely consisted of ancient rent receipts and various paid bills relating to property repairs on the estate. Another compartment held a bundle of official looking documents emblazoned in fine copperplate writing with the name of Ingleby and Son. As they were neatly tied with pink ribbon he concluded that in all probability they were deeds to some of the estate property, so he didn't bother to examine them further. He picked up a pile of papers from a compartment in the centre of the desk and started to idly leaf through them but as he turned them over in his hands he became aware that this compartment was not quite as deep as the others. Fascinated, Charles felt inside the small compartment. The sides seemed quite solid, but when he pressed the back he discovered that it yielded to pressure and sprung open to reveal a small recess. Putting a couple of fingers inside, his heart quickened as he wondered what if anything was hidden there. Then his fingers encircled something small and metallic. Drawing it into the daylight, he found that he was holding the double cross he had found in the beck that day all those years ago when he was only ten. As he turned it over in his hands, he still couldn't understand why his father should have become so angry when he showed it to him, and further more why he should have been so insistent that he tell no one of its existence. In spite of his threat to his father that he would no longer feel bound to keep its existence secret, he had in fact stuck to his original promise and told no one.

As he turned it over in the palm of his hand, he wondered if by any chance there might be some sort of connection with the Slade's, especially when he remembered how angry his father used to be whenever he saw the same design emblazoned on the Slades farm building. As he rotated the cross between his thumb and index finger he marvelled at its carefully rounded edges which gave it such a tactile feel. In order to examine it more closely he withdrew a handkerchief from his pocket and began to rub it vigorously until such time as he had removed some of the black tarnish and he could decipher some of the inscribed letters.

Intrigued, he walked over to the window, in order that he could study the detail in a better light. By turning the cross, first one way and then the other, he found that he was able to make out part of an intricately engraved inscription. When he found the cross all those years ago he had deciphered what he thought was a capital J followed by the letters auny, but now that he had cleaned it, he found that he was able to see the inscription more clearly. Although the lettering was partially worn, he thought he could decipher the engraved lettering to read Guy DeSauny, followed by another name in even smaller print. Could be Lorraine Conduite he thought. But what was the significance, he mused, between discovering a silver cross in the bed of the beck and the same design prominently displayed on the Slade's farm building?

As he continued to turn the cross over in his hands he felt that he would probably never know the solution to the riddle, as the answer almost certainly lay with his dead father, so he dropped the cross into the neck of a small green vase that stood amongst the papers inside the desk and carried on examining other old papers.

1890

Ever since the death of his father and his move back to the Hall, Charles Vavours name was frequently mentioned by aspiring mothers when they discussed which of the eligible bachelors in the county would make suitable husbands for their daughters. In spite of his name being romantically linked to many of those young ladies, Kate Slade was the only girl that he had ever had eyes for. It was perhaps an example of the greater enlightenment that was beginning to change society, but most certainly not because of it, that Charles proposal of marriage to her was happily accepted. Four years earlier in 1886, despite being only eighteen at the time, Kate was invited to assist the music teacher at Hoult Grammar School. Her winning smile and sunny disposition, coupled with her caring consideration for those pupils who found music lessons more challenging was universally appreciated by everyone at the school. So it was fitting that such a delightful couple should be blessed by a glorious day in June 1890 to celebrate their marriage.

Not for them a flamboyant ceremony in the large church in Hoult where his father had married, but much more in keeping with the ethos of the pair, the ceremony was held in the simple parish church that adjoined the Hall grounds. Sam proudly gave Kate away whilst Charles cousin and best friend Joseph Ingelby was best man. The reception that followed was held in a marquee erected on the lawn on the south side of the Hall where in complete contrast to Charles forbears, villagers represented a high proportion of the guests. Kate was more than overjoyed to see that in spite of the many dreadful things that had happened over the years, her aunt Rachael was there along with her other cousins. She was especially delighted that her grandmother who had become increasingly frail following her injury all those years ago, and was now permanently confined to a wheelchair could attend, which she felt cemented the Slade's new position in the community.

The previous autumn, Kate's brother Tom married Sarah Maitland, whose father had an enviable reputation as one of the leading Shire horse breeders in the county. Inevitably Sarah had accumulated a wealth of knowledge regarding the pedigrees of the most successful Shire horse families, so she was able to bring along valuable expertise to further Sam and Toms stud. Even though Kate had spent many happy hours giving recitals with Louise at the Hall before she was married, there was one room she had never entered, and that was William's old upstairs study. Years later, when as a result of her illness she was left with so much time on her hands that it was perhaps inevitable she should reflect on some of the pivotal events that had changed her life. Her marriage to Charles for instance meant that for the rest of her life she would follow a completely different path to the one she may have taken if she had married someone else. And then there were those turning points that seemed to come completely out of the blue. ....Was it pure chance, she wondered, or was it always meant to be, that having decided to follow a certain course of action that it would quite unexpectedly lead to doing something completely different. Well that was certainly the case she reflected when she entered Williams old study. If farming had remained more profitable, then it was most unlikely that she would ever have had the necessity to ever enter the room, and if so she would never have discovered the talisman that was clearly her destiny to find...

The more she thought; the more she felt that it must have been preordained for events to unfold in the way they did. She remembered that it all came about as a result of the Estates declining income. The price of farm products that had started to fall at the time of The Great Exhibition continued their relentless decline as the century progressed. Unfortunately this had a direct bearing on the rent the estate could extract from its tenants, consequently Charles was reluctantly forced to make severe reductions in the number of staff he employed in the Hall, in order to balance income against expenditure. Kate therefore was only too willing after her marriage to take on some of the domestic duties previously carried out by paid staff. It was while she was going through some of the little used rooms that she unlocked the door of William's old study. In some ways she was curious to see what lay inside, but from a practical aspect she wanted to see what work would be entailed in returning the room to a bedroom once more. Rather like Charles when he had entered the room years earlier she was appalled by its filthy state. Clasping her handkerchief to her nose in an effort to not only ward off the unpleasant musty smell, but also avoid breathing in the dust that rose in clouds from dusty papers strewn about the floor, she stepped across the room to William's old desk. In common with the surrounding floor, she found that the inside of the desk held an equally chaotic jumble of papers. Flicking through a few of the old documents she made a mental note to have a word with Charles in case there might be something of merit among them, when she noticed a small green vase half hidden by papers in one of the small compartments. Attracted by its colour she picked it up to inspect the glaze and look for any damage. Satisfied that it was sound, she was in the process of turning it over to examine its base to see if it carried any distinguishing marks when something fell from inside. "What do you know about this"? She said, swinging the cross by its cord when she met up with Charles later in the day. "Has it been in the family a long time"?

"Well no, I found it in the beck years ago. Where did YOU find it"?

After Kate told him how she had come across it, he continued.

"Of course I remember now. After father died I dropped it in there for safe keeping".

"But I thought you said you found it in the beck?"

"I did". Charles said taking the cross by its cord from between her fingers. "But to be honest, I had completely forgotten all about it when I took a look in his study after his death to see if there were any important papers that I should see".

"Well did you manage to find any?"

"Not really, there were plenty of old bills and other odds and ends, and of course, as you would see there was plenty of rubbish. No if there were any, then I never found them, but unexpectedly I did find my cross hidden in a sort of secret compartment that lay behind one of the cubby holes".

"But why would he want to hide it from you, especially when you'd found it?"

"Well I didn't know then, and furthermore I'm still mystified to this day why this little thing, which I suspect judging by this leather cord must have been some ones lucky talisman should have provoked the reaction that it did with him. You know I still remember how excited I felt when I found it and how I rushed home to show it to him. But it was his reaction when he saw it that upset me the most. I can still see his face when he first caught sight of it, and how he was so insistent that I should never tell a soul what I had found. Not even mother. Anyway after all these years you're the first person I've told".

"How bizarre", Kate said. "But you know the strange thing is that when I was a little girl. I saw a similar one to this in granny's bureau. I remember asking her about it, but all she would ever say is put it back where you found it because its evidence".

"Whatever do you think she meant by that"? Charles said turning the cross over in his fingers.

"I don't know unless this is the same one which would explain your father's reaction".

"Come to think of it I'd always wondered why that unusual design should be picked out in different coloured bricks on the gable end of your father's farm buildings, but now I'm beginning to see that there may be a connection".

"Well there's something about it that's very strange. I need to visit granny and see what she can tell me".

Her curiosity aroused, Kate went to visit her grandmother the following day.

"Yes you'll find it on the top shelf of the scullery", Rose replied when Kate asked her about the crosses whereabouts.

"I remember putting it right at the back of the shelf for safe keeping", the old lady remarked positively. "What do you want it for"?

Kate remarked that if she could find it, she would tell her grandmother why she wanted to see it. Teetering on a wooden stool, Kate felt among layers of dust, discovering long forgotten objects that at the time were considered too precious to throw away, because there was a possibility that they may be needed in the future, but almost invariably never were. Realising that none of the items remotely resembled what she was looking for, she was just about to abandon her search, when her fingers touched a piece of paper. She quickly realised it was an envelope that had become hidden in the dust, but just as she was removing it her attention was drawn to another envelope lying directly beneath. Stepping off the stool she blew away the dust covering the top envelope, and excitedly opened it to reveal a similar cross to the one that she had found in Charles study. The second envelope appeared to be much older and was secured with a cracked, brown coloured wax seal.

"I've found the cross Granny and another old envelope", she said passing both objects over to her Grandmother.

"What can you tell me about the cross, I remember you once saying when I was very small not to touch it as it was evidence, what did you mean by that"?

Rose didn't answer her at first as her arthritic fingers carefully turned the unopened envelope over so that she could study the seal. Finally she inserted a bent finger under it and removed two sheets of paper that were inscribed in the very finest copper plate writing.   Rose looked at the pages for a while then with a deep sigh closed her eyes and passed the document across to Kate.

"Read it aloud Kate I'm afraid my eyesight's not up to it".

"It's dated October 26th 1846", Kate read, unfolding the page of script.

"On this day of our Lord October 26 th 1846. I, James Vavour, in the presence of Simon Ingelby and George Slade, do solemnly make the following confession. James Vavour, in the accompaniment of the said Simon Ingelby did deliberately set a mantrap on October 28th 1831 with the sole intent to trap a man.
I the afore mentioned, and the said Simon Ingelby were so desirous to trap any person passing through the woods that we disregarded the terrible injuries that the trap might inflict on a person so trapped.
With the assistance of the afore mentioned Simon Ingelby, I James Vavour retrieved the said mantrap from the rafters of the great barn at the Hall farmyard and did set the said mantrap in such a position between trees on the beck side where we knew a person would pass by.
On the morn of October 29th 1831, John Cane a keeper on the estate discovered the dead body of Tom Slade trapped by his leg in the said mantrap".

Kates voice trailed to a whisper as she sat down heavily in a chair by the fireside, before continuing...   *My father Henry Vavour, instructed the said John Cane that he should never reveal to a mortal soul what he had witnessed. In consideration of his silence we appointed him to the position of head keeper and agreed to pay him a sum of money.*

"What treachery", Kate murmured, "This is my grandfather and Charles grandfather and great grandfather, did you know any of this Granny"?   Without waiting for a reply she went on.

"My father, the afore mentioned Henry Vavour and I James Vavour, collected Tom Slade's straw cart from the flailing yard on the pretext of accompanying the afore mentioned Tom Slade with a cart load of straw for the game birds in the wood.

We travelled to the woods unseen whereupon we picked up the body of the afore mentioned Tom Slade and transported it to the track beyond West Field. We carefully placed the afore mentioned Tom Slade's body across a deep rut in the track with the avowed intent to deceive those who would discover him. We ran the afore mentioned cart wheel over his legs to give the appearance of it being an accident.

On our return to the Hall farm buildings we accosted two of the labourers to whom we informed that we had left Tom Slade delivering the remainder of the load of straw to other game birds in the woods.

Finally in order that we remove all evidence of our evil deed, we cast the afore mentioned mantrap within a deep pool of the beck where we were desirous it remain hidden from human sight for ever.

John Cane removed the special cross that Tom Slade habitually wore to keep it for his own gratification. Out of remorse he cast it to the waters of the beck in a final act of redemption in the year of our Lord 1839.

The colour drained from Kate's face as she continued to read the document. Rose, her eyes tightly closed, slumped even deeper in her wheelchair as Kate turned the page to read the last two paragraphs.

"IN RECOGNITION OF THE DISTRESS CAUSED TO YOU AND YOUR FAMILY WE HEREBY AGREE TO PAY YOU, GEORGE SLADE THE UNENCUMBERED SUM OF ONE THOUSAND SOVEREIGNS. IN ADDITION WE AGREE TO assign forthwith all title and deed relating to the fifteen acres previously rented to Fred Hoyde.

I further admit to falsifying facts, endorsed by the afore mentioned Simon Ingelby, that led directly to the imprisonment of the afore mentioned George Slade.

Finally I admit that with collaboration of the afore mentioned Simon Ingelby I deliberately set the afore mentioned mantrap once more with the avowed intent of trapping the afore mentioned George Slade, and then if not already dead, killing him and burying his body in the wood".

"Signed, James Vavour. Simon Ingleby. 26TH OCTOBER 1846.

"Did you know about any of this"? Kate enquired, bending down to Roses level.

"Yes I knew little bits. Father was always aggrieved at being demoted,-- by as he described him, that, shifty fellow Cane. Then of course your grandfather

Slade told me much more, but this is the very first time I have seen this paper and heard the full story. You do know how I got injured by William Vavour when he attempted to run over me and your aunt Rachael".

Kate looked puzzled as Rose explained the circumstances of the accident concluding, "In return for us not pressing charges, James Vavour agreed to build new farm buildings for your Grandfather.

"But I still don't understand why this cross is evidence", Kate persisted rotating it in her hands.

"Ah that's something else", Rose said with a sigh of resignation. William attempted, and almost succeeded in poisoning our cattle with arsenic in the winter of 1859, but your father tackled him as he ran away, and although he managed to escape, he was able to grab the cross you're holding from around his neck. Of course it could never be positively proved that it was Williams, as the figure was hooded but your father was sure enough that it was him, and of course he had the cross as evidence".

Kate was shaken to hear all this, particularly as she knew William had been imprisoned for deliberately spreading cattle plague to her father's cattle.

Later that evening she discussed the day's revelations with Charles. "It's all beginning to make sense now", he said. "Father must have thought that the cross I found was the one that your father had snatched from around his neck, and that would be the reason he swore me to secrecy, for fear that if it was produced he would be convicted of poisoning your fathers cattle".

"But it was in fact my great grandfathers and this one that I have brought back from Grandmothers was in fact your fathers that he evidently got somewhere else". Kate reasoned.

As they compared the two crosses it soon became apparent that although they were both made of solid silver and designed in the shape of The Cross of Lorraine, they were totally different in the quality of workmanship. The cross that Charles had found in the beck was an item of exquisite miniature craftsmanship whilst the one Kate brought from her grandmother, although well executed was far inferior.

"I think that now we've established the correct history of each piece we should keep them both together to symbolise the union of our two families'", Kate concluded. "Surely it must be our destiny to bring these two talismans together".

"Judging by that confession, I'm appalled by the way my grandfather and father treated your family over the years", Charles said despairingly, "How can you ever begin to forgive us".

"It's not you my darling" Kate said throwing her arms around him. "You are everything that they weren't".

It had devastated Charles, on learning the contents of James confession, to think that his own Grandfather could have contemplated, let alone execute such a devastating series of atrocities against the family of his wife. The actions of his family disturbed his sensitive nature to such a degree that he felt totally ashamed of his family's past conduct, and resolved that he would do his uppermost to make amends for past outrages to his wife's family.

"Thankfully the changes the present government are introducing in this new local government act will put an end to some of the past abuses of power", Charles said glancing up from his paper a few days later. "It's ridiculous to think that just because someone owns a large estate that it should automatically qualify them for a position of administration".

"You're starting to sound like one of these new socialists", Kate joked.

"Well at least it'll have a big effect on the new councils when they are elected".

"You'll still be a magistrate though", Kate queried.

"I expect so, pity they're not changing the justice system as well, there's some individuals I see at Hoult who tend to administer punishment on an emotional basis, rather than on some sort of national guidelines".

"So what's going to happen to the tithes then"?

"Now that's a bit of a sore point", Charles said rubbing his chin. "You know for centuries, they've had the effect of being an additional rent for impoverished tenants to pay, but now that they're being transferred as an obligation for the landlord to pay, it's going to seriously affect our income".

1894

In March 1892, Kate had a son, that out of respect for Kate's great grandfather, they agreed to name Thomas, followed just over two years later by a second son whom they named Edward. It was a sad day for all the family when during the bitterly cold weather of February 1894 that Rose died. In spite of outwardly always remaining cheerful, in all reality she never fully recovered from her horrific accident with Williams gig all those years earlier.

There were nods of approval in the packed church when Charles Vavour, in his moving eulogy, described the way her fortitude shone like an inspirational beacon for others to follow when faced with similar adversity. Charles with his usual candour concluded by saying, "I'm heartily disgusted that any human being, let alone a member of my own family with all the wealth and privilege they enjoyed, could so abuse someone as good and honest as dear Rose".

Kate followed Charles passion for the natural things in life, liking nothing better than a stroll through the woods by the side of the beck, observing the changing seasons as reflected by the exuberant new life of spring, or the melancholy stillness of a winter's day. She thought the beck, as it meandered through the wood had such an endless variety of moods and colours that irrespective of the season or time of day there was always something different to see. "I would dearly love to place some sort of memorial at the spot where great Grandfather met such a terrible death". Kate said one evening after they both arrived back at the Hall following one of their walks. "Only thing is" she added, "I'm not sure how easy it might be to find the place".

"What a good idea, I need to do that if only as an act of penance for my Grandfathers brutality". Charles said opening the front door for her to pass through. "You know when father had his accident it was thought he must have tripped over a piece of rusty metal, but I just wonder, --- if there was any connection", --- leaving the rest of his sentence unfinished.

It was on a bright winter's day in January 1891, when Charles and Kate, both well prepared for the cold, decided that they would see if they could discover the site of the tragedy. Although seven years had elapsed since his father's accident, Charles felt reasonably certain he could remember whereabouts in the wood it had occurred. "I'm sure its somewhere here", he announced triumphantly; when they arrived at a particularly sharp bend in the beck. "I recognise the way the trees are aligned alongside the beck to create a natural pathway". With the aid of a couple of sticks that Charles had snapped from ash saplings , they set about the task of swishing aside dead foliage, fully expecting to quickly discover the piece of metal that had been responsible for causing William to trip.

"Everything looks much the same colour", Kate called out rather dejectedly, after spending several minutes parting dead nettle stalks and prodding among decaying leaves with her stick.

"I never thought it was going to be easy", Charles replied from his side of the clearing, as he continued to flail his stick from side to side, as if he was mowing the dead vegetation. "We've just got to hope that it's still here". After more than an hour of fruitless searching Kate was about to give in.

"I think it's a waste of time", she called out, "It's either no longer here, or else we're looking in the wrong place".

Charles, who was probably sharing her doubts, had decided to move a little further on. "Remember it's going to be buried under several years of dead leaves", he called back, "so we'll probably only realise that we've found it when we touch something metalic".

"Hey, I think I might have found something", Kate yelled excitedly after several more minutes of fruitless searching. "Come here quick and take a look".

Charles rushed over, and then by using his stick rather like a scythe, managed to flatten more of the dead nettle stalks to expose what she had found.

"Well you're certainly right about the metal", he said kneeling down, as he began to use his hands to clear away a combination of twigs, rotting leaves and roots that was covering it.

"Do you think it's what we're looking for?" Kate enquired anxiously, as she bent over to get a better view of the object that he was slowly unearthing.

"I'm not sure" he said breathlessly as he tugged at a tangled mass of nettle roots, "but it would certainly be capable of causing anyone to trip if they caught their foot in it". Before long he exposed a hooped piece of metal, so gripping the top of it he gave it a pull for all he was worth. Suddenly, the pressure he was applying overcame the resistance of nettle roots, allowing the object to break clear, sending Charles sprawling on his back. "By God this is it", he announced triumphantly, brushing lose soil and weeds from his trousers.

"What an evil looking device". Kate whispered, as she stared in horror at the instrument that had killed her Great Grandfather, and might have killed her father.

"It must have been somewhere near here where your Grandfather died", Charles said, "We know from James confession, that he brought it back here with the intention of trapping your father".

"What are we going to do with it now"? Kate asked.

"I'll carry it home", Charles said, "Then to ensure that it will never again fall into wrong hands I'll see that the wretched thing is broken up".

• • • •

Charles kept to his promise of wishing to make amends for the evil deeds of his ancestors, by carrying out sweeping changes to the land that the estate itself farmed. In spite of the economy's he had already introduced at the Hall something further needed to be done, otherwise rising debt would reach unsustainable levels. In an endeavour to effect two solutions at the same time, Charles offered Sam and Tom the tenancy to the 250 acre Hall farm at a rent that was slightly lower than other rents on the estate, but would give Charles a much greater return than he was receiving at present from farming it in hand. Both Sam and Tom were delighted to have the opportunity to substantially increase the area they farmed as it would enable them to utilise even more of the new farm machinery that was constantly being developed. Charles told them that tenancy of the Hall farm would naturally include the range of well maintained farm buildings along with the large farmhouse situated adjacent to the farmyard.

When Sarah first saw the old farmhouse, she immediately fell in love with the place and insisted that she and Tom live there. She adored the thick walls and the casement windows with their internal shutters that she felt certain would keep them snug during the winter nights, even if Tom, judging by the way he winked at her had other ideas on how they might keep warm, as they manoeuvred a double bed around the winding staircase. As Sam helped Tom and Sarah carry the last of their furniture into the big kitchen, he pointed out to them that although the 17th century house was tiled with locally produced clay pan tiles, originally it would have been thatched judging by the steeply pitched roof. Two hundred years of exposure to the elements had bleached the bricks to such a degree that it had given the old house an overall mellow hue. Sarah loved the roses that bloomed against the front wall and even the sound of masonry bees boring deep in to the soft mortar had a satisfying sound. As the farm house was situated a mere 100 yards from the Hall, it was little wonder that eventually the children of the two families, would become the best of friends as they grew up.

Unfortunately at fifty nine, Sams health was beginning to decline with the onset of arthritis. In many ways it was unsurprising, considering the days he had spent in a trench with his feet squelching in water, that he should be suffering the effects of a lifetime's hard physical work. His poor health frustrated him as it limited the physical work that he was able to do on the farm, but his foresight and clear vision for the future of farming, gave Tom enormous guidance and moral support. It was Sams pioneering vision that had led to the introduction of their two sail reapers, so it was unsurprising that one spring day in 1892 he should propose to Tom that they purchase one of the new Deering binders from America. Like the earlier sail reapers, the Deering binders were also horse drawn, using a ribbed bull wheel under the machine to provide the motive power. But there the difference ended, because instead of the cut stalks being left in a trail behind the machine, they dropped on to a canvas belt which conveyed the crop to the binding or tying mechanism.

Once a sheaf was tied it was discharged from the side of the binder, where it could be picked up and stood on its end to dry, before being carted home and stacked prior to threshing during the winter.

"It sounds a good idea, but don't these binders have problems tying the sheaves"? Tom was quick to point out.

"Well it's true that that was the case with some of the early machines, but they tied the sheaves with wire". Sam replied. "These Deering machines are quiet different because they use twine".

"I have to agree that it would make good economic sense to get one" Tom said scratching his ear, adding, "but you know if we cut a farmers corn then we ought to be able to thrash it as well".

"You're quite right there are plenty of small farms in the district that have nothing like enough acres of their own to warrant purchasing this sort of specialised machinery, but with lower prices for farm produce this is one way they can make savings on labour".

"But then we would need a new thresher, these new machines are so much bigger than they used to be".

"Ay and you'd need something a damn sight better than a horse walking round in a circle to power it". Tom added with a chuckle.

"How about a steam engine"?

"It wouldn't be very easy moving it from farm to farm".

"All right then, what about a traction engine then? I've seen pictures of em towing mobile threshers in America"?

"Nothing really, except the cost, have you any idea how much we would have to pay for one"?"

"I know it would be a hell of an expense, but remember how much land we're farming now, and furthermore, if we carried out more work for some of these smaller farms, then surely we should be able to justify the expense". "I've got to agree it's the way forward, because traction engines have enabled threshing machines to be constructed on a much larger scale, and of course now that they've put wheels under em they can be towed from farm to farm".

In spite of more acres being put under the plough as increasing mechanisation pioneered by farmers such as the Slades was reducing some of the hard work involved in growing grain, breeding livestock still remained the backbone of farming in the area around Hoult. Naturally animals required a constant supply of fresh water, so over the centuries a network of ditches had been constructed throughout the area to not only drain flood water away after heavy rain, but equally important provide a means of conveying drinking water for stock whilst they were out at grass. The principle source of the local water supply originated from a spring in Hoult that in turn led into a ditch flowing eastwards towards the sea. At the point where the ditch entered the western boundary to the village on estate land, the water supply was split by means of a carefully constructed division that precisely divided the supply into two equal parts. One half of the water went to farmers in the adjoining parish, and the other half supplied fields and farms that in the main were farmed by the estate or its tenants. Downstream from the division, the ditch was subdivided further, allowing the precious drinking water to flow past even more farms and fields as it gravitated eastwards to the sea. One arm of the sub divisions led water through a series of channels that eventually fed the moats and ponds surrounding the Hall before finally discharging into the Halls small lake. If for any reason the supply of water in the ditches was interrupted it soon became a matter of major concern for anyone with livestock, as animals were unable to survive long without water.

Consequently as he was passing through the village one day Charles was seriously concerned by what one of his tenants had to say when he was waved to a stop.

"We've run out o watter"? The poor chap declared in a highly agitated state. "The daykes bone dry".

"But surely isn't it fed by a spring in Hoult"? Charles said, never knowing a time when the ditch didn't have a good flow of water.

"It must all be goin yon road". The chap continued, "Their side o the partins lower than ours".

The seriousness of the situation was soon apparent when Charles saw that the usual flow of water down the ditch had dried up, to leave small pools of muddy water in the ditch bottom. As if to emphasise the problem he could see a drove of the estates own cattle milling around their watering hole, desperate for a drink.

"You need to get up there at once and see what's happened", Charles instructed Will Brown, the estate manager.

"Some devils dug an ole in the bank on their side the partin, so that all the watters gone their way". Will reported on his return. "I've spaded the ole full of muck and the waters comin our way again, but it'll tek more than alf a day for it to get down ere though. The beast are dry, so we'l be lucky if some on em don't brek out".

Charles was extremely worried, realising that in view of the water divisions isolated position it was going to require nothing short of someone watching over it on a permanent basis, if in fact there was somebody out there who was determined to cause mischief by diverting the flow. Charles was well aware that despite all the good works he was doing to appease for the cruelty and sharp practice inflicted by his predecessors, there were unfortunately some folk, who continued to bear a grudge against the Vavour family. Some of them found it hard to forgive and took every opportunity, despite his generosity, to be downright hostile. He realised that it needed the actions of only one disgruntled individual to just as surely ruin the estate as if they were being robbed. Thankfully later that afternoon, after commencing as a mere trickle, it wasn't too long before a full flow was water was coursing down the dried up ditch bed to bring relief to parched animal's throats. Sam and Tom, who after all were in exactly the same position as everyone else in the village who relied on a constant supply of drinking water in their ditches for their own stock, were delighted when a full flow of water was restored. Over the course of the next week Will Brown inspected the division each morning, but found nothing untoward. To the contrary everything seemed completely normal with a good supply of clear water flowing happily down the ditch. In view of the division's remote location, it entailed Will having to travel by foot around the edge of several fields of growing crops to reach it. Inevitably, after a lengthy walk to inspect it for several days in succession and finding that everything appeared normal, complacency began to creep in, so that after a week he resorted to making his inspection every other day. After a further week when nothing untoward happened, Will began to believe that perhaps the person responsible for the original sabotage was satisfied that he had made his protest or alternatively had been warned off, consequently he decided to make an inspection every fourth or fifth day.

The farming year moved on into August and demands on labour became stretched to their maximum. It always seemed to be the case at that time of year there never seemed to be sufficient hours in the day to carry out all the work that needed doing in such a short period of time, with the result that Will, in the absence of nothing further happening, stopped visiting the weir. However on one particularly hot afternoon, as Tom Slade brought another cartload of sheaves to the farm for stacking, he noticed that the cattle were restless as they bellowed and milled around the watering point by the ditch. He quickly discovered to his dismay that the water supply had been cut off once more. Other farmers further downstream were soon experiencing the same problem, with one instance of cattle smashing through a fence and flattening a field of standing corn in their desperation to seek water. Charles decided that he needed to accompany Will Brown to the division and see the problem for himself and what they might do about it.

"They've dug a damn site bigger ole this time", Will said pointing to where the bank had been dug away. "Yer can see ivery drop o watters goin their way".

Whilst Will spaded earth into the breach allowing the upstream water to rise, before once again flowing equally over the plank of wood, Charles pondered what he could do about it. "Whoever's doing this", he remarked eventually, "is determined for whatever reason to inflict the maximum amount of disruption to not only our estate farms, but also to other farmers downstream. This person obviously knows everyone's busy harvesting at this time of year, so it's virtually impossible for someone to keep an eye on things here twenty four hours a day".

"By God if I could lay me ands on the devil what's doing it I would owd is ead under the watter until he begged for mercy, then e might realise the effects that water ad on is own ealth". Will declared between clenched teeth, as he took hold of a tussock of grass on the bank top to scramble out of the ditch.

"Have you any idea who might be doing this"? Charles enquired, his brow furrowed with concern, as the ramifications of the sabotage became all too apparent.

"Well yer know that yer late father and grandfather before im did some pretty orible things to a lot of folks, so it wouldn't surprise me if wasn't some bugger arbouring a grudge. They maybe reckon yer`e an easier target than what they wus, and this might be one way of getting one ower yer".

"We've got to stop whoever's doing this as soon as possible. If cattle don't have water to drink, especially in this hot weather, they'll be breaking out all over". Charles said.

"Yer right", Sam Slade told me this morning ow their beast brok out last night and trampled ower a field of wheat. E reckoned they ed an ell of a job getting em too watter in the moat".

"Look, as I'm not directly involved in bringing in the harvest, I think I'd better take it on myself to catch whoever's doing this". Charles said rubbing his chin in a reflective manner. He could see that there was a considerably greater opportunity for him to avoid detection if he was to hide behind the thick hedge that ran alongside the ditch bringing the water from Hoult and continued along the ditch side leading to the estate farms, whilst the ditch leading from the division to the neighbouring village was fairly open, with only isolated hawthorn bushes to afford any cover. Kate was worried when Charles announced what he intended doing, but reasoned that the seriousness of the situation meant that something had to be done, otherwise farmer's livelihoods would be at stake.

As dusk fell Charles made his way unseen using the natural cover of trees and hedgerows until he arrived at a spot on the other side of the hedge overlooking the division. From his secluded position he had a clear view of the other two arms of the ditch, feeling reasonably confident that the saboteur would approach the division either from Hoult or the neighbouring village, but even in the unlikely event that he came from his direction, he felt that he was safely out of sight. Charles never believed a night could be as long, when at long last he saw the first pale streaks of dawn lighting the eastern sky heralding the promise of another fine harvesting day. Charles checked the division just in case he had nodded off and missed his adversary, but discovered to his relief that it was intact having suffered no nocturnal visitors to disturb the flow of water. He made his way wearily back home, only to repeat the same exercise the following night. Once again with negative results prompting Kate to remark "I think your man knows you`re waiting".

"I don't think so, I'm certain that given time he will do it again". Charles replied undaunted.   I'm sure he'll be back, I just need plenty of patience". He occupied the same uncomfortable position under the hedge for the next ten nights with negative results.

As another long cold night gave way to yet another dawn, he reluctantly began to think that perhaps Kate was right after all. It was quite possible, he thought, that having caused the maximum amount of trouble by denying a supply of water to Charles and his tenants, that whoever had been responsible felt he had satisfied his objective. On the other hand it was possible that the man knew he was lying in wait and was merely biding his time. The eleventh day had been grey and overcast with a keen wind blowing a sea fret inland from a cold North Sea, when in spite of Kate's protestations, he declared, "I'll spend one more night there, and if I don't see anything I'll do as you say and call the whole thing off". Charles shivered, as he drew his fleece lined coat tighter around his shoulders and once again commenced his nightly vigil. The fret seemed to eddy like ghostly galleons as it almost cleared, then wafted across in much thicker swirls. The extremely fine droplets of water collected in lace like filaments along spider's webs, and dripped from twigs and branches along the hedgerow. He constantly had to keep rubbing his eyes as the fine mist settled on his eyebrows, and dripped drops of water down his face. Everything he seemed to touch was wet and cold, which only added to his discomfort, especially when he thought that instead of being stuck here under a cold wet hedge, he could be tucked up in a warm bed beside Kate. The constantly moving swirls of mist made him lose all sense of distance, as he began to imagine all manner of fanciful creations emerging from the gloom.

All of a sudden he was on edge as a figure armed with a spade appeared through the mist from the direction of Hoult and after scrambling down the dike side into the ditch bottom, stood only a matter of feet from where he crouched. Even though, at long last his wait was over, he knew that if he was perfectly honest, he had really dreaded this moment, little wonder therefore that his heart was beating so fast he felt sure it was bound to disclose his position. He could only partially see the man through gaps in the leaves of the hedge, but what he could see did little to ease his unease, as he saw a tall individual wearing a rough type of smock coat. Charles couldn't see the man's face as his back was turned, but in any event, even if he had turned in Charles direction he would still have found it difficult to see his features, as the brim of the man's hat was turned down to partially obscure it. The man waded through the water until he stood by the bank leading to the other village, and immediately began to furiously excavate a tunnel in the bank around the brick base of the division. It wasn't too long before he had removed most of the earth that Will had replaced almost two weeks earlier, allowing water to gush through the gap. Not satisfied with that he began to widen the hole, throwing great spades of soil on to the bank top. Charles nature was to be placid and not seek confrontation, but it incensed him to see the feverish manner in which the man was going about the destruction of the carefully regulated water division. Having seen enough, he quietly picked up the stout ash stick he had brought with him for the express purpose of defending himself if the saboteur should turn violent. His back turned, the man, one foot resting on the wooden sill of the brick division and the other in the dike bottom continued to dig away furiously completely unaware of Charles presence. "What the devil do you think you're doing"? Charles roared, fired up with adrenalin, now that at long last he faced the saboteur.   Silently he had moved to a gap in the hedge that brought him directly opposite the man. The last thing the fellow was expecting was to hear someone speak, so it was a natural reaction to turn in the direction of the voice, but unfortunately in his haste to spin round he hadn't reckoned on how much effort was required to pull his foot from the sucking mud at the bottom of the ditch.   Consequently when he did finally pull his foot clear, he overbalanced and fell backwards into the muddy water.

"Drop your spade", Charles commanded from his dominant position on the bank top, as he looked down on the hapless individual, who in spite of Charles instruction continued to grip the shaft of his spade as he floundered in the ditch bottom. If the situation hadn't been quite so deadly serious, then Charles would have had little difficulty in seeing the funny side of what was happening. The man was attempting to scramble to his feet, his face, hair and sodden clothing were entwined with mud and strands of green weed, whilst his hat floated away downstream.

"What's your name"? Charles said, raising his stick, as a mixture of mud and water continued to drain from the fellow's body and trickle into the ditch. The man's face was full of hate as he looked at Charles towering above him. His heart raced at the shock of being discovered while his mind reeled at how he could possibly extricate himself from the position he was now in.

"Come on, speak up man", Charles commanded again, "who are you and what do you think that you're doing?" The man didn't reply, as very slowly he began to spade earth back into the breach on the bank side, his mind working overtime after recovering from the initial shock of being discovered.

"Don't I recognise you", Charles said, getting a better glimpse of the man's face as he turned his head. "Aren't you Mason, I seem to remember you came before my court last winter, weren't you imprisoned for persistent drunkenness". Still the fellow remained silent as he sullenly spaded more material in to the bank he had so recently breeched.

All of a sudden he dropped his spade in the water and bent over as if to retrieve it.   But then in what seemed like a continuous motion, he twisted his body sideways whilst at the same time trawling his hand through the water into the mud below, and in the process collecting a handful of black glutinous slime which he hurled in Charles direction on the bank top. Perhaps as a consequence of not only being cold and wet, but also immobile for the previous five hours, Charles reactions were just a little too slow in avoiding the filthy substance. The result was that the man's handful of mud caught him fair and square on the side of his face, immediately blinding him in one eye. Bending down quickly, Mason retrieved his spade, and then swung it in a wide arc catching one of Charles leather boots with a glancing blow from the steel blade. In spite of feeling intense pain from his leg and blinded in one eye with the mud, Charles reflexes reacted swiftly as he instinctively swung his stick with all of his might in the direction of his assailant, before collapsing to the ground in agony. More by good luck than judgement, Charles stick gave a glancing blow to Mason's upper arm, with the remaining force of the stroke expiring on the side of his head, resulting in Mason, rather like a tree that had just been felled collapsing face down in the water. Using his coat sleeve, Charles was able to wipe the thick of the mud from his eye, although the only way he was going to see properly was to bathe it in water. He bent down to feel his shin, relieved to find that although it throbbed with pain, it didn't appear that any bones were broken. As stars danced before his eyes, he realised that his adversary, who was laying somewhere in the darkness at the bottom of the ditch wasn't moving. Seized with panic that if he hadn't actually killed the fellow with his stick, then he was likely to drown down there, Charles hurriedly scrambled down the bank into the ditch bottom.

Mason was laying face down in the water, so Charles managed to turn him over and drag him into a partial sitting position, whereupon much to Charles relief he began to cough and splutter. Very slowly, amidst further bouts of coughing, Mason started to regain his senses, before a spasm of violent shivering threatened to over balance them both into the water. As Mason's composure began to return to something approaching normal, Charles got him to rise shakily to his feet. Terrified that the man would collapse once more into the water, Charles pushed from behind, enabling the man to scramble up the ditch bank where he immediately crumpled into an untidy heap.

Completely sodden, with an aching leg and an eye that felt as though it contained a bucket of grit, Charles pulled himself out of the ditch, to sit a few yards away, facing his adversary. "Who put you up to this", Charles said sharply, once it was apparent that the man's senses seemed to be returning to normal. "Come on man, out with it. You'd better tell me now or I'll see to it that you get a severe lashing followed by a lengthy prison sentence for sabotage and endangering the welfare of animals, to say nothing of violently assaulting a magistrate". Mason cradling an arm with the other, shivered uncontrollably as he began to speak in a voice little louder than a whisper. "You Vavours tricked us out of our family business taking it for your own; my father died last year in the workhouse. My mother lives with me now in my cottage behind the canal in Pond Street". Charles knew the filthy hovels that were situated down a narrow alleyway. The open sewers stank at this time of year with piles of vermin infested rubbish rotting in heaps by the entrance to the low cottages.

"I know it all happened over fifty years ago in my grandfather's time, when father was a young man, but to his dying day he said that because of the way your family swindled him out of his business he would get even with you lot, and then when you sentenced me to prison it brought it all back". Mason went into another bout of coughing, before continuing in a voice that was even lower than before. "Lying in my dark cell during those winter nights I had plenty of time to think how I could get even with you, and then it came to me like a flash. I reckoned that if I cut off your water supply it would cause you and your tenant's endless trouble, especially if I did it in the middle of summer when cattle are out at grass. You see I knew about the way the water divided up here, because as a lad I had followed the course of the water from the spring in Hoult, so I reckoned that as it was in such an isolated spot, I could easily creep up here undetected. Only thing was though, I hadn't reckoned on you laying in wait for me".

"For what my forebears did I'm truly sorry", Charles said, his leg now starting to throb with a vengeance, "But I can't turn the clock back for injustices that they may have carried out". Rubbing more mud from the corner his eye he looked across at the sorry figure of Mason, who had lost all his will to fight and was obviously in considerable pain from the injuries he had sustained to his arm and head, and must now be contemplating even more pain from another flogging and an even longer prison sentence.

After a while Charles said, "Go home now and come back to the Hall tomorrow morning, by which time I'll have decided what I'm going to do with you".

• • • •

"I've given the matter a great deal of thought since we met last night", Charles said to Mason in his study the following morning. "In view of the fact that you obviously get a great deal of satisfaction by working with a spade, I'm prepared to offer you a job digging ditches on the estate, providing you promise me that you will never do anything of this nature again, If you agree to that condition, I shall take no further action in what you've done, and that will be the end of the matter. Charles rose from his chair and with a look of steely determination on his face gripped the edge of his desk for support as he stood resting one foot on the other in order that he might ease the throbbing in his leg.

Mason had had the rest of a sleepless night to consider the serious position that he now found himself in and was consequently fully resigned to the fact that he would be spending the next few years in prison, so he was totally overwhelmed with emotion when he heard Charles magnanimous gesture.

190

1900

Six years seemed to pass by incredibly quickly, as Charles standing in the community scaled new heights with his benevolent concern for the welfare of his tenants becoming a byword for ideal landlord tenant relationships. Local farmers were relieved that following the restoration of the water supply that harvest time six years ago, there had never again been an interruption in the water supply. More perceptive folk, felt that Charles knew a great deal more about it than he was prepared to let on, and even some of those closest to him, weren't altogether convinced by his reassuring answer, that the reason for his limp, was as a result of his horse kicking him whilst removing the saddle. Others, who liked to gossip couldn't understand why Charles had suddenly found work for Bill Mason; surely they reasoned he was a "wrong un". They knew Charles had a compassionate nature, but surely this was taking it a bit far, especially when he found a home for both him and his mother in an empty cottage in Peddars Row. Will Brown though held his council, only permitting himself a wry smile whenever he spotted Mason with a spade over his shoulder. Peoples concerns soon evaporated, reasoning that perhaps as a result of the country air and a regular job of work, that Bills character really had taken a change for the better, shifting from a lifetime spent bemoaning the injustice that his family had suffered at the hands of the Vavours, to publicly declaring to anyone who cared to listen, what a wonderful man Charles Vavour was.

Kate however, wasn't fooled by Charles assertion that a horse had kicked him, but was too considerate to challenge him, realising that if he wanted her to know how he had hurt his leg, then he would tell her in the fullness of time. From the moment Kate moved into the Hall, she became a gracious hostess supporting local and national charities by allowing the Hall and its spacious lawns to be used for regular money making events. Her two boys Thomas and Edward, rather than be educated by a governess in the Hall, joined their three Slade cousins; Andrew, William and Grace along with other village children at the village school were they were taught values of equality and compassion for others by the very able headmaster Mr Brady. Unfortunately, although she had few problems during her pregnancy, the birth of her younger son, Edward, didn't go at all well.

Despite Charles ensuring that she receives the finest medical attention during the birth, complications arose from which she was fortunate to survive. With careful nursing she slowly regained strength, but the trauma which had so nearly killed her left her drained of energy, yet in spite of always feeling tired she remained cheerful with a friendly smile for everyone. Her doctor advised that she must have plenty of fresh air and rest, particularly if her feet and legs started to swell. Even though she had the best possible medical attention her health continued to deteriorate, to such a degree that it wasn't long before it became an effort for her to walk across the lawn to the garden seat overlooking the lake.

It distressed Charles to see the way that even the slightest exertion of walking those few steps left her out of breath. As she sat exhausted, he desperately wished that she was able to take a walk by the beck with him. He remembered how she always seemed to find something fascinating to see around every bend.

The distant war in South Africa didn't really impinge on any of their lives, or at least that was the case until Charles felt it his national duty to respond to what Chamberlain described as, "the greatest war facing Britain since the Crimea".

"I tell you that's a man in a thousand", Sam remarked to Tom one morning, after learning of Charles intention to support the country. "Especially when I know how dreadfully worried he is about your sister's health, so it must have been an agonising decision".

"I'll bet there won't be many men of his age volunteering to go in any case" Tom said. "It certainly takes some guts to do what he's doing".

"Well the least we can do is offer any help, but I know that he's got some good staff on the estate and they'll do their level best to ensure the smooth running of the farms".

As Kate bade Charles a tearful farewell on the platform of Hoult station she reached in the pocket of her coat and removed the cross that Charles had found in the beck all those years ago. Fearful that she may never see her husband again she tenderly slipped it over his neck and whispered so that only he could hear, "You have brought so much happiness to me my darling, and also to so many other people, wear this always as a constant reminder that wherever you might be, you will constantly be in our thoughts until you are safely back home with us once more". Kate had a great belief in the fact that things didn't just happen; rather they were ordained for a purpose. After all she reasoned what other explanation could there be for two almost identical talisman to end up in the possession of their two families, and then play such a pivotal part in the turbulent history of their relationship if it wasn't part of their destiny.

With Charles gone she became even more steadfast in her belief that if she always wore the other cross then no harm would befall Charles. So retrieving it from the drawer where it had lain since she had brought it back from her grandmothers, she placed it around her neck vowing never to remove it until such time as he returned.

In South Africa, General Roberts, the Commander in Chief of the British forces, took great pains to explain the logistical and practical difficulties facing them in a rural terrain. He said their adversaries were a plain- clothes army that had the ability to melt into the countryside and reappear as peaceful agriculturists, yet only needed a horse and ammunition to re-emerge as soldiers. He warmly thanked Charles and those like him with rural backgrounds and leadership skills, for being among the volunteers he needed to suppress the 60,000 Boers. Out on the veldt, Charles caring attitude to the men under his command was soon evident as he endured with them the privations of bitterly cold nights, frequently under sustained sniper fire. During those occasions he was reminded of his lonely vigil up at the water division when his nerves had jangled at the slightest unusual sound.   He reflected on how easily everything could have had such a different outcome.   If Masons blow with his spade had been slightly higher, then he might have been severely injured, if not killed, or conversely, he dreaded to think what the outcome might have been, if his stick had struck higher and Mason had suffered a lethal blow to his head, then it might have been difficult to prove self defence. The privations and long anxious days of trekking in hostile terrain were followed by the triumphant defeat of Cronje's forces at Paardeberg, soon to be followed by the exhilaration of relieving Ladysmith. Although many men under his command were killed or injured Charles remained unscathed and returned back home during the winter of 1901.

In recognition of his exemplary leadership skills he was decorated by the new King in London and made a Knight.   A well deserved honour trumpeted the local paper, reflecting the high regard in which Sir Charles was held. Characteristically, Sir Charles, as he became known, didn't want any fuss, as he heaped praise on the gallant soldiers under his command that had lost their lives.

The new century proved a turning point with the passing of Victoria, as it ushered in the beginning of a new social order to further erode the viability of many of the country's smaller estates such as that of Sir Charles Vavour's Hall.

Sam Slade although crippled with arthritis was immensely proud of Tom and his daughter in law Sarah whose combined efforts were confirming their leading role as one of the county's most enterprising farms. They now employed fourteen men to look after their various enterprises, with two gangs of men employed for much of the year running two threshing sets that were powered by their two new steam traction engines.

Another two men were permanently employed travelling their Shire horse stallions around the country.   Such was the power that the Slade's had bred into their stallions that their superior blood lines were now in great demand by farmers and breeders, who were confident it would be reflected in their mare's offspring.

With the start of a new century the countryside seemed to be filled with new hope, especially when the price of grain reversed its long slide in price and began to make hesitant moves in the other direction. Improving prices provided the incentive for some of the more enterprising farms, such as the one Sam and Tom Slade's had now become, to invest in more labour saving machinery, in spite of the fact that even after its introduction, work on farms would still be incredibly hard, involving a great deal of hard, repetitive handwork. In spite of the improved prosperity in agricultural, business on the canal continued to decline, as people preferred the much quicker service provided by the railway. With little money available for reinvestment, the canals limited capacity began to render it increasingly irrelevant, resulting in the channel becoming clogged with weed and mud, turning what had once been a thriving watercourse into a rural backwater of little economic importance.

Fortunately Ben Ingelby had had the foresight to move his business away from the canal and on to the railway, with the result that he and his son now had one of the most important agricultural supply businesses in the county. Many of the redundant warehouses by the canal basin, that had originally been built to handle cargo transported by water, took on a new lease of life as storage warehouses for land based traffic as steam traction engines steadily replaced horse drawn transport.

1905

Rapid industrialization within Europe coupled with a rampant Germany created a strong market for hardwood timber from Britain's deciduous trees, a fact not lost on Sir Charles who recognised that if the estate could sell some of its timber; it would make a valuable contribution to reducing his substantial overdraft, without resorting to increases in his tenant's rent. The woods by the beck were composed principally of large elms whose timber was extremely durable under wet conditions making it highly sought after for use in the mines. It was with mixed emotions that Sir Charles reluctantly agreed to the sale of the trees, after all, ever since he was a child, the trees with the beck meandering through them had been a special place where he had gained such a love of the natural world.

Before long the quiet tranquillity of the wood was rudely shattered by the arrival of massive traction engines belching smoke and steam, their wire ropes straining to breaking point by the pressure of hauling the massive trunks. The beck that for hundreds of years had remained cloaked under a canopy of overhanging branches was soon denuded of its trees, by gangs of axmen chopping the difficult grained timber. Then they were gone and the beck assumed a primeval look as though it had gouged a deep fissure through the raw earth on its passage to the sea.

The Hall meanwhile, gently mellowed, as for the first time in its history there was now an uninterrupted view of villages to the south. The lake that for years had provided fresh fish for the Hall slowly became choked with bull rushes, as each year their fleshy stalks seemed to advance a little further across the water to leave a raft of brown vegetation in their wake which in turn provided a refuge for moorhens, ducks and other water loving creatures.

When the time came for Thomas and Edward to leave the village school, they joined their three Slade cousins and half a dozen other children for the walk to the next village, where they caught the train to the grammar school in Hoult. Even though both Kate and Charles had set such a good example of kindness and generosity for their sons to follow, it was a great disappointment to them to find that only the younger one of their two sons should inherit those traits. If it were at all possible for Thomas to get someone into trouble without drawing attention to himself, then he seemed to take a perverse delight in doing so. It was therefore unsurprising that Edward should allow Thomas to dominate him, as he was always fearful that if he didn't comply with his wishes then he could be guaranteed to exert his revenge.

It concerned both his parents that in spite of all the good works they had done in trying to improve the Vavour name in the eyes of the community; it might all be thwarted by the feckless actions of a son who was beginning to exhibit some of the worst aspects of his ancestors. It's just possible, Charles thought later, that if he hadn't been quite so preoccupied carrying out public work or if Kate, bless her, had enjoyed better health, then they both might have been able to spend more time with him, and if that had happened then the worst elements of his nature may well have been curbed. The situation wasn't improved by Thomas being such a big lad for his age, little wonder therefore that he could quite literally throw his weight around, soon gaining a reputation among his fellow pupils as not only being a bully, but also something of a tyrant to anyone he considered to have come from a humbler background. Unfortunately for Andrew Slade, it appeared to him that no one suffered a deal more from Thomas' spiteful actions than him. He felt that it wasn't so much a case of him being a year younger, nor was it because he was smaller that Thomas seemed so intent in trying to get him into trouble. No, he suspected that the real reason for his spite and vindictiveness had more to do with the fact that he considered a Slade to be inferior, even though his mother was a Slade and maybe, just maybe that was the real cause of his attitude.

Andrew had good reason to remember one such incident at school, when unjustly he received a beating in front of the class for deceit. The truth only surfaced later when another pupil, frightened of what Thomas might do to him if he reported to the teacher what had happened, told Andrew how he had seen Thomas remove a ruler from a fellow pupil's satchel and conceal it amongst Andrews possessions. In spite of denying all knowledge of how it had got there, the teacher didn't believe him, so in order to act as a deterrent against other pupils thieving he received a thrashing. This was so typical of Thomas' insidious knack of lying and shifting blame for any of his despicable acts on to others, and particularly his three Slade cousins.

Grace, who was the youngest of Tom and Mary Slade's three children, was a slight girl who invariably seemed to be holding a handkerchief to her nose. Little wonder therefore that when she became old enough to join the others at the station, following her move to the girl's grammar school in Hoult, she should become an easy target for his abuse. One morning as they waited on the platform for the Hoult train an incident occurred that was typical of Thomas' vindictive manner in trying to get someone else in trouble for something he had deliberately done. Ever an opportunist he seized his moment provided by the sight of a group of farm labourers making a lot of noise as they tried to force a drove of cattle over the railway lines at the adjacent level crossing. Whilst everyone else on the platform was fascinated by the impromptu show, he gave Grace a violent push in the back to send her sprawling forward into a nearby coal bunker, whilst he slipped quickly sideways. As the little girl began to sob, with tears coursing through the coal dust on her cheeks, Thomas was quick to condemn Andrew claiming that he had witnessed him pushing her.

"You damn liar, you know full well I didn't do it. I'm fed up with the way you pick on her." Andrew said, " Why can't you leave her alone and pick on someone your own size."

Seeing the way the coal dust had left black marks on his sister's dress and face, Andrew was furious. In spite of knowing that Thomas would be sure to take his revenge on him probably sooner than later, he threw caution to the wind, deciding that he had had quite enough of the bully's lies.

"So what are you going to do about it squirt? Thomas replied, crowding over Andrews's small figure. With that Andrew clenched his fists into a ball and without giving a second thought to the consequences thrust all his pent up anger into a punch that was as remarkable for its power, as it was for its unexpectedness. Propelled by Andrews's furious onslaught, Thomas reeled backwards, narrowly avoiding slipping over the edge of the platform to the line below. Rather shamefacedly, to the accompaniment of muffled guffaws from some of the other children who were quite delighted to see that Thomas was getting his comeuppance for once, he scrambled to his feet, shaking his head in disbelief at the unexpectedness of Andrews's reaction.

Humiliated he retreated behind a coal bunker constructed of railway sleeper's, to nurse his wounds and collect his thoughts. Without warning a handful of coal dust shot over the top of the sleepers to rain down on the three Slade children, covering them and their clothes in a film of black dust. Grace already distressed by Thomas' actions, descended into more tears as she found even more coal dust on her hair and clothes. Thomas emerged from behind the coal bunker, looking rather like the sweep that swept the Halls chimneys, except that a trickle of blood from where Andrew had hit him on the lips, had cut a narrow trace across his blackened chin. "You've picked on her just once too often", Andrew remarked as he gently comforted his distraught younger sister, unrepentant at his fortitude at hitting Thomas.

"You Slade's are nothing but jumped up peasants", Thomas leered, forgetting in the heat of the moment that his mother was a Slade, "you all need putting in your place".

Edward was acutely embarrassed when Thomas said, "You saw it all, you saw Andrew attack me for no reason, you'd better back me up or you know what you can expect". Although Edward was a great friend of Andrew he was immensely fearful of his older brother who from past experience could make his life a misery by manipulating the true facts.

So it was that once again Thomas escaped justice whilst the blame was heaped on to Andrew for starting a fight and in so doing ingraining their school clothes with black coal dust.

1907

Over the previous two years, Kate's health had continued to deteriorate, to such a degree that she became exhausted following the slightest exertion. Even though she had always derived enormous pleasure by looking across the lawn to the lake, it wasn't too long before her lack of mobility made even that impossible. It soon became an effort to get to and from her chair beside her bed. Eventually even that became too much, so that she became permanently confined to her bed requiring the constant supervision of a nurse to attend to all her needs. In spite of always remaining cheerful, never once complaining about the illness that was steadily but surely debilitating her, the vibrant young woman that everyone loved so much was slowly sinking away.

Charles was devastated to see what was happening to his beloved wife. He always put on a brave face, but those closest to him; particularly Edward with his sensitive nature saw the effect it was having on him. Unfortunately all of this seemed to pass Thomas by. With his mother's illness dominating his father's thoughts, his bullying if anything, became worse. Even though Charles had grave misgivings about Thomas's behaviour, he found that on occasions he was left with little alternative other than to leave both boys to amuse themselves when he was away on either council or magisterial duties. Although at thirteen, Edward was only two years younger than his older brother, his kindly nature made it all too easy for Thomas to dominate him, but considering he was family and in any event was always compliant with anything he wanted doing, Thomas was careful never to humiliate him in quite the same way he treated non family members.

When Thomas's attitude did eventually change, it came about, it in a most unpredictable manner, or certainly that was the case as far as he was concerned, though Charles when he studied the circumstances leading up to it, felt there was a certain irony about the way it happened. It had been a wet Saturday afternoon and Sir Charles was away for the day. He had left home quite early that morning, to attend a function in his capacity as chairman of the bench. Edward had invited his cousin Andrew over and they had spent most of the day on the top floor of the Hall, looking through boxes of old relics from years gone by. Thomas meanwhile, spent the day in the south drawing room working on his Geography homework. Hoping to discover some additional information, he went into his father's study to look for a book in the bookcase. By pure chance he stumbled on a key concealed on a hook under one of the shelves. Curious to see if it fitted any of the locks on his father's desk he walked across and tried the key in the drawers. A gentle pull on the handle of the shallow drawer above his knees established that it wasn't locked, but as it only contained an assortment of rulers, pencils and other odds and ends there would have been little need for it to be locked in any case. Then he turned his attention to the two much deeper drawers, on either side of the desk. The two on the left were unlocked, but again they only contained bundles of old papers. Bored with what he'd found he idly tried the top drawer on the right, but this one like the others contained more papers, except that some of these appeared to be field maps. He was just about to return the key to where he had found it, when he half heartedly pulled the handle of the bottom right drawer, but found that it wouldn't budge. So this is what the keys for, he thought, putting it in the lock. Again the drawer, rather like all the others he had previously opened held more papers, only this time they were in bundles tied with pink ribbon. He untied one, only to discover that judging by the legal jargon it must relate to title of land. Idly flicking his hand through them he presumed they were all something similar, so that would be the reason he concluded for the drawer being locked. But then by chance, his fingers touched something metallic. Intrigued, he removed the top bundles of papers and there at the bottom of the drawer lay two identical looking strange shaped crosses. He vaguely remembered that when his father was away in South Africa that his mother had worn something similar around her neck, but as he was quite young at the time it meant little to him. Intrigued by their unusual design he picked one of them up to examine it more closely. All the crosses he had previously seen, notwithstanding the one his mother had worn when he was a small child, had had just the one horizontal bar, so he wondered why these should have two. He turned them over in his hands examining every possible angle, puzzled by why his father would want to lock them away. Then he made an amazing discovery when he found that by holding it at a certain angle, it caught the light enabling him to detect a feint inscription exquisitely inscribed on both of the two cross bars, but try as he might he could only properly decipher the word "auny".

Deciding to examine it later, he put the cross in his pocket and picked up the other cross, but surprisingly, in whichever way he turned it, he was unable to detect the slightest sign of an inscription. He was about to replace it back in the drawer, when an odd shaped piece of paper with some kind of faded red seal on its front caught his attention.   He had been intrigued by the sight of the two crosses, so what was this about? Picking it up, he unfolded it and began to read James confession of how Tom Slade had met his death. "So that's how the devils got their money" he murmured between clenched teeth. "By God that George Slade must have had us over a barrel". His twisted logic seemed incapable of understanding the seriousness of what his ancestor had done.

The cross in his pocket seemed so tactile that he couldn't resist continually rotating it between his thumb and fore finger, yet the document that he had just read clearly stated that a cross had been thrown into the beck! There must be a connection between the confession document and those crosses, he mused, otherwise why place them together? But there again why are there two of them?

Which, if any, was the one that Cane had thrown in the beck? And if one of them had come from the beck, where had the other one come from?

Thomas took the cross from his pocket and once again compared it with the other one in the desk. There was something about the design of the crosses that had troubled him ever since he had seen them, and then all of a sudden the connection hit him like a bolt of lightning. "Why of course", he exclaimed aloud, "It's the motif on the gable of the Slade's farm buildings". He had often wondered why that unusual design was picked out so prominently on the gable end. And then there was the quality of the brickwork. Even he could see that its quality was comparable with many of the larger houses in Hoult, let alone the miserable thatched roofed structures with their mud and stud walls that could be found on practically every farm in the village, including several on the Halls estate farms.

His mind spun with intrigue realising that with the discovery of the two crosses, along with that confession locked away in his father's desk, there were a great many other issues involved between the Vavour and Slade families that he didn't know about.

It still rankled, the way that Andrew Slade had humiliated him on the station even though he personally had managed to escape the blame. But after reading that confession it made him even angrier to think that Andrews's father, in addition to all the other benefits that had arisen from his family, was now tenant of Hall Farm, the largest farm on the estate. What if?... He mused, re-locking the drawer and replacing the key where he had found it, as the outline of a plan started to formulate in his head.

• • • •

A biting north easterly wind, that must have originated from somewhere in the frozen wilds beyond the Arctic Circle, if its intense cold was any indication of where it had come from, funnelled unfettered between the rows of corn stacks surrounding Sam and Tom Slade's farm buildings. The January night was not only black as pitch, but was also freezing so hard, that the boot sucking mud surrounding the entrance to the cattle buildings had assumed the characteristics of solidified lava. Neither event however, seemed to trouble Sam and Toms new herd of red cattle who were lying contentedly within the sheltered walls of their crew, whilst the Shire horses in the top stables occasionally stamped a foot as they nosed the meadow hay in the racks above them. Floss, Jess's granddaughter, was curled up tight into a black and white ball at the rear of her kennel. With little more than her head showing above her bed of wheat straw, her nose twitched, giving little growls of sheer delight as she dreamed of running at breakneck speed around the rear of a group of grazing sheep. Although appearing to be fast asleep her senses never entirely switched off. So, even though the wind made strange moaning noises as it whistled through the farmyard, her ears pricked up when she detected a slightly different sound. Believing her territory was being violated, Floss was instantly awake as she bounded from her kennel barking excitedly. Unable to get further than her chain would allow she leapt to her hind feet, her keen senses trying to identify the source of what had aroused her.

Finding temporary shelter from the biting wind by the Slade's threshing machine, Thomas was beginning to think that what had originally seemed such a brilliant idea to get Andrew into really serious trouble and knock the Slade's down a peg or two didn't seem anything like so appealing now. It was bad enough being frozen to the marrow, but what he hadn't counted on was the racket that dog of theirs was making. If the damned thing continued to bark its head off, then surely someone would hear it, and be bound to come out of the house to see what was happening. As he crept into the farm yard, he had spotted the bulk of one of their threshing machines drawn alongside a corn stack, so he paused beside it for a few moments to collect his thoughts. In order to properly execute the next part of his plan it was essential that he planted the evidence that would convict Andrew of wrecking his father's desk and stealing his money and cross, so he reasoned that in spite of the obvious dangers, it was no good giving up now, especially considering what he had done during the afternoon.

· · · ·

In view of the bitterly cold weather, Andrew had once again spent the afternoon with his cousin Edward in the Hall, where they had both been kept amused sorting through more boxes of fascinating relics stored in the disused second floor rooms. Meanwhile, with Charles away for a couple of days in London and Kate's nurse having the afternoon off, the household was unusually quiet. Even Alice after serving their midday meal remarked that as soon as she had washed up, she would be away until later in the afternoon, as she had to visit a sick aunt. With Edward and Andrew upstairs, he decided to go to the south drawing room and get on with some outstanding geography homework. It was only when he needed to look up a place name in an atlas that was kept on a shelf in his father's study, that Thomas realised how the present circumstances presented him with a unique opportunity to execute the plan that had rarely left his mind since he had unlocked the bottom drawer of the desk.

Deciding that it was now or never, he went down to the coach house and picked up a large screwdriver that he had previously spotted in a box of tools. Back in the study he didn't find it too difficult to force the blade into the slight gap between the top of the locked drawer and the edge of the desk. By wrenching the screwdriver sharply upwards, the front of the drawer smashed away from the lock, enabling him to easily pull the remainder of the drawer from the desk. Rather like a fox, once it had tasted blood, he seemed incapable of stopping his orgy of desecration once he had started. Just whether his twisted logic was telling him that this was a perfect way of taking his revenge on Andrew for humiliating him at the station or whether there was some other deeper motive, it was difficult to tell, as he seemed intent on inflicting as much damage on the desk as possible. In what soon resembled a wild frenzy of wanton destruction, he no sooner pulled out the drawers than he set about stamping on them with all his considerable strength, until they resembled little more than a series of boards. Very soon the floor was littered with splintered wood from the broken drawers along with their contents. Breathing heavily from his exertion, he only paused in the mayhem he was causing, when from the corner of his eye, he spotted a small tightly wrapped bundle enclosed by a green rubber band, that had rolled across the floor. Realising that it must have come from the locked drawer, he picked it up to examine it further, thinking that perhaps it may be connected to the crosses he had found on his earlier visit. After removing the rubber band he discovered to his amazement that he was holding a wad of brown pound notes drawn on Blades & Co's Bank in Hoult. Turning them over in his hands, his mind buzzed at this fresh discovery and whether it would be possibly to get Andrew or even his parents into even more trouble. In spite of carefully rummaging through the bundles of papers littering the floor to see if he could find anything else of interest that he might use against them, he was forced to conclude that that was it, so putting the roll of notes in his pockets he continued to inflict even more damage to the drawers. Rather like a glutton faced with his favourite food, the more damage he inflicted the more his appetite seemed incapable of being sated in his rabid desire to create ever more mayhem. The narrow drawer under the desk top was the next to receive his venom. No longer satisfied with merely flattening it, he stamped his heel on the base of the drawer, smashing it to matchwood. Having wreaked his havoc on the five drawers he turned his attention once more to what was left of the drawer where he had discovered the two crosses. Although he had taken, what he considered to be the better of the two, when he had made his original discovery he picked up the other one and pocketed it alongside the roll of notes.

The sight of the second cross reminded him of the envelope containing James confession, so he rummaged among the papers until he came across the stained envelope with its faded red seal. Removing James confession from the envelope he read it once more, before laying it on top of the now cleared desk. Quickly crossing the study he took the curved dagger from the wall that his grandfather had brought back from the Crimea, and in one final fit of vandalism stabbed it with the dagger, impaling it to the desk top.

• • • •

Recalling the events of earlier that day he approached the back of the house with a great deal of trepidation. Was it just his nerves, or was that wretched dog barking even louder now? Surely, he felt, they must hear it, anyway if someone left the warmth of the living room for a trek to the privy at the bottom of the garden, then it really would be all up for him. He became so tense, that in his desire to move quickly and complete the job so that he could get away, he neglected to pay sufficient attention to where he placed his feet, or at least that was the case until it was much too late to do anything about it. The first he was aware of his error was seeing a flash of brilliant stars, when the shaft of an upturned brush whacked him on the side of the head. Then, as if to compound his discomfiture, the same foot threaded into the loop of a boot scraper felling him to the floor in an untidy heap.

Floss's frantic barking increased his feeling of panic as he became convinced that the noise would surely see the back door flung open any second, and he would be faced with having to explain what he was doing there at something past eleven o'clock on a freezing cold winter's night?

Fortunately no one emerged so he was able to slither past the back door, and then ever so gently, to avoid making a sound, lift the latch of the adjoining scullery. The hinges creaked as he pushed the door inwards, stretching his already taut nerves to near breaking point. Once inside the comparative safety of the room, and out of the wind, he began to relax a little, believing it unlikely that anyone was likely to enter at this time of night. He had taken the precaution of bringing along a box of Vestas, just in case he was unable to see what he was doing, but to his relief, as his eyes slowly became acclimatised to the poor light within the room, he discovered that he could make out what he was after, thanks to a feint yellow light entering the scullery from the nearby kitchen window. He could see that a line of coats hung on pegs along one wall, whilst below them he spotted a row of boots, some of which gave off the distinctive cloying smell of damp leather and sour cattle manure. As he paused to cast his eyes along the line of coats, his heart raced, unsure exactly if the feint murmuring he could hear was someone talking or whether it was just the wind playing tricks with his imagination. Temporally conquering his fear, he put those thoughts to the back of his mind as he looked for the distinctive plaid coat that Andrew had been wearing. Spotting it on the last peg he was delighted to see that Andrew, methodical as ever, had stood the pair of high sided boots that he had been wearing that afternoon, and left at the front door of the Hall, were placed on the floor directly under his coat. With adrenalin coursing through his veins, Thomas opened Andrew's coat, and then, extracting a small pen knife from his trousers pocket, proceeded to cut a slit just large enough in the garments lining for him to pass through the roll of pound notes he had brought with him. Then he carefully removed the inferior of the two crosses from his coat pocket and dropped it into one of Andrew's inside coat pockets. His coup de grace, he reasoned was pressing a few fine splinters of wood into Andrew's boots at the point where the uppers met the sole. The deceit accomplished he beat a hasty retreat back to his bedroom at the Hall.

• • • •

Charles returned home in the early afternoon of the following day and immediately went to his study to deposit a bundle of documents in his desk, before he went upstairs to see Kate. His mind was still on other matters, as he opened his study door to be confronted with a scene of desecration. Picking his way through the carnage inflicted on his study to his ruined desk, he was stunned to see his father's Crimean dagger impaling a document that he believed had been securely locked away forever. With mounting concern he picked up bundles of papers from the floor, placing them on top of the desk. After standing the larger pieces of drawers to one side, he anxiously ferreted amongst the remaining bits of torn paper and broken wood to find the two crosses and roll of pound notes; until he was quite satisfied they definitely weren't there.

With anger rising by the second he rushed into the passageway.

"ALICE , - COME HERE QUICKLY". He shouted at the top of his voice. The frightened maid, with the tails of her mop cap billowing like a sail rushed into the hallway, fearing some awful tragedy.

"What is it sir?" She cried anxiously, drying her wet hands on her pinafore.

Seeing her distress, Charles asked in a much calmer voice. "Have you been in my study Alice"?

"No sir, Ever since Lady Vavour's illness I only manage to get in there once a fortnight. I certainly haven't been in since you went away".

"Do you know who else might have been in there then?"

"I don't sir, what's happened?" Alice said, her bottom lip beginning to quiver, at Charles line of questioning.

"No please don't upset yourself" Charles said sympathetically. "It's nothing really and certainly nothing that you've done. There's just a few papers scattered on the floor, so I wondered if you might know who's been in there. I don't suppose you can remember who's been in the house since I've been gone"?

"Well, on account of the bad weather, I don't think anybody's been to the house Sir". Her face furrowed, trying to recollect events over the past two days. "Mind you, I'm not counting Sarah though; she comes and goes to your wife's room all hours of the day, but there again, she only slips in the side door, and go's up the back stairs. Now let me think, Thomas and Edward. I know they stopped inside both days, oh, and young Andrew came to play with Edward yesterday afternoon".

After checking on Kate, he quickly established that everything seemed as normal in the other rooms with nothing else apparently missing. Mystified as to why such a frenzied attack should have been carried out on his study, and in particular to his desk, he could only conclude that someone else knew of the crosses whereabouts, but whom? He knew that Kate was aware of not only the location of the crosses but James confession as well, but, she was bedridden, incapable of even getting out of bed without assistance. As he drove along the Hall drive, he had spotted his two sons playing on the far side of the Park with two other boys, which he assumed, though he couldn't recognise them from that distance, to be their two

Slade cousins. The front door banged as excited chatter announced the boy's arrival back in the Hall.

"I would like a word with you boys", Charles announced, as he led them into the south drawing room. "Have any of you been in my study whilst I've been away", he said in a matter of fact voice.

To a succession of "No father", from his two sons, followed by "No sir" from the two cousins, he studied their blank faces as they all vigorously shook their heads.

"Why what's happened"? Thomas asked.

"I've just arrived back home", Charles explained, "and I find that whilst I've been away someone has forced an entry into my desk, not only destroying it in the process but taking certain items. Do any of you know anything about it?"

"Well today is the first time that I've been in the Hall for ages" young William piped up.

"What about you other three then"? Charles enquired, "Alice tells me that you were in the house all day yesterday; did any of you hear anything unusual?"

"I was here in this room all the time doing homework for school" Thomas said.

"And what about you two", Charles said, looking in the direction of Andrew and Edward.

"We were on the top floor father, discovering all sorts of things in boxes at the back of the old schoolroom", Edward said.

"I felt sure I heard someone in the hallway once" Thomas said, glancing in Andrew's direction.

The glance wasn't missed on Charles as he asked Andrew directly, "Did you go in my study?"

Andrew immediately sensing some sort of trap and knowing Thomas's vindictive nature felt he was blushing.

"No sir, I have not been in your study".

"I thought I saw some papers sticking out of your coat pocket when you left to go home last night". Thomas said, with a smirk on his face.

With that Charles went into the entrance hall and looked at the pile of coats and boots lying untidily on the floor.

"Which is yours"? He asked, looking at Andrew. Before he had an opportunity to answer, Thomas, almost salivating in anticipation said, "It's the green plaid one over there".

Charles picked it up and quickly ran his hands through the pockets finding them completely empty bar a short length of string and a horn backed pocket knife.

"Check inside", Thomas said a little too eagerly.

Turning the garment around Charles examined the inside pockets but found nothing.

"The lining, check for any holes in the lining", Thomas said completely mystified why nothing had been revealed.

"Well there's a small slit here", Charles remarked as he spotted the cut that Thomas had made at the base of the lining. "But somehow I don't think it's going to conceal very much. Anyway there's nothing in here" he said running his fingers around the edge.

"You seem very knowledgeable about Andrew's coat, what makes you so sure he's taken something?"

Thomas was mortified, his carefully crafted plan in tatters. His mind raced, how could Andrew have possibly discovered the planted objects? And if he had found them, how was it that he was acting so composed.

"Oh, I just thought that you needed to thoroughly check Andrew's coat so that he was no longer under suspicion", he replied, as colour drained from his cheeks. His plan had seriously backfired, as there was no evidence pointing in Andrew's direction. Furthermore he knew that Andrew had the money along with the double cross. Charles for his part in order to be even handed examined the other three coats, and then asked all four boys to empty their pockets. Thomas was relieved that he had taken the precaution of hiding the other cross on the top of the heavy mahogany wardrobe in his bedroom.

He would have been staggered if he had really known how transparent his carefully crafted plan had been.

• • • •

Floss's growls and subsequent chain rattling had aroused Tom as he lay contentedly snoozing beside the fire. Moving quickly without showing more lights, he slipped on his jacket and stepped smartly through the door leading to the rear of the scullery. Moving across the room towards the outside door he was astonished to hear the latch give a click, so he made a hasty retreat to find cover under a coat that hung alongside an old table that had been relegated to the scullery. The door opened slowly illuminating the unmistakable figure of Thomas silhouetted against the faint light from the kitchen window. Crouched beside the table, barely wanting to breathe for fear of making a noise he dearly wanted to see what Thomas was up to. Tom and Sarah of course, were all too familiar with Thomas's behaviour to Grace and the way he regularly got Andrew into all manner of trouble at school. Very slowly he crouched even lower, the ancient coat above creating a perfect camouflage, as Thomas moved further into the room. From his limited perspective, he saw the way Thomas appeared to study all the coats, before selecting Andrew's plaid one. Even if Thomas had been facing him, given the poor light, it would probably have been difficult to see exactly what Thomas was up to, but as his back was turned, naturally he saw nothing, until he saw him replace it where he had found it. Just as he was about to leave, it seemed almost as an afterthought that Tom saw Thomas extract something else from his pocket and then selecting one of Andrew's distinctive boots, rub something onto one of them. With that Thomas turned and quickly left the way he had come.

When he was quite certain that Thomas had gone and unlikely to return, he, collected Andrew's coat and boots and took them inside the house for closer inspection.

"What have you got there?" Sarah yawned; turning in her chair to see what Tom had brought into the room. She was still only half awake from a couple of hours of sheer bliss, no doubt induced by the hypnotic flickering of the log fire.

"I heard Floss barking", Tom replied by way of explanation, "so I went in the scullery to get my boots so that I could see what was upsetting her, but before I could even reach them, the outside door opened and who do you think crept in?

"What someone breaking in the house? Sarah said suddenly wide awake.

"I just had time to hide behind the coats, when I saw it was young Thomas".

"The young devil"! Sarah exclaimed. "What was he up to?

"He went across and did something to Andrew's coat here, and then bent down to do something to his boots".

"Pass it over here and let me take a look". Sarah said her voice now full of concern.

Feeling in an outside pockets she looked mystified as she produced the silver cross.

"What's this?" She said swinging it by its leather cord.

"It's a long story", Tom sighed, "that cross has caused the family trouble for nearly a hundred years. I last saw it at Granny Roses as a boy.

You'd better check if there's anything else. He seemed to be quite a long time with it whilst he had his back turned to me".

Sarah was about to say there was nothing else when she discovered the slit in the lining and extracted the roll of pound notes. "Well I'll be damned", she said, settling down heavily in her chair, "This is serious stuff, however much must there be here? I wonder where he got it? You know he's done this sort of thing before in order to get Andrew into trouble, but never on this scale".

"I'm sure he's carefully planned this for someone else to find it on Andrew", Tom said. "I suggest we don't mention anything about either what we've seen or found to Andrew so that he will be able to quite truthfully say he knows nothing about it if he's questioned".

"There's a good chance that if we keep quiet, and take good care of these items that it will rebound on the young devil and maybe teach him a lesson that he won't forget in a hurry", Sarah concluded.

The boots perplexed Tom as all he could find on them seemed to be brown wooden splinters; never the less he removed all the bits and finally returned both items to where he had found them.

Sir Charles was no fool, as he strongly suspected, that in spite of his vehement denial, his knave of a son was responsible for what had happened. Judging by his suggestions of where to look, it was fairly obvious that he was trying to get Andrew into trouble, but short of calling him a liar he couldn't prove his suspicions. Both he and Kate before her illness were concerned about Thomas' aggression, and his bullying, particularly of those smaller than himself.

But now he was faced with a dilemma. Should he contact the constables in Hoult and report a serious robbery? After all it was a substantial sum of money that had gone missing. Or should he bide his time, as he was reasonably certain that the money along with both crosses would resurface at some point in the future. Perhaps then Thomas would show his hand by his inability to give a satisfactory explanation on how he had paid for certain goods. Given the few people in the house at the time, he was confident that the constables would be much more direct in their approach asking leading questions that he personally might hesitate to ask, and thus quickly break his sons resolve. Once in the hands of the law, he visualized the likely headlines in the local paper.

"VAVOUR SON CONVICTED OF THEFT".

No he reasoned, he couldn't go down that route as it would destroy at a stroke all the good will and trust that both he and Kate had painstakingly built up over the past few years. Charles knew that faced with the same situation, his father and grandfather would have taken a much more physical approach, tearing the truth out of Thomas. With Charles, patience was most certainly a virtue, realising that given time events would unfold to vindicate his tolerant and caring nature.

Andrew narrowly avoided colliding with his father as he raced into the house. "You know what", he yelled, "Someone's broken into Uncle Charles study. They've wrecked his desk and stolen some things".

"Steady on, just calm down a bit. How do you know this", Tom replied.

"He came home this afternoon, from London I think", Andrew said, taking deep breaths of air. And said his office had been destroyed and that certain items had been stolen".

"Did he say who might have done it?" Tom enquired.

"No, he questioned us boys and asked us if we knew anything, then went through all of our coats after Thomas said that he thought I had some papers in my pocket as I left for home last night"

"Well did you?

"Of course not, it was just Thomas as usual trying to get me into trouble".

"That confirms it", Tom said to Sarah later that night. It's quite obvious that the rotten young devil planted them in Andrew's clothing to deliberately get him into trouble".

"Don't you think we should tell Charles?"

"No, I don't think so. I think we ought to put the cross and money away for safekeeping and let master Thomas stew for a while. I know Charles has his plate full with Kate, but even so, he's been far too soft with that boy for too long; he should have reined him in years ago".

"What a good job you heard him, and saw what he was up to". Sarah said glancing up from her darning.

"Well we've Floss to thank for that, if she hadn't made such a racket, then I doubt I'd have heard anything".

"He must be in a bit of a quandary now", Sarah smiled. "I'd like to have seen his face when Charles failed to find either the money or the cross in Andrew's coat".

"He would be banking on his father making the discovery", Tom added, "So naturally Andrew would have got the blame for wrecking his desk".

"So as long as those items don't turn up" Sarah said removing her glasses and putting down her darning mushroom, "he's not going to know what to do. He certainly can't say anything, otherwise he's going to incriminate himself, nor can he accuse Andrew without some sort of proof".

"So until they do turn up he's not going to know what to think", Tom laughed.

1910

It was so typical of Charles to minimise what had had happened to his desk, that the event became something of a seven day wonder and became relegated to the back of people's minds. Even Alice who had been seriously worried when Sir Charles had made his discovery had almost forgotten about it, particularly as the days and then the weeks passed by with no further developments. However as the weeks passed into months, Thomas lived in dread that Andrew who had obviously discovered the planted items in his clothing, was biding his time before he said something. He was only too conscious that Andrew, if and when he so wished, had all the evidence that was necessary to get him into serious trouble. Consequently he feared that if he attempted to carry out any further spiteful acts to either Andrew or his siblings, then it was a near certainty that Andrew would choose that moment to reveal what he knew. Therefore feeling suitably chastened, Thomas went out of his way to prevent the slightest possibility of any event on his part being interpreted in such a manner that it might provoke an adverse reaction from any of the Slade children. What he couldn't understand though, was why Andrew was able to show such a complete and total indifference to him for what had happened, never once giving the slightest hint on what he had found. As for his father, ever since the event, he always felt uncomfortable in his presence, as he felt sure he had an idea who was responsible for the desecration of his study and theft of the money and two crosses. Charles for his part, felt disappointed, that with the passage of time Thomas hadn't shown his hand, but latterly his mind had been on other things as Kate's already poor health declined more rapidly.

It was only as a result of the doctor administering ever larger doses of Laudanum that her constant pain could be relieved, which regrettably caused her to hallucinate causing even greater distress to Charles and all who cared for her. Although a relay of nurses attended to all her needs, it upset him to see how the vibrant girl he had married only twenty years earlier had descended into a pit from which there was no escape. Finally one day early in May, at a time of year when she would have been so excited to see the very first red roses on the south wall of the Hall coming into bloom she died.

Her burial, a week later was in a grave on the south side of the church within sight of The Hall in one direction, and The Hall farmhouse, where her brother and his family now lived in the other. Kate's crowning achievement was to link the two families', whose history had been one of severe hardship and struggle against adversity on the one hand, whilst the other had all the trappings that went with privilege.

Social change was gaining momentum in the new century as reformist governments started the long haul of redistributing wealth by increasing taxation that started to chip away at the fortunes of landowners with large estates. Sir Charles, like many others with relatively modest sized inherited estates up and down the country, was caught in the impossible position of finding that the estate was unable to generate sufficient income to match expenditure. As large buildings such as the Hall aged, they required ever increasing amounts of money spent on maintenance, and that was just to keep pace with routine jobs, let alone any major repairs.

Much earlier of course, Sir Charles had found that the estate farms and rents from his tenanted farms were incapable of generating sufficient funds to employ the number of staff that had previously been required to run the household. But now that he was faced with increased taxation, and the cost of repairs to his tenant's houses and farm buildings, to say nothing of some of his more progressive tenants requesting investment in new buildings in order that they could keep their farms viable, he was faced with a serious problem.

Thomas left school to begin his articles with an old established firm of Land Agents and Agricultural Valuers, thirty miles away in the county town. He hankered for a position where he could have authority over others, so thought being a land agent might satisfy his ego. As he prepared to pack, he pulled his suitcase from above the wardrobe in his bedroom, and in so doing dislodged the silver cross that he had hidden from view more than three years previously. Sitting on the edge of his bed he fingered its tactile edges, as once again he tried to decipher the carefully crafted letters inscribed along the arms of the cross. Memories flooded back, as with the benefit of greater maturity he realised how incredibly lucky he had been that the whole episode seemed to have blown over with no further ramifications. He gave a rue smile as he dropped the cross into the bottom of his case; perhaps it had brought him good luck after all, especially when he considered how badly things might have gone.

His father had quietly brought in a cabinet maker and furniture restorer from Hoult, who had carried out such a good repair on the desk that it was difficult to see that it had ever been damaged. Andrew and William completed their grammar school education and joined their father on the farm allowing William, now that the farm was of a certain size and could merit expenditure in the latest mechanical aids, to pursue his passion in growing crops.

Andrew on the other hand enjoyed working with animals. He found it hugely satisfying on a cold winter's night to walk among his cows lying contentedly chewing their cud on a bed of clean straw. He particularly enjoyed stroking one of his favourite placid animals or gently talking to another cow that was more nervous, Edward Vavour, although the brighter of Charles two sons didn't fancy a professional type of career such as the one his brother was following, as he much preferred to be with his cousin Andrew on the farm. It was little surprise to Tom one day, particularly as over the years they had become such firm friends and had become almost inseparable, that Andrew should ask if it would be possible for Edward to join them on the farm.

Tom of course was more than happy to agree to the proposal as Sarah's experience with Shires had given their stud such a boost, that the farm was able to expand in other directions, requiring their presence at both horse and other agricultural shows throughout the county.

Sir Charles of course, was completely devastated by Kate's untimely death, missing everything about the wife he loved so dearly. One evening a few weeks after her funeral, he sat wearily on the garden seat where she would often have joined him on a warm summers evening such as this, and they would both marvel at the antics of the swallows swooping over the lake. It wasn't until the shadows lengthened and the chill evening air forced them to retreat inside the Hall that those magical moments drew to a close. He missed those joyous walks he took with her along the beck and her shared enthusiasm of the natural things in life that he so loved. Sitting here reminded him of the time, when holding her finger to his lips to prevent him speaking; she had taken his hand to show him a robin's nest that she had just discovered in the creeper by the front door. He missed her so much that he felt that if he closed his eyes really tight he might be able to visualize her smiling face standing on the steps with a tray of cool drinks. He remembered so clearly how the slightest of evening breezes would ruffle her hair and then her engaging smile as she handed him a glass.

But then the spell was broken, as opening his eyes reality returned, when his attention was drawn to half a dozen rooks cawing amongst the trees surrounding the churchyard where her body lay. The massive stones of the churches rectangular tower seemed ageless, yet as he looked at them he wondered how many other scenes of despair and hopelessness, contrasting with joy, hope and optimism they had witnessed over the years. What he wouldn't give just to have her back, her symbolic act with the two crosses had been a tangible link uniting them both whilst he was in South Africa, but now, even they were missing as if to emphasise how all of the important things in his life were falling apart.

1914

"Well are you going to come with me or not""? Edward said somewhat disappointed by Andrew's lack of enthusiasm. Full of excitement he had just rushed across to tell Andrew he was volunteering to go to France.

"I don't know", Andrew replied cautiously after listening to all Edward had to say.

"What's making you hang back? It's a chance in a lifetime to travel abroad and see something different".

"I can't think it will be the glorified holiday they're making out". Andrew maintained, "Anyway don't you think that those chaps with pointed helmets will be doing their best to spoil it for you".

"Well maybe if we're very unlucky, but the recruitment officer said it'll be like a walk in the park. He reckoned it was only a question of us going over there and showing that Kaiser fellow we mean business".

"I'm still not convinced", Andrew said.

"Well if you don't go you're going to live to regret it". Edward said exasperated by Andrew's lack of enthusiasm.

"At least I will still be alive" Andrew replied laughing at his pun.

"Anyway most of our old friends from school are going". Edward said as a final clincher to convince his friend.

"But how will your father and brother manage at the Horse Fair, if you're not there to show Daisy"? Sarah countered, when he told his mother that he was thinking about joining Edward.

"It's only for this autumn mother" Andrew said defensively. "In any case if I'm not quick I'll be too late, Edward says that they think the whole thing will be over before the end of the year".

"However short it might be, don't forget its war". Sarah cautioned. "Remember soldiers fire bullets and people get killed. I can't believe they're going to send you all on a free trip to France without there being a catch in it".

"But everyone's going mother, even Thomas boss at the land agents is letting him go. It'll probably be one of the few chances I'll ever get to travel and see somewhere different. Apart from going down to the coast by train, which doesn't really count, I've only been to Lincoln a few times, and I've never been to London, further more I don't know anyone that's actually been to the continent. It just doesn't make sense to miss out on such a marvellous opportunity to travel abroad". He said in a final attempt to pacify his mother.

In spite of Sarah doing her level best to get him to have a change of heart, it was all to no avail as his mind was made up. She knew full well that whatever the popular press might say about the power of Great Britain and her French allies going to war against Germany, it was unlikely to be quite as simple as they were making out.

• • • •

Thomas had almost completed packing the few personal items he would be taking with him to France, when he sat on the edge of his bed, and probably for the first time since joining the army, began to wonder if perhaps the sceptics were right after all when they raised doubts about it not being quite so easy as everyone was making out. As he gazed through the window, everything appeared timeless. The trees lining the drive across the Park looked exactly the same as he remembered them being when he was a child. Even the huddle of houses that made up the central part of the small village beyond had barely altered during his lifetime. In reflective moments such as these, he felt there was a strong possibility that rather like lemmings heading for collective annihilation, he along with his fellow young recruits, had been seduced by the gung ho raz a ma taz of the recruiting officers, who thought the British were invincible against a weak adversary.

Then his eyes were drawn to the Slade's farm buildings, and to be more exact, the bricks that formed the distinctive double cross on the gable end of the one nearest the lane. It must be something to do with the angle of the sun, he thought, because he could never recall it standing out in such sharp relief against the dull red of the other brickwork. In spite of being some distance away, there was, nevertheless, something about its bold outline that disturbed him, even though he may be reluctant to admit it of course, that it might have had something to do with discovering his Great Grandfathers confession in his father's desk and what subsequently happened. Ever since he had read the contents, it rankled with him that his family had been usurped by the Slade's, who had gained their present position largely at his family's expense.

Wasn't that the real reason, even though he wasn't aware of the confession at the time when he thought back to his days at school, that he'd always tried his damndest to get Andrew into trouble, and had secretly been so delighted when, despite pleading his innocence, Andrew had received a totally unjustified punishment. He hated the way people admired the family, even to the extent of despising his mother when she had told him as a child, how her grandfather had struggled so hard to get ahead. And then rather like couch grass, that still managed to keep growing until every last vestige of root was removed, so his thoughts reverted once again to what could possibly have gone wrong, when he thought he had devised such a foolproof plan to get Andrew into really serious trouble. He still couldn't understand why Andrew had never mentioned anything about the incident, it was as though he was holding on to the information until such time as he could turn the tables, and reveal the true facts of what had happened. Countless times he had poured over the possibility of Andrew seeing him in his father's study, but always came to the same conclusion, that if he had been seen then surely Andrew would have told Edward and his parents. And as for placing the cross and money in Andrew's coat, well he was certain that he hadn't been heard either, otherwise someone would have come out the house, if only to discover why their dog was barking. The trouble was that instead of Andrew being the prime suspect, it had completely backfired on him, to such an extent that he felt certain his father, although never mentioning it, suspected him of being responsible for wrecking his desk and stealing not only both crosses but the roll of pound notes as well.

The more he thought about it, the more he felt that was the real reason the sight of the cross on the Slade's building unsettled him so. Perhaps it was gently mocking him for trying and failing miserably to humiliate Andrew. Yet, ever since he had removed the silver cross from the top of his wardrobe, he had been so fascinated by it, that it had rarely left his pocket. There was something strangely calming about fingering the talismans contoured edges, that led him to believe that in some mysterious way it was connecting him with the many people who must have handled it over the centuries. Because it felt so strangely reassuring he decided to slip it around his neck as he became convinced that it couldn't fail but bring him good luck. It was possible, he reasoned, that whilst he was in France he just might get an opportunity to visit the area of Lorraine that it originated from, and perhaps even discover the identity of the mysterious de Sauny.

A few weeks later following a period of training, the young recruits were barely able to contain their excitement, as cheering wildly they leant from the open windows of the train that was about to leave Hoult station for France. They waved to parents, wives and girl friends, and in some instances to envious friends who by being hesitant had missed out on the glorious opportunity to join them. Many a mother standing there that day, whilst caught up in the general euphoria of the moment wiped away a tear as they realised, even if their sons didn't, that it perhaps wouldn't be quite as easy as they were all making out. Andrew, along with his two Vavour cousins and other local young men who had joined the train in Hoult, formed a very small portion of the British Expeditionary Forces five divisions of about 100,000 men that were being sent to France to support their French allies. Thomas, perhaps because of his age, but more likely the influence of his Land Agent employer, was quickly promoted to the rank of sergeant.

Upon landing on French soil he was instructed to meet his superior officer in a building overlooking the landing quay in Calais.

"Unusual name", the captain said by way of introduction. "When I saw you all for the first time this morning, couldn't help noticing that cross you wear around your neck. Good friend of mine in the South African campaign, same name as yours, wore something similar, never kept in touch with the fella though, you not related by any chance"?

"Well yes Sir. Sir Charles Vavour`s my father; I've always wanted to know more about the cross's origin. I know it's the cross of Lorraine and Lorraine is part of Germany now. It's been in the family a long time, so I hoped that during my time over here I might learn a little more of its origin".

The officer rose from his desk and walking over to the window, silently studied the feverish activity on the quayside below. Pretty well as far as he could see, ships were being unloaded at a frantic pace to form enormous stacks of supplies stretching the full length of the harbour. Over to his right he could see lines of khaki clad soldiers slowly disembarking from a vessel. Once on the quay, they marched a short distance before lining up in ranks. Further along, he could see what appeared to be hundreds of horses tied to a long rail that disappeared out of sight beyond even larger mountains of supplies.

"Damned front extends over four hundred miles now", the officer said in a dispassionate kind of way, as though his mind was focused on something totally different.

It occurred to Thomas standing there, that the officer was either very tired, or he was suffering from some form of nervous affliction, judging by the way he had a habit of blinking several times in quick succession.

After a lengthy pause, he turned from the window and focused his eyes on Thomas once more. "Oh yes," he said at last, abstractedly rolling the ends of his moustache between his thumb and forefinger. "Let me see where was I. Oh yes it goes from the Channel coast to the north of us here, all the way to the border with Switzerland. Hmm let me see. Owe your father a favour for his kindness to me in South Africa. I'll see your units transferred to the eastern end of our lines adjoining the French in the Ardennes. Tricky part of the world though. The French claim that Alsace and Lorraine are there's. Bally Prussian's took it in 1871 so they want it back. Damn lands kept changing hands over the centuries".

"It's hard to believe that only a couple of days ago we were back in Hoult", Andrew remarked, his eyes glued to the carriage window as their train trundled through the French countryside.

"You know if we hadn't seen all those supplies at Calais, it would be hard to believe there was a war on at all", Edward replied, sounding slightly disappointed.

"I must say I'm beginning to wonder what all the fuss was about. There's certainly no sign of fighting that I've seen."

"Well what do you expect when everyone seems to be going about their work normally".

"So do you think that we`ll be seeing any action?" Andrew said.

"Not according to some of the men I spoke to last night as we waited for our train".

"Why, what had they got to say?"

"They'd heard the Germans had turned scared and gone back. They said if it wasn't over already, then it would be very soon. Somebody else reckoned he wouldn't be surprised if they didn't send us all back home by the weekend".

"Well what do you expect when they knew we were coming", Andrew said with a chuckle.

Ever since landing on foreign soil, he had been fascinated by the sights and sounds of France, even the houses and churches with their peculiar shaped spires seemed so different to those he was familiar with back home. As the train swung around Paris and headed in a more easterly direction, he was constantly amazed by the sight of vast fields that seemed to go on forever across the rolling countryside. Everything about the journey fascinated him. Before long he was excitedly attracting Edwards's attention, pointing out what he presumed were grape vines growing along wire trellises. Eventually the train came to a halt by the banks of a sizable river that someone said was called The Meuse. With usual military precision they disembarked and marched in orderly fashion to a wood not too far distant.

"It reminds me of our wood back home" Andrew said as they dropped their kit within a large clearing, "except that most of these trees are beech and oak, whilst ours are mainly elms".

"Trust you to be thinking about what trees we're under", Edward laughed. Still it's hard to believe there's a war on when you hear the way the birds are singing".

"That's if you disregard the sound of guns". Andrew joked.

"What guns? Edward scoffed a slight edge to his voice. "You're beginning to let your imagination run away with you. That's not guns, its thunder you can hear"!

The section captain drew them to order. "We need to consolidate the area, so your first task is to dig yourself in. The deeper you dig your trenches the greater chance you'll have of surviving an exploding shell. I know it's rather unlikely you will encounter the enemy, but nevertheless I'm placing you on a state of high alert. Your sergeants will detail the strongest and fittest of you to digging the trenches whilst the remainder of you who won't be tired out from digging will be posted around the circumference to keep a lookout. Remember", he concluded, "be vigilant, the Huns an evil beast, he could be lurking behind any of these trees at this very moment taking careful aim at any one of you".

"By heck that captain didn't half put the wind up me", Edward said, a worried frown on his face, as he dug yet another spade of earth from the trench.

Thomas walked across to his section of men as the germ of an idea started to form in his brain. "You'd better keep digging, because you've got to complete this length before nightfall". He said pointing out how far they needed to extend their trench.

"It's only like digging grips*" Andrew said with a smile. "Only I hope this one doesn't have water in it".

"I didn't believe you when you said it was like being back home", Edward remarked with a broad smile. "Now you've got your wish".

"It is, except we wouldn't be digging a bloody great trench like this in the

Grips - Underground land drainage

middle of a wood" Andrew laughed, just a touch of concern creeping in his voice.

As the last of the daylight gave way to darkness, flashes, reminiscent of sheet lightening could be seen reflected on the bases of distant clouds, whilst there was a constant low rumble in the background, rather like the sound of distant thunder that Edward had put it down to earlier. Occasionally there was a much louder muffled boom, as if to remind those in doubt that the sound they could hear really was guns. Cramped together in the bottom of the trench, tension grew among the new recruits. Gone was the bravado and feeling of invincibility that they had enjoyed on the train earlier in the day. Some of them nervously smoked a cigarette, whilst others talked in hushed tones to their immediate companions.

"We won't stand a cat in hells chance in this bloody trench if a shell drops in it", Edward said in a barely audible voice to Andrew.

"Ay and we'll be sitting bloody ducks if we get out of it, especially if there's a German marksman somewhere in the trees out there". A wag said further along the trench.

"How the devil do they expect us to rest down here". Edward said, finding it virtually impossible to get half comfortable in the narrow trench. "God I'm hungry as well", he complained. "When do you think we'll get something to eat".

"Not tonight mate", someone else remarked.

"An you'll be damn lucky if yer get ought to-mor'er either", another volunteered.

The night closed in and apart for an occasional muffled cough, it all went quiet, which was probably unsurprising, as very soon it became difficult to distinguish the bottom of the trench. Sometime before dawn to add to their misery, it began to rain. It didn't take too long before their great coats were soaked, making them feel like leaden blankets. As the drizzle intensified water began to dribble down the sides of the trench to gather in little pools in the trench bottom, turning the soil into a boot sucking morass.

"I'm sure the sound of those guns is getting nearer". Edward whispered into Andrew's ear, who in spite of the wet, he could see was probably tolerating the conditions better than most.

"Don't worry", Andrew replied reassuringly, "sound always seems to travel further at night; you heard what the captain said the main battles are miles away from us".

"Out Slade" Thomas suddenly commanded. "You can go on guard duty now".

"Hang on he's been digging the trench along with the rest of us", Edward replied angrily.

"I can do without your yelp", Thomas snapped, luxuriating in the fact that without fear of reprisal, he was about to get one over Andrew at long last.

"You heard what the captain said about those who were digging didn't have to go on guard duty", Edward added, undaunted by Thomas. "Other platoons have a separate rota for guard duty. If he goes out there he could easily get shot by mistake".

"Another cheep from you and I'll have you on a charge. Come on Slade get a move on or I'll charge you with disobeying an order".

"You bastard Thomas, it's suicidal and you know it". Edward said as Andrew got ready to clamber up the side of the trench.

Andrew thought that in spite of the rain, dawn was approaching, as he could just about decipher the form of individual trees from the dark mass of the forest. Suddenly the still air was shattered by a tremendous whoosh, followed milliseconds later by a blinding flash and an ear bursting bang that instantly sent shards of red hot shrapnel screeching in all directions. Andrew immediately ducked back into the trench, as several more explosions followed in rapid succession turning what had previously been a tranquil camp into one of confusion.

"What the hell's happening"? He could hear Edward yelling in a high pitched voice beside him.

A distant voice from somewhere towards the end of the trench yelled, "We`re under attack, take cover", followed by the command being repeated several more times further down the trench.

"The buggers are over - ", someone else was yelling, as a shrieking whistle, followed milliseconds later by an explosion cut off the remainder of his sentence.

Someone else yelled "Retreat".

As Andrew clambered from the trench he could hear Thomas yelling at frightened soldiers to "Move for God's sake".

Concerned about Edwards safety he glanced over his shoulder, pausing just long enough to be satisfied that he was following tight behind, before making a mad dash for the safety of the trees across the clearing.

"Run like hell", he could hear Thomas shouting, as he became conscious that both brothers must be following close behind him.

But then when the situation could hardly get any worse, as more of the frightened soldiers scrambled from the trenches and started running to the safety of the trees, the air became filled with the sharp crack of Mausers, which judging by the flashes of their rifles, indicated that the enemy was among the trees to their rear. All of a sudden there was a blinding flash followed almost simultaneously by an enormous explosion, but before Andrew had an inkling on what was happening, he found himself being hurled in the air, before sprawling on the ground with a burning pain in his right shoulder. Strangely, as he lay stunned, everything about him seemed to go deathly quiet, whilst all he could see were flashing lights before his eyes. After a little while the flashing lights were replaced by a series of still images, that reminded him of the time he had been in the nickelodeon in Hoult, when the projectionist had failed to turn the handle quite quickly enough, resulting in the action being slowed down to a series of pictures, each one slightly more advanced to the one previous. However, as he returned to something approaching normality he looked about him and in spite of the poor light, was able to see the sprawled bodies of his two cousins. Even though Andrew had never seen a dead body it was immediately obvious that Edward was beyond human help judging by the distorted angle in which he was laying. He couldn't understand why, but for some reason he found it imposable to dispel the image from his mind, of his two cousins with their arms flailing, being flung into the air before crashing down onto the still smoking earth. He suspected that whatever had floored them must also have been responsible for what had hit him, yet curiously he felt no pain, it seemed almost as though he had become detached from the rest of his body. The strange thing was though, that in spite of smelling the acrid fumes of cordite in his nostrils and seeing smoke rising from exploding shells all around him, everything was silent; it was as though someone by turning down the sound of the battle, had given him an almost detached view of the surrounding mayhem. As if in a dream, Andrew continued to gaze about him, then his eyes focused on Thomas's motionless body which looked rather like an abandoned doll balanced precariously on the side of a still smoking crater. He could see that one of his legs was twisted back at an unnatural angle and that he must have some sort of injury to his chest judging by the dark patch spreading across the front of his torn tunic.

All he could see about him were fresh mounds of upturned earth where shells continued to explode among the bodies of dead and injured men. It seemed hardly possible that it was only yesterday afternoon that they had been laughing and joking as they moved into the clearing and he had remarked to Edward about it being such a haven of peace and tranquillity. Some idyllic spot now, he thought bitterly, as he looked about him at faces contorted in agony, and then as his hearing started to return he began to hear the screams of men enduring the most horrific of agonies. Gripping his shoulder Andrew pulled himself to his feet and began to make his painful way to where Thomas lay.

"For God's sake help me" Thomas croaked, bringing Andrew sharply out of his reverie.

At first all he saw was the dreadful desperation in Thomas's eyes, but then as he moved closer his mouth filled with bile and he was violently sick when he saw the extent of the injury to his old adversary's chest.

"I feel cold", Thomas muttered, shivering uncontrollably as Andrew using his one serviceable arm, did his best to staunch the worst of the bleeding by placing part of Thomas's torn tunic against the gaping wound.

God have mercy on me", Thomas cried with tears running down his cheeks, "I've done some rotten things to you over the years, but now out of the goodness of your heart I implore you Andrew, please help me, I'm so scared". Many of the despicable deeds he had enacted on Andrew seemed to flash before his eyes as he looked up in desperation for Andrew's help.

Somehow Andrew struggled to get him on one leg, then by using his upturned rifle as a crutch, managed to support most of the heavier man's weight, as they made erratic progress to the shelter of the forest. Andrew became completely exhausted, as they both collapsed by the trunk of a massive beech tree.

Thomas continued to have violent spasms of shivering, as Andrew removed his great coat and fastened it over his shoulders, after which he withdrew two cigarettes from the pocket of his tunic, and after lighting them both, placed one between Thomas's pale lips.

"You're going to be alright", Andrew reassured him, "lay still and don't fret whilst I find a medical orderly". Thomas' head slowly tipped forward, before coming to rest on his chest. Before Andrew could get to his feet to fetch help, a long sigh escaped from his lips, as his cigarette dropped from his mouth and his head lolled sideways, allowing a trickle of blood to fall onto the damp earth. A sense of hopelessness engulfed him, as in the space of a few short weeks his life had been transformed from the gentle pace he had known back home, to the carnage of a brutal war over here in France. Furthermore, his best friend along with so many others he had known since his school days lay dead or injured. Even though he was certain there was no chance whatsoever, it was so typical of Andrew's caring nature that rather than be thinking about saving his own skin, he should be doing his best to save his old tormentor. It would never have crossed his mind of course, that if their roles had been reversed it was most unlikely that Thomas would done the same for him.

Unbuttoning the neck of Thomas' blouse, Andrew was just about to place his hand over Thomas chest in the remote chance that he could feel a heartbeat, but as soon as he saw the extent of his appalling injury, he didn't bother to carry it out, as it was quite obvious that Thomas in common with his younger brother was also dead. Andrew was about to rearrange the dead man's shirt when he spotted the double cross of Lorraine hung around Thomas' neck. In a scene reminiscent of previous occasions when it had changed hands, though the irony of course was lost on him, Andrew, like Cane and his Great, Great Grandfather before him, removed the cross and tucked it in a trouser pocket, though in Andrew's case, he thought that were he to survive the war then he would be able to explain the circumstances of Thomas's death to Sir Charles, and return an item that Thomas had evidently held dear. It was doubly ironic that once again it should pass from one soldier to another, on a battle field separated by little more than one hundred years and one hundred miles in distance.

With his sound arm holding his useless one to his chest, Andrew got to his feet and began a stumbling walk that would take him deeper into the forest. Once among the trees he found that the ground sloped upwards before dropping away into a shallow valley with another wooded hill beyond. He seemed to lose all track of time as he made his way through the trees, reasoning that as long as he kept the sound of gunfire behind him, then every step he made must be taking him closer to safety. If it hadn't been for the thought of what the enemy may do to him if they managed to catch up, then he doubted he would have been able to summon up the extra strength to carry on, especially when he found it necessary to keep stopping and take increasingly long rests. The trouble was that the pain in his shoulder was making him feel so weak that without that conviction; it would have been all too easy to give up and stay where he was.

Considering that it was less than a day since he had been relaxing on the train with Edward and the other members of the Hoult platoon, it seemed barely conceivable that within hours, many of them, including his best friend, would be laying dead, whilst others were coming to terms with horrific injuries. Leaning against a tree after climbing yet another wooded slope, he paused once again to catch his breath, remembering how excited he had felt when the train left the station in Hoult, on what he thought was going to be such a wonderful experience. Well, it was an experience alright, he thought ruefully as he'd soon discovered in the most brutal way possible. If only he hadn't been quite so headstrong and spent just a little longer listening to his mother's words of caution, then he might have realised that she had a point, when she said that they weren't going to be giving away foreign trips unless there was a catch. Looking at the massive trees around him, reminded him of the train journey. Of course it had been a marvellous experience to visit a foreign country and see so many different sights. There was the rolling countryside with its forested hills, the pretty villages interspersed with fields of grazing cattle and from time to time sited either close to or actually on a hilltop he remembered seeing isolated turreted houses that Edward said were called chateau.

As he left the trees and emerged onto a grassy meadow it was therefore no great surprise to find a line of clipped yews by a gravel road that led into what appeared to be to some sort of courtyard and stables, with a large house beyond. It was only sheer will power that kept driving him forward as he staggered down the gentle slope to the rear of the property. Although he felt that he might gain some sort of sanctuary there, he was in no condition to notice that the turrets and walls of the chateau were constructed of grey coloured stone, any more than he was aware of who it belonged to or for that matter what significance that might be. As he got closer, he was not aware that a middle aged couple were standing in the rear courtyard, a look of anguish on both their faces as they watched Andrew's erratic progress down the slope towards them.

"Mon dieu, you poor fellow, come this way", the silver haired woman remarked in a heavily accented voice. Her instructions though, fell on deaf ears as Andrew seeing all manner of flashing stars before his eyes, crumpled to the ground before their feet.

• • • •

He wasn't exactly sure how long he had been awake, or indeed if it was part of a dream as a haze in front of his eyes made everything appear blurred. Slowly, rather like a mist lifting, his vision began to clear allowing his eyes to focus on his surroundings, which if anything only made things worse because he couldn't understand what he was doing lying in the church? The grey coloured stones of the walls at first glance seemed familiar enough, yet the more he looked at them, the more he began to think that there was something about them that wasn't quite right, though he couldn't put his finger on what it might be. It was only when his eyes came to rest on an intricately carved post extending towards the ceiling that he began to feel even more confused. He was back in the church, of that he was certain, but for some reason it had changed. He could never recall seeing that post, nor for that matter that window, and further more what were curtains doing on either side of it? It was at that point he became aware with something of a shock that he was covered with a white sheet and realised he was in bed, and that confused him even more.   What was he doing in bed?   --- In the church.

Was he dead? But surely he reasoned, if he was dead, it was hardly likely that he would be in a bed, so he must be in a coffin. But there again he had never known a coffin like this one. It was while he tried to make sense of it all, that very slowly it started to come back. There was something about the station platform, and yes, he remembered running down the carriage to secure a compartment, and then there was the ship, yes he remembered the red funnel and then, -- then his memory became hazy, was there another train journey, he just couldn't be sure, but there were those strange church spires. Trouble was, he was uncertain whether it was something he remembered seeing, or whether it was something he had dreamt.   However much he tried to remember his mind was a complete blank. He tried to turn over to get a better view of the other wall, but when he moved he felt an excruciating pain deep within his right shoulder. It must have been his piercing shriek that brought the sound of feet rapidly ascending a wooden staircase, quickly followed by a door bursting open and a breathless, middle aged lady rushing to his bed side.

"Oh, I am so pleased that you have come round at long last", she said in a voice that although heavily accented, was full of relief at seeing him awake. "We have been so worried about you" she added, as she hurried across the room to his bedside. After selecting a white napkin from a bowl standing on a small table she sat on the edge of the four poster bed and began to gently mop beads of perspiration from his brow. "My husband bandaged your chest", she said eventually, noticing that Andrew had opened his eyes once more. "He said you needed complete rest for it to heal, but we never thought your fever would last quite so long".

Slowly the pain began to subside sufficiently for Andrew to gingerly feel with his left hand where the pain was coming from, but all he could feel were bandages over his chest. "What happened? Where am I"? He muttered between cracked lips.

"You are safe, with friends", she smiled sweetly, at the same time continuing to moisten his face. "You've been very poorly for more than a week. Do you remember anything about the battle"?

Then it started to return, though confusingly he couldn't be entirely certain if what he was remembering had actually happened, or whether it was just his mind playing tricks.

"A great many of your brave soldiers unfortunately lost their lives" she continued.

So perhaps it wasn't a dream after all that Edward had been killed and maybe that vision of Thomas' horrific wounds actually happened as well. "But where am I"? He repeated completely confused, still trying to reconcile being in the church, with what was happening. Maybe this was all part of a dream after all.

"You are in the Chateau de Sauveur, you collapsed on our doorstep and we took you in. My husband's a doctor and he dressed your wounds. Martine, our daughter has watched over you all this time till your fever went". She lifted a glass of water to his lips and continued, "See if you can rest now, and perhaps after a while you might try a little food".

Later that evening, after a fitful sleep, Andrew opened his eyes to find a beautiful young woman wearing a white apron and holding a small bowl, sitting on the edge of his bed.

"My name is Martine", she said in a soft lilting voice when she saw his eyes flicker open.

He immediately noticed her sweet smile and the way her long hair was drawn away from her face to be neatly tied in a bun above her head.

"I am so pleased to see you awake" she said smiling broadly. Father says that your wounds are starting to heal, so perhaps in a few days you will be able to get out of bed. Do you think that you can manage a little soup"?

Andrew, feeling a good deal more lucid than when her mother had spoken to him earlier, nodded his head. "I just can't thank you enough for what you have done. I will forever be in your debt". He caught a waft of fragrance as Martine bent over to straighten the top sheet of his bed, then her hair brushed his cheek as she gently wiped away a film of moisture from his brow.

As Martine left the room to go downstairs, a tall, distinguished looking man entered the room and introduced himself as Monsieur De Sauny. After enquiring as to how Andrew felt he said, "The German soldiers searched the Chateau but fortunately didn't find you".

"But why? I don't understand why didn't they find me"?

"We feel in your pockets to see if we find your name. I'm sorry but you must excuse my English", Monsieur De Sauny apologised, "it's some time since I speak. Anyway we remove, how you say, suit".

"Uniform" Andrew corrected, not appreciating until that point that he was hardly likely to be laid in bed still wearing his uniform.

"Of course, uniform! We hid your uniform in a safe place where we knew it would not be found. But first we find your Croix de Lorraine in your pocket which we put around your neck. When the soldiers searched the chateau they naturally found you here".

"But I still don't understand why they didn't take me, if they came looking for me?"

"It's because of your Cross of Lorraine. The doctor said gently, as Andrew ran his hand to his neck and began to carefully finger the object that he had barely glimpsed when he had removed it from Thomas' neck, but which may well have saved his life.

Martine, who had just entered the bedroom with a tray, immediately spotted the difficulty Andrew was having with one hand as he attempted to get a better look at the cross. So placing the tray on the side table she reached over and carefully slipped it over the back of his head, placing it in his hand.

"Can you tell me how it came in your possession?" the doctor enquired.

As Andrew looked down at the silver talisman in his hand, bits started to come back.

"I removed it from Thomas' neck". He said hesitantly as he furrowed his brow trying to remember what had happened.

"Thomas?"

"Yes he's my cousin. I think he died. Yes, that's right, I remember now. He was badly injured and I helped move him. I was going to get help, but before I could go he died. I took it with the intention of returning it to his father when I returned home and would be able to explain to him how Thomas died".

Although this was the first time, he had examined it properly; there was something about the unusual design that seemed familiar". He closed his eyes trying to remember where he had seen it, then like a thunder clap it came to him.

"Of course I remember", he said with a start, wincing as he attempted to sit upright, "that design is picked out in different coloured bricks on the gable end of my family's farm buildings".

Monsieur De Sauny sighed as he stepped back from Andrews's bed and sat down heavily in a chair. "This cross has been with our family since the days of Joan de Arc", he explained with great deliberation.

"Then what was it doing around my cousins neck" Andrew said mystified.

"Guy De Sauny, was a famous man in our family. He stood for everything right and proper. He abhorred the way that Joan was how do you say martyr".

"Yes that's right martyred, it's the same word in English", Andrew added helpfully.

"He vowed that this cross would symbolise all he respected. So it was passed down through many generations until my great grandfather lost it when he was killed at Waterloo".

"How can you be so sure that this is the same cross"? Andrew remarked, when this is the first time that you have seen it."

"I know this it", Monsieur De Sauny said, "I've carefully examined it with a magnifying glass. There's not a shadow of doubt in my mind that it's the one he lost, pointing to the rounded base underneath the vertical bar cross". If you look very carefully, it's just possible to see our family crest is minutely carved there" he said, adding, "I believe it was made by one of the very finest craftsmen in medieval France. See just below the words Joan of Arc conduit, its even got Guy De Sauny, printed in much larger letters".

Good food and careful nursing by the De Sauny family helped heal his shoulder wound sufficiently for him to get about, even though he was left with limited mobility in his right arm.

"Do you have any other brothers or sisters". He asked Martine, whilst they chatted one day.

"Oui of course" she replied, but then tears started to run down her cheeks, "I only had one brother. His name was Phillipe. He was called up soon after the war started and was sent to the border with Lorraine, but tragically he was shot soon after he arrived".

Andrew tenderly reached across and touched her with his sound arm as she quietly wept on his shoulder.

"I am so sorry" he said",

"No", she said drying her eyes, "it's me that should apologise", I should be strong, but I was so close to Phillipe, we did so many things together, and now, he's gone forever".

Andrew grew to enjoy the company of this caring young French woman with her laughing eyes. He knew she must have sat patiently for hours on the side of his bed during the time he was unconscious, but now that he was growing stronger by the day she wanted to know all about his home and family in England. As the advancing German troops passed by, the Chateau fell behind their lines, so the main body of the building was requisitioned by German officers forcing them to move into the coach house across the courtyard. Andrew for the sake of all their lives had to assume the identity of their dead son Philipe. Fortunately both he and Phillipe were about the same age, so as the majority of Phillipe's identification papers were still at the Chateau it was relatively easy to assume his identity. Under Martine's excellent tutelage, Andrews French language skills improved so quickly that it wasn't too long before he became a competent French speaker, easily able to pass himself off to the predominantly German speaking officers as Phillipe De Sauny.

• • • •

And there the position may well have remained until the conclusion of the war now that Andrew had assumed the identity of Martine's dead brother Phillipe. In the eyes of the Chateau's German occupiers, he posed little threat as his injured shoulder was an obvious impediment to his effectiveness as a soldier. In spite of Andrew wishing to rejoin his British comrades, he was extremely reluctant to do anything that might further compromise the risks that Martine and her family had undertaken on his behalf.

1917

By 1917, with soldiers on both sides suffering unimaginable casualties, the war had reached an impasse, bogged down in the stinking squalor of trench warfare on the frontiers of France, Belgium and Germany. Strangely enough considering what lay ahead, it had all started so well in the late summer and autumn of 1914, with the confident assertion of those who ought to have known better that it would all be over by Christmas. Little wonder therefore that young men like Andrew and his two cousins should have been swept along by the feeling of euphoria that encouraged young men to do their patriotic duty by joining the army, for what was a rare opportunity to travel abroad at the government's expense. What made it so much worse was that before too long those euphoric scenes of departing soldiers were transformed into the harsh reality of warfare, as shell shocked men with broken minds and bodies returned by train to hushed platforms lined with silent grieving families.

Sarah, in common with so many other local mothers, was still haunted by the memory of seeing Andrew in the company of his excited young friends jauntily waving from their carriage windows at Hoult station. Unfortunately it did little to lessen her feeling of grief when Tom in trying to comfort her, reminded her that he shared her hurt, but unfortunately they wouldn't be the first parents to lose a son, nor judging by what was happening in France would they be the last either. Sir Charles, in common with other families in the area was totally devastated when news of the action involving the Hoult men reached his ears. The loss of his dear wife had been a big enough blow to bear, but to learn that both his sons had been killed in action shook him to the core. If all of that wasn't bad enough, then his misery was compounded by the news that his favourite nephew Andrew was missing presumed dead. Even those who would claim to know Sir Charles really well, never fully appreciated how the rapid succession of blows had knocked all the stuffing from him.

Believing that all purpose in life had deserted him, he felt that as the Hall held so many painful memories, he couldn't bear to live there a moment longer. Knowing how desperate the country was to find properties far away from noise and bustle, where badly injured men could recuperate in peace and solitude, he decided to contact the army and offer them the use of the building as a convalescent home for injured soldiers returning from the front. It wasn't long therefore before he had the rooms cleared of their contents, storing them in the now empty coach house.

The tide of battle that had largely stagnated further north, was more fluid further south, and none more so was this evident than in the area around the

Chateau, following the enemy's initial onslaught in the autumn of 1914. However in early 1916, French forces began to regroup leading the German officer corps who had requisitioned the main body of the chateau, to abandon the property and retreat further east. Fearing for their safety, now that the chateau lay effectively in no man's land, Monsieur De Sauny was faced with an agonising dilemma, as there was now a very real danger of the chateau being hit in the crossfire between the two sides. For the previous nine months they had lived rather uncomfortably in the adjacent coach house, but at least they had food and a roof over their heads. In the final analysis it was a question of balancing the risk of staying where they were, or taking to the road as refugees, if they thought the risk of the chateau being hit was too great.

If they decided to leave, then it would be a question of how much they could take with them to ensure their survival? Andrew, in spite of making a good recovery was still in no condition to lift much more than a small suitcase, and as for the rest of them, well there was a limit to what they were physically capable of carrying. When the doctor expressed his concerns about staying in the cramped conditions of the coach house, Andrew was left with very mixed emotions. On the one hand he was naturally delighted that, at long, long last he might be able to make contact with his own people and remove the constant fear of someone inadvertently revealing his true identity to the enemy. On the other hand he realised how desperately he would miss living with the family, who at great personal risk had cared for him and undoubtedly saved his life by treating him, as though he was their recently departed son. In reality though, if he was really honest, he knew that he didn't want to be parted from the girl whose companionship he had come to love in so many ways. Whenever he had felt down, and there had been plenty of those moments early on when he found it extremely difficult to maintain the pretence of being Philippe, Martine was always there to lift his spirits.

Martine's father had said enough about the enemy's brutality, to remove any lingering doubts he may have harboured about the severity of the outcome they might expect if the deception they had been maintaining was disclosed. Little wonder he had always been on edge whenever a German officer spoke to him. He was never entirely certain if their questions were seemingly innocuous enquiries made out of boredom, or whether they had a more sinister purpose. Those were the times that he was so thankful of Martine's almost permanent presence by his side. He knew that but for her timely intervention, he may well have said a wrong word that would have immediately aroused suspicion, the outcome of which didn't bear thinking about. Over the months her bright smile and cheerful enthusiasm had lifted his spirits on so many occasions that he could hardly envisage a time when she wasn't about, so it was almost inevitable that he began to dread the time when they would be parted.

That wasn't to say that he didn't desperately miss his family and being back home, though his pain of longing was always relieved by Martine's genuine interest when she wanted to know everything about his life in England and particularly all about the farm. Curiously enough he always felt less homesick following one of their long talks, as though by answering her detailed questions he could imagine for a short while being back on the farm as he enjoyed telling her about the animals and how he missed some of his favourite cows that he had come to know so well. It didn't stop there because Martine seemed so genuinely interested in all he had to say, even when he talked about mundane things such as fields and hedgerows. Then he told her about Hoult and some of the struggles his family had endured in the past, although there was little more he could add about the talisman that he now wore about his neck. When this was all over he wanted her to come back with him to England so that he could show her everything he had described. Dare he hope, even though he never discussed such an outcome with her, perhaps she might just be willing to stay with him. But all of that of course, lay in the future.

For now, if the happy times they spent together whilst she patiently taught him French was any indication, he was more than satisfied that she evidently enjoyed his company, just as much as he enjoyed being in hers. It was only natural that there had been plenty of times over the months when they had talked about his home that he became very nostalgic, desperately wanting to share some of his recent experiences with his mother and the rest of his family. But for all of that, the thing that most distressed him was to think that his parents, on hearing he was missing, would have feared the worst, expecting him to be dead. He knew how grief stricken his mother would have been when she thought that she would never see him again.

Eventually one morning, the decision of whether to move or stay put was taken out their hands when the chateau received a direct hit. The blast was so powerful that in addition to destroying the major portion of the house, it removed part of the coach house roof, to say nothing of shattering all the windows. Luckily, apart from being badly shaken by the suddenness of the explosion, and being covered in dust, none of them suffered any more than a few minor nicks and bruises caused by splinters of glass and bits of flying debris. It was only after they had picked themselves up and begun to collect their thoughts that they looked across the courtyard at what remained of the chateau, when they all began to realise how incredibly lucky they had been.

"Well at least we can thank the Germans for something". Martine said with a broad smile.

"I don't see how", her father replied, giving her, the sort of luck he normally reserved for patients who were beginning to lose their faculty's.

"Simple really, if they hadn't been in the chateau, then we would still been living there".

Following the Germans hurried departure; they had delayed returning to live within the chateau itself, just in case, as Martine's father pointed out, another group might suddenly want to move in and turn them out again. Fearing another hit, the Doctor had no hesitation in insisting that they quickly gather a few things together and not only leave, but leave quickly or perhaps they wouldn't be quite so lucky next time. "Remember we are limited by what we can carry, so we need to concentrate on only taking things that are essential for our survival" he cautioned. "Obviously we need to take all our cash, and I think it would be a good idea if you two bring along your jewellery". He said looking in the direction of his wife and Martine, both of whom, despite Martine's levity, were still quite badly shocked by the explosion. "The problem is that we don't know what we might have to buy. We also need all our personal documents and that includes Phillipe's for you Andrew. I will leave it to you ladies to bring some food that ideally will keep awhile. Also we need to take some warm clothing along with something to keep us dry."

A little later, the four of them, each carrying an old suitcase made a pathetic looking little group, as they left the ruined chateau to join others on the road who were in a similar position to themselves. It was indicative of the high esteem in which the doctor was held locally, that when they caught up with another small group of desultory looking refugees that they should automatically look to him for leadership and guidance. Rather like the four of them, most of the other sad looking people, clung to an odd assortment of bulging suitcases, whilst the women with babies, and even some that didn't, pushed an odd assortment of prams and wheelbarrows containing as many of their personal possessions as they could possibly take with them.

Whenever Martine caught sight of one of the small children's tearful faces looking towards her, she became overwhelmed with sympathy because apart from giving them a reassuring smile, there was so little that either she or indeed any of them could do to relieve the anguish they were experiencing. The smallest children, held their mother's hands or in instances where there were additional slightly older children in the family, looked bewildered by all that was happening about them, as they clung to the hems of their mothers coats. If ever evidence was needed about the misery created by war, then the sight of this small section of humanity was ample testament. With only the smashed remnants of isolated tree trunks, or a pile of stones to act as a reminder of a house or community had once existed there, Martine was distressed to see how the familiar landscape she had so enjoyed walking through as a child had become an almost unrecognisable sea of pock marked bare earth.

It was unsurprising therefore that as a result of more than two years of near constant gunfire, that so many of the farms and villages that the doctor had passed through visiting patients had been blasted to oblivion. After spending a restless night in the ruins of one of those destroyed farm buildings, they resumed their journey as soon as it was light enough to travel safely. Following a couple of hours of steady walking when at best it was doubtful if they had managed to cover any more than seven or eight kilometres, Monsieur de Sauny drew the group to a halt for a short break. Standing his case on the ground, he pointed to a ribbon of dust in the far distance. "That's where we need to go. Once we get on `La Voie Sacree` we can follow it to Bar le Duc, where it's fairly certain we will be able to stay".

"The Sacred Way", Martine whispered in Andrew's ear noting his blank expression, then turning to her father asked, "What do you thinks making all that dust"?

"Trucks" he said as everyone narrowed their eyes to gaze in the distance at a seemingly endless stream of canvas covered small trucks. "They're carrying men and supplies from Bar le Duc to the French troops defending Verdun. I've heard that there are so many, that they do say, one goes by every fourteen seconds".

"How far's Bar de Duc?" an elderly man enquired, leaning heavily on his stick.

"About seventy kilometres I should imagine, but I'm afraid that's where we need to go". He sighed.

Before long they joined the road, but because of the sheer volume of traffic, created by the endless procession of trucks that even if it were possible to walk by the side of the road the choking dust made it extremely difficult to breathe properly. Consequently people on foot, and that included a great many French soldiers, were obliged to walk in the fields alongside the dusty road.

"There's never been a pause, whether it's night or day", Martine remarked as they took a rest, a couple of days later.

"Good job there's so many holes in the road, or they'd travel a good deal faster", Andrew replied. "As it is they're not going a deal more than a brisk walking pace".

In addition to the stream of trucks there seemed to be an almost endless line of people, who rather like themselves seemed to be heading in the direction from which the trucks were coming. It was quite obvious, that judging by the exhausted and hungry looking faces of some of the more elderly or infirm refugees, that they were getting to the end of their tether. Even with his doctors training and calling to help others, the doctor had to admit it was a hopeless task to stop and offer some form of assistance. The trouble was there were so many folk who required care and attention that it would have been virtually impossible to know where to begin, even if he had the means to carry out the help in any case. After a few days food and water became a constant issue, so it became a God send to reach a village with a pump and clean fresh water. Fresh food though was always a problem as it became necessary to supplement the food they had brought with them by eating what they could scavenge from hedges and fields. In spite of encountering all manner of appalling conditions along the way, eventually Monsieur de Sauny along with other members of his bedraggled group reached Bar de Duc and their nightmare of a journey ended. Even though they had taken the sensible precaution of carrying documentation to establish their identity that in itself presented its own difficulty's.

With the absence of papers to the contrary, the French forces were reluctant to accept the fact that Andrew was in fact English as his identity papers clearly showed that he was Phillipe de Sauny. However after much wrangling, he was at long last able to rejoin his own forces, but in view of his injuries he was invalided out of the army to enjoy a hero's welcome back in Hoult. Meanwhile, Martine and her family travelled on to Paris, where they found shelter in the Parisian home of Monsieur De Sauny's brother. - Until the conclusion of the war.

1918

Although the war raged on for almost another eighteen months, Martine and Andrew managed to correspond regularly. Then early in 1918 an opportunity arose for Martine to travel to England to meet Andrew once more.

Tom and Sarah were only too delighted to meet the young lady who undoubtedly had been responsible for saving his life. For more than a year without hearing a word of Andrew's whereabouts they had become resigned to the fact that he had been killed at the same time as Thomas and Edward and his body like so many others had never been recovered. After the army medical core vacated The Hall in early 1919 Charles who now had no immediate male heirs, following the death of his two sons decided to be rid of the responsibility of running the estate, so he resolved to give all of his tenants the opportunity to purchase the freehold of their property, be it farm or cottage. Tom and his two sons bought the freehold of their rented farms in addition to purchasing another four hundred acres of land that other tenants declined to purchase, making the Slade's one of the largest and most successful farmers in Hoult and district.

· · · ·

APRIL 27th 1920 *continued*

Perhaps Kate was right after all when she said it must have been my destiny to find the talisman that day, Sir Charles mused. With the sale of the Halls contents due to take place the following day, he was taking a final nostalgic look around the various lots displayed in the marquee that the auctioneers had erected in the courtyard.

Leaving the auction staff attaching numbers to the various lots, as they completed their final preparations for the sale, he made his way through the archway into the garden. It saddened him to see the level of neglect, when he was forced to stoop to avoid catching his face on the briars trailing from the rambler roses. Even the lawn that used to be an immaculately mown stretch of grass leading down to the lake resembled an overgrown meadow. As he walked by the side of the Hall towards the French doors leading into the south drawing room he spotted the garden seat where both he and Kate had sat on still summer evenings long ago.

Taking a seat to rest his legs he noticed that it carried a sale number, so he assumed that owing to its considerable weight, the auctioneers must have decided that it was much easier to sell it in situ rather than try to move it.

Momentarily closing his eyes, his mind became filled with nostalgic memories, as he tried to recreate a vision of those happy times. He remembered how they both delighted in watching the shadows lengthen as they listened to the sights and sounds of water fowl on the lake. As dusk approached and the rooks returned to roost in the large trees surrounding the church, they loved to watch their quarrelsome antics as they squawked for territorial positions within the branches. He remembered that whenever they had discussed the way the cross had come into his possession, he had always been rather dismissive of her deeply held belief that things are preordained and are meant to happen. But looking back now, when he thought about the many events involving the cross that had subsequently occurred, he was beginning to have second thoughts, so he was willing to concede that she may have had a point after all.

Opening his eyes once more, his nostalgic train of thoughts were temporally broken, when he spotted his first swallow of the year. As the tiny bird with its swept back wings swooped and soared over the lake, in its seemingly effortless search for flying insects, it reminded him of how Kate used to be so thrilled when she caught her first sight of the sleek little birds. Like her, it never ceased to amaze him that after their incredibly long journey, the same birds somehow managed to return once again to nest under the eaves of the coach house roof. Even though this first sighting was generally a good indication that the long warm days of summer were just around the corner, he noticed that the sharp northerly breeze still had a keen edge to it, which was a reminder that winter could still have a last fling.

A kaleidoscope of thoughts began to flood into his mind, as he thought about the generations of his family who had lived in the Hall. And that reminded him of a similar spring day fifty years earlier, as his mind went back to his walk by the beck all those years ago when he made his remarkable discovery. Gripping his walking cane for support, he slowly got to his feet, his mind still on the many things that had happened to the cross after he had rushed home to show it to his father. If I hadn't decided to go along the beck that day, he mused, then it's a salutary thought that much of what occurred later as a result of finding the cross wouldn't have happened.

He remembered that when he had turned into the Park for probably the last time, he couldn't help but be impressed by Tom and Andrews's herd of fine Red Cattle. He felt immensely proud that the sight of those animals would have gladdened Kate's heart, but really she couldn't have had a finer legacy than her nephew Andrew who was the living embodiment of all she had ever sought. Lowering his gaze he looked towards the Hall farmhouse and its group of farm buildings beyond. It didn't seem all that long since the estate farmed it, but it was obvious that under Tom Slade and his two son's direction that the farm was prospering. In the stack yard he saw a wooden ladder propped against a stack of straw and presumed that Andrew was about to cut a square of straw for the remaining cattle still inside the cattle yards. Then his attention was caught by the sight of a slim young woman, who he instantly recognised as Martine emerging from the front door of the house with a clothes basket tucked under her arm. He watched her walk down the path to a clothes line suspended between two posts at the end of the garden. After selecting a handful of white napkins from the basket she began to peg them on the line to dry in the brisk wind. Seeing the confident young woman going about her tasks reminded him so much of Kate, and the way that she also refused to let adversity get in her way. As she bent over to pick another item from the clothes basket he saw something glint as the rays of the sun reflected on something around her neck. Of course, the talisman he thought, as he recalled what Andrew had told him about them finding the talisman in his pocket when Martine's family took him in and started to treat his wounds. He felt certain that but for it and the bravery of this remarkable young woman and her parents, it was unlikely that Andrew's life would have been saved, especially when it was done under the very noses of the Germans living in the Chateau.

Maybe Kate was right after all, when she said that some things are meant to be, he thought. If he hadn't found the talisman that day then it would never have been placed in his father's desk...... for him to find .... then Thomas to find .... Without the talisman, there was little doubt in his mind that it would have proved far more difficult to establish Andrew's false identity. As it was it showed remarkable courage on all their parts, he thought, as he watched Martine continue to pin more clothes on the line. It must have placed an incredible strain on them, when they knew that the slightest slip of the tongue would lead to an outcome that hardly bore thinking about.

As Sir Charles made his way to the hand gate leading into the churchyard, he thought about his journey across northern France a little over a year earlier, to attend her wedding to Andrew. He respected Martine's steely determination, when she insisted that as a practical demonstration of the way they would rebuild their lives, that once the rubble was cleared from within the nave of the ruined church, she wanted the ceremony to take place there regardless of whether the church had a roof or not. And then as he thought about the wedding, his thoughts drifted to Martine's sad face when she showed him all that remained of the house where she had grown up. It had been flattened into an almost unrecognisable ruin in a featureless landscape, rather like almost everything else in the district that had once risen above the earth's surface.

He felt so proud of his nephew when Andrew showed him where both his sons had met their death and the cemetery where they were buried. He remembered how it had brought a lump to his throat when he had met one of the survivors of the attack back in Hoult, when he said how he had witnessed Andrew, despite his own severe injuries, doing his best to help Thomas. It was a special sort of person who could offer such compassion, he thought, when he cast his mind back to some of the despicable acts that he knew Thomas had done to make Andrew's life a misery over the years.

Passing into the church yard reminded him of the emotional moment, when Andrew on his return to England had immediately brought him the cross that he had taken from Thomas' body. He recalled how he had insisted that Andrew keep it.

Little wonder therefore that he wasn't the only person choking with emotion, when the priest conducting the marriage service told the assembled guests some of the turbulent history surrounding the silver Cross of Lorraine which Andrew held in his hands.

As long as he lived, he knew he would never forget Andrew's stirring words to Martine after they had exchanged vows and he had placed a ring on her finger.

He remembered the way Andrew had delicately lifted her veil and placed the cross around her neck and how in a clear voice, heavy with emotion, said such stirring words that immediately brought a lump to his throat whenever he thought about it.

"This cross has witnessed many events during its seven hundred year history, but none more so than in the last one hundred and thirty years. Not only has it seen violent death in both our families, but more importantly for me, it was instrumental in saving my life, and in so doing enabling me to meet my courageous beautiful bride Martine. As I place this Cross of Lorraine around your neck my dear, I do it as a symbol of unity and hope that you will proudly wear it as long as you shall live". After a slight pause adding with deep feeling, "The Chateau de Saveur was indeed my saviour".

Judging by the sound of handbags opening and hands delving into pockets for handkerchiefs he didn't think he was by himself in shedding a tear, as he remembered that wonderful moment. Glancing back to the unkempt grounds around the Hall, he was acutely conscious that the steps he had put in place signalled the end of a way of life that had existed for centuries. Tomorrow the drive across the Park would be thronged with not only potential buyers, but the curious who just wanted to gawp at the dispersal of The Halls contents. He knew that many of those folk relished the opportunity of a sale as a means of demonstrating their newly acquired wealth to as wide an audience as possible. Pony and traps would mix with a minority of folk who had invested in one of the new cars increasingly making their appearance in the streets of Hoult. So much has changed, he thought as he made his way among the gravestones to Kate's grave.

Following the sale of the contents of the Hall, the marquee would be taken down so that the team commissioned to demolish the Hall itself could commence their work. He knew he would be saddened to see the Hall demolished, but unfortunately that was the only realistic outcome for a property of that size. It was neither large enough to be considered a stately home, nor was it small enough to make a family home. In any event it required a vast amount of money spending on it to deal with minor repairs let alone anything major. He recalled his conversation with the local firm of auctioneers who were selling the contents, when they said the building as it stood was unsalable. It will come to more money if you demolish it and sell the building materials they confidently predicted. Regrettably therefore, in another three month's time another sale was due to be held when the very fabric of the building itself would be placed in lots and auctioned to the highest bidder. Where, Sir Charles pondered would the fine sweeping staircase be re-erected and what grand building would stage the white marble slabs of the entrance hall. Once the demolition men had done their work, and everything had been removed it would close the curtain on an era and allow the grounds to decay into a haven for wild life.

With eyes closed in quiet contemplation, he stood beside the grave of his dear wife whose life had been so tragically cut short. He remembered the all too brief period that he and Kate had been together and the sorrow that he still felt at her passing. Then glancing further to his left he saw the serried rows of gravestones, the more recent ones standing erect, whilst many of the older ones rather like people as they aged, were stooped and leaning, with inscriptions increasingly difficult to decipher. He saw the fine black Italian marble grave stones commemorating his Vavour ancestors, the most recent recording Kate's death, then a little further back, his fathers, and inscribed below was the date of his mother's death. A little further on, partially obscured by the branches of a spreading yew was yet another that recorded the death of Henry in 1848 and also of his devoted wife Constance three years later. Further across the churchyard, his eye was drawn to a line of simple pale brown sandstone memorials where the action of wind and rain had almost obliterated the inscriptions recording the passing of generations of Slade's.

He walked across to one particular stone that leaned at an even greater angle than the rest. Bending over he carefully teased away strands of ivy, delighted to discover that it had protected the inscription carved into the soft sandstone. Now as the bright rays of the early morning sun struck obliquely across the stones surface it enabled him to decipher the name of Meg Slade, who the stone recorded had died tragically in 1820, and further down the stone, an inscription relating to her faithful husband Tom who had been tragically killed in 1831. I know something about Tom's death but what were the circumstances of Meg's death he mused? It must have been, that Tom Slade, who had brought The Cross of Lorraine back from the body of Martine's Great, Great, Grandfather at the battle of Waterloo, what a great story he thought, if it could all be told.

With a head full of memories he slowly picked his way, between tufts of grass as he made his way across the church yard to the gate leading on to the lane.

This is purely a work of fiction set against events that actually occurred. The characters are also purely fictitious and if they bear any resemblance to people alive or dead then it is purely coincidental.

Ralph Needham. August 2013

This is the opening extract from the second book in the trilogy

DECEPTION POINT
June 1920

"Mon Dieu", she screamed waking up with a start. Feeling completely disorientated she couldn't decide whether it was the loudness of the crash, or just the fact she had woken so quickly from a deep sleep that was responsible for her confusion. After such a resounding thump, at the very least, she expected to see some damage, but to her astonishment, she was surprised to see that everything at first glance appeared perfectly normal, that is apart from a trickle of plaster falling from a crack in the ceiling. Convinced there had been a massive explosion somewhere close by, it just didn't make sense that there was so little sign of damage. But then her thoughts turned to Andrew, what if something had happened to him? Trouble was that even after maintaining the deception for so long, she knew it would only take the slightest indiscretion or slip of the tongue to invite suspicion, the outcome of which didn't bare contemplating about.

She would never admit it to others of course, but she knew in her heart how deeply she had come to care for him, especially after those first difficult weeks nursing him back to health. The longer he stopped with them, the more she knew she would miss him, so it appalled her to think that as a result of dozing off, something could have happened to him. Temporally putting thoughts of Andrew to one side, her gaze returned once more to the ceiling, as she tried to weigh up in her mind what might have happened, but there was something fundamentally wrong, though she couldn't just put her finger on what it was.

And then all of a sudden it hit her. "I can't believe I've been be so stupid", she remarked aloud. "Of course it's the bacon hooks. Come to that, what's happened to the flagstones"? I must be dreaming she thought, because even the windows are different, what on earths going on? Then her eyes focused on the scene through the kitchen window. If she hadn't been disorientated before, then what she was seeing now left her completely confused. She realised with a shock that it wasn't the familiar scene of the cobbled courtyard and the clock tower, but for some peculiar reason it was replaced by her garden in England.

Just what was happening? Surely it couldn't be a bad dream, --- or---- could it? The funny thing was, she had been totally convinced she was back in her family home, but now she wasn't so sure. Suddenly, rather like pulling a set of heavy curtains aside to let light flood into a room, it all came flooding back as she remembered her infant son. In near panic she rushed across the room to the pram, only to immediately relax when she found that in spite of the crash that had completely disoriented her, he continued to sleep peacefully. Satisfied that he was perfectly safe, her mind began to return to normal as she looked through the window to see a cloud of grey dust slowly clearing from a pile of rubble at the front of the Hall, making it instantly obvious what had caused the crash and woken her from what must have been a very deep sleep. As the dust continued to settle she began to see that a gap existed now where once a winged eagle had proudly stood atop two magnificent Corinthian columns, all of which had been carved from the finest Portland stone to create the impressive centre piece of the Halls imposing west front. Now though, rather like an elegant butterfly that had somehow metamorphosed in reverse, a thing of grace and beauty had been transformed into something totally unrecognisable.

Until seconds earlier she had been totally convinced she was back home at the Chateau, little wonder therefore that her mind should drift back to happy memories spent walking alongside the gently flowing Meuse and seeing the spectacular views from the ridges of the nearby hill tops across to the Argonne forest in the west, and the wooded hills of Douaumont in the east. She recalled with sorrow how everyone's life had changed irrevocably in 1914 when the German army attempted to seize Verdun and how the pleasant countryside that she knew so well was reduced to a landscape that was unrecognisable. Incessant shelling had blasted complete villages off the face of the earth, and the woods that the family had picnicked in on warm summer days were reduced to mangled tree stumps, poking through a cratered landscape. She shuddered, recalling those times, still finding it impossible to comprehend the sheer volume of trucks carrying soldiers and materials that she had seen passing along La Voie Sacree. Ah, the sacred way she mused, recalling those times.

Noticing a couple of workmen picking their way over the rubble brought her back to reality once more. The Halls demolition in some ways seemed to symbolise the end of an older order of privilege and in particular an abuse of power by earlier generations of the family living there. Sir Charles Vavour however, who had been the last owner, was a gentleman of great integrity in complete contrast to many of his predecessors. He was universally liked and respected, but following the untimely death of his beloved wife Kate and then the loss of both his sons in the Great War, had retired a broken man to a town house in Hoult. The latch on the outer door leading into the scullery lifted and Martine could hear the familiar sound of leather boots passing over the brick floor to the sink. The kitchen door opened and Andrew still drying his hands put his head around the corner. "I've put the eggs in the back", he remarked in a matter of fact voice. Martine hurried across the room and pressing a finger tight to her lips, indicating that he should speak quietly. "I have just had a terrible frayeau", she whispered, temporally mixing her French and English words. "I must have been so very tired, because after I cleared away the pots and washed up, I sat by the fire and fell sound asleep. Next thing I knew I heard such an enormous crash that I really thought I was back in the chateau.   I had forgotten all about the workmen at the Hall".

Andrew put his sound arm around his wife's slim figure and kissed her lightly on the forehead, then with his other hand lifted the silver Cross of Lorraine from inside the neckline of her dress and held it to his lips.

"You know if it hadn't been for this silver talisman it's more than likely that I wouldn't be here today, in which case I would never have met the beautiful girl who saved me".

"It must have been our destiny to meet" she said with a faraway look in her eyes, hooking her arm in Andrew's and gazing out of the window at the pile of rubble where the Hall once stood.

CHAPTER ONE
November 1940

With a mournful sigh the steam hammer gave one last thump for the day, then as the hiss of escaping steam was replaced by the crash of waves breaking just yards away, half a dozen men, who had spent the day erecting scaffolding, prepared to walk back to their lodgings. The scaffolding errectors had been brought in at short notice that summer, to erect a continuous line of scaffolding along the flat expanse of the Lincolnshire foreshore with the aim of providing a deterrent against invasion. In many ways viewing the structure from the sand hills, gave the appearance of it being a long grandstand devoid of its seating. The rawness of the November afternoon was made worse by a sea fret that although it had retreated off shore for most of the day, was rolling back with a vengeance now that the tide had turned. None of which was going to trouble the scaffolding errectors, who with their backs turned to the sea, were only too pleased at long last, to be heading for the comparative shelter of the sand hills and relief from the numbing cold. In spite of being warmly clad and used to a life of working outside, there was something about being by the North Sea in winter that was making even the hardiest of them wish they were back on their usual type of work in the midlands, all of which added to their keen anticipation of a hot supper and pint of best Hewitt's in front of a blazing fire at their lodgings in the Fox.

With warmth and food dominating their thoughts it was perhaps understandable that they were oblivious to the sight of a small man wearing a grubby mac and grey hat pulled down to his ears, who had slipped furtively through the Marram grass on to the edge of the now deserted beach. Although the light was fading rapidly, the man withdrew a large scale map from an inside coat pocket and set about marking the extent of the construction that had taken place since his last visit. Finally he withdrew a sketchbook and carefully drew the shape of the structure being constructed. His instructions had been quiet precise. Look, listen and record, but under no circumstances draw attention to yourself.

That afternoon he had caught Elgins bus in Hoult and from the anonymity of a seat towards the rear of the bus, had noted a new gun emplacement that had been strategically constructed on a corner to give the gunners a clear view in both directions. A little further along the road, he took note of fifty gallon drum sized concrete blocks that had been so positioned behind trees on a bend, so that they could quickly be positioned to block the road.

"What do you reckon then, Fred", the youngest member of the erecting team suddenly remarked, gesticulating with a chip in the direction of an older man. Fred, exercising his right as the oldest and most experienced member of the team, sat by the log fire, in the one easy chair provided by the landlord in the public bar of The Fox. With his flat cap skewed rakishly over his left ear, he took two long draws on his pipe, then looking through a haze of white smoke responded in measured tones.

"Buggered if I know, can't see how it's going to work".

"It'll tear the tracks off a tank", Joe enthused knowingly, selecting another chip from within the layers of newspaper, much of which had become transparent as a result of absorbing the grease surrounding his fish and chip supper. The others, who were either finishing their fish and chips or contemplating the amber liquid in their glasses, looked unconcerned as Joe unperturbed continued.

"I saw this attack at the pictures; I reckon it was somewhere like". - He paused to look up at the wooden beams spanning the ceiling, as though among the swirling clouds of tobacco smoke the word he was seeking might miraculously materialize. - "Spain". His voice exploded at long last with the satisfaction of making an important memory feat. "All these tanks started coming ashore and then they got caught up in the stuff like what we're building, well the guns started to ammer ell out on em, and then the mines started going off".

"It's different ere", Fred interrupted looking completely disinterested.

"Firstly what makes you think they'll land ere when they can just nip across the channel on the south coast, and secondly they wouldn't dare to invade us anyway, after we give um such a good 'idin last time".

"Walls ave ears" Joe said looking at a poster behind the bar, "I saw this picture last year, where this spy saw everything that was 'appening and sent secret messages to his contact".

"And then what 'appened", Fred said, taking a long draw on his pipe, settling deeper into his chair.

"Well somebody saw 'im and reported 'im to the police; they cornered 'im and shot 'im".

"Serve the bugger right, father told me about cases in France during the last do where anyone suspected of being a bit too interested in our trenches were put agin a wall".

"I reckon the governments woken up at long last". Frank said leaning over the bar polishing a glass. "You don't have to be a brain surgeon to see that these are flat open beaches, ideal to mount an invasion. That's the reason they've brought you chaps here in such a rush to build defences, and try and slow em down if they come here".

The small bar continued to fill as men from local farms, having finished their tea came in for a game of darts or dominoes over a pint. Others were quite content to enjoy their drink, whilst smoking and chatting to colleagues. Frank, business like as ever, left the bar to throw another shovel of coal on the fire, which made a haze of sparks shoot up the chimney as a tongue of flame burst through the fresh coals.

"Don't get too comfortable, or you won't want to leave at closing time" Frank said semi seriously as he was forced to side step over Fred's outstretched legs.

There must have been something strangely addictive about the smell of stale beer, when combined with sweaty bodies and tobacco smoke, that made Fred's regulars want to be crammed in to such a small room that in other circumstances they would have complained bitterly about Little wonder therefore, that in that slightly stupefying atmosphere nobody should pay too much attention to a little man in a grubby grey mac who sidled up to the bar and asked Frank for half a pint of shandy. Unobtrusively he made his way from the bar to take a seat on a brown, pew like, wooden bench set against the far wall of the small room. He felt in an inside pocket of his jacket and extracted a small, well worn, silver coloured tin. He gave the appearance to other drinkers of being just another sad little man who was drowning his sorrows in his drink and a fag, whilst in fact his ears were highly attuned to the varied conversations going on around him. With great dexterity he carefully removed a cigarette paper from a packet within the tin, then sticking it to his upper lip delved into the tin once more, but this time removed a pinch of his favourite Ogdens tobacco. Although seeming to be preoccupied with his task of rolling an incredibly thin pencil of tobacco, it enabled him to concentrate on what was being said without making it seem obvious he was listening to the conversations going on around him.

• • • •

"I reckon you'll be all right now", Phillipe said aloud as he fluffed up the straw around Sara, one of his favourite cows. He felt a deep sense of pride as he watched the pair of calves he had helped deliver just over 24 hours earlier. Both calves were now swishing their tails contentedly, one on either side of their mother as they luxuriated in the plentiful supply of warm milk. As he closed the stable door he gave a final glance in the cows direction who he was satisfied to note was contentedly chewing the hay he had just placed in the feed rack in front of her. Nevertheless he made a mental note that when he made his regular late night checks around the crews later that evening he would check her once more.

Phillipe Slade was a fine young man a little past his twentieth birthday. His easy smile instantly warmed him to everyone that came in contact with him, whilst his tall aristocratic features were a living proof of his mother Martine's French ancestors. Although he had been brought up on the family farm in England he was completely bilingual, just as happy conversing in French to his parents as speaking English to all his friends and neighbours. As he walked across the farm yard to the back door of the farmhouse he could see that the light that had never been particularly good throughout the short winter day was fading fast. Passing into the scullery he made his way across to the brown sink under the window where he set about washing his hands. On opening the kitchen door he was greeted by a fire blazing in the grate, and the inviting smell of a dish his mother was removing from the adjoining side oven.

Finishing drying his hands he good humouredly tossed the towel across the room towards his younger sister, Laura, who was sitting by the fire reading the local paper. Twisting her face into a grimace, she hurled it back to him with a flourish, "Where have you had your hands Phillipe"?

"Ar if only you knew", Phillipe replied with a laugh in his voice.

Although only two years younger than he, she had the figure and looks that turned heads as she went about her work in the Town Clerks office in Hoult.

Phillipe half thought about throwing it back to his sister, but quickly dismissed the idea, realising that once was enough. He knew from past experience when to quit. She could be quite a handful if she became sufficiently annoyed. Instead as shadows from the kitchen fire danced up the walls chasing away the last vestige of daylight, he walked over to the window and pulled across the internal wooden shutters.

"Do you think we will have a frost tonight"? Martine asked, turning up the wick on the ceiling lamp.

"I wouldn't be surprised, there was quite a nip in the air when I left the calves" Phillipe replied, casually picking a piece of crust from the end of one of his mothers freshly baked loaves.

"I hate the cold" Laura remarked giving an involuntary shiver as she toasted her hands by the fire. "It's not often I catch the four o clock bus. I don't know what came over Mr Sloan when he said we could leave early".

"He's only being kind. You've worked late for him plenty of times in the past" Martine said taking a handful of cutlery from the drawer under the table.

She had baked bread that afternoon in the traditional French style so that now as the loaves began to cool on the table the appetising smell percolated throughout the house. It was only natural that she should have inherited her cookery skills from her mother at the family chateau back in Lorraine, consequently her dishes were a constant delight to friends and relations who enjoyed dining with them. It had taken her sometime to become acclimatised to English customs that were so different to those that she had grown up with in eastern France, but nevertheless she passed on a certain Gallic twist to the traditional local dishes of stuff chine and rook pie, and her eels marinated in spiced red wine were a taste to savour.

The familiar clang of a bucket handle heralded Andrew's arrival in the scullery. It wasn't long before the living room door opened to reveal the man who had so captivated her during those dangerous times more than two decades earlier. Andrew's facial features belied his real age, though the grey hairs appearing around his temples gave an indication that he would soon be 46. However he carried mental scars much deeper than the physical ones he had incurred when he went to France in the autumn of 1914. Andrew had inherited the farm from his father Tom, but had been saddled with a crippling debt during those difficult inter war years. He knew of many good farmers in a similar situation to his, who had become unable to meet their liabilities and subsequently become insolvent losing everything. Andrew's father had purchased the freehold of the farms that he had previously rented from Charles Vavour back in 1920, when as a result of the death of both of his sons and his wife during The Great War, had decided to sell the estate and demolish the Hall . All that now remained to indicate where the magnificent building had once stood was a forlorn tangle of briars and scrubby shrubs set amidst mature trees that overlooked a grass field still known as the Park.

"Do you think that we're going to be invaded", Martine said, a worried frown creasing her forehead, when a little later they sat around the table having their evening meal.

"The grocery man says that some farmers have decided that they are not going to plant crops for Hitler".

"To be perfectly honest I sometimes wonder if we are doing the right thing producing food and breeding animals for the Hun", Andrew said, adding "just look at the way they devastated Poland and took everything that the Poles could produce".

"It makes me so afraid when I remember what happened last time",she said with passion in her voice.

Andrew stood with his back to the fire rubbing his injured shoulder that had a habit of starting to ache with the onset of colder weather. "The government must think there's an increased risk, because they were saying at the L D last night about gangs of men erecting scaffolding pipes at the seas edge. That can only mean they think an invasion's imminent".

"Going in to work this morning I noticed that what looked like rows of cylindrical concrete blocks have been positioned on the roadside by Turners bend", Laura said, adding, "We have all been issued with instructions on how to keep the town council services operating as normal if an invasion does occur".

"And what about the trenches they are digging across any of the long marsh fields", Phillipe said. "Presumably they're intended to deter gliders from landing. Makes me wonder if I'm serving the country to the best of my ability"?

"You've got to remember that producing food is just as vital for the war effort as in being in the front line firing bullets, after all an army can't fight without food", Andrew said picking his glasses case from the mantel piece.

Deep in thought he sat down in the Windsor chair that had been in the family from the time of his great grandfather. Hooking a frame over his ear he said. "You know if I were the German military looking at Britain from their side of the water, I reckon I would encourage the enemy to think that I would invade across the shortest distance, from say somewhere like Dunkirk, but do something completely different, remember if our army could escape from there, then it must be an equally suitable place to mount an invasion from". Cutting a slice of bread from the still warm loaf that Martine had placed on the table he ran a wedge of butter over its surface. "The Lincolnshire beaches have a lot to commend them. They're in the centre of the country. They're flat, and they've got a sparsely populated flat hinterland that would provide excellent mobility for all kinds of vehicles, that could travel in any direction.   Furthermore they're close to a range of deep water ports in the river Humber to bring in supplies. And lastly but by no means least Lincolnshire's in the centre of the largest concentration of bomber bases anywhere in the world, what a coup if they could be taken out and at a stroke eliminate the bomber raids on German soil".

As the rest of the family continued with their meal, no one spoke as the full realisation of what he had said sank in.

After a while Phillipe broke the silence, "I wonder......."?

CHAPTER TWO

A long, mournful wail, echoed around the hillsides, momentarily overriding the rhythmical sound of the trains wagon wheels passing over joins in the railway line. Suddenly the note changed as the trucks began to pass over points. With rising tension, half a dozen men waited patiently on the side of a ridge that overlooked the railway track in the valley below.

"What else do you think its carrying", a haggard looking man, wearing a leather jacket and grimy beret, enquired of his older, more muscular colleague.

"Don't know, but you can bet that whatever it is it won't be to our advantage."

As the noise from the train started to recede, the sound of the wheels passing over the steel rails changed pitch once more as the train moved on to a bridge crossing the river. One of the men crouched close to the ground with a separate wire held in either hand, whilst another had a pair of earphones clasped over his ears.

"Now". The man with earphones commanded.

Suddenly, a sheet of flame exploded into the night sky vividly illuminating the surrounding countryside, followed by a resounding boom that seemed to echo and re echo as the sound was bounced back and forth from one wooded hillside to the other. And then as if in slow motion the incredulous onlookers saw the fruits of their handiwork, as the trucks that the train had been pulling continued to fall off the now shattered bridge into the waters of the river below.

"Well done fellows" Maurice beamed, with a wide grin over his face, "now make yourselves scarce, there'll be hell to pop after this lot, we've well and truly poked a stick into the wasps nest, so I reckon somebody's likely to get very badly stung".

"Remember what happened to Raymond", Emile the thin faced chap remarked, "and how they got a confession out of him". The others shifted their feet uneasily as they recalled the sight of their friend's mutilated body.

"I hope none of you'll forget that day in June when the devils recaptured Verdun once again".

"So much for the generals who reckoned that the Maginot line with its line of forts was impregnable, because they simply by passed it by going north through Holland and Belgium instead" Maurice added ruefully.